D1648354

A

DREAM

OF

DARKNESS

A
DREAM
OF
DARKNESS

BY
CORY KRUSE

FIRE'S EDGE
PUBLISHING

Fire's Edge Publishing
310 N. Derby Lane PO Box 800
North Sioux City, SD 57049

First Edition: October 2019

ISBN 978-1-7330694-1-0 (hardcover)
ISBN 978-1-7330694-0-3 (e-book)
Library of Congress Control Number: 2019911129

Typesetting & Interior book design by Anamaria Stefan
Map by Carlos G. Rios, RemyArt
Original illustrations by Obigas and Cristina Tanase

To learn more, visit AuthorCoryKruse.com.

Printed in the United States of America

For my family,
Who, through all these years,
Helped keep the dream alive.

Your belief was everything;
Your love, an anchor and a light.

Every word's for you.

CONTENTS

A

DREAM

OF

DARKNESS

THE
HISTORY

In the darkness,
A single candle can
Cast the brightest glow.

But so, too, can it uncover that which is hidden—
That which is slumbering
With a sliver of one eye cracked.

A single candle
Can wake the darkness.

In a world very much like our own in times past:
A sweeping expanse of oceans and mountains and trees;
A world teeming with animals and creatures of every variety and sort,
With humans and their rising kingdoms,
People living off the plough and under the sword—
In a world such as this, our story begins.

In the year 1299 (by the Welte Calendar),
An explorer, Rufus Milgrin—
Who'd ventured further north than any person
And who had discovered iron and gold
In the previously uncharted Remos Mountains—
Gathered together a group of fifty families,
Of all races, genders, and means,
Anyone sharing his disdain for the unending spree
Of war and conflict of the past two decades,
Sparked by the great divider of humankind: religion.

Fed up with corrupt politicians and depraved city living,
Milgrin and his Fifty ignored the warnings of the wise and of the priests
(Who spoke of ill fortune, death,
And a living Darkness in the North)
And bartered their way into a contract with the king:

As long as they partook in commerce—
Trade centered around lumber and ores—
They would be free to do as they wished, to govern as they pleased,
Unhindered by the shackles of politics, religion, and greed.

Bolstered by the terms of this contract,
The families set out in the spring of the year 1301.
Swearing off the ways of the South,
They left its great coastal cities behind.

They journeyed northward for months,
Passing over ice-capped mountains and through endless wood.
Overcoming sickness, starvation,
And every hardship bestowed by an untamed wild,
Milgrin's Fifty finally reached a fertile valley nestled against the sea.

Commemorating their good fortune,
They began at once constructing a town,
Keeping watchful eyes on the surrounding woods,
And flickering torches burning at night.

But their first year passed without incident,
As did the next, and the next,
And the following century drifted by in peace and virtue—

Until the townspeople, growing fat off exported lumber and ore,
Forgot the warnings of the past altogether and
Gradually turned those watchful eyes off the woods,
And onto their fellow Man.

While around them,
The Darkness waited in silence,
And *grew...*

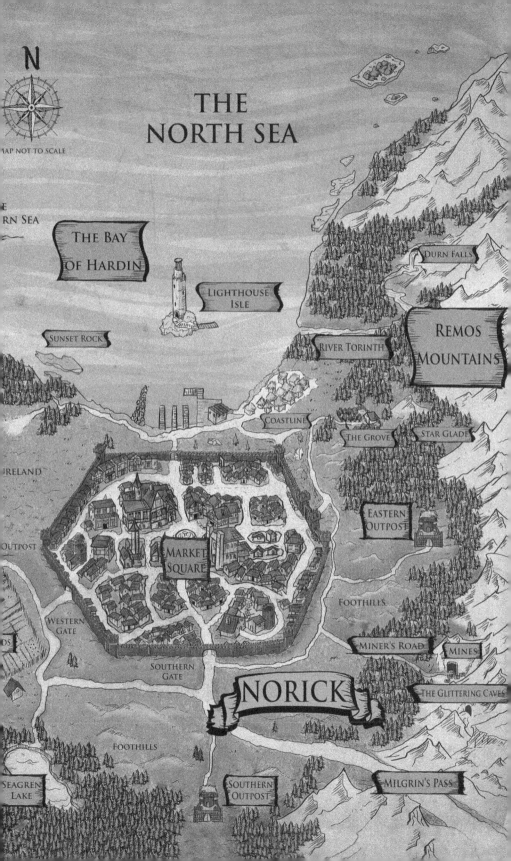

PART ONE

THE DARK
BENEATH THE LIGHT

(1401)

Ours is a world of noise.

The daytime swirls
With commotion and sound,
All the frantic flurries
Of lives lived,
Of labors toiled,
Of loves professed.

The world grumbles and creaks as it turns.
It sings.

But the daytime isn't alone in its symphony;
The night, too, contains a voice.

Ours is a world of noise;
Often, the darkness speaks loudest of all.

CHAPTER ONE

The man in the cloak approached the wall at a crouch.

Ahead, two guardsmen dozed against the gatehouse. Little more than a shadow in the descending twilight, the man in the cloak slipped past them, unseen.

Inside, the town of Norick was in uproar: Its nine hundred or so residents celebrated in unrestrained mirth—some dancing, their cavorting bodies casting wide shadows in the torchlight, others meandering to and from barrels of ale set up beneath richly embroidered tents. All across the Market Square, families reclined at tavern tables repurposed for picnic, small children wolfing down hunks from sugared bread loaves while their parents nibbled at turkey legs and curried lamb meat.

"Courtesy of Norick's festival committee and the humble magistrates of the High Council: All food and drink free of charge—festival night only," the council spokesman had announced earlier that week, in preparation for Norick's hundredth anniversary celebration. The townspeople had christened it Milgrin's Day in honor of the late intrepid explorer, by whose courage this valley was found; by whose wisdom, its abundance seized. While it was now difficult to parse fact from fiction (some claimed he'd wielded a ten-foot pike of pure ivory, others that he'd called up the walls from the sea), Milgrin's exploits were known intimately by every man, woman, and child in town. In their eyes, they owed him everything. He had founded this sanctuary, this paradise, this home. He had discovered a new world; he'd given his people hope.

All afternoon, Norick's citizens celebrated the blessing of their inheritance, fawning over an assortment of tournaments and feasts and a dawdling, grandiose parade. Three plays were conducted on the stage elevated over a corner of the Market Square. The productions, light-hearted affairs that satirized the ways of the South while also poking fun at all of them here in Norick, were performed by members of the town's theater company, The Brocade of Lights, which was headed up by a plump, half-blind man named Lerrick Rose (whom the younglings called "Night-Eyed").

Before the townspeople knew it, the climax of the day's festivities was upon them. At sundown, the actors took their bows and ambled off the stage as singers from the Emerald Choir filed in behind. Comprised of both children and adults alike, the choir breezed through a rendition of the town's anthem (penned by Rose's late father, Rylin) while a brilliant display of fireworks flared and sizzled over the harbor. The crowd, many of whom had never seen pyrotechnics before, gaped at the brilliant red and green incandescence erupting from the lighthouse. At the finale—a great culmination of sound and light, like a thousand rupturing stars—the gathered citizens cooed and *ahh-ed*. Afterward, the adults unleashed dignified cheers while their younglings squealed.

The colorful streamers faded and vanished, and the platform's occupants were shuffled anew. As the Emerald Choir departed, the chancellor of the High Council, Skylar Higgins, stepped up to deliver an address. Grinning triumphantly, he prattled on about the town's heroics, the merits of virtue, the surety of their collective future. He concluded with a fist raised high while the townspeople lauded him and themselves with jubilant applause. Ever the gracious host, Higgins next welcomed a troupe of musicians to the stage and implored them to take up song. A brisk melody found their fingers, and the crowd cheered once more. Soon, even the most conservative among them had fallen to dance.

The remainder of the night, unscheduled, was theirs. For many, this equated to dancing and frolicking themselves into a stupor, aided by the numbing embrace of excessive food and drink. Young and old alike roared in laughter as they danced to the musicians' frenetic strumming; lovers, drifting from the throng, clung to each other in darkened alleyways and whispered promises of eternal affection. All cares were forgotten amongst the townspeople, all sadness and anger cast away.

On this night, the people of Norick felt immortal. They felt *alive*.

Not realizing, thought the man in the cloak as he moved among them, that death was coming.

That it had already arrived.

Keeping to the fringes, the man in the cloak glided toward his destination. He hugged the line of wood-framed houses bordering Norick's narrow cobblestone streets and kept his eyes lowered, hidden beneath the reach of his hood. Thus far, he'd avoided detection with remarkable ease: The townspeople were either unconscious of his presence or far too distracted to offer him more than a passing glance. As predicted, he was effectively invisible.

Even when he had tarried at the edge of the Market Square, they failed to notice him. Crossing the eastern edge of the courtyard, he found himself faltering after only a handful of paces, his ears tuned to the stage erected at the opposite end. Lerrick Rose was in the middle of delivering an impassioned soliloquy. He spoke as if he were Rufus Milgrin himself, gesturing over the audience and pretending to stare off, with measured bravado, into some vast, inhospitable wild. The man in the cloak had been using a row of four-poster market stalls to shield his passage across the square; at Rose's monologue, he hesitated between two vacant booths and angled his cowl toward the stage.

He drew in a heavy breath through both nostrils.

He kept moving.

The rest of his journey passed without incident, as they'd known it would. He circled the square twice. He spotted the magistrate but did nothing. Not yet. Slinking into a grime-encrusted alleyway, he watched him— watched them all—and waited for the appointed time. Finally, it arrived: The fireworks sizzled over the harbor, Higgins blathered out his speech, and, last of all, the musicians took the stage.

With the townspeople's attentions duly fixed, the man in the cloak stole away. He crept deeper into Norick, street by street, block by block, drifting like a wayward shadow. It was only as he was ascending the stairs to the magistrate's house that he drew the knife from his cloak. Rusted and nicked, with a grooved handle of yellowing bone, it felt almost weightless in his grip. He slid the dull curve of its blade against his palm without so much as a pause. He made two more cuts. On the third, he pushed the blade down until both hands were sticky and warm.

He returned the knife to its sheath. For an interval, he simply let himself drip.

A stillness descended upon the empty street. Nothing moved, save the fat droplets leaching from his fingers to stain the smooth stone of the stair below. The magistrate's windows, likewise empty, revealed nothing but darkness. This far removed, the sounds from the festival were all but muted. The man in the cloak let himself recede into the relative hush. He let the evening air inflate his lungs. The darkness gathered about him in whorls. The voice lingered nearby.

Painted a lurid shade of emerald with ornate silver grooves running up either side, the magistrate's front door was a heavy, expensive thing. Its surface felt cool and firm as the man in the cloak pressed his palm to the engraved wood. He extended each of his fingers while applying further pressure. Once he removed his hand, a wet, trickling imprint remained.

The note came next. With a separate knife, hardly more than a letter opener, he jammed the piece of parchment into place just over the leaking handprint.

He turned without rereading its message. Following the swirl of his cloak, he glided down the stoop and returned to street level. A ripple of noise from the celebration wafted over the rooftops. As the cobblestone clacked beneath his boots, the man in the cloak's hood tilted in the direction of the sound, back toward the Market Square.

He paused.

Considered.

The man in the cloak approached the wall at a crouch.

He slipped past the guards, unseen.

CHAPTER TWO

"Fuck you," said Captain William Breeve as he faced down the flagon of wine perched on the railing. "Fuck *you*."

His lips were trembling, whether because of indecision or because he hadn't yet had a drink today, and so were his hands. The air of the Eastern Outpost festered with his body's stench: a reek of stale breath and souring sweat. With tears pooling in his eyes, he fumbled for the pommel of the sword at his waist, anything to help steady the wobble in his fingertips.

You don't need it, he told himself as he blinked away the tears. *You don't need it.*

As always, he wished he believed that.

He had procured the flagon that morning from the town's only winemaker, a portly, rosy-skinned fellow named Marcus Calvin. His store, The Wandering Cask, sat cater-cornered to the Market Square and was abutted next to Trinity Weston's shop. William hadn't expected to encounter Calvin at that hour; typically it was the bungling, simpleminded Artie Layman who covered the early shift. But alas, as the door's string of chimes jangled, William observed it was the peevish vintner standing behind the counter.

A scowl lingered on William's face just long enough to be seen.

Calvin's cheeks, as pockmarked as the shop's pitted doorframe, brandished a grimace of their own. He flattened his palms upon the varnished wood of the checkout counter. Between his lips, the stem of a roven weed twisted and swirled.

"Can I help you." It didn't possess the cadence of a question.

"Milgrin's courage," William said in greeting. Blinking toward the floor, he stepped from the shop's threshold and approached the counter; an overpowering rush of odors assailed him as he went. Some were sweet, a few dry. Others seemed only a few degrees off from vinegar. At any rate, the flood of smells was enough to mask the pungent earthiness coming from the herbalist's shop next door, an aroma fragrant with bitterness and its own brand of syrupy decay. For William, the mingled scents were somehow both alluring and fundamentally off-putting: There was a rot in his stomach, but so too was there a craving for a drink.

"No Artie today?" he asked once he'd reached the counter. He ignored the urge to pull his cloak tighter about his guard's uniform as he fidgeted beneath Calvin's stare.

The vintner inspected him with dead eyes, as cold and distant as the stars. With his tongue, he shifted the roven stem to the opposite side. "Out sick. I reckon the little shit's playing me for a fool, it being Milgrin's Day and all. Starting to think I'd be better off employing my halfwit of a boy."

"Shame." William fiddled with the hem of his cloak. "Can't trust the youth nowadays," he added, in an attempt at solidarity. "Lazy, the lot of them. Bloody helpless."

"Can't trust anyone nowadays."

William didn't hear him. He was glancing over his shoulder at the rows of shelving stretching out toward the back of the store. Laden with receptacles, each case loomed at least a foot over William's head. Light filtering in through the far window, besmirched with grime, cast the shelves in a tawny glow. Reflected dapples covered the ceiling in an inverted crown. "Well..." said William, "just my usual then. Normally, Artie—"

"I know what you get." Calvin scratched at the scraggly folds of skin that encased his throat. He was still scrutinizing William with those impassive eyes. "I'm aware of all my clients' tastes."

"All right, then I'll just—"

"Almorian red. Got it. Will you be paying with coin or leveraging it against your tab?"

"Coins, I—"

"Twenty joricks."

William started speaking, then stopped. "Wait ... what? That's *double* what I paid last week."

Calvin pretended to pick at a loose hangnail; his cuticles were yellowing, incrusted, and chewed. "Is it? Ah, well. The market, you know." He offered a hapless shrug.

Thoughts of discretion vanishing, William clouted a fist against the counter. A handful of trinkets, carved talismans from the Dobë forests further south, rattled with the blow. "Oh, come on. That's horse*shit*. You know it same as me. I'm not some bloody youngling, Calvin. I won't have you swindling me."

Craning his eyes up from William's hand, Calvin smacked his lips in an even drawl. "It's Milgrin's Day. Either buy something or get out. I won't have my time wasted by the likes of *you*." He fixed the captain with that stare, what was less deadpan now and more quietly brimming.

"What are you implying?"

Calvin didn't bother answering the question. He made as if to turn away.

"This isn't right." William realized, without caring, that his voice contained the slightest of wavers. "You're a filthy cheat."

The floorboards groaned as Calvin wheeled back. "Is that so? Huh." The vintner gave a scoff before reaching up and yanking the roven weed from his lips. "Curious, a member of the Guard purchasing wine." Calvin shot a glance over the edge of the counter, appraising William up and down. "The captain, too—and in his full uniform, no less. As if he has a shift coming up."

William tensed. Knowing himself outmaneuvered, he pinched his lips shut.

"Huh," Calvin persisted, as if he were genuinely intrigued. "Indulging on duty. None of my business, that, but I wonder what the Council would think."

William's fists disappeared into the folds of his cloak. He dug his nails into a thigh.

Seeming to enjoy himself, Calvin continued picking at his own cuticles with a maddening nonchalance. "Not that it truly matters, I suppose. Your lot doesn't do much up there in those outposts anyhow. Have you ever even had cause to draw your sword, Breeve?" Calvin peeked up from his pudgy fingers. When William didn't respond, he went back to grooming. "Interesting. How 'bout a bear? Ever seen a grizzly up there?"

A clammy sweat had broken out upon William's spine, the droplets adhering themselves to his tunic. Already narrow and cramped, the wine shop now felt outright suffocating.

"Ever seen any monsters? Wandering spirits? Fiery demons?"

"No." His voice came out a rasp.

"Strange. I thought that's why the Founders originally organized your lot. Some dark presence inhabiting the North. Isn't that how the legend goes? An evil entity waiting to swallow us whole?" Calvin laughed, a horrid, scathing cackle snuffling out from his nostrils. "Superstition, that's all that was. And we're the bloody idiots still funding their delusions."

William didn't argue. As a military man from the South, he generally agreed. Even before he'd emigrated here, he had paid little attention to stories of spirits or ghosts or other supernatural beings. He simply didn't believe in them, nor in any of the other rhetoric spewed by the fanatics. He'd witnessed many wars—genocide even—started from such oratory, helpless mothers and babes cut down in the name of various dogmas and creeds. Nay, the supernatural and all of its accompanying ideologies were merely tools used by avaricious men to further their aims, whether they themselves knew it or not. The world was what it was, nothing more.

"Makes a man wonder, though." Calvin leaned against the cabinets along the back wall. "Has the Guard ever protected the town in any tangible way? Truly? Done anything—whatsoever—to keep us safe?" This time, the word wouldn't emerge from William's throat at all.

"Nah," Calvin continued, with a theatrical lilt to his eyebrows. "Far as I can reckon, the Guard is the biggest waste of coin in Norick's history. Soldiers?" The man gave a scoff. "More like a bunch of wet nurses. And pathetic ones at that."

Some part of William was livid, but he could hardly detect the emotion beneath his desperation and the hard truth found in Calvin's words. The man was right: William's and the rest of the Guard's jobs were strictly precautionary. In its hundred-year history, Norick had never once been attacked or looted. Never even had a murder, as far as records showed. The town's greatest threat was posed by nature itself—rare summers of drought, the occasional tempest, winters of almost wanton brutality—but that was nothing his men could solve. In the end, this valley was generally safe.

And those rumors of a living darkness infesting the woods?

Silly fantasy.

"The Guard's a joke, Breeve," said Calvin, "and as far as I reckon, you're to blame. A bottle of wine is only as good as its vintner. I want no part in helping you erode this town's safety even more than you already have. I won't endanger lives because of your carelessness."

William couldn't meet Calvin's eyes for the smirk lodged there.

"All right," he said. "Truce." Agitation coiled in his gut like a living thing. What if the shopkeeper truly meant not to sell to him? What if he couldn't stop this shaking in his hands? Worse yet if Calvin dragged the moment out, forcing William to wallow in his shame. He needed this done. Right now. By all the gilded spires in the South, he needed this damned thing over with.

William eased his hands over the counter, as if he were settling an agitated beast. "I spoke in haste. I see that now. I'll pay your fee, whatever it is. Let's just look past all this, then we can both be on our way."

Calvin bathed him with a cockeyed frown, one desperate to be a sneer. "I don't know, Breeve... Wouldn't be in good taste to indulge your—clearly destructive—vices."

William pulled in a breath through his nose. He could feel that coil of agitation tunneling deeper, and the shop's dingy walls pressed in close. *Don't you dare*, he scolded himself as waves of heat broke out over his flesh. *Don't you fuckin' dare.*

Amused, Calvin simply watched as William lost control. Even when his tears started rolling, the vintner refused to look away. It was only as William was making his way to the entrance, wearing humiliation like a garment, that Calvin relented. With an exasperated sigh, as if he were dealing with the tantrum of a youngling, he offered a wave. "Fine, fine. Breeve, wait." William trundled to a halt, his legs threatening to topple. He didn't turn. "There's no need to pout," Calvin said. "Just get what you need, then go. No jest. Hurry up—but first, show me the coin."

And William, shaking all the while, did so. Despite Calvin's apparent change of heart, the spiteful bastard counted out each coin meticulously, laying them flat upon the counter with a dull clang before stacking them off to the right, a smug non-expression plastered to his cheeks.

Finished, he deigned only to give William the curtest of nods. He retrieved the proper vintage, weighed it, then festooned The Wandering

Cask's customary silver ribbon about its neck. With similar muteness, William seized the flagon from the counter, squashed it against his leather chest plate like a medallion hard-won, and beelined for the door.

He elbowed the slab open. Beyond, townspeople bustled through the Market Square, cheerfully stringing banners, roping off activities, erecting tents. The sight instantly made him claustrophobic. Gulping, William moved to cross the threshold and slip away, but Calvin surprised him by calling out. "Breeve."

William's stomach clenched. He closed his eyes, steeling himself for the trap. The shopkeeper's voice, however, was soft now, if not gentle then a strange mix of solemn and curious. "Why don't you just leave?" Calvin paused, and though he couldn't see him, William knew the man was shaking his head. "No one wants you here. *You* don't want to be here. Look at ya—you're as decrepit as old Ferny. Why not go back to the South? After everything that happened … why keep reminding yourself?"

Caught between the shop and the lively preparations beyond, William froze. A crease between the square's cobblestones filled his vision. Blurred. Having no words to express his ineffable mooring, William instead choked out the only thing that came to mind: "*She* was from here."

Calvin scoffed. "Bloody sunken hells. That's foolishness, you dolt. Can't you see that? It's been four years. It's not noble what you're doing. It's not even sane. It's just pathetic. You're torturing yourself, and for what?"

No doubt viewing himself gracious, the vintner let out a sigh. "Norick's not your home. Never has been. Staying here accomplishes nothing. She's gone, Breeve, you hear? *Gone.* Do yourself a favor and just *go.*"

William stood frozen. From some distant realm in which his body dwelt came the sensation of the Almorian red, moist with perspiration, slipping from his grasp.

"What say you?" asked Calvin. William heard him prop a meaty elbow on the counter. "You know I speak the truth; you may as well accept it."

William shored up his hold upon the flagon. "Thanks for the wine."

Head bowed, he staggered from the shop.

You don't need it. As always, he wished he believed that.

The glass flagon, nearly as round as it was tall, glimmered across the tower's veranda in the wavering lamplight. Its contents, a fluid the shade of evening crimson, caressed the vessel's tapering lip. Earlier, as he'd popped the cork, William had spotted—then fixated on—the haggard face reflected in the glass. He took in the taut, inverted nature of the cheeks, which stretched in stark contrast to the purple bags drooping like canopies beneath both eyes. He inspected those orbs—dark as charcoal—and the scrubland of stubble darkening his chin. The tufts, patchy as a clump of weeds, were moldering from a thick black to a shale-gray. Not recognizing the man returning his stare, William took a step back. Only to reveal a wider image, distorted by the flagon's bulbous curve.

A rolled paunch flopped at his midsection, circling the crest of his hips. It retained its shape not from an ingestion of food (he rarely ate more than a slim portion each day) but from a regular helping of ale and, following bimonthly wage distributions, wine. Further up, the spokes of his ribcage protruded sharply: skeletal, incongruent with the whole. Calvin had likened him to ancient Mary Fern, who hobbled her way through Norick on that twisted pinewood cane of hers. An apt comparison, except she was likely to be of a sharper mind. Only forty-four, and William was wasting away. Not some damned fool, either, he understood what was causing the decline. He'd seen its effects in other men. He knew the toll it exacted.

Even so, that wine called to him like an old promise. He didn't even have to take a sip; it was inside him already, whispering its assurances. *Just once,* its song crooned as it floated through his head, poised to swell at the slightest provocation. *What difference will it make?*

He'd never drunk on duty before, that's what. Always he had held off until after the shift. Had made a vow to himself, even. Aye, he'd stood watch hungover often enough, but this was different. This was a merging of two disparate worlds, a dangerous intermixing. William understood what such a merger would signify. If he did this now, it would truly be over. Drinking that wine was a forfeit.

He didn't need it, he didn't need it…

He crumpled to his knees.

"Help me, Ellen," he pleaded into his clammy palms. "Please, Elle…" The only answer was a smarting ache rising into his kneecaps. Vaguely, he could make out the muddled din of the festival, drifting up from the valley below. *They're celebrating; why can't you?*

It was those distant, featureless voices that returned his attention to the flagon. The receptacle was staring at him, William was certain of it. Even with his eyes closed he'd been able to sense its presence, as if the flagon were exuding some kind of aura, visible in both body and spirit.

Now it practically *beamed* at him from its perch. It crooned.

He blinked at it through splotchy tears. His mouth, rather suddenly, flared with a cottony dryness, and his stomach roiled. Across from him, the wine giggled in glee.

William averted his eyes before his body could lurch rebelliously forward. *Look at me*, he thought, face buried, limbs braced. *What've I become?* A military man from the South; the *captain* of the Town Guard, with over twenty men heeding his call: laid low by a simple flagon of wine.

No… he thought, over its hypnotic song. *I won't.*

Just one sip won't hurt, insisted another voice in his head. It hardly sounded like his own. *It's Milgrin's Day. You deserve this. One time—then never again. What can it hurt?*

Someone has to be on duty.

For what reason? What's going to happen?

Anything. Nothing. I don't know.

You want to.

Yes. No. I…

This is who you are now. This is all you are.

No. Ellen—

…is gone. This will help you forget her. Just for a while.

I don't want to forget. After my watch—

It doesn't matter. You're holding out for nothing. Today, tomorrow, thirty years hence… one day you will give in on duty. Now or then, the outcome's the same: You're alone.

"No!" William rocked back onto his haunches; with a snarl, he pushed himself up. Wobbling, he teetered his way to the balustrade and, in one smooth swipe, whacked the flagon from the railing. It tumbled over the ledge, end over end, and down the side of the tower.

Its glass surface caught a final shimmer before it vanished.

William heaved in air as he watched it fall. His palms dug into the balustrade, catching splinters. There must have been a collision, but he couldn't see it. Over his ragged breaths, he could hear neither a shatter nor an obvious *thunk*. But he'd done it… It was gone now, out of his reach. Even now he could feel its presence receding.

The moment had passed.

William buckled to his knees. Calling out to Ellen, he started to weep.

The thought came later.

A little thing, at least at first, tickling at the back of his skull. Seated against the balustrade, William became aware of it gradually. It was a vague curiosity—trivial, really. Especially after the commitment he'd just reaffirmed. Yet as the minutes passed—and it kept on nagging and nagging—the thought acquired a heightened degree of urgency.

It didn't make much of a sound when it hit, he thought, blinking into the torchlight. *That's odd… Could a flagon survive a fall like that? What if it did? What if it's just rolling around down there, waiting and intact?*

Perhaps…

Perhaps—just to be safe—he should go check and see.

CHAPTER THREE

Mary Fern, nearly a hundred and four years old and one of the first people to set foot on this plot of land a century earlier, braced her feeble legs atop the seaside jetty, leaned heavily on her cane, and squinted into the darkness.

She stood alone but not alone, and *knew.*

On the horizon, a storm brewed. It was little more than a gradual thickening of the nighttime gloom hanging over the Western Sea. There were a few pocketed flashes, at intervals, of severe white light, each of which revealed a silhouetted mass of thunderheads, all smooth contours and undulating mounds—rising, rising, rising.

With the storm's approach, something else drew near. Perhaps it was there already. Perhaps it had always been there and was merely awakening.

The fireworks over the harbor had ended minutes earlier, not that she had cared to watch. Facing away from the town and out over the bay, Mary held the ocean's countenance with her own: hard lines and wrinkles and sun-leathered skin, draped in a thick cascade of snowy white hair. She blinked for the first time in minutes, inhaled, then ground what remained of her rotting teeth.

Things felt different tonight; things had changed. She could feel it in the air, in the cold ocean gusts gradually building from the west. In the hollow ache lodged in her gut. She didn't know what it would be exactly, or how or why she knew, just that she did. Just as she always did. Something wasn't right; nay, something was decidedly wrong.

Mary Fern was certain now: Tonight would be the night.

CHAPTER FOUR

"I hate this shithole."

Thomas Calvin, fifteen, swung his legs back and forth over the edge of the rampart and reached for the pilfered jug of ale at his side. Technically, not stolen since food and drink were apparently free of charge thanks to the Council (*All worship and honor to their bloody highnesses, oh how infinitely generous are they*).

Not that the original owner, Victor Jacobson, would have seen it that way, what with it being his handmade, ornately carved jug and all; what with Thomas having taken it right out from under the potter's nose (*Stupid wretch*). Thomas wouldn't lose sleep over it, that much was sure. As he saw it, his father had left him no other choice. As the only winemaker and brewer in Norick, Marcus Calvin had overseen the distribution of alcohol during the celebration; as a hypocritical drunk who treated his children like varmints in need of constant management, he strictly forbade Thomas and his sisters from ever partaking themselves. He'd even instructed some of the Guard to inform him straight away if they saw Thomas drinking (*Good luck with that, Father*).

Hence here he sat, on a secluded section of the walls between two of the cresset-like torches placed at intervals along their length. From here, a short distance from the Market Square, he and his four friends could keep eyes on the celebrating masses while still avoiding detection. Hence the stolen jug. He took a swing then passed it to the lanky teen, shadowed in gloom, who lounged on his right.

Natalie Willow, a fisherman's daughter, gulped for a full five seconds before handing off the ale to the next teen in line. She wiped her thin lips with the back of her hand. Her strawberry-blonde hair, which she wore pulled back in a ponytail, swung with the movement. "*I* hate the bloody people."

"Aye," Thomas agreed as Betsy Til and Walter and Frederick Reins took their turns with the jug.

"...including you," Natalie added with a sidelong glance and a smirk.

"Don't make me throw you off this thing."

"Fred has fat ankles. I'll find something to grab on to."

"Then I'll push him over as well."

"Great, some cushioning for me to land on."

"I'm not fat," said Frederick. His jowls bounced with the reply.

"My ass," said Betsy through a face full of freckles. She made an *oinking* noise, then they were all laughing together and passing the ale again.

Walter burped. "*I* like the bloody ale." Foamy traces of it clung to the patches of hair beginning to sprout from his round face.

"Aye," the others agreed with further chuckling.

"Still a stinking pit."

"Aye."

"With stinking worms for people."

"Everyone crawling all over each other, and for what?" Natalie added.

"Thinking they're *so* important," said Betsy.

"So blind and stupid, that's what they are."

"Acting like everything is always so perfect. Everyone's happy, all the time."

"Nothing is *ever* wrong."

"We are a moral people with moral lives! We shine with virtue in an unkind wild."

"We live together, as one," Betsy chimed in, imitating Thomas's tone of proud rectitude. "In unity..."

"...in justice..."

"...in peace..."

"...in *love*."

"Making a better future..."

"...for ourselves..."

"...for our children..."

"...*for the world!*" Thomas, Natalie, and Betsy finished the creed together, a town motto they had heard the citizens declare more times than they could possibly count—all their lives, in fact. The words held a resonance of history, of memory, beyond mere tradition. They were statements wrapped up into the framework of the people's lives, in how they sought to live and conduct themselves. Or so their parents said.

Down the line, Frederick and Walter hadn't noticed the chant. They were busy trying to spit on a statue of one of the Fifty rising nobly far below. Christina Lyons? Rian the Craftsman? Thomas couldn't remember which of the Founders the sculpture depicted. Whoever it was, Walter's third attempt landed with a *plop* on his or her stone head, and the two shared a cheer.

"I want in on this," Betsy said, hacking for some mucus.

"We really are alone, aren't we?" said Thomas, ignoring the game. He was glancing out toward the looming Remos Mountains, a sheer track of craggy alpine peaks ascending as far as the eye could see. During the day the range was a hazy, iridescent multitude beyond counting. Tonight, it towered like a collection of black monoliths. For all but three months out of the year, shimmering fists of snow clenched themselves about the summits; each daybreak, the sun rose unhurriedly, almost timidly, over those peaks, yielding prolonged mornings of shadow.

"Ain't much out there." Natalie had joined him in ignoring their friends' game and followed his gaze to the valley beyond. Norick resided in a shallow basin encircled by heavily wooded foothills, though wide swaths of deforestation now carved their way through the trees. Combined with the knolls, the mountains' precipitous rockface fashioned a formidable barrier surrounding the town on three sides, like a bowl with a serrated lip, broken only by the coastline to the north and Milgrin's Pass in the south. "It's almost like a cage."

"It's suffocating."

"Everything's so big, but there's nowhere to go."

"I wonder what the South is like. Endless cities, castles of the brightest stone. Kings and queens; the royal court. Can you imagine, Nat?"

"Palm trees," she added. "Deserts. Warm, lazy seas."

"Not a hint of winter."

"New faces. Stuff actually *happening.*"

"New faces..." murmured Thomas. Then: " 'Don't you dare drink, boy,' " he intoned in the husky drawl of his father. "Piss off, *Marcus*. Can you believe him? Biggest drunk in Norick, and he has the audacity to tell me I can't partake. Hypocrite." Thomas traced his eyes across the throng of townspeople milling about in the square. He wondered where the vintner was now (*Passed out, I'd wager*). From this distance, a few streets over, he couldn't make out much going on within the courtyard. Just a pulsating blob of humanity of which he'd never felt a part.

"They're all hypocrites," said Natalie, casting him a sympathetic glance. At this height, Norick looked almost miniature, spread out inside the walls in a disorganized grid. Dimly lit streets branched this way and that. Some avenues ran straight; others curved and meandered like wayward forest paths. Rows of houses were scrunched together, layered into clustered town blocks. Most were narrow and constructed of wood, ascending to slanting apexes and thatched roofs. Those belonging to the wealthier members of the community stood tall with firm shingles and smoothly carved mountain stone.

"Every last one of them," Thomas agreed.

"So much for virtue."

"Stumbling around like a bunch of younglings."

"Dancing like fools."

"Squealing like pigs."

"Idiots."

"Worms—bunch of filthy worms. Blind to the fact they're constantly eating their own shi—" Thomas squinted at the shadowed corridor immediately below their feet. He could just make out the shape of two adults, male and female, stumbling around the bend. The two were clinging to one another and laughing erratically. Thomas gestured to the others, then pointed at the scene: "Hey, shhh. Guys, look. Look at that. By Milgrin…"

Natalie—and now the other three—followed his finger with a frown. "What? It's just some drunk adults."

Thomas squinted some more; he was certain now. "Yeah. But look who it is." He'd dropped his voice to a whisper, hoping the others would follow suit.

Natalie shifted her weight forward. "Millons? Is that Gregory Millons? The stable head?"

Thomas nodded. The other three weren't impressed.

"So what?" Betsy said.

"I'm almost certain that's not his wife."

They squinted harder. "How can you tell?"

"Ain't tall enough."

"Not the same hair, either," Walter added. "And she's not dragging her leg like Rebecca does. Like the damned thing's busted."

"So who's the whore?" Betsy asked.

"Looks like Mayrin to me."

"Nah, that's definitely Priscilla Hawkins."

"No... I don't know. Maybe."

"Looks half his bloody age."

They watched in silence as the pair, hugging the far line of unlit houses, continued along the street in lurching spurts. Every so often, they paused to bring their faces—and their hips—together. Their hands were lost in the shadows. "Look at all that virtue," Thomas said. "Never seen such *virtuous* adultery." Natalie snorted, then stifled further laughter with a hand. At the last house on the block, the couple half-staggered, half-pulled one another to the door and shoved it closed behind them.

"Good for him," Frederick said.

"Don't know how he does it," Walter said. "He's as old as a bloody kalikan."

"Kalikan don't exist."

"Do too," Walter said. "Our pa was telling us about 'em. They haunt and torture their victims for hundreds of years."

"How? The person would already be dead."

"They keep them alive. Unnaturally." Walter whispered the last word as if he were reciting a particularly spooky campfire story.

"That's a load of rubbish," Thomas said. "A youngling's tale."

"Our pa—"

"You're an idiot."

"Whore," said Betsy, still peering down at the home the couple had entered. "I can't count the number of adults I've seen slobbering all over each other tonight. In *public*, too. And who knows how many of those were cheating slime."

Natalie nodded. "Me too. What's gotten in to them?"

"What do you mean?" said Thomas. "They're hypocrites. Liars, every last one of them."

Natalie shrugged. "Yeah, yeah, I know. But they've never been *this* bad before, not like tonight. Not out in the open anyway. I mean, yeah, they all pretend everything is perfect all the time—"

"Living in denial," Thomas interjected.

"—yeah, but I don't know. Tonight just feels different somehow. Like all of them have lost their need to hide it. Usually they at least pretend."

"They're just drunk. You know how the adults love their festivals." Thomas frowned. What was she getting at?

"Aye. But it's more like … they suddenly don't care. Like they forgot everything that's important to them, how holy and virtuous they all claim to be. I don't know. I just find it strange, that's all."

Thomas supposed Natalie was right: The townspeople's inhibitions did seem lower tonight, perhaps even unnaturally so. Even his own felt lacking (*Not that they were all that high to begin with*).

"Even my mother and father," Natalie said with a frown and a faraway look.

"What about 'em?"

"They're just different. I tried speaking to them earlier and they wouldn't even look at me. It was like I wasn't even there. Like they were under some kind of spell."

"They've never exactly been talkative."

"Yeah, but they were especially quiet tonight. Distracted. Maybe even sick of me. I don't know, tonight just feels odd."

"I agree with Natalie," Betsy said, turning away from the twins. "I feel it too. Everyone's acting … strange. They're distant. And it's allowing … it's like this sense of … chaos or something, just below the surface."

"Chaos?" Thomas cocked an eyebrow.

"Waiting to unleash," Natalie added.

"Like anything can happen—and maybe should. No consequences."

Thomas scoffed and glanced toward the twins. "You two hearing this nonsense?" They weren't; Walter had his lips locked around the jug while Frederick stared off toward the Market Square in a world of his own (*Dim-witted morons; why do I keep them around?*).

Meanwhile, Betsy was still talking, almost to herself. "It's the strangest thing," she said, "it's like there's some kind of *desire* in the air."

"Desire?"

"Aye. To do something wild, something … bad."

"Keep it in your trousers, Betsy. None of us are gonna take ya to bed." Frederick's oafish ears perked up (*Of course he's listening now*), but Betsy didn't seem to hear the retort. Her eyes were fixed on some distant point. Beside her, Natalie sat in silence; Thomas could feel her thinking.

"You're both raving mad," he said after it became clear neither wished to say anything more. "Or drunk. They are all horrible wretches, every last one of them. Drunk silly fools, that's all there is to it. No point making it more than it is. Tonight just goes to show that—"

"Hey. Hey!" Frederick was pointing down the wall. A figure, short and heavy around the middle, was rounding the curve and lumbering toward them. He was less than a hundred yards away. "It's the Guard."

"Time to go." Thomas stood; a gust of wind (*Bloody storm must be coming in*) forced him to pause and check his balance. Regaining it, he crouched and shuffled toward the stone rampway that slanted down the wall in a three-point zigzag. He glanced back. The others had snapped out of their contemplations and were moving to join him. Still positioned between the wall's perimeter lights, they might have a few seconds to scatter before the guardsman noticed them.

"I was getting bored anyway," Betsy said from behind Thomas.

"Me too," said Walter.

"Let's find some more ale," said Thomas, gesturing toward the empty jug Frederick held.

"Aye," they all agreed.

A punitive shout rose into the air, carried on the wind like an echo: "Hey, you! Stop. You can't be up her—"

They turned and gave the still-distant figure a passing glance. Betsy lifted an obscene gesture, snickering all the while. "Look at him. He looks like a damn roly-poly." She raised her voice and kept her hand extended. "Hey! Insect man—come get us!" Quieter, she added, "Fat ass."

"Hey," protested Frederick.

"Let's go," said Natalie.

And then they were descending the ramp, into darkness.

CHAPTER FIVE

Peter Ash could hardly breathe, much less think.

He cowered at the end of a darkened alleyway whose three sides rose above his head toward a patchwork of stars. The narrow corridor was formed by a pair of angular structures on either side, Remy's bakery to his left and Lucas Illhap's place on the right. Ahead, the passage opened to the far corner of the Market Square, which teemed with dancing torches and swaying bodies. Enthusiastic voices called out to one another; slurred, intoxicated singing rose above the commotion, dragging slightly behind or rushing ahead, not quite on pace with the up-tempo strumming of the musicians.

Peter—heavyset but not fat, with a wide forehead and angular mounds for cheeks—heaved air from his lungs. Out and in. Out and in. His stomach twisted in knots and seemed ready to come toppling out at any moment. He closed his eyes, overcome by the endless concave circles spinning in his head, then cracked them open again. He needed to vomit— whether from the hefty portion of ale he'd consumed that night or from the discovery of the parchment, he didn't know which. He tried pulling it up from his stomach, failed. Tried again. *Breathe,* he told himself, *just breathe.*

At forty-six, Peter served as a senior magistrate on the High Council, Norick's official ruling body. He'd recently been elected to his fifth term. As the master of trade, he oversaw the exportation of Norick's chief commodities: lumber, gold, and other minerals of worth, all mined from the heavily laden Remos Mountains. Another facet of his job involved the supervision of Southern imports. His days were endless examinations and inspections, transactions and legalities; his language was duties and fees and the legal jargon of negotiation. Throughout his twelve-year tenure as master of trade, he'd seen much—seen it all, he sometimes thought. He had been cheated and bribed; he'd been cursed at and assaulted and even taken as a prisoner by a band of pirates (a voyage to the Stanris Islands he wouldn't soon forget, all to establish an ultimately meager trade deal with the locals). There wasn't much that surprised Peter anymore; life, like the market, fluctuated in dips and crests, drops and turns. As long as one prepared himself for the inevitable fluxes that came with the seasons, then nothing could prove truly shocking or devastating. Life, despite all of its changes, was ultimately predictable.

But *this*... This he hadn't planned for at all.

He had spotted the blood as he was ascending the stairs of his front stoop. He'd returned home to retrieve a shawl for his wife, Sara, who always seemed to suffer from a lingering chill. ("Even in the midst of summer," Peter had muttered before setting out; Sara had just pretended not to hear him.) He hadn't been thrilled at the prospect of parting from his fellows and from the celebration; Milgrin knew, the opportunity for Peter to unwind came scarcely enough. Leave it to Sara to tarnish what had so far been an impeccable night.

Leave it to her to be needy in the middle of a damn party.

Irritation had kept him preoccupied as he strode down their block. Lit only from the cressets mounted on the walls, the houses on either side gave the illusion of stretching away boundlessly, like a tunnel leading into some black oblivion. Hands stuffed into the pockets of his trousers—strangely cold himself now—Peter had moved along the thoroughfare and hadn't bothered checking his surroundings. So distracted was he that he'd failed to notice the blood until his boots had connected with the stoop and he was reaching for their doorknob.

Peter jolted where he stood.

Just above his eyeline: a splash of ruddy color beveled by the distant torchlight. The sight—something out of place, an emergence that didn't belong—immediately truncated his thoughts. Peter blinked into the darkness and tilted his head toward what must surely have been a trick of the dim lighting, a mere figment of his preoccupied mind...

His mouth fell open.

There it was. Not a trick of the mind or a game of the shadows, but cold inscrutable reality, tangible and unmoving and peering at him like a contemptuous riddle. Sara and the festival forgotten, he squinted at it, his frown deepening. As he'd originally speculated, his mind jumping to the worst: *Blood.*

Splayed above the brass knocker, it assumed the rough shape of a handprint, with four vertical smears running through its center and trailing down, as if whoever had placed it there had pasted the hand for a count and then dragged his or her fingers toward the floor. The result was a splotchy coat of burgundy with the desultory effect of a child's sketch. As he stared at the blood, a chill crawled up Peter's spine. On impulse, he glanced down the vacant street, which no longer felt so empty. He couldn't pinpoint from where, but the sensation was unmistakable: He was being watched.

Dozens of windows leered down at him. Alleyways cut thin slits into the buildings' lineup, trailing off like portals into the unknown. A gust of wind, what sounded like a wraith's agonized shriek, funneled down the road.

Suddenly sweating, Peter whipped his head toward the door. *Blood...* It was not the quantity that unnerved him, for in fact there was very little. What'd sent his stomach plummeting was its very presence, its gloating simplicity.

The way it had appeared right before his nose.

Peter swallowed and, in a daze, stretched a finger toward the thickest portion of the symbol: the rounded belly of the imprinted palm. Carefully, at the crawl of an earthen slug—as if he were about to come into contact with something foreign and mephitic; as if by doing so he would set into motion something he could neither control nor understand—he tapped his fingertip into the blood. The liquid squished about his nail. He removed the finger and slid another along the corresponding digit of the symbol. His whorled skin came away red, moist.

The blood hadn't yet dried.

Which meant the intruder wasn't far from the stoop. Chances were the interloper still lingered somewhere nearby, observing him. Not daring to turn back, Peter absentmindedly rubbed his middle finger against the callus of his thumb. He could feel the skin sticking, stiffening.

It was then that he'd finally spotted the sheet of parchment pinned beneath the handprint. Peter's eyes narrowed. Jagged along three edges as if torn off in a fit, the note fluttered in the breeze. With smeared shaky fingers, he snatched it from its perch.

He stretched it taut before his eyes.

I know what you did.
Grove. 1 Hour.
Or the rest of them will too.

Peter's veins went cold. Dropping his arms abruptly, he hurled the parchment from his body, as if its edges were aflame.

The implications of the message tumbled in his mind like a ball of daggers. A tremor rattled his sternum. Seizing the note from the stoop, he read through its message once more. Finished, he darted a glance either which way along the street (feeling observed all the while), then yanked the note's knifelike rivet from the door.

He took off toward the Market Square.

And now Peter found himself alone in the alleyway, which was hung with the smell of warm bread, dead fish, and rotting meat. Behind it, the faintest hint of excrement and stagnant water, puddles of which vibrated within small depressions in the dirt, leftovers from a recent late-summer rain. Peter lifted his gaze from the muddy floor; his breathing, labored but slowing, fell in rhythm with the pounding of the heavy bombi drums outside. He worked at isolating the note's threat from his own emotion, forcing himself to view it objectively, as a merchant would, taking in all the facts and figures and turning it over in his mind as he would any market calculation.

This meant… But how? Impossible.

No. It couldn't be. No one knew. They *couldn't* know. The two of them had been so careful, so thorough. Surely no evidence remained, if any had ever existed at all. They had both sworn an oath; he recalled the words precisely. There was no reason for a cessation of that promise now. But what if she *had* told someone? *Then I'll kill her.* And if that wasn't it? If, in the end, they simply hadn't been as careful as he'd thought? *Then I'm ruined.*

He hadn't given much consideration to the possibility of being found out. The prospect had always seemed abstract, a concern belonging to a lesser man. Now the potential oversight haunted him, leaving Peter feeling flustered, exposed. Had he truly been so careless? So blinded by his ego? *What did I miss?*

His shock was swiftly curdling into rage.

The sheet of parchment crackled in his fist. Peter balled his hands tighter about the thin material and, before long, his nails punched their way through. Still he could see those words; they danced before his eyes, baiting him—and filling him with fear.

What am I going to do? But the question was a rhetorical one. What choice did he have? He was caught at the bargaining table with his purse open. There was only one play here: He had to go. As the note commanded, he would venture out to the Grove, where he would learn the blackmailer's demands—and his own fate.

He nodded to himself, feeling almost calm. The resolve held for a minute, then a moment more. Then it crumbled beneath the furnace-rush of heat funneling through his veins. He shredded the parchment into two pieces, three. It was reduced to fluttering scraps whirling about the alleyway before he was done with it.

So what. He'd done what he'd done; what of it? He wasn't about to let some coward blackmail him. Milgrin knew, dumb blokes had tried it before, ruffling up 'dirt' and demanding ransom to buy their silence. Oh, but this fool had something coming if he thought Peter Ash, magistrate of the *High Council*, was going to just lay down and be jerked about by the likes of him. *Oh yes. Yes, he does...*

Peter would not be made a fool of, not like this. Not now, not ever.

He knew what he had to do.

Pushing off from the wall, he rolled toward the square. A course of action cemented itself in his mind as he went, driven by a thousand vindictive voices hollering for retribution. It was as he was reaching the crest of the passage—mind lost on his upcoming counterstrike—that a child darted in from the courtyard and impeded his path. Seconds from stampeding over her, Peter glanced down, felt his heart leap, and pulled up short.

Her eyes widened; breathless, she smiled up at him. White-blonde hair, cut just below the shoulders, swung with the movement. "Papa, there you are. I've been looking for you—they're having a pie-eating contest! Let's go see if— What are you doing in here, Papa? Why are you all by yourself?"

Peter closed his eyes and released an exasperated sigh. Time was moving too slowly. In his head, the voices continued to rage. *Do something. Do it now, before it's too late. Catch him by surprise, whoever this scoundrel is. Arrogant bastard. Let him see what happens to people who cross you. Hurt him, hurt him, hurt him.*

He placed an unsteady hand on the crown of his daughter's head and maneuvered around her. He swept the Market Square left to right then traced his eyes back a second time. The courtyard was noisy and crowded, overflowing with sweaty townspeople. Wooden market stalls were pushed back along the edge, barrels of ale beckoned at convenient intervals along the footpaths, and blazing fire-pits coughed up sparks, casting the scene in a sensuous glow. "Not now, Heather. Run along."

At the dismissal, Heather, only ten years old, crinkled her freckled nose. "But Papa, you didn't let me go with the other children to play earlier... Why can't we do this now?" Peter ignored her. He scanned the stage at the far end of the square. It had served as a focal point for the day's festivities; currently, six flamboyantly garbed musicians (looking like court jesters from the South) manned the elevated platform with an intense and focused rapture, their limbs and fingers awhirl.

"Papa?"

Peter glanced down. "What?"

"You didn't let me go with the other children earlier."

He waved her off and kept his attention on the square. As of yet, nobody stood out (or seemed to be surveilling him). "We've been over this already. You know I forbid you from leaving the walls at night, and that's always how that lot ends up spending their time. I won't have it. Now go watch the musicians."

"Is something wrong, Papa?"

"Go, Heather."

"But..."

He looked down at her, finally affording her his full attention. He lifted a reproachful finger. "Child, I said no!" His patience was cracking, as was his nerve. "Understood? No." But this time his voice held little force.

Could he really do this, what his mind had planned? Could he, what with his daughter standing right here, practically begging for him to stay with her? And if he failed—what would he tell her then? How would he explain any of this? *If you're smart, you won't have to.* He wiped at the perspiration leaking into his eyes. He could still contain this. If he acted quickly, caught this blackmailer by surprise and did what was necessary, then Heather (*and Sara*) wouldn't have to know a thing.

Damage control, that's all this was. Mitigating his losses.

Just business.

Peter regarded the crowd, tracing a guardsman patrolling the walls with a lumbering gait. As he watched the soldier's indolent movements, nervous fury overtook him. Pushing away any final reservations, Peter gave in to the inner voice calling for reprisal and prepared to depart.

Heather hadn't moved. "But I wanted to dance. Can we dance later, Papa?"

Peter ignored her and stepped from the alley. He slid into the crowd; a man and a woman threw up their hands as he elbowed past. Moments later he hesitated, stopped, and turned back, guilt pricking at his conscience. It was a tiny sensation beneath the force of his rage, but it was enough to give him pause. The couple cursed and sidestepped out of his way, scowling venom as they charged past. Dumbfounded, Heather stood in the dim opening and watched the interaction with her pale green eyes. Peter studied her for a breath, just taking her in. His heart softened. Sighing, he fashioned his lips into a sad smile.

"Go find Mother."

Then, before he knew if she'd heard him or not, he edged his way back into the throng, refusing to think about anything but the task at hand. *Make him pay. Make him hurt. Make him suffer.* It was like an unholy cadence in his head, falling in time with his harried step, satisfying in its simple, methodic urgency.

Make him pay. Make him hurt. Make him suffer.

Peter hurried toward the harbor gate. The crowds thinned as he zigzagged through the narrow streets, moving further and further from the

Market Square. Further from the celebration, from the music.
From the lights.

CHAPTER SIX

As some part of him had always expected, William discovered the flagon waiting for him at the base of the tower, glimmering and unharmed.

Upon descending, he spotted the glass container at once. It stood upright upon its circular base—as if, William noted, someone had arranged it that way. *That's not possible,* he thought with a slow crank of his neck. *No, that's not right at all.*

It's a sign, that swirling voice inside of him whispered. *You're supposed to drink it.*

Maybe he was.

He knew there existed a logical explanation for the flagon's survival. From the corner of his eye he could see an ox cart, recently delivered up from town, encumbered with a load of straw. Clearly the flagon had fallen into that padded mass then tumbled to the ground. By mere coincidence had it landed upright. Coincidence and nothing more.

William knew this. He understood the rationality in such an explanation. And yet... It didn't feel right. More reasonable was the possibility that the wine was calling to him. That it *wanted* him to drink it, to finally accept his fate.

As perplexed as he was, as terrified, who was he to refuse?

Eyes affixed, he wobbled a step toward the flagon. His hands were shaking again.

What about the Guard?

The Guard. It was all he had left: this one solitary, monotonous, unfeeling job. But at least it was *something,* a current of routine and habit that, once abandoned, could only be filled by days of emptiness. He didn't have friends; even his comrades detested him. It was a vacuum he'd carved out for himself and chosen to linger in, like the hollow of a cave he'd entered years before and had ever since refused to leave. If he did this now, he would condemn himself to isolation for the rest of his life.

From a great distance, William felt himself stoop to retrieve the flagon. He stared at it blankly.

Around him, the compound looked on in an expectant silence. The place felt rearranged, foreign. Its three buildings—a diminutive barracks, stable, and the watchtower itself—were draped in a molding of shadow. A ten-foot palisade—stout tree trunks held together with thick strands of rope—enclosed the structures. One gate served as the only entrance.

The place was empty, but, just then, William didn't feel alone.

On quivering legs, he started back toward the tower, clasping the flagon like a prize.

CHAPTER SEVEN

Mary Fern shook and, despite the chill, let her cloak hang loosely about her knobbed shoulders.

The storm rumbled closer, ever closer. And still Mary hadn't moved. She couldn't have even if she wanted to. Her legs were no longer her own, her body an unusable abstraction. Standing on the furthermost boundary of the harbor, beady eyes clenched shut, she willed her thoughts beyond— and they went, echoing out amongst the wind. Soon she could no longer feel the bitter, driving gusts, nor hear the lapping of the waves along the slime-covered boulders. What she could feel was the *awareness* and, with it, a torrent of fear sloshing like poison in her gut.

It threatened to overcome her, to drown her.

Still she searched beyond herself.

She saw nothing, and then everything at once. A presence encroached from the trees. It swirled there, and here: beside her and around her and in her. Twisting along the streets, eager and searching, it lurked amongst the townspeople. Mary followed it as she could, and it led her up and away. Up to a sky that had been ripped open and was now hurtling toward the earth in a cacophonous rage: an expanding hole of crooked angles and jagged peaks, all of it spinning, spinning, spinning.

Tilting.

Many years before, the people of Norick had sworn off the unseen. The supernatural was nothing more than a figment to them, an elaborate fiction they'd cast aside. But here—in their garden of reason and virtue, after all this time—it had found them anyway.

Here, it would make itself known.

PART TWO

WANDERINGS

The night has a voice.

Listen close,
And you'll hear it
Calling out your name.

Like a whisper upon the wind,
It summons those with wandering eyes.
It murmurs to the lost.

It beckons not, the night,
With promises of beauty or warmth or life,
But with the cool hands of the unknown,
The freedom found in darkness deep.

The night has a voice.
It always speaks.

CHAPTER EIGHT

Julie Temult, twenty-six with jet-black hair, pale skin, and a tiny, almost shrunken nose, knelt behind a decorative waist-high partition dividing the two properties and kept her dark eyes trained on a house across the street.

She studied its first-floor window and the bald, broad-chested man moving within. Washed in a wavering orange glow, he paced contentedly while clutching a goblet of wine that shimmered in the candlelight. Julie thought he looked like a specter, moving back and forth with no legs.

Skylar Higgins. The chancellor of the High Council and mayor of the town. The elected voice and leader of the people. Well-dressed, well-spoken, and generally well-liked.

Pompous wretch, Julie thought.

She had known him only from a distance until recently—until two nights ago, when he had come into The Hooks, Norick's only tavern, for the first time since she'd started work there. He'd entered alone, cheeks rosy, and paused in the threshold, his massive presence instantly seeming to fill the space. Turning from the three ancient bear-sized harpoons adorning the back wall (the tavern's namesake), his eyes ran up and down the rows of thick oaken tables, searching faces. The smoky, wood-ceilinged great room was nearly empty but for a few patrons scattered here and there; it was late, and just days before the festival. Most of the townspeople were at home asleep, resting from a long day of setup. The following morning promised plenty of additional preparations. The tavern's owner, Lucas Illhap, had even called it an early night, entrusting The Hooks to Julie.

None of those gathered seemed to give Higgins a second thought. Satisfied, he proceeded toward the bar, plopped on a stool, and beamed at her from across the counter. "Milgrin's courage," he said.

"Milgrin's courage."

"How are you doing this fine evening?" His voice, which was known to boom during his speeches, lilted slightly higher that evening. His breath—a hint of oaky wine and seasoned meat—fogged over her nose as he leaned forward. A meticulous goatee hugged his lips. He continued smirking like a fool, and Julie forced herself to smile back. She couldn't stop herself from dwelling on the chancellor's luminous white teeth—preserved so by an expensive substance made from the leaves of a teelyle plant—nor from thinking of her own, yellowing and crooked, two of which were missing from when she'd slipped on a spill and fallen face-first against the counter.

"I'm doing very well, sir," Julie said, despite her exhaustion and the fiery ache burning in both feet. She wiped her palms on the faded apron cinched about her waist. "And yourself? Is there something I might get you right away?" Her eyes passed over his teeth once more; she noticed a small chunk of meat lodged between the two positioned near the center. *Not so perfect after all.*

"Oh, I'm doing fine," said Higgins, widening both hands. They were positively *huge*—veiny and thick with monstrous, tubular fingers. Julie reflected just how easy it would be for them to crush her windpipe with a single squeeze.

He laced his fat digits together. "Actually, that isn't fully true. I am doing quite well, just a tad worn out. That's why I'm in here now, I suppose, a short reprieve from all the madness. It's been a long fortnight. So many preparations, you know. So much planning. A festival of this magnitude doesn't occur without a tremendous amount of labor beforehand on my part. I'm happy to sacrifice, but I would be speaking falsely if I said I wasn't just a little ready for all of this to be over."

"I can only imagine the amount of time and energy you've given." A memory of countless laboring townspeople flashed through Julie's mind; she couldn't recall seeing Higgins among them.

"Aye. The responsibility is a great one. But one I cherish. Soon enough all of my toils will be rewarded." Higgins nodded to himself. "Yes. Soon enough the citizens will come together, fill their bellies, and celebrate one hundred years of virtue and prosperity. Really, what more could I ask?"

Julie listened and tried to appear interested. With her fingers, she played with a soiled rag beneath the counter.

"That is, other than some of your finest wine, my dear." He chuckled, fiddling with one of the ornate gold rings wrapped about his fingers. "*And* some of your company—finer than all the wine in the world, I'm sure."

Pretending to be flattered, she offered a giggle before turning her back on him. "Absolutely. I'll be right back with that. And you're very gracious to praise me, sir." She shuffled toward the wooden shelving lining the wall behind her. She reached for the top ledge, where they kept the Southern imports.

"No need for such pleasantries, my dear. I don't expect you to acknowledge me with 'sir' all evening. My real name will suffice."

"Very well, Mr. Higgins." She chose their most expensive selection and poured it into a chalice, watching the crimson liquid fall from one vessel and rise in another.

"Ah, so you *are* aware of who I am." Higgins chuckled. "I realize I practically revealed as much already, but I'm just never certain with some people, you know. I'm told I appear differently out and about in town than I do up on stage during gatherings. Must have something to do with the elevation or the ceremonial dress." He sighed thoughtfully. "Alas, I'm just like any of you. People often see only the leader but forget the man."

Julie took the two strides back to the counter and proffered him the chalice. His eyes were on the oaken rafters above, leaving her to hold out the wine awkwardly and wait. "Perhaps it's my own fault. Not being as public and accessible as I should be. I used to come in here all the time, but I rarely get the opportunity now. The demands of my position just keep me too busy, you understand. What with our recent growth and all of our developing trade interests. Governing is no easy task, even for a town this size. And keeping those jackals on the Council in check is no simpleton's game either."

He snickered and brought his gaze around. Finally, he accepted the chalice—just as her arms were beginning to tremble. "*And,*" he continued, serious once more, "it's paramount, as chancellor, that I provide a good example for everyone in Norick to follow. It's not just words, you understand. Our morals truly do mean something. Our honor is what's preserved us all these years. We've evolved as a people. That's what the upcoming festivities are all about: a celebration of our rise to greatness as a community. Our transcendence. The Founders' ideals live on in us. Our spirits are pure and our ways are true. A hundred years hasn't changed that, and a hundred more won't either." Lacing his fingers around the neck of the chalice, he inspected it before offering a smirk. "Not that a little wine isn't warranted every now and then." He lifted the vessel, nodding in her direction. "I suppose, it also allows me to mingle with the common folk, which is always a delight." He pressed the rim of the cup to his lips and took a rumbling gulp. "Delicious. Thank you. The South does get some things right after all."

Julie was still fixated on his use of the phrase *common folk*. Her eyes narrowed.

After that, Higgins began rambling on about the various regions of the South and their particular breeds of wine and how he had sampled nearly all of them over the years. He lectured her about how each variety paired better with certain dishes than with others and how to decide between them. As if she hadn't already known that. As if her very profession didn't hinge on her ability to do so. She thanked him for his advice then refilled his chalice. He barely heard her, already transitioning into a long-winded spiel about his responsibilities as chancellor. Julie just continued to nod politely when it seemed appropriate; she was used to this kind of treatment, to being a silent, anonymous face patrons could speak at when they wanted to feel important.

But she also couldn't ignore how something twisted inside of her every time Higgins opened his mouth. She didn't know what it was exactly, but she felt herself growing furious. Standing across from him, she washed cups and tableware in a soapy basin of water; her hands were bone-white as she scrubbed a rag across the utensils, back and forth, back and forth. She refilled his chalice twice, three times. By the third, the chancellor's proud posture on the stool had acquired a sway. Additionally, his voice had risen with each subsequent pour; he was practically shouting at her now.

"So, my second cousin Eustace—Eustace from the coastal city, you remember? The mayor I mentioned earlier? The ardent gambler? Nearly four hundred pounds, that wretch. Has all these scars from those boils he had when he was a lad. One ugly bloke, I tell you what. Can't miss that hideous goblin when he waddles through the streets."

Julie wished others could see Higgins now: face a smoldering red, hollering officiously like some common fool. But the last few patrons had cleared out nearly an hour earlier, and she was left alone with the chancellor. (She wondered briefly if she should be frightened of that fact. *No, he would never.* Despite his vanity, Higgins at least held himself to be a virtuous man. He was the *chancellor* of Norick after all, a town founded on the notions of goodness and purity. Surely that would prevent anything from happening. Right?)

She barely heard him as Higgins rambled on about his relative. "So Eustace somehow gets in good with the king. Well...I believe the two knew each other when they were lads, when he was just a prince. Something or other. Well connected, that wretch. Anyway, for his birthday—his fortieth—the king presents him with a vase made of the purest gold. The two of them are that intimate. It's the most beautiful, radiant vessel your little mind can fathom. Its surface positively *lusters* in the sunlight. And the whole base is jewel-encrusted—rubies, emeralds, these absolutely splendid pink stones from the Tarmron region. It's the most wonderful thing I've ever seen."

Julie didn't know what his point was, but she wished he'd get to it.

"So, the fool brings it with him three months ago when he comes here on holiday. I can't imagine what possessed him to take such a gamble, lugging such a precious treasure by ship over such a distance, but I guess he deemed the chance to show it off to his lowly cousin worth the risk. It's unfortunate that he has yet to master a sense of humility like those of us here in Norick."

Julie turned to conceal the roll of her eyes.

"Anyway, as you'll remember,"—she did not—"Eustace spends a good deal of time here with us, surveying our humble little town, learning our customs. Frankly, I believe he found it all very curious, our life here in the wild. It certainly has its disparities with city living in the South. Though things have changed over the years, of course. We're not as primitive as we once were."

Higgins chuckled to himself and took a long gulp. He used the back of his hand to wipe at his thick lips. "On one of the last nights, the wretch desires a game of chance." He put a palm on his thick chest. "I'm not a regular gambler myself, mind you. I find that style of entertainment infantile. But I decided to humor him; it was his holiday, after all. So, we play—dice, so adolescent, if you ask my opinion. But I indulge him. We wager back and forth for several hours, and finally, at the end, for one last round, the fool offers to win his money back—I was up handily by then, you understand, and had come out with quite the haul. But I knew immediately I couldn't deny his request, because I knew just what I would ask for: the vase."

He said those last two words with gusto, like a schoolmaster coming to a particularly tantalizing point.

"He had shown it to me the previous evening, gloating as usual—Southerners really do have such poor manners—but I'll be frank: I was envious, to a degree. Any human being with functioning eyes would've felt the same. I knew I wanted it—not for the monetary value alone, mind you, but for what it represented. Such prestige, such honor. Royalty made manifest."

He gave his head a nearly imperceptible shake. His eyes went distant for a moment; Julie knew he was visualizing the vase, with all its vibrant, sparkling gems, sitting in a place of honor. *The wretch probably has it on his mantelpiece.*

"So Eustace, drunk as he is at this point, begs me for a chance to win back his money. Double or nothing. His bet is the vase.

"Of course, I *must* accept. It'll serve him right for gloating. The vase, when I win it, will be a constant reminder of the importance of humility—and will make my hearth room all the more pleasant." He leaned toward her, his bald head catching the firelight. "Chancellor or not, every man needs a pleasant hearth room, a space he is proud of.

"We agree on best out of three. Simple, straightforward. Fair. We're sensible folk, Eustace and me. Just us and pure, unbiased chance.

"We begin. Together … we roll the dice. Once"—he stabbed a finger out—"I *win*.

"Twice"—another finger went up—"he wins." Higgins made an *uh oh* expression with his mouth.

"Three times … and I jump madly from my seat!" Higgins flailed his powerful arms in mock re-enactment of the scene. "And—as you're probably already guessing—I win." His smug, self-satisfied look was almost enough for Julie to reach across the counter and slap him.

The chancellor dropped his arms. "Aye, what a moment it was… What a moment, indeed. And now the vase sits proudly atop my mantelpiece"

—*Knew it*—"and I can barely contain my pleasure when I hold it, which isn't often, I can tell you. No sense smudging it. Nay, only on special occasions. Hard not to catch myself staring at it, though."

He sat silently for a moment, waiting. Julie realized she was expected to say something. She fumbled for words, trying to remember the last thing he'd said and how to respond. Flustered, she stammered out, "What an excellent story, Mr. Higgins. I reckon you're very proud of such a hard-won prize. A very deserved one, I might add."

He glared at her. Remembering himself, he offered a sudden grin. "Aye, indeed I am. Eustace was none too pleased, though. I don't believe he'll be holidaying this way again anytime soon." Silence fell once more. Again, Julie didn't know what to say; her mind was concentrated on trying to steady her thumping heartbeat. She'd seen that look—that sneer—and it frightened her.

Oblivious of her unease, Higgins yawned. "Well ... there's still plenty of work to be done in the morning. I'm afraid it's time for me to take my leave." He reached for the chalice and finished off the last dregs. He set it on the bar, slid back from the counter, and stood, rocking from one foot to the other. He looked truly miserable then, pale and whiskered with dark silhouettes hanging beneath both eyes. His teeth were stained crimson. "Tell Illhap to charge the wine to my tab," he continued, slurring somewhat. He patted at the pockets of his trousers, removed something solid, and placed it on the counter. "For your service, my dear."

Julie arrived at the door a second before he did. He pulled up and waited as she reached for the latch and lugged the slab open. A surge of fresh summer air, crisp that late in the evening, pushed in through the entrance. For the first time, Julie realized how stuffy the tavern was, how claustrophobic.

She gestured ceremoniously. "Thank you for your patronage this evening, Mr. Higgins. And for your generosity. I'm very grateful. Please come back again soon." She simpered at him (without showing her teeth) and tried to ignore the pulsating ache in her heels, reignited by her sudden dash across the tavern.

"Yes, yes, you are very welcome." He made a half-hearted effort at a bow. "Now I must take my leave. Goodnight, dear barmaid." She couldn't have cared less what Higgins thought of her, not really, but his use of the title stung.

"And to you, *sir.*" Julie's lips withered into a grimace. She lowered her gaze to hide the expression, clenching a clammy fist at her side.

But Higgins didn't seem to notice. Without another glance in her direction, he crossed the mud-caked threshold—*I'll have to scrape that before I leave,* Julie noted—with a burp and a swirl of his sweat-dampened tunic. His monolithic figure fell to shadow as he marched across the Market Square. After a handful of paces, he ambled down a side street and vanished.

Julie studied his outline until she could no longer make out his hulk among the darkness. She swung the thick tavern door closed and threw the latch into place. She realized she was struggling for breath, without knowing why.

Stooping, she reached for her leather sandals and pulled them off. "Finally." Hiking up her dress—gray-blue and hemmed short—she sagged onto the stool Higgins had occupied a minute earlier and flexed her wrinkled toes. She closed her eyes, took a calming breath. She could feel the spool of tension unwinding in her gut. *Just a short break. A couple minutes, then I'll finish closing up.*

She didn't want to think about how early she had to be there the next morning. She didn't want to consider her final patron that evening nor his superior manner. She wanted—no, *needed*—to just sit. And so she did, massaging her throbbing heels. She sighed and let the kneading sensation dominate her thoughts.

At last, she glanced at the chancellor's tip. She'd been in such a rush to escort him out the door that she hadn't yet tallied it. Now—rubbing her aching feet, which had carried her for well over sixteen hours and felt like the center point of all the exhaustion and stress in her body—she examined the tip eagerly, reflecting that, despite having had to put up with Higgins's bullshit all night, she would at least come out okay. He was the wealthiest man in town, after all.

Julie dropped her foot with a thud.

The coin was jagged, oval, and roughly the size of her thumb: a fleetle. *One fleetle,* she thought with a surge of anger that surprised her. Her ears grew warm, and her shrunken nose flared with a sudden intake of breath. *One. Bloody. Fleetle.* Her hand darted across the counter and hurled the pathetic coin as far as she could manage. With a whistle of metal against metal, it ricocheted off one of the tavern's three hooked harpoons before coming to rest near a half-empty chalice.

One fleetle. It wasn't enough for a single slice of bread.

Two nights later, the evening of Milgrin's Day, Julie crouched across from Skylar Higgins's home and felt her stomach toss at the memory of his visit.

She readjusted her stance behind the stone partition. Whether imagined or not, she felt the meager weight of the fleetle shifting in her trousers' front pocket. Its movement sent revulsion tingling up her spine. Keeping her eyes on the candlelit figure inside, Julie stabbed a hand into her pocket and clenched the coin between two fingers. She remembered why she was there.

Their encounter had churned in her mind for the past two days. She'd been slighted by customers before—been cursed at and slapped and called every name known to the human imagination—but this was different. This she couldn't let go.

Early that morning while she had hauled yet another barrel of ale to the Market Square—sweat leaking down her temples and beneath her armpits, the summer heat already sweltering at dawn—something had fractured inside of her. She'd felt it in her chest; had felt it in the air. It grew in force throughout the day: a feeling of recklessness, desire, and contempt, turning itself over and over in her mind until, at nightfall, her inhibitions dissolved completely. Unbidden—like a strike of lightning amid a quiet spring rain—a plan took shape.

She would pay Higgins a visit that night. She would make a little trade.

The chance arrived sooner than expected. Mr. Illhap let her off early. "Go enjoy yourself," he said, nodding toward the door and the celebration beyond. "You've done enough. You deserve it." What he really meant was, *We're not busy—everyone is outside in the square dancing, not in here drinking—so go.* But if he wanted to feel good about himself by thinking he'd done something nice for her, so be it. Julie thanked him and, depositing her grime-coated apron beneath the counter, left The Hooks. After that, she stood in the center of the Market Square without moving, the crowds flowing around her. A sense of detachment consumed her; she felt outside of herself, numb and fiery at once, a sensation equal parts strange and thrilling. The feeling contained an adopted quality, as if it belonged to someone else.

Julie spotted him by chance. Higgins, dressed in a scarlet vest and a finely-embroidered cloak, loitered next to the stage clutching a goblet of ale. He laughed heartily with a group of council members. He was as boisterous and charming as usual: ever on his game, ever the center of attention. Julie crept closer, using vendor tents and scattered throngs to obscure her path. She watched as the chancellor delivered a final riotous joke before excusing himself and tramping across the square. He angled toward the street he'd used two nights prior. *He's heading home,* Julie thought with a clarity she couldn't explain—and, without realizing she'd taken another step, she moved at an accelerated clip to follow him.

Before long, she found herself crouching alone on a dimly lit side street. The neighborhood was deserted; the echoes of the celebration, several blocks over, filled the air but without distinct form. Just buzzing white noise. Lurking in the hush, Julie reflected how *good* all of this felt. How daring, as if for the first time she were truly alive.

More than alive: unstoppable.

Movement caught her eye. Julie shook herself from her thoughts. The candle in Higgins's window had been snuffed out; the door to his home swung open. Dressed in a silk vest (*He changed?*), the same jewel-studded black cloak, and a trio of golden necklaces, Higgins strode onto his front stoop.

Julie threw herself against the stone partition, palms pressed flat against the muddy sidewalk, and kept just the slits of her eyes over the ledge, hoping the darkness and the quiet would conceal her. If it weren't already too late. She held her breath, felt certain the chancellor would hear her anyway.

Sweat beaded on her forehead. The pit in her stomach stretched.

Higgins adjusted the cloak about his broad shoulders. Satisfied, he turned and pulled the door closed behind him. He started down the steps.

Julie ducked and scrunched her eyes. *Please don't see me, please don't see me, please don't see me...* How could she explain being knelt here, or even being on this street to begin with? Higgins would assume mischief on principle alone.

She waited, her knees aching from the crouch. She could hear his footsteps growing closer. She could make out the swing of his weight and the heavy pull of his breath. Her own lungs were on fire. She set herself to counting—something to distract her, to keep from gulping at the air. *One... Two... Three... Four...*

A new sound emerged on the street. It was partly shrill, partly melodic. Unable to resist, every muscle in her body prepared to spring and bolt away, Julie lifted her eyes over the partition, ready to find Higgins waiting there with a venomous scowl and a cocked fist.

Instead she was met only by vacant air. Puzzled, Julie craned her neck until she found him. He was marching away from her toward the harbor gate. Whistling. Julie plopped onto her rear and gave the night a hearty exhale. *Thank Milgrin.*

She waited until Higgins had disappeared altogether. Resuming a crouch, she ran her eyes up and down the neighborhood. All of the houses were quiet, infiltrated with darkness. A peek back confirmed the same for the homes behind her: not a candle in sight. For the time being, the street was empty.

It was time to move.

A prickle of fear reared its head, but she suppressed it with a grunt. A goading whisper had returned to her mind, and it urged her on with a wicked spew of assurances. *Just do it. This is your chance. Nobody will ever know. There's no one around. You're safe. And he deserves this. Show him he isn't better than you. Show him his arrogance has a price.*

Just do it, just do it, just do it.

Julie straightened and, to the whisper's cadence, darted across the street. She wasn't turning back, not now, not after making it this far. Not with this detached, dizzy feeling pulsing inside of her. She felt positively intoxicated by the rush of adrenaline, by the euphoria that waited once all of this was over.

She was on the steps then, rising swift and light on her toes.

At the entrance now, standing before the door. It loomed over her in shades of red and gold that reflected the walls' cressets. She reached forward and tried the knob. It turned with ease.

The fool had left it unlocked.

No one will ever know. He deserves this. You *deserve this.*

Julie shoved the door wide. It squeaked on its hinges before rebounding against the far wall and starting back. The splay of her shadow fell onto the stained wooden floor beyond. A rush of warm air and silence spilled out.

She stepped inside.

CHAPTER NINE

The toils of the virtuous are always rewarded, Skylar Higgins mused as his vaulting steps carried him to the harbor gate. He'd left his modest three-story home minutes earlier, whistling, eager for a few more moments of solitude before he returned to the Market Square and its lingering festivities. Right then, he could think of no greater company than the harmonious lapping of the sea. Ahead, it roiled black against the wharf.

Two members of the Town Guard, standing as rigid as stone pillars on either side of the gateway (Higgins knew the sentries had straightened only with his approach; he'd spotted them slouching like vagabonds as he rounded the bend in the street), hailed him with upturned palms, keeping the others clasped around their rusting spears. Trying to appear formidable, no doubt. And useful. *Which they are not.*

"Evening, Chancellor Higgins. Milgrin's courage."

"An honor to see you, sir. Pleasant night."

Chest inflated, eyes squinting in the semi-darkness, Higgins regarded each of them in turn. The lads—by Milgrin, he couldn't recall their names—wore light studded armor over olive green tunics. A scarlet insignia (a torch hovering above a cresting wave) was stamped to their breasts, and a pair of tanned leather helmets far too large teetered on their heads. One had slipped forward to rest on its owner's nose, obscuring all but the whites of his eyes. The poor wretch appeared too nervous to dare adjust it.

Shoddy. It was the only word for it. The Guard had devolved into a mockery of late: ill-equipped, ill-trained, and ill-prepared to handle anything of serious import. And all because of its leader, William Breeve. The captain was a drunk, pitiful man. Truly, Higgins felt that for him: pity. How unbearable for one to lose his wife and child as Breeve had, all in an hour's span—and to have been alone ever since. But Higgins's pity only went so far. Like all weak men, Breeve had made a choice to fester in his grief. He was a blight on Norick now, a sob story the citizens had long since lost patience with. Spineless, dejected, and about as pleasant as a corpse, Breeve offered nothing of value to the town; as the captain of the Guard, he had become a liability. So, while the man had Higgins's compassion, he certainly didn't have the chancellor's respect.

It wasn't as if Higgins couldn't empathize, either. He had lost his own wife, Teresa, almost two decades earlier after the sudden emergence of that lump on her throat. It'd been a globular, ulcerous thing, like a ball of compacted dirt buried just beneath her flesh. Later, it looked almost spider-like, with lengthy feelers reaching for more of her, eager to multiply. For a time, Higgins had known a sorrow like death itself. Could death really be so much worse than this gaping emptiness inside of him? Than her eternal absence? Like all things, though, these feelings had eventually passed. The Earth and its bustle kept moving; life went on. Losing your wife wasn't something you ever truly got over, but Higgins had tried (especially for the sake of Brade, who'd only been an infant at the time), and it was this act of trying that'd finally liberated him. The greater tragedy, he came to believe, would have been if he'd let her demise destroy them as well. No matter how difficult the circumstance, people had to find a way to pull themselves from despair. They *had* to. Anything else was purely shameful—a waste of life.

Which was precisely what Breeve was enacting: a squandering of his life. And this, by extension, was weakening the rest of them as well. In many respects, what the captain was doing was selfish. *Weakness festers only in the hearts of unworthy men. Self-pity is a plague.* Running his eyes over the scrawny guardsmen, Higgins decided it was time for some improvements. At the next council meeting, he would insist on new (properly fitting) uniforms for the Guard. And he would address, again, the issue of its leadership.

"Gentlemen." Higgins offered them a curt nod—they weren't fully culpable for their ineptitude, after all—and strolled forward through the open gate. "Let's stay alert now, shall we?" Behind him, he sensed the guardsmen stiffen. His tone held a warning they wouldn't dare ignore.

"Aye, sir," came a timid reply. "Absolutely."

"Aye, Mr. Higgins."

He glanced over his shoulder. "Unobstructed vision may assist in that, lad. Just so you're aware." Higgins marched on toward the wooden docks as the fool shuffled the leather helmet up to the peak of his forehead.

"Thank you, sir!" he stammered.

"Shut your trap," hissed the other. "Just be quiet."

The wind swallowed the last syllables of the retort as Higgins's boots clacked onto the smoothed planks of the wharf. Higgins pulled up, surveying the scene before him. The pier on which he stood was one of several gangways extending out from the shoreline. They cut through the harbor in long parallel lines, separated by slices of seawater that acted as shipping lanes for the various trade cogs, carracks, and fishing vessels that navigated into port. Berths for mooring were fixed at intervals, ready for the sailors' heavy ropes. At present, there was only a handful of small local craft, as the larger trade vessels from the South weren't due yet for another few weeks.

Along the perimeter, a cluster of open-faced warehouses were swollen with the tools of the trade: folded sails, riggings, oars; extra pieces for the masts, corroding anchors, buckets of tar. A guardsman—a pale-skinned fellow with abnormally thin legs, incompatible with the rest of his frame—lounged on a stool against a pyramid of freshwater kegs. His torch was set into a nearby mount; its oily flicker illuminated the sentry's closed eyelids and wide, drooling lips. *Is there no end?* Higgins suppressed the impulse to charge over and throttle him awake. Having dealt with enough incompetence for the moment, he vowed instead to scold the imbecile on his return and then proceeded up the pier, keeping his eyes pointed out toward the bay.

A storm approached. The wind had risen from the west, cold ocean sheets slapping against the exposed heel of the coast. Off into the distance, cracks of thunder boomed portentously as a mass of thunderheads churned their way toward Norick. Whitecaps crowned the black seawater, weltering in the air before perishing with a splash. The air smelt thickly of rain.

To possess the strength of nature... ruminated Higgins as he reached the end of the pier and settled in to watch the night come alive. *Such power; such unyielding, indomitable force.*

He would need to ensure the harbor crew secured the docks ahead of the storm's arrival. It looked to be a formidable one; the last thing they

needed was loose debris thrashing around causing damage. Nevertheless, Higgins paused to enjoy the sense of isolation the scene afforded, the
smallness he felt. Isolation and smallness and power—

Higgins frowned. *What in Milgrin's name?*

A short distance away, a figure loomed on the harbor's jetty. Higgins squinted, trying to make sense of the image. The figure, whomever it
was—a woman, he decided after a vein of lightning zigzagged across the
sky, illuminating a waterfall of snowy-white hair that reached nearly to her
waist—stood parallel to him across the water. Her body was angled toward
the bay; she appeared to have her neck thrown back. Like some kind of
scarecrow, her arms were extended out in a rigid fixture of lines. The woman looked positively wraithlike in that moment, as if she were communing
with the sky. A flicker of apprehension wound its way through Higgins, a
distant remnant of the small boy he'd once been: thrilled but terrified by
local legends and ghost stories told amongst his friends.

Shoving reason to the forefront, he peered closer.

Mary Fern. It had to be. Higgins knew that trailing white hair, and
he thought he could just make out her birdlike face from the profile. He
didn't know where her pinewood cane was; how she was supporting herself on those white, straw-like legs—which seemed unfit to carry her on
the most docile of terrain—he hadn't a clue. But it was her, all right. Mary
Fern: older than any in town, than any on record, standing alone on a per-
ilous stretch of seawall and exposed to the elements. In little more than her
undergarments, no less. A holdover from a previous generation, the frail,
eccentric matriarch was often believed to be quite wise, though Higgins
found her antics vexing and juvenile. She spent her days aimlessly wandering Norick and meddling in others' affairs. What some viewed as a cryptic
sense of wisdom, Higgins saw an exasperating tendency to dance around
inquiries and avoid providing direct answers. It was always riddles, cloaked
language, and platitudes with her. Always a stubborn fixation on the supernatural, on leading others astray. *Infuriating.*

Founder though she was, Higgins had little time for the woman. Yet
there she stood and, if he wasn't mistaken, she appeared to be trembling,
almost writhing in the wind. There was a chance her mind had fled her
altogether or that she was suffering from a bodily fit. He would have to
investigate, lest she lose her footing, stumble, and plunge into the water

and drown.

Higgins ignored a passing satisfaction—and temptation—at the thought and retraced his steps. *A good leader—a righteous one—can put aside personal feelings. A good man never hesitates to lend aid.* Arriving at the end of the pier, he retrieved a torch and started off along the water's edge by the light of its flame. On his right, rocky beachfront cowlicked with seagrass widened in a crescent toward the bay. Beyond it, the jetty stretched into the night. Its boulders were ragged, slimed, and damp from the spray. Puckered starfish and the occasional mussel latched themselves to the leeward sides. Leading with his expensive leather boots—which were already soaked—he took short painstaking steps and made his way up the seawall. If he weren't careful, he would break an ankle out here. *Or end up sopping wet.* Twice the storm's wailing gusts nearly sent him careening into the surf—and cursing loud enough for all the valley to hear—but his balance held true. After what seemed an age, he lifted his eyes and found her standing before him, her arms outstretched, her hair tossing in the wind.

The old hag didn't seem to notice his approach. As suspected, little convulsions ran up and down her sagging flesh. An unsightly gray tunic, tattered at the edges, shuddered with the movements. Her cloak was nowhere to be seen.

"Mary?" said Higgins, moving closer. He spotted her crooked pinewood cane lying within a nearby nook. "Is that you? Are you feeling well? What madness urged you out this far?"

Impossibly, the founder's limbs seemed to stiffen even further. A series of tremors juddered the lumpy tissue of her back, and she heaved a great sigh. Her arms, suddenly going slack, plopped down. "I am Mary Fern," she said, almost a question.

Neither of them moved. Mary's breathing had steadied, though she was still inexplicably staring out to sea. Higgins got the sense she was deep in thought, mind far from the jetty. *Deep in thought—and waiting for something.*

"It's Skylar Higgins, Mary. The chancellor."

"I know who you are." Still she hadn't turned. If he were a different sort of man, he might have classified the scene as eerie.

"It's considered uncouth not to look at someone when they address you. I don't know what fantasy you're playing at, but I won't let you stay out here. You need to head back to shore and join the rest of us in the Market Square. Reasonable enough? There's a storm coming in."

"I am aware of the storm."

"I'm serious, Mary. It's not safe."

"Nothing in this valley is safe."

"Are you certain you're feeling—"

"My health is stable."

Higgins didn't bother concealing his groan. He was growing damper by the second, and cold. "Enough of the games. It's time to head in." But Mary didn't respond, instead choosing to continue her showdown with the bay. As if expecting at any moment for something to happen. Higgins scowled as he took the final paces to her side—slipping once more, though catching himself before he fell. Recovering, irate, he snapped a hand forward. "Mary—"

His fingers clasped a bony shoulder. He spun her around. She rotated without protest, but when her face arrived, its pale beady eyes carved into him. Despite a desire to demonstrate his authority, Higgins found himself thinking less on her poor manners and more on the current condition of those eyes: little blue orbs, a shade so soft almost to be gray, that were sunken into her face like miniature river stones. Currently, they somehow looked both empty and full, clawing through him while also searching beyond to some distant point. Beneath them, Mary's rivuleted cheeks shuddered with a sneer.

Higgins dropped his arm, feeling as though he were a youngling who was being reprimanded and wasn't clever enough to understand why. He found himself taking a hasty step in retreat. "It's happening," Mary croaked—before turning her back on him with a sense of finality. In seconds, she'd resumed her watchful stance, as if *she* didn't have time for *his* antics.

Higgins started to say something then thought better of it. Something about that look—surprisingly lucid and utterly serious, with a mixture of cavernous dread—stopped him short. Any previous indignation had all but vacated his chest. For the first time in many years, Higgins didn't know what to do.

Should he just leave her out here? Declare good riddance to those who refuse help? Or was there perhaps more occurring on this seawall than he'd originally thought? *It's happening.* What did *that* mean? Cryptic old hag. *What* was happening?

Loath to let the mystery elude him, Higgins made a show of clearing his throat, hoping the sound would reclaim her attention (and some of his lost composure). But right then old Mary Fern may as well have been deaf to the world: At the sound, she did nothing. Didn't take a breath, didn't even twitch. It was as if he weren't even there. Unable to stop himself, Higgins leaned forward—not daring to touch her, not yet—and darted a glance between her shoulders and the sea.

"Mary," he said with the slightest of stammers hobbling his breath, "what on earth is going on out here?"

CHAPTER TEN

Darkness didn't scare Christopher Willow; storms, however, were a different story.

As a lifelong fisherman, he'd spent many a lonely night aboard his diminutive, flat-bottomed skiff far from the lights of town and the comforts of home. Often, he knew no company other than that of the stars, their wistful light imprinting a shimmering falsehood upon the waves. Some nights there were no stars at all, just varying degrees of darkness between the sky and sea.

Christopher didn't prefer to remain out past dark, but tracking the schools of yuki-yuli fish on which his livelihood depended often necessitated late-night voyages. The creatures, bloated in shape and vibrantly colored, with scales like glittering diamonds, fed in the evening on pockets of fluorescent green algae. Hence, Christopher had grown accustomed to the night and harbored no fear of it, but whenever storm clouds came billowing in over the horizon, a trawl of dread scooped through his chest. His father had been killed in such a storm, many years before. Christopher had come down with a stomach fever that morning; moaning and digging his nails into his belly, he'd begged his father—a stern and quiet man called Old Joe, who communicated as much with looks and grunts as with the spoken word—to allow him the day off from the sea. Finally, the old man had relented, offering Christopher a nearly imperceptible nod of his leathered forehead. Shoving open their cottage door, Old Joe let it fall shut behind him with a meaningful clatter.

Christopher twisted the blinds in their home's one window—a square opening barely large enough for his head to pass through—and watched as Old Joe's skiff pushed out to sea. He observed its progress until the white sail was no longer visible, disappearing in an iridescent haze that was building on the horizon. It was the last time Christopher saw his father alive.

Late in the afternoon, rancorous storm clouds gathered out over the Western Sea. Serpents of lightning streaked across their billows, and gales roared toward the coast. Christopher noted the changing weather with knots in his stomach, tightening now for another reason altogether. He begged that sail to reappear. And he knew, with a deepening certainty, that Old Joe was in trouble.

They discovered the wreckage the following day. A search party of fellow fishermen, no more than a half-dozen boats, set out at dawn, impelled not by any particular degree of friendship but by an unspoken kinship shared amongst their ilk. The skiff was found capsized and ruined; there was no body in sight. Even so, those fishermen told Christopher, Old Joe's fate was all but certain. As Old Joe's son—and as the coward who'd left him to die alone—Christopher had refused to believe such a jaded proclamation, refused to give it even a moment's credence. "But he could still be out there! We can't stop searching now. We have to save him."

"He's gone, lad," sighed a whiskered sailor known collectively as Bait. "The storm and the waves… There were fifteen-foot swells."

"It's not true. He's waiting for us!"

"He drowned, lad. *Drowned*. He's under a thousand foot of ocean by now. There's no riddle about it. It's best if you work yourself into accepting that. Not a pleasant way to go, but at least he went down with his craft. There's an honor in that." Bait, gaunt and weathered, removed his gray cap and placed it across his breast in a salute. "He's gone, boy. I'm sorry. He's gone."

For a long while, fear and guilt kept Christopher from entering the ocean. At night, he was haunted by the same recurring nightmare: his father, floundering out amongst the waves, his hair hanging into his eyes like strands of black seaweed. The dream would at first offer an overhead vantage, but then the scene would change, and Christopher was no longer just observing Old Joe, he actually *was* him, gasping and shivering and barely staying afloat, growing weaker and paler by the second, taking in gulps of water at first by accident, and then by design…

Tonight, Christopher could smell the tempest brewing, and he felt that old fear. It pulled him from a daze, jangling his nerves like a loose anchor. Feeling foolish—but not enough so to stop—he slipped away from the square and from his wife, Janae, who was caught up in her own trance as she watched the hypnotizing movements of the musicians. Sniffing at the air, almost tasting the destruction to come, Christopher hustled through Norick's winding streets. Two guardsmen, Brennen Varis and Tyler Prian, were arguing as he arrived at the harbor gate. One soldier stood as rigid as a mast; the other slouched against the wall, arms crossed against a scrawny chest.

"Stand up, you slug."

"Would you relax? There's no way he's coming back—not yet anyway. And I don't see what all the fuss is about; a little sitting's not gonna hurt anyone. Don't know if you've looked around lately, but there ain't shit happenin' out here."

"Doesn't matter."

"Why do they all get to have a bloody good time while we bust our backsides? We deserve to celebrate as much as the rest of them."

"You signed up for this, same as me."

"Yeah, because Delire told me old Breeve has gone soft as silk and doesn't enforce shit nowadays. I didn't think I'd be on duty for the biggest night of the year."

"You're a bloody *guardsman*. Who else is going to keep watch?"

"It ain't fair, is all I'm saying. Once-in-a-lifetime festival and we're missing out. I won't even have a story to tell my lads one day."

"Would you rather be shoveling pig shit in the sties? Because that's what'll happen if Higgins comes back and sees you slouchin' like that. He might even sack me too, out of spite."

"Least the wages are similar."

"I'm serious."

"Oh, come off it."

"Stand. *Up*." The more disciplined of the two, Tyler, had spotted Christopher plowing toward them. He jerked his head in the fisherman's direction, trying to be subtle.

"I told you—" Brennen caught his mate's gesture and glanced over. "Oh." He scrambled to his feet before puffing out his chest, clutching his spear with new purpose. Christopher strode by without saying a word,

giving each a passing glance. Brennen grunted at Christopher's scowl and
trailed him with a stare of his own. "What you lookin' at, leatherskin?"

Christopher speared the guardsman with a look vehement enough
to cause the lad to lower his eyes. Grunting, Christopher pressed on. *Little
sea rat's not worth your time.* Once through the gate, he took a moment to
study the looming squall before veering off toward a cluster of thatch cottages dotting the shore.

Coastline, they called it. A simple, uninspired name, but one they
more or less agreed on. As the homes of fishermen and other laborers, the
seaside hamlet represented some of the lowest class of citizens in Norick.
Unable to afford the more expensive property within the walls—long occupied by the wealthier families of town, descendants of the original Founders—many of the newer settlers had chosen to construct their homes out
here, along the gently sloping foothills. Cleared of trees over the years, the
terrain was moderately rocky with scattered patches of seagrass. Here and
there, ripening lilac clusters waved at passersby. In the neighborhood itself,
cooking pits forged shallow depressions in the dirt, and brine-encrusted
wash lines latticed their way between the cottages. Half-naked younglings
ambled about looking feral—and often sickly, with a flurry of sores, haggard cheeks, and sunken, guarded eyes. The adults were hardly better. But
it didn't matter: Coastline offered them a haven, their own little kingdom,
no matter how unkempt or destitute. Here, separated from Norick proper,
they were free to do—and be—as they pleased.

The place smelt of fish, sweat, and sea clover: all the scents of home.

Christopher's cottage, a dilapidated hut in sore need of repairs, consisted of two small bedrooms (created by a tattered curtain that was all but
see-through) and a communal living space. Once belonging to his father,
the cottage was now shared by Christopher, Janae, and their two children,
Jacob and Natalie. He wondered what the two of them were up to. Jacob,
the youngest, always seemed to be running off and making himself scarce
(and always just when Christopher needed him most), while Natalie was
a force of teenage stubbornness, tenacity, and a frightening degree of wit.
He'd come to accept he had little hope of understanding, much less con-
taining, her. Of late, he found it a challenge to even speak with the girl.

Christopher arrived at the hut. Moving around back, he left behind
thoughts of his children—whose unfathomable behavior sometimes made

him question whether they were actually his kin—and returned to the task at hand.

Earlier in the week he had lugged his skiff from the water and deposited it in the long seagrass sprouting behind their cottage. He propped the craft, with its sharp, pointed bow and boxy stern, onto a pair of braces. He wasn't one for sentimentality or gaudy displays—he couldn't give two gyriah shits about what other people thought—but Janae had all but demanded a renovation of the skiff. For weeks she'd nagged him about its ugliness—the coarseness of the wood; the bland shade of its hull; the way it seemed to bumble around through the waves like an overturned beetle. Didn't he realize how embarrassing it was for her to have the other wives looking down on it—and on *her*—with all their snide remarks? Didn't he realize a fisherman's boat was the source of his pride? The other men's hulls were decorated, artfully painted as tradition dictated; why wasn't his?

Relenting at last, Christopher had set to work on an overhaul. While it served no practical purpose for his fishing (again, he didn't give a damn how the bloody thing looked as long as it *worked*), he hoped the renovation would satisfy Janae and finally earn him an ounce of peace. *I swear, the whims of women...*

And, the dumb blokes who give in to their bidding.

With the lethargic help of Jacob, who would've much rather have been running off in the woods with his friends, Christopher had reinforced and sanded the hull, replaced some old sailing rope and a splintering oar, and stitched together several small imperfections in the sail. Finally, he was in the process of painting the whole thing a bright cheery red, Janae's favorite color—or so he had told her when pressed on his decision to paint it such (in truth, he'd purchased that particular dye because Trinity Weston had brewed an abundance and was selling it for half price). He had put on one coat already; tomorrow he would apply the second.

The mounted skiff drew into view, lit faintly by the distant lights of town. Planning his next moves, Christopher moved toward it, the knee-high seagrass tickling his calves as he went. He would secure the craft as much as possible before the storm arrived and ensure all the loose tools were safely stowed away. Perhaps then this simmering panic would abate.

Christopher knew something wasn't right the moment he came around the edge to the aft. He sensed it immediately: Something was missing. He had left four or five horsehair brushes, as well as the jugs of red dye, on a workbench in the grass. Both the containers and brushes were now gone. *I'd swear an oath I left them right there...*

He *had* left them sitting there, he was sure of it. He was a careful, or-dered man; he wouldn't have forgotten moving the tools. Which could only mean someone had taken them.

A fresh anxiety snagged him. Christopher quickly combed the area around the skiff, finding nothing. Next, he looked within the boat itself, checking to see if anything else had gone missing. The two oars were there, as were the netting and fishing line and the disassembled mast. Beside it, the thick mooring ropes and his flaying knife were both...

...gone.

Christopher blinked into the darkness. Somebody had stolen his brushes, dye, several cords of rope, and a knife? Earlier, disquiet had coursed through him like a chill; the harpoon of anger splicing into his chest now was like a fountain of flame. *Bastards.*

He whipped his head toward the village, searching for a thief despite knowing there'd be none to find. Whoever did this was long gone.

It made no sense. None of the items were worth much; sure, the ropes *could* fetch a price, but they were old and fraying. Why, in a town of mo-rality and virtue, would someone risk punishment for such a lousy haul? *Probably some drunk bastard trying to entertain his mates.*

More likely, some of Norick's younglings had done it. Christopher's thoughts returned to his children. Jacob wouldn't have—at least he didn't think so. The boy, despite his maddening aloofness, seemed to understand the reverence Christopher expected to be shown to his tools. That left Na-talie. Christopher didn't think she would risk his ire, but then again, she'd been spending a lot of time lately with that winemaker's boy. Maybe he and that cohort of his had something to do with this. Perhaps they thought this was some sort of game.

In either case, Christopher wouldn't stop until he got to bottom of it. *I'll lash 'em,* he thought. *I swear I will. By the nine seas, whoever did this is gonna receive a proper beating.* But for now: the storm.

Scowling, Christopher set to work safeguarding his boat against the incoming tempest.

Damn kids, he thought with a sigh.

CHAPTER ELEVEN

Heather Ash, ten years old with a bob of white-blonde hair, soft freckles, and two missing baby teeth, was just entering her family's home and swinging the door closed when she heard the wailing.

Her heart stuttered, both fearful and relieved at once, and she froze in the gloom of the entranceway, her small fingers clasped around the doorknob. She listened, lips parted. The noise—shrill and full of anguish, more animal than human, like the squalling of an injured doe—came from deeper within the dwelling. To her right opened the hearth room, glowing a hazy red from a few dwindling embers. A narrow staircase, set in the corner, led to the sleeping quarters above. The dreadful sound came from that opening.

On trembling legs, Heather stepped forward and angled for the stairs.

After her father, the master of trade, had left her in the alleyway, a vindictive twist to his face, Heather hadn't known what to do. His distracted, restless manner had perplexed and frightened her. His disregard had stung in a way only love could.

Papa had been increasingly withdrawn of late, spending more and more time away from home. Gone were the days when he and Heather had spent entire afternoons down on the mossy banks of Seagren Lake, sketching mud paintings of lions and dolphins on their forearms and wrists. Their giggling at their crude images had given way to deep belly laughs as they'd hurled mud back and forth with cheerful tears pooling in their eyes. Now, he was perpetually busy with negotiations, late-night meetings, and prolonged voyages to the South, all byproducts of a burgeoning economy (or so he'd told her). While Heather was acutely aware of the new lines of stress etching themselves into his forehead—as well as the growing sense of distance—she continued to hold out hope that things would change, that his apparent indifference would reach a tipping point and swing back into warmth and affection. She'd hoped that tonight, the evening of Milgrin's Day, things would go back to normal. That she and her parents would enjoy several hours together, just the three of them, free from obligation and stress and the unspoken cloud of heaviness that hung over them all.

Tonight they could be happy.

But then he'd sent her away. Again. With a lump wedged in her throat, Heather had slouched in the alley for a long while, biting at her lip to keep the tears from coming. Eventually, she decided it didn't matter. *She* would have fun, with or without him. Swallowing, she pushed aside Papa's dismissal (and the urge to follow him) and returned to the celebration.

She meandered through the crowd. Most of her friends weren't around; even Kel Pollor, her best friend, was absent. Companionless, Heather settled on watching the pie-eating contest from the sidelines as the ten or so contestants, arms looped behind their backs, buried their faces into the gooey fillings. After a winner was declared, she set off for other parts of the festival, pausing to examine the wares at the market stalls, speak to other townspeople, and try her hand at the assortment of carnival games set up for younglings. She drifted toward the stage, drawn to the musicians capering upon it. It was there, standing in the throng beside Christopher and Janae Willow—both of whom were looking sour, spaced at least a foot apart—that Heather, losing interest, remembered her father's command: "Go find Mother."

Heather wondered where Mumma could be. She hadn't spotted Sara's shoulder-length curls once in the last few hours, and glancing about now, the woman was still nowhere to be seen. Heather frowned. A feeling of dread passed through her, similar to the one she'd felt at that wild look in Papa's eyes. What was going on? Had something happened? Why were they both missing?

Sliding between the sweaty bodies, clustered around the stage like moths to a flame, Heather squeezed her way to the edge of the courtyard— scanning flushed faces all the while—and searched the adjoining streets.

Nothing.

She retraced her steps, crossed the Market Square once more, and checked the other half of town. She searched the tavern, the stable, the infirmary. She even ascended the walls (stealing upward once a chunky guardsman had sauntered by) and peered out over the open pastures. Her mother used to enjoy riding ponies in the meadows when she was younger. The quietly rolling grassland, a luminous lime-green in the summertime, presented a striking view of the coast, severed only by the western reaches of the Remos Mountains. Heather wondered if her mother had gone out for a walk alone—she'd done so in the past when particularly tense or lonesome—but now that she was here, Heather didn't know what she'd expected to see. The fields lay in darkness, all but obscured by night. Even if her mother were out there, Heather would never know it. Unless she ventured out herself.

Which was unthinkable. She couldn't. Not only because her father strictly forbade her from doing so, but because she still had the nightmares. Almost all the children in Norick got them at one point or another. They were lucid, disquieting things; there were a dozen variations, but most were filled with shadowy figures, garbled whispers, and probing hands. In Heather's, she found herself alone in a barren field while beasts of the night swirled and snickered about her. She could never see them, though, could only ever feel the rush of air as they circled. The creatures were always just out of reach … while she screamed and screamed and screamed. Norick's parents—who'd gone through the dreams themselves when they were younglings—simply attributed the nightmares to the local legends and ghost tales still whispered around the hearth. They were merely side effects of those old stories, things every child had to go through. In time, the dreams would pass.

For Heather, this had yet to occur. And so she hesitated, standing there on the rampart, her pale green eyes searching the darkness in vain. The Western Outpost glowed with lamplight in the distance, but it seemed an impossible expanse away. No, there was nothing for her to do but return home and wait. Her parents had to turn up eventually. *Unless something bad has happened…*

She didn't dare think about what that might mean.

Descending to street level, Heather started off toward the opposite side of town. She took the back streets, not in the mood for the congestion of the Market Square. She doubted her mother had suddenly shown up there anyhow. She reached their house without delay: two stories of polished stone, cut and painted into an ornate blue façade. Out front, a small square yard was edged by manicured rosebushes. The arched windows above were empty, and dark.

Heather took the stairs two at a time—then froze. On the surface of their door, a bloody handprint leaked toward the stoop. Heather eyed it as her stomach wheeled. She shook her head, refusing to accept the image, then spun the brass knob and pushed inward. The door squeaked, ever so slightly, and she couldn't stop herself from imagining it was the handprint making the sound.

Not looking back, she hurried across the threshold and was closing the door behind her (thinking one of her friends must be playing a trick) when she heard the wailing, coming from deeper within their home.

Wailing. Like the squalling of a wounded doe.

Heather's stomach ached more than ever.

She started toward the black void of the staircase, its outline lit by an insipid afterglow swiftly dying in the fireplace. The hearth room itself appeared ethereal, sinister, its numerous portraits glowering down at her. The one of Rufus Milgrin, a distant relative, domineered with its deep-set eyes, a beaklike nose, and a heavy though neatly trimmed goatee. The armchairs, elongated by darkness and shadow, sat like hulking beasts waiting to come alive. Even the two bookcases and their tomes were forlorn and cryptic tonight, arranged about the room's perimeter like faceless sentries. The books, from which Heather normally took such great wonder, seemed ready to tumble from their shelves at any moment.

Taking it all in, Heather hugged her thin arms against her torso as the wailing seeped through the ceiling. *Mumma.* It sounded like Sara. At least Heather thought it did. Maybe. There was the faintest suggestion of her mother's natural voice, layered beneath the keening. Heather bit at her lower lip. If that was Mumma, what could make her cry like that?

Heather took another step; the wooden floorboards groaned beneath her. She nearly turned and fled. But no creatures of the night came barreling toward her, so she pressed on, deciding she needed a light. Too much remained hidden.

Slinking forward, she felt her way past the armchairs and her mother's sofa until she drew level with a decorative side table covered to abundance with nautical maps, navigational tools, a stack of parchment, and an unlit candelabrum. Yanking a waxy candle from one of the half-dozen golden tines, Heather swiveled toward the hearth's expiring embers and thrust the candle inside. The wick sputtered in protest before igniting.

She allowed herself a smile, face awash in the glow, and headed for the staircase. Holding the candle out from her body, she let the soft light do its work: The space and its features dawned into focus, the tiny sphere of yellow chasing the darkness to the corners of the room. Milgrin, in his oil portrait on the wall, still appeared hawkish and menacing, but overall Heather was satisfied: She could see.

She was moving before she let herself consider the situation any further. She peered up the length of the staircase, candle extended like a weapon. The wooden steps, edged by two straight-lined walls and a cylindrical handrail, rose steeply toward an upstairs hallway. A pool of shadow draped beneath each step, looking like bottomless pits waiting to swallow her.

Heather started up.

She reached the top without incident, though she'd expected at any moment for something terrible to appear at the summit. She didn't dare look back at the darkness she'd left behind. The sensation of being followed—pursued—had hurried her step, and now she tingled with the feeling of being watched. Despite herself, she risked a glance. She couldn't see anything but felt it all the same: a presence loitering just beyond the reaches of her candle and sight.

One of the steps near the bottom released a grumbling creak. As if someone were mounting the staircase after her.

Heather went rigid. *It's not real,* she thought with a harsh intake of breath, *it's not real. It's all in my head.* The words were a mantra her father had given her late one night after she'd woken up screaming. Sitting beside her on her rumpled bedsheets, Papa had instructed Heather to repeat it to herself every time she felt the monsters encroaching. "There's nothing to be afraid of, dear. You have to trust me. The darkness is only scary if you let it be. That's its power: the unknown. But you have power, too. Every time you're afraid, I want you to say this to yourself: 'It's not real. It's all in my head.' The more you say it, the more you'll believe it. And belief can go a long way." He'd leaned forward then and kissed her brow. " 'It's not real. It's all in my head. I'm stronger than these fears.' Remember that."

She did remember it, but right now it didn't seem to be working. Nothing visible moved below—and no other noises followed the first—but the terror remained rooted in Heather's gut. The blackness down there was gaping; her mind whirled with what was left unseen. A gust of wind shook the rafters above—a labored groan of timber—and Heather fled down the hallway, away from the opening. *It's not real, it's not real…*

Ahead, the wailing had faltered. Heather, finding it hard to breathe, stopped and listened. The sudden quiet was almost as disconcerting as the original sound. Hounded by thoughts of what could even now be creeping up the stairs behind her, Heather dashed the final paces to her parents' bedroom door.

No light came from beneath the wood. The sobs inside were unmistakable, though. Her mother was in there. Steeling herself, Heather reached for the handle and gave it a measured turn, her palm clammy and tender against the glass knob. She pressed the door inward.

It opened with a shriek from its hinges. Heather stiffened, pulse spiking, but continued pushing. She peered around the edge of the door, using it as a shield. The room lay in murk; the shutters were rotated flat, their accompanying drapes likewise drawn. A dark mass towered in one corner, what Heather knew to be a wardrobe. Two rectangular shapes rose from the floor: her parents' beds. Several feet of hardwood lay between them, a recent development. The candle next revealed a nightstand, a dressing table, an armchair. A small hearth. A bearskin rug, thick and expansive, stretched toward the windows. And, last of all, there was the rough outline of a person lying on the floor. Heaped like a collection of filth.

"Mumma…?"

Sara Ash didn't respond. Instead, her quiet sobs continued their ricochet around the bedchamber. From what Heather could see, Sara hadn't moved with her daughter's arrival. Not even a glance in her direction. A wave of unease swelled in Heather's chest. "Mumma." She opened the door further and stepped into the room. The candle's warm, if feeble, glow allowed her to inspect Sara closer. The woman lay in a ball, angled toward the shuttered windows. Her knees were tucked to her chest, and her face was pressed into her palms. Makeup and tears combined in a smudged waterfall, while sandy-blonde hair wandered this way and that. A blanket hung about her shoulders; beneath its wooly covering, Sara's crying continued, interspersed by low, tormented moans.

Concern propelling her forward, Heather locked the door behind her and crept deeper into the room. "Mumma?" she whispered, afraid to disturb the woman but scared, too, of not knowing. Again there was no answer. It was almost as if Sara couldn't hear her—as if Heather weren't even there. "What's the matter? What happened?" She trod closer, feet shuffling through the fibers of the bearskin rug. Louder this time: "Mumma!"

"Get out of my head."

The outburst, rasped between clenched teeth, arrested Heather where she stood. Ignoring the urge to turn and run, she took another step forward. "Wha … what are you talking about?"

"Get. Out. Of. My. Head."

"You're scaring me, Mumma." Sara was now digging her fingers into her tousled hair, yanking at her scalp. "What are you doing? Stop it, Mumma!" Heather waded closer, nearly standing overtop the woman now. "What's going on? What's wrong?"

"Get … out … of …"

Her mother froze, her limbs snapping taut and her words stunting off, immobilized mid-speech. A thick silence followed as the woman went completely stiff.

Heather looked on in horror. Even when Sara returned to sobbing, her body once more folding in upon itself, Heather couldn't bring herself to move. A part of her wanted to kneel and place a hand on the woman's shoulder, to comfort her and make sense of this nightmare scenario, but she didn't dare. That spasm just now had been … unnatural.

Startling her, Sara rolled over. She didn't look at Heather yet—her face was still buried in both hands—but she finally seemed to register her daughter's presence. Heather normally considered Sara to be quite beautiful with her long lashes, high cheekbones, and shoulder-length hair; tonight, the woman appeared haggard and ill, almost hollowed out. At last the woman spoke, little more than a murmur between her cupped palms. "It knows everything," she said. "Everything I've ever done. *It knows.*"

Heather was focused on keeping the candle aloft. "Who?"

"It showed me everything, Heather. I've *seen* it."

"What are you talking about, Mumma? Seen what?"

Sara was crying now in earnest. "The fire. Your father. The rope. It's coming for us. All of us. It'll drag us into the dark." Heather swallowed as a chill spread through her body. She glanced at the closed bedroom door. When she turned back, she found Sara caught in another spasm. The woman lowered her hands, dragging her nails across her cheeks. Her red-rimmed eyes—puffy, overwrought—bore into Heather with a feverish urgency. "You need to leave. Before it's too late. Get as far from here as you can." She was practically spewing her words. "Go—before it finds you, too. I'm begging you. Please, go."

Heather stumbled back. She bumped into a mattress and yelped, toppling onto its spread. The candle nearly fell from her grip. Too startled to move, she remained seated.

"It's coming." Sara's shimmering eyes regarded her through the twilight. There was a leer in them now Heather didn't recognize. The woman's tangle of hair, illumed by the candle's anemic flame, framed her face like a mane. She was, of all things, laughing. "It's coming, Heather," she said between the cackles. "I can feel it... It'll have all of us before it's through."

"You're scaring me, Mumma..."

Sara continued to laugh, nasty little chortles tapering to a deranged giggle. Fighting back tears, Heather lifted herself from the bed and lurched blindly toward the door. "Please, Mumma," she begged as she backpedaled, "stop this."

Gradually, her mother stilled. The hysteria receded. When next Sara spoke, she did so calmly, with a clear sense of purpose. "Listen to me, Heather. Listen to me closely. You need to go—*right now.*

"You need to run."

CHAPTER TWELVE

It was the anger that did it.

Slumped on the outpost's covered veranda, Captain William Breeve regarded Norick and let his fury build.

Who do they think they are, celebrating? What right do they have?

He hated them. Every last one of 'em. Those arrogant pricks on the Council. The other soldiers in the Guard. All those in town he had thought were his friends before they'd drifted away. All the bloody younglings running about with their laughter and games.

All those bright, awe-filled eyes.

The reasons were simple: for being so cheerful; for witnessing what'd happened to him—what *was* happening to him, day after day, a deterioration like the dulling of a blade—and doing nothing. He hated the unfairness of it all. How they carried that unspoken sentiment in their eyes: *Better him than us,* as if he somehow deserved what'd happened, as if it were *his* fault and his present failings proved precisely such.

Those self-righteous eyes. The pity.

The anger consumed him then, and he let himself seethe. The pity: a sentiment he abhorred above all others. The townspeople leveled it at him as if they were doing him a favor, as if they just couldn't *bear* to regard him without it.

William was trembling now in full. He was ready to stand, depart the outpost, and march down there to give them a piece of his mind.

Instead he reached for the flagon at his hip. The stopper came off with an airy *pop.* He let it bounce on the wooden inlay beneath him. Closing his eyes, William raised the container and swigged.

It was a beautiful sensation, that first slosh of wine lapping down his throat. He hardly tasted the liquid itself, but he didn't need to. Better was the buzz of dreamy warmth spreading through his chest. More immediate was the release that accompanied it: the relief of letting go. Why had he waited so long to do this? Didn't he see now how *great* it felt?

You're confirming what the town thinks of you, a whisper inside of him warned. *Calvin, the Council—all of them. You're proving them right.*

He didn't care. If they could celebrate, so could he. What had he even been holding on to? Routine? His pride? *No,* that logical part of him corrected, *your honor.*

The honor he was meant to impart to a son.

William froze, and the flagon lowered as if of its own accord. A son, he thought. *The one who was stolen from you.* Ah, yes. *That's* what he was waiting for. What he'd always been waiting for, what had ripped this yawning hole in his chest from the start. William felt for the flagon again. He threw back another gulp.

Landon, he thought. That would have been his name: a good name, a respectable one. One he and Ellen had chosen together, bodies entwined in the early hours of some crisp spring morn. She'd giggled when he whispered it for the first time, tracing a finger over her naked abdomen. "Landon." He'd gently set his ear upon her stomach, already swelling with a slight bump, and listened. "What'd you think? Our Landon…"

A cough erupted from William's throat, tearing him from the memory. He sputtered into the night, his body clenching, and straightened the flagon before it could spill. Recovering, he just as quickly tipped the container up for another drink. *Our Landon,* he thought. *Our boy.*

It was going to be a long night.

At the Eastern Outpost, drinking and remembering, Captain William Breeve studied the surrounding woods and the approaching storm and, almost beyond his control, like sinking from one inky haze into another, he fell asleep.

He dreamt.

It was the same dream he'd had for many months now, more a feeling of fear and helplessness than anything else. It came with the sensation of being smothered, suffocated by some invisible weight.

During the course of the dream—in fact, a nightmare—he could usually see nothing but darkness. Could hear nothing save a low buzzing that seemed to arise from the very fiber of his being. The nightmare rarely took the shape of any concrete image, but when it did, he would see the face of a young child, a boy, with curly black hair and round hazel eyes. It was only later that William began associating the face, one he couldn't recall seeing with his waking eyes, with that of his stillborn son.

When that face appeared, the vague quality of the dream would morph into a kind of clarity—that of sadness, a blanket of yearning, which would itself soon transform, this time into a boiling mass of fury. The rage was aimed at the universe and at himself—and at Landon and Ellen, for stealing one another away from him.

Often the nightmare manifested as an overwhelming urge to join his family in death. He envisioned lying down beside them in that shallow grave near Seagren Lake and never emerging. He dreamt just how he'd do it. It would be so easy, one little flip of his knife across both wrists ... and then he would drain away, leaking back into the earth, dissolving from existence.

But tonight the dream was different. The feelings were the same, aye, but there was something else there. Something new. It was a presence he hadn't felt before: the sensation of being watched, scrutinized.

Come, the voice said, and it was then that he realized it was indeed a voice he was hearing, a voice apart from his own; and not just a feeling of being watched, but of being caressed, pulled.

Summoned.

Numb, unwilling to resist, William followed. He felt his consciousness detach and become weightless, drifting upon the warm embrace of the darkness. He knew himself helpless against the pull of that voice, just as he'd been helpless against the wine. Both rang again and again in his head, cutting deeper and deeper within him.

Come, William, the voice said. *Come and see what I have to show you. Come, come, come...*

CHAPTER THIRTEEN

Two hours and a few pilfered jugs of ale later, Natalie Willow, Thomas Calvin, and their three companions found themselves drunk in a dank wall-
side alleyway. Together they surrounded a short, whimpering adolescent,
two or three years their junior.

How'd we get here? wondered Natalie. The question came unbidden;
try as she might, she couldn't suppress it. How had they gone from having
innocent—okay, perhaps not so innocent, but what was ultimately harmless—fun, to *this:* flocking around a youngling like vultures and taking
turns at him with a stick?

Mere hours before, they had denounced the behavior of the town, its
looseness and apathy. Yet here they were, enraptured in their own wicked
revelry. *I should know better,* Natalie reflected. *We all should know better.*
But she found she didn't care.

She knew, on many levels, that she was enjoying this.

The boy, whom Natalie recognized as Lerrick Rose's son, Vernon,
cowered against the wall, his eyes red-rimmed and wild, his orange hair
tousled and standing on end. Dirt and mud blotted his jawline. Loose gravel clung to both brows. Swelling and enflamed, his limbs were pulled in
tight, scrunched together like the wings of a broken bird. Natalie couldn't
stop herself from thinking how pathetic he appeared.

(Deep down, she hated herself for the thought.)

The five of them had chanced upon the boy ten minutes earlier as
they wandered the streets far from the Market Square. They'd been lost in
each other's company, in the rapture and vitality of the night. In its peculiar
numbness. In its desire. Speaking too loudly and too often, they took turns

with the jugs. They told jokes. They sang songs. Their laughter bounded up and down the deserted lanes with a vicious flair. They cursed at their parents. They threw stones at windows. They smeared raspberry pie on statues of the Founders and pissed on Trinity Weston's carefully manicured garden. And they found this boy, Vernon Rose.

He was departing his home with a grin plastered to his freckled face. No doubt running an errand of some kind and eager to return to the festival. Vernon had a beautiful voice—high and pure, Natalie recalled from a performance he'd given earlier in the day during one of his father's productions. Perhaps that was where he was heading now, to sing.

Walter spotted him as the boy's short stubby legs carried him down the stoop. The twin slapped a palm against his brother's portly chest. "Fred, Fred, look. Thomas." He pointed eagerly like a hound marking its quarry.

By then all of them had turned. Natalie squinted. Something about the sight immediately made her angry. *How happy he looks*, she decided.

"Well, well, well. Would you look at that." Thomas had a strange glint to his eye. "This could be fun."

"Look at his stumpy legs," Frederick said.

"Check out that hair," said Thomas, "could start ya on fire just by lookin' at it."

"Natalie, that could be your brother," Walter said. "Or your father."

"He's like twelve, you moron. Maybe thirteen."

"So what. Has your mother been coupling around?"

"Shut your trout face before I slice you."

Walter raised his hands defensively. "I'm just saying. Look at 'im. That hair—" Natalie's scowl, sharp as a blade, sliced toward the twin.

Thomas chuckled as he listened to the exchange. "Long-lost brother it is, then."

"Dwarfism doesn't run in my family. And my hair's much lighter than that; it's basically blonde, you halfwits."

"He's not a dwarf. He's just a runt."

"Wonder what the fat little runt is up to," said Betsy, drawing their eyes back toward the boy.

"Let's find out," crowed Thomas. None of them needed to voice assent; Natalie knew they'd come to an unspoken agreement the moment they'd laid eyes on him. Eagerly would they prey on Vernon, like a pack of wolves to a lost sheep. Why? She didn't know. They'd never tormented anyone before—especially nobody younger than them, especially not a *kid*—but tonight was different.

Even in the short time since they'd left the wall, something had changed. The others didn't look like themselves; their faces were somehow both gleaming and haggard, caught somewhere between coy grins and ominous sneers. Even their forms were altered: Tensed and hunched up, their collective gait was a lurking shuffle through the darkness. Normally these facts would have been cause for concern, but Natalie suspected she appeared much the same. She knew she didn't *feel* like herself now. She hadn't since they left their elevated perch two hours earlier. The recklessness and indifference they'd wondered at then—a decadence observed in their fellow townspeople—had seemed strange and perplexing. It now felt infectious.

Tonight, that feeling told them, they were free. They were powerful. They could do whatever they damn well pleased. Rising to a crescendo, these notions consumed them the moment Vernon came frolicking down that stoop. Pouncing on the boy was simply the next logical move.

They were on him before he could turn for the sidewalk. Vernon jumped at the sound of their approach, regarding the pack with apprehension. The grin fled from his cheeks.

"Heya there," purred Thomas.

"Hello," said Vernon, uncertain. He did a quick scan of the group, and his body instinctively clenched. Natalie knew they must look a menacing lot. The others' faces were slightly manic, sinister even. As, she sensed, was her own.

"What ya up to, little boy?" said Betsy.

"Just returning to the Market Square," Vernon replied. "I was grabbing someth—"

"Why ya all alone?" Walter asked.

"Yeah, don't you have any friends?"

"You like being by yourself, huh, torchhead."

"I— No. What ar—" They didn't let him finish. As if rehearsed, they badgered the boy with questions, barely allowing him a word in between.

"Where your parents at?"

"You a virgin, runt? Ever been with a woman?"

"How tall are ya, dwarf? You *are* a dwarf, aren't ya?"

"Not around the middle, he ain't!"

"Nor the rear."

"Want some of the Earth's drink, boy? Thirsty? Bet we can get ya pissed and stumbling."

"No, thanks, I—"

"Is that your house there? Anyone inside?"

"Got any coin on ya, torchy?"

"Don't you have any friends? There has to be *someone* you hang around with."

"Why's your hair so bloody *orange*?"

"Why ya sweating so much? It's not even hot out."

"Want to have some fun? We sure do. You can help us."

It wasn't long before embarrassment overtook Vernon's face—usually moon-pale, his cheeks deepened to a glossy pink then a deep shade of red, visible even in the gloom. Though young and by all appearances naïve, the theater head's son clearly knew when he was being toyed with. And when he was vulnerable.

He backed away from them, trying to slip off toward a bend in the street. "I gotta go now. I'm sorry, okay. I'll see you guys later…"

They pursued him. Their insults now spewed openly. As he led them down the cobblestone, huffing air with frantic breaths, they stayed tight on his heels, mocking the way he waddled and how the sweat was soaking through his tunic. They laughed at his splotchy freckles, at the birthmark besmirching his neck. They ridiculed his father's failing eyesight and the way Lerrick sometimes crashed into stalls in the Market Square, dumping their wares. They mimicked Night-Eyed's hurried, stammering apologies and the sheepish down-twist of his gaze. Enraptured, enraged, the teenagers supplemented their insults with physical prods: pinches, slaps, kicks. Vernon jogged forward, flailing his arms, trying to free himself. Every now and then he gasped. Natalie felt her palm collide with the boy's shoulder. The blow sent a satisfying jolt up her arm. *That felt good. This feels* right.

An alley appeared, radiating darkness and reeking of animal shit. On its left and right were two darkened homes; further down stood the stable, though it, too, was closed up for the night. *Perfect.* They herded Vernon toward the passageway, twice dragging him to his feet by his collar.

They shoved him inside.

At present, Vernon half-crouched, half-slumped against the masonry over a squat drainage gate, its corrugated rods glinting from a torch far above. Hardly able to stand, the boy was covered in mud and filth and a web of purpling bruises.

Thomas, ever the leader, stood in the center of the pack. He clutched a thick, multi-fingered tree branch, discovered just inside the entrance when they'd first arrived. The five of them had passed it amongst themselves ("Not his face," Thomas warned Frederick. "Nothing too noticeable. We don't want old Night-Eyed fumbling after us."). They all panted from their efforts. Frederick and Walter stood with arms crossed; the latter wet his lips. Betsy leaned against one of the houses looking bored. Thomas, standing closest, prepared himself for another go.

"Please," Vernon begged. "Please…"

His voice was little more than a whisper. His flooded eyes implored each of them in turn. "Don't… Please, no more. I can't…" Thomas didn't seem to hear him. Despite smiling, his face had an empty appearance to it. He studied Vernon silently, holding the tree branch waist high. He twirled it with his mud-caked fingers.

Vernon's pleading gaze slid from Thomas to Natalie. Their eyes locked … and then she looked away, fixing her stare on the uneven pattern of brick to her left.

Thomas prowled forward.

Natalie would remember this moment, later on. The moment she could have done something, could have simply said *Stop* and ended this boy's suffering. The others would've listened to her, surely; in some ways she was more a leader than even Thomas. They would have paused, seen the logic in her reasoning (Which was what, exactly? That she'd felt something stir within her when Vernon had met her eye? That all of this was actually *wrong*, so terribly wrong?), and together they would have moved on to other activities. But she didn't. Despite how the evening was making her feel, she still made a choice. She remained silent, and this passivity would haunt her late in the coming nights of clarity and remorse, a smothering of guilt and shame that would crawl along her skin like pond leeches on an exposed heel.

Thomas was close now, towering over the boy. He lifted the branch.

Two hours and a few pilfered jugs of ale later, Natalie Willow, Thomas Calvin, and their three companions found themselves here, drunk in a dank
wall-side alleyway. No more than children themselves—jaded and broken,
but hopeful—they'd decried the hypocrisy of their parents and the town.
They'd each yearned for a different world, a better one, a Norick aligned
with the promise they'd been raised to believe in.

They were the dreamers, the idealists, the cynics; they were the innocents, with goodness residing in them still.

They were children, transfixed by the breathlessness of violence and
power; by a short, whimpering adolescent, a plaything, ensnared for their
amusement.

Over and over Thomas lashed the boy.

His blows struck them all.

PART THREE

THE NIGHTTIME
VISITOR

In every absence of light
There is darkness.
In every setting sun,
A growing shadow.

The dark is not empty.
The dark is not alone.

Evil waits in the night.

CHAPTER FOURTEEN

"Mary, what on earth is going on out here?"

The two balanced themselves on the rutted boulders of the seawall, which were slick and slimy with the intensifying ocean spray. To Higgins's irritation, the old hag still refused to terminate her silence. She was no longer as stiff and unyielding as when he'd first approached, but even the wind seemed incapable of fazing her. Buffets of it seethed over the jetty, and yet Mary stood motionless. The only part of her that moved was her hoary strands of hair, tossing about like snowflakes in a blizzard.

Higgins streaked a massive palm across his brow, sponging at the moisture gathered there. He spit toward the rocks below; salt coated his tongue and he wanted nothing more than to be rid of it. He tried spitting again; some of the saliva, caught by an updraft, spattered back onto his cheek. Cursing, he scrubbed off the mucus then smeared it along the front of his pants, already damp themselves anyway.

He'd had enough of this. Yet, despite his frustration, Higgins couldn't bring himself to turn away. That previous stare in Mary's eyes kept his stomach in loops. Whatever she thought was happening out here, she believed it sincerely. And it seemed to terrify her. Could it be true? Did she know something he didn't? Or, more likely, was she losing her mind?

Uncertain either way—but hoping for the latter—Higgins felt for a level boulder and maneuvered forward. He stole a look at her face. The woman's chin was angled skyward, her turret of a nose sucking in breath. Floppy wet cheeks wobbled on brittle bones.

Her eyes were closed.

Higgins debated stretching forward and tapping her. Mary's response earlier, however, caused him to hesitate. He wasn't eager to receive that look again: belittlement imbedded in a reproachful glare. But he needed to know—and as chancellor, he would not be scolded for investigating his town's affairs. "Mary?"

Her eyelids stayed shut. One cheek offered a rhythmic twitch.

"Mary." He grunted the word, growing increasingly aggravated with every smash of the surf. Thunder cackled overhead, and, with it, a tremor ruptured in his chest. "*Answer* me. Quit playing the fool and converse with me like an adult."

She said nothing. That passing tic rose to a veiny eyelid and the orb underneath seemed to roll. Otherwise Mary remained blind, and silent, to her surroundings.

"I know you can hear me. What's going on out here? What did you mean, 'It's happening'? *What's* happening? What delusions are you nurturing?"

Her tiny lips parted, revealing a thin black cavity filmed in mucus. She took a shallow breath, breaching the bubble. Then her lips were moving once more—up and down, as though she were speaking—but Higgins couldn't hear a thing.

He studied her mouth's rise and fall, feeling the soft vapor gathering on his bald scalp, the salt-tinged saliva collecting at the back of his throat. "Speak louder, woman," he demanded. "Enough with the games!"

Nothing.

"I am your chancellor—open your eyes and look at me!" Higgins nearly lurched forward then and struck her. But her eyelids' sudden rousing froze him mid-swing. He stopped, arm suspended, and they regarded each other coolly.

Mary's eyebrows narrowed. "What is it that you need, *Chancellor*?"

Higgins again got the sense he was being reprimanded. *How dare she...* But those pale, beady eyes: He saw madness and delusion there, but also clarity, reason, and a maternal rage. He found himself blundering for words. "I... I..." He glanced away, out toward the heaving sea. He swallowed, composing himself. Swore internally. *No.* He would not be struck petrified by some kook. Oscillating his arm—which was hanging gracelessly in space—Higgins leveled a finger at her. "I want to know exactly what you're doing out here," he commanded with all the authority he could muster. "Right now. Or perhaps a night in the stocks can help spur your memory."

Mary kept her focus on him, ignoring the finger. There was contempt in those eyes, Higgins was certain of it. "Don't you know already?" she said. "Can't you feel it?"

With a groan, Higgins rolled his neck toward the sky and gave an exasperated wave. "No, I do not *know*, Mary. That's why I am out here on this sodden jetty talking to you. Now, for the love of Norick, explain yourself." He placed both hands on his hips and waited.

Mary's expression remained fixed, her eyes as impenetrable as ever. "If you let yourself," she crooned, "you will feel it."

His spade-like hands found the air again as he rocked toward her, heat emanating from his cheeks like a cloud of steam. "Feel *what*?"

Her grating rasp was as resolute as before. "Feel *it*. Among us now. It's happening, Chancellor."

"*What* is happening? Out with it."

"The awakening. We've woken the darkness, and now it's come. You need to sound the alarm, you fool." Those cryptic eyes peered up at him beneath their wispy brows. "The hour grows late."

Higgins dug his fingers into his temples, as if attempting to squeeze out a headache. "*What*, Mary? What! No more riddles."

"We're being chosen," she murmured, her lower lip protruding like a rat's. The nubs of her teeth were just visible. "Hunted. It sees. It hears. It knows. Each and every one of us. Every man, woman, and child in this town—and it knows us well."

Squinting at her, Higgins drew back.

The drone of the waves occupied the space between them. A colony of gulls overhead braved flight only to be battered back by the wind as if by some great invisible hand. Then Mary was leaning forward, slinking closer as though she were a town gossip divulging some scandalous secret. "The water has been drowned with blood. The shroud has been lifted, the passage rent through. None of this is coincidence, don't you see? It cannot yet take material form, but it matters not. It doesn't need to. It has us." Her eyes widened in their furrowed sockets. "It has plans, Chancellor. Even now working them into fruition. Even now."

Letting Higgins process that, Mary pulled away, her pupils shifting down and to the left, onto the stack of boulders on which they stood. She muttered something into the wind. Higgins missed the first strand but turned his ear for the second. "…evil only needs one."

" 'Evil'? What in Milgrin's name—?"

Her eyes were suddenly glued to him again. The manic, overwrought appearance had returned, as had the urgency. "Milgrin? *Milgrin!*" Mary scoffed. "It will destroy us," she said, accentuating each word, "like it destroyed him. The past does not die, Higgins. Make no mistake. We cannot run from it. We cannot hide. Every sin knows a return."

"I don't understand—"

"It will consume us all."

His gaze settled on her wraithlike face. Concerned in spite of himself, he threw up his arms. Mary just looked at him, almost sadly. Overhead, the clouds jostled and swirled while the waves seized and roiled, massacring their own against the shoreline. Lightning flared over the harbor and just as quickly vanished: light revealing dark, and dark swallowing light.

Mustering the wherewithal to proceed with the interrogation, Higgins bent toward Mary and seized her by the shoulder. "Explain yourself, woman. What's here? What's the threat?"

The matriarch's eyes burrowed into him.

"*It.*"

CHAPTER FIFTEEN

People are sure acting funny tonight, thought twenty-four-year-old guardsman Riley Ford as he rounded the southeastern bend in the wall and continued up its weathered length for the countless time that night, sweating despite the rising chill.

Shaped like a rotund beetle, with short burly limbs, a mound of stomach, and a tangled growth of coppery neck beard, Riley lumbered forward and gazed down at the Market Square, where the Milgrin's Day festivities carried on despite the threat of rain and storm. The townspeople, oblivious or uncaring, were dancing themselves into a stupor. Riley had never seen them quite like this, so absorbed in their revelry. They frolicked and flounced, their energy seemingly inexhaustible. Their voices erupted with spurts of laughter and cheers—the latest, from what Riley could make out, coming from a group of citizens standing in a line gulping ale: a drinking contest. The winners—for two of the lot genuinely appeared to finish at the same time—shrieked their glee, then turned on one another with comic absurdity. Riley sighed. He hoped he wouldn't have another quarrel to break up.

He had intervened in two fights already and wasn't eager for a third. The encounters had left a bad flavor in his mouth, as the involved parties had seemed to completely disregard his appeal for maintaining harmony, a lecture any respectable guardsman would've given. Instead the brawlers had shared eye-rolls, growing strangely unified as Riley spoke.

Plodding along the wall now, Riley couldn't negate the derisory way those men had made him feel. He should have gone after them, should've given them a real speaking to (*Y'all want to spend a night in the stockade?*

I'll do it, I'm tellin' ya. Don't think I won't). Closing his eyes, he could almost picture them trembling in their boots, desperate to apologize.

Almost.

With more candor, he mused, *If I keep up my training ... and lose some of this weight ... then they'll* have *to respect me. One day when I'm captain— why can't I be?—they'll learn to appreciate the Guard and everything we do for this town. I'll just keep getting stronger and faster and...* His strides along the wall were increasing in pace. "It's not just a job, you know," he lectured to an imaginary audience. "It's a calling. Being on the Town Guard is a sacred duty. We are the defenders of Norick—*and* her ideals."

That wasn't to say the Guard didn't have its flaws. The chief of which was its leadership. Like all guardsmen, Riley knew the tales of Captain Breeve's valor in the South. But it was hard to reconcile the war hero with the man he knew, someone keen on wasting away drunk and alone in his cottage. Not that Riley had ever seen the man drinking on duty, but still: What kind of example was that? What kind of leader? Despite a baffling insistence on working the night shift, Breeve's duties as captain seemed an afterthought to him—perhaps even a nuisance.

The Guard deserved a better leader, a more disciplined one; someone, wholly motivated, who cared about its tradition, its values, and everything it represented. Someone who cared as Riley cared, who would devote his life as he would.

One day...

Coming upon the wall's northeastern flank, Riley pulled up. He was panting in soft spouts of air, heat flaring along his neck. Admittedly, he'd pushed his pace a bit there. *Can't carve a statue in an hour,* his father, a craftsman, liked to say. There was wisdom in that, Riley knew. He could afford to take it a little slower.

He bent to tug the legs of his trousers up over his kneecaps and sighed as the wind swooshed against his calves. Balancing his torch in the crook of an elbow, he set to work rolling his sleeves as well.

Finished, Riley returned the torch to a moist palm and continued his watch. His gaze tracked from the incensed sky to the collection of dilapidated structures comprising Coastline. He peered up toward the Grove, a cluster of fruit trees arranged in loose rows. There weren't any torches positioned that way, so the orchard was lit only from the town's runoff. The outermost reaches were an ethereal orange; within, darkness held reign, the trees like a gallery of shifting black columns. Riley found the sight inexplicably eerie. He knew what the shapes were and why they were moving, but he couldn't rid the notion that the branches were somehow alive and scheming, plotting a conspiracy against him and the town. Furthermore, he sensed movement *between* the rows, phantom motion just out of sight. He imagined something sinister lurking.

Riley shook his head, knowing these thoughts foolish. Eager to be rid of them, he allowed himself a heavy blink. But when he opened his eyes, he found the thoughts were not only still present, they were receiving their confirmation.

He stepped toward the parapet and craned his neck over the ledge. *What in Milgrin's name?* After his superstitious musings, surely his eyes were just playing tricks. Another handful of blinks, however, produced no change.

Beyond the edge of the Grove, a figure had appeared. Enveloped in black, the figure—a shadow really, little more than a black oblong shape— weaved its way from the orchard's perimeter and halted, facing Norick. *Whoever it is*, Riley noted, *they're wearing a hooded cloak.* The garment billowed as the person stared toward the town. Riley's stomach plunged at the realization that the figure appeared to be staring *at him.*

Glaring, in fact.

He gulped. This wasn't the first person he had seen out beyond the walls tonight. Earlier, the master of trade, Peter Ash, had departed from the harbor gate and looped his way east. At the time, Riley had found the behavior odd, but it wasn't his place to question the comings and goings of a council member, no matter how strange it was for one of Norick's wealthiest citizens to be out wandering alone at night. Now Riley wondered if this new emergence was related to Ash's earlier departure. Was there something illicit occurring out there in the Grove?

He squinted at the figure—a blurred silhouette; a haze; the shadow of a shadow. It *could* be Ash, but Riley didn't think so. The master of trade hadn't been wearing a cloak, and this person stood at least half a foot taller than Ash. Riley supposed it could be Brade, who was quite tall himself, heading to take over at the Eastern Outpost. But the chancellor's son had no business being in the orchard, nor this far north. And the person didn't appear to be wearing a uniform.

Who, then, might this figure be? And why in Milgrin's name was he or she staring up at Riley so determinedly, as if caught in mischief and deciding what to do next?

As if deciding what to do *about* him.

Riley shuddered. Swallowing, he determined he would march down there and investigate—*After calling for reinforcements, of course*—but then the figure moved.

It shuffled for a step, turned parallel to the wall, and drifted from Norick, almost seeming to float upon the air. After a series of gliding paces, it turned once more—what Riley thought was its back now turned toward him—and angled for the woods.

Eyebrows scrunched, Riley watched it go. He knew his eyes to be playing tricks, but he now got the impression it wasn't a cloak obscuring the person but something else entirely. It was as if there were a human core at the figure's center—solid, corporeal—but around it draped a cloud of shadow, thick and oily with tendrils of patterned smoke. The figure compressed, shifted, and swirled before Riley's eyes—*I'm imagining this; it isn't real. It can't be real. I'm simply seeing the cloak flapping in the wind*—and he got the sense he was witnessing something strange and unknowable. Something private. Something obscene.

As if reading his thoughts, the figure lifted a black-clad arm and motioned a gesture that felt expressly for Riley. Mounting the soft ascent of foothills surrounding the town, the figure's hand tightened and smoothed above its head in a lethargic, five-fingered wave, each individual digit curling and climbing like rolling ocean swells.

Riley's mouth closed upon itself at the gesture, only a whisper of breath drifting through. He placed a trembling hand across the width of his chin, and then, unable to help himself, he glanced down at the windswept rampart on which he stood.

When he looked up again, out toward the edge of the forest with its copious underbrush and gnarled limbs, there was nothing to be seen.

Like a fog, the figure had vanished.

PART FOUR

SUCTION
AND RELEASE

The child
Sees a wolf
And knows no fear.

Enthralled, he stares,
Oblivious to its hunger,
Its bloodlust,
Its rage.

The child stands fascinated
As the beast, ever cunning, steals close.
With awe he regards its eyes,
Its tail,
Its fur,

Missing entirely, in his wonderment,
The horrible glint of its fangs.

CHAPTER SIXTEEN

For little Codiah Longford, there were only two things in Norick that could capture his undivided attention: fire and horses.

Fire, because as the seven-year-old son of the town smithy, Restin Longford, he spent numerous languid afternoons watching as his father toiled in Norick's squat, diamond-shaped forge. Located just a block over from the Market Square, the workshop was a realm of unparalleled delight, enchanting with its dim lighting, brick oven, and funneled hood. The tools of the trade, when furnished in the nimble hands of his father, were no less than the instruments of a sorcerer. That's how Codiah viewed the profession: a kind of thrilling magic, one he didn't understand but knew to be real. One that could transform brute lumps of ore into shining pieces of wonder.

And it was all because of fire. Sprawled belly-down on one of his father's workbenches—situated just close enough to monitor the activity without taking the full brunt from the furnace—Codiah would chart the flames' movement with a dreamy sense of detachment, mesmerized by the immensity hidden in every lurch and crease. He couldn't quite put to words the emotions that sight evoked—infinity laid bare, trapped in a confined space—but later on he would come to regard fire as something vast and unfathomable, a force of both inhale and exhale, suction and release. The secret to life could be found in that furnace: a cycle of creation and destruction, chaos and order. Death begetting life. The old world burning up so that a new one could rise.

Codiah lost and found himself when staring into those flames. As difficult as it was for him to express, he felt as if he were, in some strange way, peering within himself.

He couldn't spend *all* of his time at the forge, though—at least according to his father. A cultivated man, Restin advocated for a wide range of life experiences, especially for younglings. And so, the latter half of Codiah's two unyielding passions: horses.

As the nephew of Gregory Millons, the stable head, Codiah was granted unrestricted access to Norick's in-town stable, a triangular structure pushed up against one of the town's walls. He found the building, with its long gallery apportioned into pens, nearly as captivating as his father's workshop. Like the forge, the stable rested in a perpetual state of gloom, lit only by a few lamps and a row of windows that never managed to catch much sunlight. The floors were smoothed by wear and almost always dirty. Mud, grime, and flakes of chaff covered the flagstones, finding recess in every corner and nook. The musk of man and beast coated the air like a cologne.

What really summoned Codiah to the stable—and kept him returning—were the animals themselves. He found horses to be magnificent creatures, somber and deeply elegant. Their eyes always seemed distant and sad to him, even lonesome. Often, he spent untold minutes simply stroking their coned faces and staring into those eyes, mumbling a word or two. They shared a connection, the horses and him. One he didn't quite understand but cherished all the same, like an old memory he'd since forgotten the meaning to.

He hadn't ridden one yet—*When you're older,* his uncle would grunt in his brusque drawl. *Your pa would kill me if anything happened*—and in truth Codiah wasn't sure if he wanted to. As much as he adored the beasts, he also possessed an inherent fear of them. He sensed a wildness lingering in their melancholic eyes. More so he felt there was a mutual respect between them, an understanding even, and to mount up on their backs would shatter the innocence with which both parties regarded one another.

So he waited, and he didn't push the matter with his uncle. In fact, he hadn't thought about riding for months. Until tonight, until Milgrin's Day. Late into the evening, nearing midnight, he lounged with his parents at one of the long tavern tables set up in the square, watching as the musicians orchestrated a controlled chaos from the stage. His mother, Emilee, was giving Restin a knowing smile—soft, but laden with meaning—and the blacksmith, squeezing her hand, returned the look. Normally Codiah, blushing and squirming in his seat, would've turned and asked them what they were smiling about, to stop it *pleeease* before any of his friends saw, but tonight he just ignored the interaction altogether, eyes pasted on the crowd and its brazen spirit.

He felt it as they all felt it. A hypnotic sense of detachment and desire. A lurching hysteria funneling through his chest. He couldn't explain the feeling, but he wanted to partake, to be swept up in the revelry and to do something daring himself. Something crazy.

And why shouldn't he?

Reclining beside his parents—but still decidedly alone—it came to Codiah in a mad dash, like a thunderous stampede: the stable, the horses. He smirked at the thought, imagining the pull of the crisp night air; imagining the rhythmic heave of the animal beneath him, its slogging pant. Already he could feel the exhilarating rush of speed and weightlessness. The sense of freedom.

Yes. Yes—he would do this. This thing for himself, this thing of beauty, on a night of possibility and adventure. It was time, no matter what his uncle thought. Codiah had watched the stable hands plenty; he knew just how to prepare the horses and set them into motion. He was sure he could do it himself if he were to just try.

Forget what everyone else thought—he was ready.

Codiah risked a glance across the table. Mother and Father would never understand (he imagined their faces when they saw him riding the horse: fearful and angry—but also proud, he hoped), so he would go without their permission, waiting for the perfect moment to steal away.

The opportunity came sooner than expected. Restin, finishing his pint of ale, set it on the table before draping an arm across Emilee's shoulders. Gazing up at him, she scooted closer and leaned into his chest. The pair locked eyes. They shared a kiss.

Lost in each other, they failed to notice as Codiah slipped from the bench, backed from the table, and, grinning with his newfound freedom, skittered down an empty side street.

The trip through town was effortless, without thought, like a journey toward home. Before he knew it, the stable's entrance had emerged from the darkness; a cumbersome thing, the door stretched along the outer wall in an enormous iron slab sealed with a padlock. Codiah frowned as he reached for the latch: He had no idea where his uncle kept the key. As his eyes lingered, however, he noticed that the lock's curved lever was elevated from its corresponding hollow; a millimeter of black space floated in between. *It isn't locked.*

He didn't know how to interpret his good fortune. The disengaged mechanism was something of a surprise; without consciously thinking it, a part of him had hoped the building would be sealed. Then he wouldn't have had to face the impulsiveness of this scheme and he could've turned around and returned to his parents—unsuccessful, but still puffed up with the knowledge that he had tried.

Now there was no excuse but his own fear. A fact that was kind of invigorating. *Just do it*, a whisper in his head insisted. *You've already come all this way. There's no reason to turn back now. It's open; you won't get this chance again.*

He knew it was true: It *had* to be now. The restlessness in his gut and the infinite feeling of the night would allow for nothing less.

He removed the padlock and grabbed hold of the door. Heaving with all the strength his young body could muster, he tugged it open. By the time the slab was retracted completely, Codiah was sweating in full, but not enough so to miss the pungent odors scampering for open air: hay, manure, sweat, dust.

The interior lay in darkness. The glow of the town's torches spilled into the foyer but failed further in as the gallery stretched away. Rows of stalls lined either side, their occupants concealed. The hayloft, nestled into the base of the roof, was a bastion of mystery and gloom; its ladder, missing a few rungs and casting a disfigured shadow, strained for the opening above. A rustle of movement drew Codiah's eyes from the ladder to the pens.

You need a light. The thought was an obvious one, and it arrived not borne by fear but purely from necessity: If he wanted to ride, he would need to see. Not once had he considered the regular nightmare that haunted his dreams (a shrouded figure accompanied by a host of voices, as if there were a great multitude chanting around him in rasping, feverish tones). As he stood at the threshold, Codiah felt only a sense of calm. The feeling was akin to those first trancelike moments of a dream, when anything—euphoria or terror—was still possible.

Codiah recalled a trio of torches he'd seen on the way to the stable, mounted just up the block. *Grab one,* that voice in his head instructed. *Quickly now.*

Scurrying along the sidewalk, he did so. He yanked it from its cagelike socket and hustled back to the stable with the flame afloat. He caught his breath. The radiance of the fire swelled within the foyer, sending a curtain of shadow slithering to the rear. Without the burden of further thought, Codiah walked inside and wrenched the door shut.

Darkness engulfed him. He felt enclosed but liberated, and he paused to listen as the wind's lament moaned through the rafters. He stepped toward the nearest stall.

Clasping the edge, he peered inside on the tips of his toes. The pen's inhabitant, Bravia, arced her neck around, snuffled, and stared at him with enormous sparkling eyes. Codiah's own lingered on the mare's black coat, sheened in torchlight, before drifting up to those doleful spheres. For half a minute the horse and the boy simply gazed at one another, the glow in their eyes like distant starlight, bottomless and unreachable. Codiah nodded; he understood.

He turned and departed. *The tack room,* the voice said. *You'll need equipment.* The overcrowded storage space lay at the end of the gallery beneath the loft's overhang. Codiah made it only a handful of paces before his eyes again found the ladder, thin slats of poorly nailed wood grasping for sky. *Climb it. Just for a peek.* And suddenly he wanted to.

Codiah folded his fingers about one of the rungs and snuggled the torch tighter to his body. The flames were hot and bright against his cheek, but he hardly felt them; his eyes were already climbing upward, toward the wonders left unseen.

Why not tonight? It's harmless. Using his one free arm, he hauled his body up. *Just a quick look, then you can go ride.* His foot felt for the next rung. *Who said you couldn't? Not Uncle Gregory. Not Father or Mother. What do they know anyhow?* He steadied himself against the wobbly frame before feeling for another slat. *You've always wanted to see what it looks like from up there. I bet Uncle Gregory is even hiding things.* He lugged himself higher, ascending rung after rung, eyes fixed on the blackness above. Not once did he glance down. *You're gonna get a sight you've never seen, boy.*

His head crested the lip of the platform. Sweat wormed its way down his temples. Balancing himself with his free hand, Codiah glided the torch over the brink, letting the soft glow filter throughout the loft. Dust motes drifted like golden flecks of snow. Swaths of spider webs covered the slanted ceiling. Beneath it, hay rose in towering bundles. Loose stalks lay spilled and abandoned across the floor, and a chaffy thickness clogged the air.

Dizzy with the smell, Codiah scampered over the ledge.

The sight, while in every way unremarkable, seemed strange and lovely. The stacks of hay loomed in tight clusters, refracting the torchlight into peculiar shapes and shadows. Codiah wanted to climb in and lay amongst it all: lost, forgotten, consumed. To be just another anonymous piece in a larger whole.

It's yours, bestowed that voice inside of him. *Every single thing. To do with as you please.*

All mine. His eyes were shimmering. *To do with as I please.* He started forward, torch extended, and that's when the thought came—like a hammer abruptly jarring an anvil, like an eruption of sparks. It halted him before he could take another step.

For the first time, Codiah wondered what all of that hay would look like burning.

His mouth lolled open as his eyes raked over the scene. He wondered what would happen if *he* were to set it alight, right then; set it all ablaze in a rush of noise and heat. An image danced across his eyes: the ravenous swell of orange and yellow flame clambering over the stalks and licking at the ceiling; the sheer expansiveness of the fire, the endless surge and recoil of its innards; the blackened course of its ascent, death in a color, swelling up, up, up.

Codiah's gaze narrowed on the torch. The flame rustled in its spindled half-cage. Its burn suddenly seemed diminutive—seemed almost confined, as if the flame were entrapped and cheated of its full potential. As if it needed to be set free.

So set it free. And he knew, as before, that he wanted to.

In a trance, Codiah started for the nearest bale.

He didn't think of the horses below; didn't think of their bright mournful eyes and lazy, whooshing tails. He didn't consider how their shrieks would pierce the night as first the smoke and then the heat found them. He thought only of his father's furnace: thought only of its simmering rumble and the sweltering congestion of heat. Of the enchanting tumble of the flames, the ceaseless careening of color, round and round, side to side: an infinity, a multitude, a void.

Inhale and exhale. Suction and release. The world burning away.

With the faintest hint of a smile, torch securely in hand, little Codiah Longford knelt at a mound of hay.

PART FIVE

THE CRANKING
OF THE VISE

Every river
Begins first as a drop from the sky.

Every avalanche:
A stone loosened, gravel upturned,
A tossing forth from the cliffside.

All things are fuel;
All things are ash.

Every fire sparks first
Before its catch.

CHAPTER SEVENTEEN

From a darkness—from the nightmare, a stagnant pool of water rank with the funk of decay—William drifted toward the gray half-light of wakefulness, borne gently through a seepage of anger and guilt by the slinking rustle of the voice.

They're coming, William. Time to wake now; they're coming.

The voice. From out of the blackness it came: a voice from nowhere, from everywhere. From inside him and from afar; from all things at once. An ancient presence, an oily nothingness, stretching beyond his measure of time and understanding. And yet it knew him, this voice, this swelling dissonance, this whisper with the force of a shout. It knew him intimately, this presence; it called to him by name with its seductive croon, knowing all about his past and his fears and the crippling weakness keeping him rooted.

It knew about Landon, his stillborn son. It knew how William yearned—oh how he yearned, how he *ached*—for a chance, just a chance, to hold the child in his arms. To enfold and shelter him from the world, to give him warmth and protection and the certainty of being loved. To show him life wasn't so bad after all, not when they were together, a promise through touch: *I'm here, little guy. My son, my boy. I'm here and I always will be. I won't let you go. Don't you worry, don't you ever worry. I won't let you go.*

The voice knew how, in the end, William had been forced to do exactly that.

It knew all of this and more: about his time in the South fighting in someone else's wars; about the bone-deep weariness, the suffering, that had consumed him afterward. How, night after night on a cot of soaked sheets, he'd wrestled with ghosts turning circles in his mind: the faces of his fallen comrades, pale and tinted blue, whispering to him from the shadows. Their words were obscured, but the meaning was always the same: *Why us, and not you?*

Night after night, reliving those battles. There were the sights: lime-green hillsides, painted crimson; the whitest beaches, sanded with gore. The smells: flesh baking in the sun, shit leaking from a man's loosened bowels. Worst of all were the sounds, which would return at the oddest moments: the slurp of arrows upon the wind (and the reel of his heart as he waited for the barrage to fall); the clamor of steel and the squeals of the dying; the noises those women had made in that burning hayfield of Yournic, the ash drifting skyward before tumbling like a perverted snowfall.

Night after night—but during the day, also, the feeling of suffocation seizing him at random, sometimes powerfully enough to bring him to his knees.

The voice knew how, unable to stomach the torment any longer, William had traveled north, aiming to put some miles between himself and his past, hoping sheer distance and the refreshment of new scenery would do the trick. The voice knew how, beyond all hope or reason, that that was exactly what happened. That he had found peace right here in this little town of Norick, a thousand leagues into the north.

It knew how he had discovered it—finally, after so many years—in her. In Ellen.

Ellen, who, four years later, was gone. Still gone.

Ellen: a wisp of vapor, a mere memory.

The voice knew about the life they had shared, how she'd sparked his heart into motion and color, into meaning. It knew about their eventual pregnancy and the hidden danger lurking in the midst of such joy. It knew about that cursed midwinter morning nine months later, with its white avalanche sky and gray, glassy sea. It knew about the unnatural surge of blood that had seeped into the midwife's cot. It knew about the shrieks.

On the evening of Milgrin's Day, the voice drew William into the folds of these memories. It pulled him tenderly, as a schoolmaster leads a sobbing child. It paused long enough for him to look around, to see. But now the voice was releasing William, pushing him away and out, sending him floating upon the black like a wayward leaf.

He was being lifted; he was frozen in place. There was no way to tell. There was only darkness. Darkness and the last echoes of the voice, dispersing like vapor into the abyss. *Wake,* it called. *It's time, William. Awake.* He seemed to lie there forever, and for no time at all: an eternity and a blink.

Then the shell of his body was returning, materializing at a distance and gradually encasing him on all sides. The weight of his limbs returned; a heaviness bloomed in his chest. The wooden balustrade fencing the veranda pressed into his back. Fingers of wind surged against his cheeks. For a moment William's eyes remained sealed, and it wasn't so much waking as remembering. Remembering where he was—who he was. Remembering why any of this mattered.

The Eastern Outpost. Yes. On watch. Milgrin's Day. A bit of wine, perhaps too much. Landon... A weariness greater than any he could recall settled over him. He resolved then to wither back into the folds of sleep, to let the dark and its cool oblivion take him. *A few more minutes can't hurt.*

A momentous crack split the air. *Thunder. The storm.* William had observed the tempest earlier before drifting off, but sometime during his stupor he'd come to regard it as a fiction, one of many, and so had forgotten it. Until now, as it snarled over the Bay of Hardin as though indignant. *Take heed. I am real; I am here. And I won't soon be dismissed.*

Another sound materialized in the storm's booming wake. This one was much closer: a *thwack* of wood as a door was slammed into its frame. Next came a series of thuds, rising from within the tower itself.

Footsteps.

Time to wake now; they're coming.

Someone had opened and shut the door to the outpost, and that someone was now approaching through the staircase beneath him. The thread of his dreams scattered at the realization and, with a gasp, William jolted awake.

CHAPTER EIGHTEEN

Tossing and turning upon the rickety bed cot, Gregory Millons stirred awake from the sound of his own catching breath.

For a moment, thought eluded the stable head completely. Just a trace of his consciousness surfaced, drifting through the black but finding nothing firm to cling to. He wasn't sure where he was or who he was supposed to be; for what could have been an eternity, lying there in the dark with no stimuli to ground him, he simply *was*.

But this weightless suspension, a kind of peace in its own right, couldn't last.

Another wheezing snore jarred its way through his throat, and Gregory roused further. This time the awakening was accompanied by a distinct bodily sensation: a fist of pressure between both temples, what Gregory knew to be his head reeling suddenly from drink.

Drink. *Yes.* He'd been drinking. Celebrating. It was Milgrin's Day.

With a fluttering of his lids, Gregory willed his surroundings into focus. The space in which he lay was crammed with a darkness so total he wondered if he'd been struck sightless, as blind as the rothmire bats that dwelt in the Yurgen Hollows. He squinted into the black, shut his eyes, then opened them once more. As his vision adjusted, clues to his whereabouts began to emerge.

There was the coarse fiber of the straw mattress beneath him, grating against his torso. There was the itch of the wool blanket slung across his hips. The muted heave of the ocean was just audible through the walls, and a pale glimmer of light snuck its way through a rent in the ceiling. Finally there was the stuffiness of the room itself, a familiar musty odor.

And something else: the carnal, fleshy musk of their bodies. A sour-sweet fragrance of perspiration, body odor, and spent desire.

Ah, yes. He remembered now, all of it. Sliding to a sitting position, he turned to peer at the naked woman slumbering beside him. *Mayrin.* Beautiful, stoic Mayrin Malecko, who had captured his attention that night as much with her indifference as with her quiet sensuality and youth. He felt certain he would never forget that silent look she'd given him as her calloused hand led him away: away from the crowds and the music and the baggage of their former lives. Their desire had been a tide breaking, first in the stolen kisses of a back alleyway, and then in the final act itself, a hypnotic dance of limbs and sweat and flesh. He remembered it now less with specific images than with a dreamy feeling of satisfaction and warmth.

Gregory knew he should feel remorse, or at the very least shame, but he felt neither. He couldn't even muster concern over the foolhardy—and very public—way in which he'd pursued her. All that came was a sense of craving, the understanding that he would at once do it all again if only given the chance. That, and a palpable sense of regret. Not from any considerations regarding his wife, Rebecca, but for the fact that he hadn't done it all sooner.

Becca. A woman with whom he'd spent more than twenty years sharing a bed, and yet, at present, he couldn't call to mind the image of her homely face. Their relationship was built on practicality and routine; of late, he found himself possessing nothing more than a curious apathy toward her. He knew what he'd done with Mayrin tonight breached an unspoken understanding between them, but it didn't matter. There was only this room; this weightless feeling in his gut; this woman, many years his junior, lying naked before him.

It was enough; it was all he needed. Gregory was determined to enjoy it while he could.

Slithering himself next to her, he reached for the blanket and adjusted it over his belly. His drowsiness was returning; a warm curtain of exhaustion lowered upon him. Wrapping his arms about Mayrin's midsection, he spun her gently—she stirred, mumbled something incoherent—and pulled her in close. Still half asleep, she reciprocated, snuggling against the crook of his body.

Eyes closed, Gregory just held her and felt himself fade.

Already a dream was surfacing: a torpid affair of hazy golden light and the coned heads of his horses peering at him from over their stalls. Between them, arranged in curving rows along the stable floor, were candles.

There were dozens of them, laid out like the tail of some great glittering snake. Their sputtering wicks released trails of smoke that rose toward a ceiling pooled in darkness. Those black columns seemed to be upholding it—and, perhaps, acting as conduits *for* it.

Though partially awake—part of him still sensing Mayrin's weight—Gregory, the dream-Gregory, moved for the line of candles. He was drawn by a need to stand amongst them and crane his neck up to stare into the darkness above.

He stepped forward—in the way of dreams, all too quickly—and the candles were suddenly surrounding him, watching him. Orange flames with blackened cores danced in his vision. Along the walls, the horses looked on without blinking: silent, emotionless, accepting of what was about to occur. A whine, lower than that of summer cicadas, buzzed in his skull. Gregory bent and ran a hand through the nearest candle, feeling no surprise when the flame didn't sting.

It was time.

Time to look up, to do what he knew would be an irrevocable act, a last thing.

It was time for them to meet.

For there wasn't just smoke up there, gathering on the ceiling in concentrated billows. There was something else in that blackness. Some*one* else. Waiting.

Grinning.

He was arching his neck when the stampede of terror—hardly realized until now but ever present beneath the surface—unleashed itself in full. Gregory jerked awake upon the cot with a gasp. Panicked, suddenly sweating, he unwound his arms from Mayrin's stomach and, staring at the black ceiling above, sucked down breath.

He was choking. He was drowning in air.

Gradually, his breathing slowed. The tension uncoiled. And Mayrin snoozed on, unaware of his jarring arousal from sleep.

Just a dream, Gregory reassured himself. He found Mayrin's body and wriggled in close. Shutting his eyes, he listened to the rhythmic intake of her breath, the rise and fall of her chest. *Don't be a fool; it was just a dream.*

Already he could feel himself drifting. It was easy, really. His eyelids had never felt so heavy, his mind so pleasantly numbed. There was nothing to be afraid of either. For reasons that escaped him, he felt confident the nightmare had run its course and would plague him no longer. He would now find other, happier realms. Dreams awash with memories of his youth and with golden fantasies of summer: galloping with his personal steed, Serren, out on fields of green; smoking his pipe from the stable's rooftop with a clear view of the sea; and Mayrin, Mayrin, *Mayrin*... The fullness of her breasts, the fleshy curve of her hips.

No, Gregory soothed with a drowsy smacking of his lips, *it was nonsense. Just a dream. And now I'll find others.*

But as he sunk into the fog of his subconscious, a string of logic gave him pause. *Why were there candles in the stable? And why so much smoke? What's* that *supposed to mean?*

Because it was a nightmare, you fool, he eventually decided. *Nothing more. It's not supposed to make a lick of sense.*

Annoyed with himself—and finished with the matter—Gregory nuzzled his whiskers into Mayrin's coiled hair, took in the scent of her, and let himself fade. He refused to give credence to another thought that was begging for attention. Originating from a slight, involuntary crinkle of his nostrils, it surfaced in a rush. He granted it only passing scrutiny before dismissing it as just another leftover from the nightmare, one that would soon recede into the murk of sleep.

Beyond the scent of Mayrin's perfume, hovering on the fringes of air, something else?

Was that smoke he could smell?

CHAPTER NINETEEN

It was lighter than she'd expected.

Julie Temult stood rigid on the furthermost point of the wharf—a small cutout of space behind a warehouse on the eastern side, accessed only by a narrow ledge that required you to slink along at a crawl, lest you tumble into the sea. Thus shielded from view, she gazed as if mesmerized at the object clutched between her fingers.

She spun it. Twirled it, end over end. She held it against the backdrop of clouds above and squinted at its minute, opulent details. He had been right about one thing: It was indeed beautiful; exquisite even. She lowered it, admiring the way in which, even in the tenebrous darkness, it seemed to sparkle and shine.

She spat on it.

Screw him. She released her grip and watched as the vase plunged toward the storm-churned waves below. There was a plop and a splash. A glitter of golden luminescence. And then it was sinking, the whitecaps lapping over it in their rush toward the shore. In no time at all, the vase was swallowed completely, vanishing just like that. Gone into the black.

Sorry, Eustace, Julie thought.

CHAPTER TWENTY

Footsteps. Footsteps on the tower stairs.

William pitched forward, and then his body crashed back into the railing. He groped instinctively for a sheathed sword leaning nearby. Locating it, he lurched to his feet, stumbling before catching himself with a hand.

The erratic movement upended the flagon of wine—the vessel was empty now, streaked with a faint burgundy hue—and sent it skittering along the pinewood floor in a jangle of friction and glass. He tried to follow it with his eyes, but his surroundings spun. The sword, a reward from a former commander for exemplary performance in the Denmoore campaign, seemed too heavy to hold. A sludge of pressure expanded in the space behind his eyes. Lids closed, breathing fitfully into the wind, he braced himself upon the balustrade.

On the stairs, the clomp of footsteps continued upward.

William pried his eyes open and turned toward the enclosed stairway descending to the compound below. The lamps mounted in each of the outpost's four corners illuminated the entrance, but darkness held reign just beyond the threshold. William kept his stare on that black opening and listened. A slight wheeze matched the steps and was punctuated at irregular intervals by a soft spew of curses. He sighed. *Brade.*

Relaxing, William hauled in another breath. *Get ahold of yourself, soldier. Pull it together.* Fastening the sword to his belt, he rotated toward the railing and the panoramic view it offered. Brade would detect nothing of his captain's former panic; the young guardsman would find only an aloof and steely resolve, a sense that William was utterly focused and had nothing but time to spare, that perhaps he'd stick around and observe and ensure that—

An exhale filled the space behind him. "Piss, it's dark in there. Forgot my bloody torch."

At nineteen, the chancellor's wiry, dark-haired son stood nearly six and a half feet tall. He'd inherited the lean physicality of his mother—who had reportedly been almost six-two herself—rather than the burly, mountainous breadth of his father. The boy's soaring stature was no less commanding, however: He towered over his peers and, indeed, over most of the town, a fact he flaunted like a crown.

The newest recruit to the Guard, Brade hadn't been recruited through William's efforts the previous cycle. He'd been *assigned* by the Council in a move William suspected was a ploy to keep an eye on him. They were looking for an excuse, he knew, any excuse.

"Thought those bloody stairs were gonna hack my shins off," Brade said. William could hear him stepping toward the balustrade on the opposite end of the tower; he could picture the boy staring off over the valley with a possessive eye. "I'm as tender as a whore on Midsummer's Eve."

William's cheek gave a twitch.

"Well, well, well… I see you've been having yourself some fun, old man." There was a *clinking* as Brade stooped and retrieved the flagon. William's stomach tightened, and, for a beat, his eyes fell shut. In all the commotion of his rousing, he'd forgotten about the wine.

How did I forget the bloody wine?

He turned warily toward the chancellor's son. Brade was squinting into the mouth of the flagon and making a *clucking* sound with his tongue. He spun the container so that a few residual drops slipped out. "Didn't even save me any. I'm a tad hurt, Captain. Even the grunts deserve their rations, you know." He set the container down. "Bloody shame, really. You and I could've had our own little Milgrin's Day celebration up here. Not to worry, though, I brought my own." Reaching into the folds of his uniform, the boy pulled out an amber bottle and rattled it in William's direction.

William just stared at him. "Oh ease up, you old skin-rack." Brade flicked his wrist in a lethargic wave. "I understand the need for a little fun as much as the next bloke. Especially tonight. Milgrin himself would approve." The boy slid to a seat against the balustrade; with his teeth, he yanked the stopper free. "You got nothing to worry about, Captain," he slurred between the cork. "On my honor, I shan't gossip a thing."

William scowled. The boy's silence was about as likely as a northern winter without snow.

Brade spit the stopper from his lips and traced the cork as it lurched in little vaults and bounds toward the belfry. He slung his neck back and guzzled. "If I'm being honest," he said after a hiccup, "I may or may not have been indulging some myself already. Thought I'd be a part of the community and all that. You know how it goes." He flashed a small grin, droll and reflective, his teeth a luminous white. "And that was *before* my mates and I rendezvoused with the women. Let me tell you, Captain. Sunken hells. Little whores, every one of them. But Jansen Mangle's daughter most of all." He whistled and gave his head a dreamy shake. "Quite the temptress. Couldn't keep her hands off of me… And thus"—he gestured theatrically toward the staircase—"the forgotten torch."

Brade lifted the bottle for another pull. As he glowered at the movement, William's voice returned to him at last. "You know the rules, boy," he croaked, his throat as dry as a julen weed. "When you're at your post: no drink, no women, and no sitting. You're to be alert and ready for combat at all times."

Brade waved him off. "Right." He cackled as if William had just offered the most absurd of jokes. The sound whirled about the veranda and chafed along William's spine. "Aye. You're absolutely right." He swigged more ale. "Can't believe I forgot."

William said nothing, just crossed his arms and waited for the boy's hilarity to wane.

Brade's smile faltered as he registered the sullen slant to his superior's face. "Oh. You're serious. All right, let's not get your old bones all up in a twist." He set the bottle, half-full, between his legs. He lifted both palms. "Just take a breath. You sure you're all right? You look a little worn out. Maybe you're not thinking straight."

"I know exactly what I'm saying."

"Me drinking isn't harming a thing, and you know it. Just go on back to town, and I'll handle things up here. No sense causing a fuss."

"This isn't a joke, boy. Those are the rules—and you'll follow them."

Brade considered that. "Come on, Breeve. Just head home."

William found his finger knifing through the air. "*I* will decide when—and *if*—I leave. *Not you.*" William could feel the old anger boiling up, a fissure-rush of pressure and heat. "You'll dispose of that bottle, stand up, and get your ass to keeping watch. Do you understand?" Brade stayed silent. Lips sealed, he crossed his arms against his chest. "You'll do as you're told, or I'll send you back to town in riggings. Get up—and pour that ale out *now.*"

Brade's eyes had gone cold. "Is this really what you want to get riled up about? Let's not forget what you were doing before I got here. By the looks of ya, I'd wager you were even sleeping." The young guardsman shifted his weight forward, his neck extending out like a bird's. "I would *hate* for the Council to hear about that."

"You saw nothing, child."

"I saw plenty. Enough to recognize the hypocrisy standing before me. As my father always says,"—right then the boy was a facsimile of the elder Higgins, his bulbous lips drawn tight over moon-bleached teeth—" 'Hypocrisy is the greatest affliction of them all.' "

"Your father is the greatest hypocrite of them all."

A slug of a vein wormed its way up Brade's throat, palpitating beneath the sharp slant of his jawline. "Is that right? Well, I'm sure he'd love to hear about it. Don't you worry, Breeve, I'll pass on your sentiments precisely."

So there they were: words that would be an eradication of any future William had hoped to have in the Guard. He wasn't entirely sure where his outburst had come from; he knew he should be, at present, cringing at his lack of discipline and rushing forward to stammer out an apology. *A slip of the tongue only, Brade, a momentary lapse in judgment. There's no need—really no need—to bring your father into this. Please…* But, whether because of the wine or the nightmare or the boy's constant sense of entitlement, he found himself unable to care. *Fuck him, and fuck his father, and fuck the Council.*

He was done. Done with it all. Done with bowing mutely to the town's every whim. Done with seeking meaning in some inane, pointless job. Drinking that wine earlier might have been a forfeit, but maybe it'd also set him free.

May as well crank the vise. "Then you will do so from chains, boy. Just be sure to include that *you*, his son, are the most rancid waste of human filth in this whole damned valley. A little calf who can't quite pull himself off his father's teat."

Brade launched himself to his feet, toppling the bottle resting between his thighs. In much the same fashion as William's, the container jangled across the tower, clangored against the balustrade, and spun to a halt. Its contents spilled out. Strangely mesmerized, both of them watched as the amber fluid fanned across the floor. It splashed onto the planks and diverted along the cracks. Silence filled the space between them, and the moment stretched.

Braving a step toward William, Brade fumed. "You'll be lucky to get a shit-coated hovel in the woods when this is over with. Mark my words."

"So be it. But I won't tolerate another second of your disrespect. You'll be in the stocks before night's end if it's the last command I give."

Expression dark, the chancellor's son took another step. William reciprocated. He could see Brade's hand sliding toward the hilt of his blade. He could make out the red tangle patterning the whites of his eyes. *He's serious, then.* The realization brought forth fresh moisture to William's back.

" 'No drinking while on watch,' " Brade sneered as they continued tracking a slow circle around each other. " 'No sleeping on duty.' 'Alert and standing at all times.' Any other rules you've broken that I'm forgetting? Wouldn't want the Council to be cheated of any of the facts."

Their measured lurk continued. "You're sure you wanna do this, boy? I promise locking blades with me will not end well. I won't hold back." Brade had to understand he was outmatched here, that in a soldier's arena no sarcastic retort could save you. All that counted was the quickness of your swing, the heft of your stroke. As William saw it, the chancellor's son had about as good a chance as a candle in a downpour. If he were wise, he'd wait until William was vulnerable—or until he had the backing of his father and his council cronies—to finish this fight.

The two of them had swapped positions; William stood before the blackened staircase while Brade's back pointed out over the valley. "You and I both know you don't want this," William said. "Not now. So here's what's going to happen: You're going to lay down that sword, drop to your knees, and I'll take you into custody for insubordination. Understood? What happens after that will be up to the Council." He paused to read Brade's expression, which struggled to hide his apprehension. "There's no reason for your blood to be spilled tonight," William continued. "Unless that's what you want. Because believe me, I'll spill it if I have to. Hell, I don't even care if I do."

"And then you'll spend the rest of your worthless life squatting in your own piss, carving lines on a dungeon wall. *If* they don't choose the gallows. You wouldn't dare strike me."

"We'll see."

Halting, they squared off from across the balcony, hands clasped about their hilts. Perspiration clung to their foreheads in dewy droplets, and animosity tethered itself between them like a cord. *Let's get on with it then,* thought William.

"Lay down your arms," he ordered again, nodding toward the floor, "right now. This is your last warning. You won't get another chance."

Brade glared at him, considering with what seemed a moment of genuine hesitation. He sucked in a breath, and William could make out real fear behind those eyes. There was frustration there too, at having been bested. Brade glanced at his sword, at William, and then at his feet...

...before heaving the weapon from its scabbard. The steel blade bit into the nighttime air with a screech, and Brade held it suspended over his shoulder. Looking pleased with himself, the boy cocked his head to the left and flashed that infuriating smile of his, goading William with his perfectly manicured teeth. *Come on, then,* they said. *Come and get me.*

The arrogant little fool, was all William could manage to think.

Brade, long limbs drawn in tight, stalked closer. "Ah, yes. I've forgotten something, *Captain.*" His grin was dwindling; in its place, a new shade of intensity colored his cheeks. "I've forgotten one of your precious fucking rules."

They spun about one another in a methodic lurch. The howling wind shoved and tugged at their garments, testing their balance. Beneath them, the tower swayed. Still William refused to draw his sword, though he clenched its hilt with an increasingly damp palm.

"Which one am I missing? Help me here, old man. Which one?" Brade pretended to ponder the question. His eyes widened with revelation. "Oh, I know. *No women,* that's it. 'No women during your shift.' How could I forget?" He pantomimed a look of disgust. "I would hate to imagine if you'd broken that one. Now *there's* an image. I doubt you've had much temptation of late, though. I'm not sure old Ferny would even touch you now."

A shudder quaked itself across William's face. He was no longer moving—he felt incapable of doing so—but stood fixed to a single point, his eyes swollen with a venom he'd long thought buried. It rose on the sludge of the nightmare, and with it came the feel of that voice—ever present, ever listening. It purred its satisfaction. It prodded him on: *Do it. Make him hurt. Make him suffer. Make him bleeeed.*

Do it, do it, do it.

Across from him, Brade was snickering. "You two sacks of flesh going at it..." He shook his head with an exaggerated grimace. "You probably wouldn't even know where to stick it in, it's been so long. That's if you can even still get that old tool of yours working."

Do it. Cut him. Slice the arrogant son of bitch into a hundred pieces. In his mind's eye, William could imagine a clean stroke through the boy's arm, a spurt of blood, then doing the same to the other, methodically, like butchering meat. He could almost hear the visceral howl of agony that would wrench from Brade's lips...

"That'd be a bit of problem." Brade offered a shrug, but his eyes lit up as he continued. "I know just the solution, though. Pretend you're with that dead wife of yours. What was her name? Oh, yes, *Ellen.* I bet if you close your eyes and call out to her you won't have any issues getting it up." Brade watched him closely. When William didn't react, the boy let his eyelids droop. Softly, as if in a moan, he continued: "Ellen, Ellen, *Ellen...*"

William's response wasn't so much a reaction as an eruption. He ripped his blade from the throat of its scabbard and then—with a bellow, with murder in his eyes—he leapt forward, toward the son of the chancellor.

CHAPTER TWENTY-ONE

Which, of course, was precisely what Brade had intended.

Too late William realized his mistake. His impulsive movement—an ungraceful, pitching vault across the span of the tower—had drawn him off balance and overextended his body, sabotaging any chance for accuracy while at the same time leaving him vulnerable for counterstrike. His sword, gripped with both hands along its hilt, was thrust up over the curve of his shoulder and arcing downward. It was a posture that left his stomach and chest exposed.

William, carried by the weight of his momentum, knew it was too late—too late to stop himself or even to pivot. He was committed, no matter the outcome. It was as simple as that: One jeering taunt and a rash surrender to anger, and William Breeve, the best swordsman Norick had ever known, was outmaneuvered.

Brade stood planted, ever patient in that micro-fraction of a second they had left. The boy's lips skewed themselves into a thin, self-satisfied smirk. Then, at the last moment, he moved.

Taking advantage of the vulnerability, Brade jerked his free hand to his belt and, with one deft flick of his wrist, sent a dagger whirling through the air toward William. William caught its glint from the corner of his eye. With a swiftness he didn't think possible, he heaved his blade downward in one last frantic lurch—just in time. The dagger pealed against the smooth stock of his blade, ricocheted with a shudder, and clattered harmlessly to the floor.

All of which was also part of Brade's scheme.

As William stood distracted, the boy launched into motion, slashing toward the captain's head. William jerked his wrists about face and swung in a wild, madcap parry. It was too late. Brade's weapon clouted against his hilt, wedged itself beneath the cross-guard, and—before William had time to process what happened, before he could even so much as blink—sent the sword spiraling away.

It whirled and tumbled before smashing against the balustrade, out of reach.

Brade wasted no time pressing his advantage. He charged William with his shoulder leveled and ripped an elbow upward; it collided with William's chin and rammed his neck back, toward the canopy.

William felt himself falling, a horrible weightlessness. Brade came with him, his free hand grasped about William's tunic. For the briefest instant William could feel the boy's breath upon his cheek, and then the two of them struck the floor. William arrived skull-first, an impact that sent swirls of light streaking across his vision. Then came the rest of him, a nasty jolt along his spine intensified by Brade's weight.

There was a rupture of air in his lungs. There was fire through every limb.

Brade was already up and scrambling for position. He drove a knee into William's gut—a pathetic, half-whimper rattled from the captain's lips—before pulling him up by the hem of his tunic. He lowered his sword to William's throat.

The boy's face broke into a grin. He chuckled, once, then shook his head. "Can you imagine. There I was about to piss myself, and for nothing." He gave another scoff, louder this time. "*The* Captain William Breeve. An *elite* warrior. A fearsome commander. 'The best swordsman Norick has ever seen.' Huh. How many times did I hear that load of rothmire filth? And not an ounce of truth to any of it. Bloody gossips—they can't ever keep things straight."

William stared at the boy—but without focus. The back of his head pulsed with a nauseating ache, and his spine seemed rent in two. For a moment, for too long, he was helpless.

"So now what?" Brade was saying, twisting his lips in disappointment. The blade quivered at William's throat. "No struggle? No last-ditch attempt to disarm me? Come on. Surely there's more to you than this. You really are an old sack of bones. Someone should have offed you years ago."

William narrowed his eyes and tried to focus on Brade's lips. The truth was he didn't have the strength to attempt a struggle. His head reeled from its impact with the floor—but also from the shame of his defeat; with how easily, in just a few quick moves, he'd been beat.

But even this disgrace was a welcome relief. It confirmed what he'd already suspected: The last remnant on which his identity had rested— his prowess as a warrior—was gone. Which gave him the permission he needed. He didn't *want* to fight anymore; he didn't have it in him even for a soldier's death. Instead he would slip quietly from this life, without struggle, without resolve, a death befitting the failure he'd always been: a feeble, pathetic man simply pilfering breath.

He hoped Brade made it swift.

But the boy wouldn't oblige. Something shifted behind his pupils, and that same maddening smirk etched itself across his cheeks. With a show of disinterest, Brade slid back onto his haunches and glanced over the valley. "I suppose *I* could be the one to do it," he said with manufactured indifference, "but that's not quite how I want all of this to end. I think I'd much rather see you face the Council. Something about the thought of you stuttering your way through an explanation is much, much more satisfying." The boy tilted his head knowingly. "*And*, I think it will be worse for you."

William understood then that the boy had interpreted the plea in his eyes: *End this. Kill me.* Yet Brade was refusing to grant him the unspoken request, and he was doing so out of spite. William understood they were enemies, but this stung like a betrayal all the same, a treachery of the worst sort. He should have known: The boy possessed no honor. In the end, he would stop at nothing to dole out vengeance to his enemies. And now to William, he had.

There would be an inquest, a trial, and the self-righteous eyes of the Council. There would be their smug superiority, the implication that they'd foreseen this outcome from the start. There would be a cell and chains— and the inevitable gossip of the town, spreading like fire before just as quickly burning out. There would be the silence that followed, one he was well accustomed to but made all the worse because even after *deciding*, he couldn't escape.

Then, later on—whether it be days or weeks, the silence buzzing in his skull like a bee—he would finally muster the courage to do it: the last thing, the releasing.

He would do it in his hut, or in the forest, or staring out over the emerald waters of Seagren Lake; it made little difference. He would be alone, and it would be quick, and then it'd be done. By staying his hand now, Brade was compounding William's misery, forcing him to endure the looks and the shame and, worst of all, the tedious extension of what he'd already given up. Time, as the boy well knew, was the greatest curse he could inflict upon William.

Gladly was he now delivering it.

William turned away; he couldn't bear to look at him a second longer. A sob gathered in the pit of his stomach and threatened to claw its way forth.

"That's right," said Brade. "I won't make it easy for you. Not this. You'll have to do it for yourself, you coward." Refusing to acknowledge him, William kept his eyes pointed through the balustrade. The foothills beyond rose softly, unhurriedly, little black smears leaking into a muddled skyline. He willed his thoughts into their folds, their abyss. "You truly want this, don't you?" Brade bit off a humorless chuckle. "Piss stones, you're pathetic."

The first tear was sliding down William's cheek when the trees of the Grove began to move. At first this seemed neither odd nor important; his mind drifted over the valley without direction, like a puff of smoke from a dying flame. He observed those racing trees, dashing in an uneven line across the foothills, without comprehension until, finally, his mind admitted the darkness must be playing tricks with him. Trees, after all, didn't just uproot themselves and start sprinting downhill. Such a phenomenon was impossible. He was imagining it, that was all.

Again, he let his eyes wander...

...and then he heard the shouts.

Howls. A fragmented chorus piercing the night. Even in his state of preoccupation, it was clear those cries belonged to the figures hurrying from the Grove. William's ears perked up on instinct—listening, interpreting.

Brade scoffed. "Look at me, you old bastard. Aren't you man enough to meet my eye? I *said*— What are you even gawking at out there..." His voice trailed off as he followed William's gaze through the railing. His body tensed as he too registered the noise. To himself, in a puzzled near-whisper:

"What in the sunken hells...?"

Brade slid from William's torso and shambled to his feet. William followed suit, groping his way up to join the chancellor's son at the railing.

The figures—humanoid, really—disappeared behind a hill before emerging seconds later at its crest. The closer they came—and with each new flash of lightning—the more certain William grew: They were people all right; at least a dozen total, perhaps more. Several near the front appeared to be holding long thin objects that swung with their movement. A glimmer radiated from one of the tips, and William's suspicions were confirmed.

Spears.

This group of people—whoever they were—were armed. Armed and rushing toward the outpost in a frenzy. The sound sent warm frissons up William's back. *War cries.* The adrenaline-laced shouts of those rushing toward a fray, becoming something less than human. A raiding party, then? A company of soldiers sent to take out the Guard?

After all this time, Norick was under attack?

Norick was under attack.

From somewhere in his subconscious, William once more heard the voice, slinking out from the darkness: *They're coming, William. Time to wake now; they're coming.* He knew then that, all along, he had been waiting for exactly this.

Brade stood dumbfounded. "Are they...? What do you think they're doing? What should *we* do?" William ignored him. His eyes were drawn toward Norick, a beacon of shimmering burnt orange beneath a shelf of cloud. It struck him like a premonition: Something was amiss there as well. He didn't know what to expect—a ringing battalion of soldiers setting up a siege; a fleet of Southern galleys with wind-blown sails; a mob of townsfolk, rioting their way through the streets—but he discovered the source of his disquiet within seconds. None of his initial guesses, but a scene that terrified him all the same.

A great tumultuous blaze blistered over the rooftops of Norick, burning along the seaward side. Like a banner caught in a tempest, the fire whipped and snapped in a furious upheaval of color: orange and yellow with thick pockets of red and black. Ever growing, ever clawing for space, it flowed outward in a ceaseless roving current and spewed a column of concentrated black smoke.

This was it, William thought. Here, right now, Norick faced its ruin. No matter how many the flames took—he shuddered to think of it: those citizens caught unaware, or those who were too drunk to act—the fire would ensure the town's destruction all the same. In minutes, abetted by the wind, the flames would spread like fleas to every dwelling, storehouse, and wooden market stall. A spark, caught in a backdraft, would find the wharf and set it alight. Perhaps even the Grove and the forest would burn: rank upon rank of wailing trees.

Their homes, their goods. All they used to sustain themselves. All they held dear.

Gone.

William's heart stuttered then spiked against his ribcage, but not from fear. The prospect of battle after all this time should have frightened him, should have sent those old feelings of suffocation and dread needling up his throat, but it didn't. The shakes didn't return; his dead comrades didn't call out his name. This was different. This felt ordained. In the South he'd simply done what he had to in order to survive—had done his duty, deviation unthinkable; deviation as good as death—but now he would be fighting for a cause he believed in. It was time to save Ellen's town and rescue her people. It was time to matter once more, to step back into life. The wars of the past had broken him; this present struggle would make him new.

Brade's jaw had gone slack. "Shit. What's happening over there? Why isn't anyone doing anything? Can't they see it? Do you think those bastards started it? Are they trying to escape? Why come this way?"

"They're not trying to escape. They're coming here."

"Why?"

"To take out the Guard. To kill us. Probably dispatched from a larger force."

"Then shouldn't we be—"

But William was already moving. He rammed his sword into its sheath and launched himself toward the belfry. "The gate, boy," he barked over his shoulder as he unspooled the warning bell's rope. "Hurry. Get down there and make sure it's secure, then grab a bow and get back up here." He pulled the cord taut. "Seal the tower door when you come—and bring as many arrows as you can carry."

Brade didn't respond or move to comply. "Brade," William hollered, "get your ass going."

The young guardsman continued gaping at the patch of forest in which those figures had disappeared. Their cries still rose from its gnarled depths. "The gate..."

"Yes, the gate, you simpleton. Make sure it's sealed, then come back and help me defend the tower. Those walls won't hold long. We need to buy ourselves some time."

"The gate..." repeated Brade, as if hypnotized. "I left..."

"*Speak up, boy.*"

"I left it open. When I got here. I didn't think..."

"You fuckin' halfwit." William hurried to the veranda's edge. Below, the two slabs of the gate stood ajar. The assailants would stride in, unimpeded.

William charged across the tower and grabbed Brade by his shoulders. "Listen to me. Get down those stairs and bar that damn door. Use whatever you can find. We just have to slow 'em down. Do you understand?" Brade stole a nervous glance toward the compound below.

William shook him. "Do it now. We have maybe a minute. Defend those stairs with everything you got. You should be able to funnel them through the opening and get them as they come in. Fall back here if you must. I'll get the bastards from above. Got it?"

Brade nodded; real fear dwelt behind his eyes. The lad had proven himself an able swordsman earlier, but this was a different test entirely. With both hands, William shoved him toward the staircase. "Move, boy."

As Brade vanished into the gloom, William set to ringing the warning bell. Its peals reverberated across the valley and out into open air, the chimes loud enough to send a shiver through William's teeth. There, he thought, the people would hear *that*.

Satisfied, he hustled to one of the canopy's supports. His bow and a quiver of arrows—William counted only ten in their rank—hung from a wire rack. Yanking the weapons free, he turned toward the compound's entrance. One of the adjoining doors thumped against the far side of the encircling palisade. William grunted at the sight then shifted his eyes toward the forest below. A dirt path emerged from its depths and gently wound its way up the hillside.

The first ghostly forms were materializing from the woods. They appeared first in ones and twos, and then the whole pack of them seemed to emerge at once. With renewed vigor, they swept up the bluff like a tide.

The hour of chaos had come. William felt the horror of it then, but also the thrill. The world itself had gone mad—suddenly, irreparably mad. Everything was coming undone, loosening, the order of things cleaved apart. And yet, in that moment, William Breeve, captain of the Town Guard, had never felt more alive.

CHAPTER TWENTY-TWO

As all things, it started small.

Only an instant, but an instant of minutiae all the same. The torch, leaking small droplets of spent oil, was tilted, lowering toward the hay. Its flame, encased in a throne of spindled metal, furled out like fingers reaching for a prize. Then came the moment: a tender, almost hesitant contact, a conferral, as neither side gave ground. For that single instant, the fire and the stalks were one, knit together in a seamless harmony, all of nature held in perfect accord.

Then: massacre.

As Codiah's eyes lit with delight and horror, the fire betrayed its truce and surged forth. What began as a mere sputter, a crackle of flame, was suddenly more. It mutated into a horde of light and heat and slurping inhalation, drinking the very air from the room. A single fire is actually a multitude: swirling currents within swirling currents—an infinity in motion, always eager to add more.

Up: The only direction it could go was up.

The fire dispersed in a fanning ring of black, scrambling over the bundles of hay like wolves to a carcass. Those flames weren't merely hungry; they were ravenous. They were at the ceiling. They were in the timbers of the roof, gnawing through the shingles. They yowled at Codiah as he retreated from the loft, thanking him.

He felt himself within their midst. He was in union with them, a part and apart, the creator but also the beneficiary. The fire was all his, the perfect gift to himself, an embodiment of some inner kingdom of untapped desire. Even then he understood those impulses could only ever be slowed, not stopped.

The flames consumed the upper half of the stable now. He could hear them working their way through the roof. And still they rose.

While he backed from the ladder and angled for the door, the horses whinnied in their stalls, their doleful eyes dancing fearfully in the dark. They knew what was coming. They understood what he'd done. But those horses were not the only ones to be burned; the flames would find others in the building that night.

When Gregory Millons had led the young Mayrin Malecko to the stable, he couldn't have predicted what would come next. He'd certainly never imagined the consequences of simply leaving the front slab unlocked.

The couple's tryst had first led them to Gregory's home and then, knowing it unwise to chance exposure (Who could guess when homely, nagging Rebecca would show up?), they'd withdrawn to the stable, a place of privacy. Any lingering anxiety was becalmed by its darkness, its quiet, and together they'd found pleasure in the squat administrative office nestled across from the tack room. Gregory kept it sparsely furnished—only a small writing desk and a cot for when he worked late and couldn't muster the energy to return home. There they slept, two strangers united in their reticence, their desire; there they slept, unaware of Codiah's fateful intrusion.

Gregory dreamt of candles and smoke; Mayrin envisioned a yawning ocean of flame.

In their slumber, coated with drink, they knew nothing of the approaching danger. By the time they stirred—*if* they stirred—it would already be too late. Over the roar of the inferno, the harried disintegration of an entire man-made edifice, none would hear their screams.

Whether from the smoke or from the flames, the fire would surely have them.

Up: The only direction it could go was up.

And so it went.

CHAPTER TWENTY-THREE

Skylar Higgins hit the Market Square at a gallop.

Because of his placement out amongst the wind and the waves, it'd taken some time for the peals of the warning bell to register. But once they had—and once he'd noticed, too, the horrible crawl of the flames—Higgins didn't squander another breath. Turning on his heel, he sprinted away, abandoning old Mary Fern where she stood.

He could feel her eyes upon him as he went. He didn't turn back.

Arms thumping through the air, he raced across town, sweat pouring from his temples and pooling on his upper lip. He wondered briefly where Brade was, if he was safe. He decided the lad would have to fend for himself. Ahead, in the square, the music and dancing had ground to a halt, replaced by a nervous hush. Even the air seemed different, tainted somehow. The odor of meat, what had before been a delectable blend of spices and grease, now hung like a rancid coating. Earlier the torches about the perimeter had cast the scene in a hypnotic glow; now their light seemed too dim, no comfort at all. The shadows they cast felt more mysterious than liberating. As if they were concealing secrets.

On the stage, the musicians cradled their instruments awkwardly as if they'd suddenly forgotten how to play. Whole clusters of townspeople were frozen about the platform, holding one another and gaping toward the foothills. Gaping toward the Eastern Outpost, which was now unnervingly silent. Their eyes slid from the knolls to the wall of flames coiling above Norick's rooftops. It rose like a fortress, meriting both horror and incomprehension—but wonderment, too. It was an unfathomable display of power, one that was gradually, though steadily, ringing them in.

Entrapping them.

Fools! Standing there as if they'd been conjured into stone, not knowing where or even how to begin. *Don't they know the seconds are conspiring against them?* As Higgins charged toward the crowd, his eyes darting this way and that, he saw a husband's comforting hand on the small of his wife's back; he saw an old man's emaciated palm, pale as a ghoul fish, clasped against the base of his chin; he watched as a child's face lifted toward the fiery surge, her eyes wide and gleaming and full of fright. These simple images brought forth a sudden flood of emotion—a visceral, fatherly desire to keep them safe. *It's not their fault. They're like children—like lambs. They don't know any better. They can't.*

They needed guidance. They needed saving.

They needed *him.*

Higgins wrestled his way past the outlying clusters; his presence, once detected, had the effect of a snapping wire. Suddenly there was movement on all sides as the townspeople erupted from muteness into motion. The heat of their bodies and the rush of their hands enveloped him. Their collective smell—nervous sweat, curdling body odor—swarmed him like a cloud, and their shouts hammered down like a barrage.

For a terrible, sobering moment Higgins thought he would be crushed.

"Why was the warning bell ringing?"

"Are we really under attack?"

"Where? From whom?"

"The fire—what are we to do? It'll destroy *everything!*"

"Do we have enough men? Can we hold the attackers at bay?"

"Higgins, what do you know? Tell us."

"Do you think we can negotiate?"

"Will my children be safe?"

"We gotta get away from them flames. I can hardly breathe already." A grizzled old merchant, Milt Wendlan, drew in a lung-rattling cough. "Where's the bloody fire brigade?"

"We *are* the fire brigade, you halfwit," said Lucas Illhap, the gray-eyed tavern owner. "All of us. What don't you understand? We won't survive this without everyone's help."

"Easy for you to say. I have my grating joints—and my swamp lungs."

"You have an ale-belly and neglected limbs, that's all. And a slug's disposition."

"How dare you, you little—" Red-faced, the elder feinted a charge toward Illhap.

"I need to watch my children," voiced a townsperson amid the mounting scuffle.

"I gotta gather my belongings," added another. "My grandfather's antique chest ain't nothing to be sacrificing to those flames."

"I ain't good for fighting."

"I can't—"

"I need—"

"You will *all* help!" screamed Illhap, turning from Wendlan. "Every one of you. Otherwise there won't be anything left. We don't have a choice here, you fools." Not listening, the pack spun from Higgins and turned on one another. Above the commotion, a staccato of voices broke through— rising in volume, desperate to be heard:

"Where's the rest of the Council?"

"Please keep my babies safe."

"This is *your* fault."

"Mine? You have some nerve—"

"I'm tellin' ya, *I can't breathe*."

"Kel! Has anyone seen Kel?"

"I can't find my children."

"Help us! Do something!"

"Save my babies!"

A woman—Bailey Hyehill, who had shining chestnut hair and a splash of freckles—implored Higgins directly. Her soft, multi-colored eyes glimmered as she spoke. "Please. Just tell us what to do."

Higgins frowned back at her. Finally, he nodded. Their hysteria had overwhelmed him, rendering him mute, but something about Bailey's look had jarred him loose. Pulling from his lungs' deepest confines, he lifted both hands toward the sky. "Silence! All of you, silence." Then for the oblivious, lingering arguments still occurring in the back: "SHUT YOUR MOUTHS THIS INSTANT!"

And they did.

An expectant silence, nearly as unsettling as the initial onslaught, rose up in the chaos's wake. The townspeople fixed their eyes on Higgins, waiting like a company of children dreading their father's rebuke. Higgins lowered his arms, slowly, afraid the movement might unleash them once more. "Listen to me. All of you." He regarded several of the closest citizens, his voice rugged though laced with an unquestionable authority. *A composure only the truest leaders possess.* "I'm going to say this once, and one time only. We don't have the luxury for anything more.

"The warning bell rang, aye. So we must assume we're under attack—if not yet, then in due course. Until we know more, no one leaves the walls. Understood? The Guard is preparing to mount a defense. If it comes to it, we may need to reenact the civilian militia."

"But we're not soldiers!"

"Our children—"

Higgins motioned for silence; with reluctance, they indulged him. He roved his eyes across them, letting the magnitude of the situation shine through. "These are our *lives* we're talking about, people. Our *home.* Illhap's right: We don't have a choice here. If there's an army out there, we either defend ourselves or we die. It's as simple as that." He let that linger. A stream of perspiration slithered down his side. He was aware, distinctly, of the seconds ticking away.

"Our first priority is the fire. We cannot leave the walls—we can't risk falling into a trap. It's possible whoever is attacking Norick also started the blaze. I need every man, woman, and child to the northern half of town—fire brigade or not. We can't do this without everyone. Even then it might not be enough."

He pointed toward the Council Hall, a stately granite structure across the square. On one of its flanks stood a boxy addition accessed from a set of steps. "In the rear storage room there are pails, a few other containers, and some hooks. All of you—yes, even you, Wendlan—form a line at the water tanks. There are two outside Illhap's place, and, if we can still get to them, three near the stable. Start passing buckets. I need a handful of you to go house-to-house—make sure no one is trapped inside or unaware of the threat. If it comes to it, we'll use the hooks to drag the buildings down. A firebreak still might be able to impede this thing."

Higgins took a breath, knowing his words were matching the frenetic pace of his heartbeat but still incapable of slowing them. "If none of that succeeds and we're overrun, we'll evacuate to the southern half of town, against the gate. That'll give us some distance—and time. We'll wait there until we know more, and then, if we must, we'll try our fate beyond."

He ran a hand over his lips, stroking the smooth sides of his chin. "Understood?" No one said anything. "Okay. Fire marshals, take charge." He paused. Still nobody moved. They had their assignment; they were now waiting for something else.

Their courage.

Higgins drilled them with a stare, each in turn. "Norick." His cheeks felt hot, almost bruised. "My sisters, my brothers. Listen to me. For one hundred years we have thrived in this untamed wild. For one hundred years our virtue has carried us, has made us stronger. We have *evolved.* Together we have created a better community. A better world. And it shall not fail—not now, not ever." Heat rushed through his lungs like a furnace. "Aye, we face adversity, a test like no other. But we *will* find a way through it—together, as we always have. *Always.*"

He was shouting now, hands gesticulating as a vein in his temple throbbed. The townspeople's attention had never been more rapt. Most were fervently nodding along; several huffed air like soldiers rushing toward battle. Higgins let his passion intensify and sensed theirs do the same. "This—*this* is our inheritance. *This* is our home. There can be no victory without opposition. No glory without adversity. No love without threat of loss. So seize your victory, Norick. It's yours. The glory tonight will be our own, *for this is our hour!*"

A tempest of cheers; a shudder of energy through the crowd, like lightning on the wind.

Higgins nodded and then—over the ruptures of their rallying cries (already the furthermost townspeople were turning and starting away)— he delivered one final command, gesturing at the flames like a general toward a distant fray:

"Now, in Milgrin's name, go save our town."

CHAPTER TWENTY-FOUR

All at once, the shadowed figures reached the gate and rushed inside.

Above them, William aimed his bow through the spokes of the balustrade and hauled in one last breath of air, stilling himself. As those armed intruders entered the compound, his whole body went rigid, his head throbbing with a swell of pressure, every molecule and vessel prepared for some momentous plunge—a release, like fire, that would soon rush through him. Even the hair of his forearms stood on end, bowing and rising against the pull of the wind.

He was as tense as a mountain lion locked on an unsuspecting doe; he was a hunter, keenly alert, set on a single fixed point.

Ready to pounce. Ready to unleash.

He would wait until they were mere paces from the tower. Never the ablest of bowmen, he would need to leverage every advantage he could get. Each shot had to count; his meager supply of arrows would allow for nothing less.

Don't fire until you can see the whites of their eyes, that same former commander in Denmoore had squawked all those years before as the enemy had approached. William heard the words anew as if the man were standing beside him now. Their company had been surrounded, hunkered down beneath a lumpy rise of sandhills with a river at their backs. Their numbers and morale were scant; the dead and wounded were piled in clumps about the base of the nearest hill. Those still able to fight—bloodied and fragmented and far too few—were backed against the riverbank, its waterway too swift and deep to ford. Most of their arrows were spent. And still the enemy came on, another mass of cavalry barreling down upon them from the hillside. *We have none to waste,* the commander had husked to his men, blood trailing into his swollen left eye. *So you make damn sure your aim is true. I want each of your arrows to gut one of those pricks after you fire. You hear me? If we're not surviving this, then neither are they.*

Then, as now, they faced grave odds; now, as then, William hoped they could overcome.

He could feel the morsels of the seconds passing, falling away; time seemed frozen in the milliseconds before those figures would reach the tower, but still there wasn't enough of it. That trickle would soon become an avalanche and he, like the rest of the world, would be left only to see what came next.

The moment arrived. Without fanfare, without pomp, without even the shrieking howls of their ascent, the intruders reached the tower. The figures drew into the lamplight, each squeezing and shouldering their way over the courtyard before halting in their tracks. Fourteen pairs of eyes craned to where William knelt.

Fourteen panicked pairs sparked with hope.

William, bowstring pulled to his ear, felt his heart's rhythm falter. His mouth drooped open. *What in the—?*

There, clumped together like refugees, were children.

Children. A whole flock of them, of varying ages and genders and sizes. All appearing as though they'd just seen a ghost—no, something worse than a ghost. A terror beyond reckoning—not merely an emotion but a living, physical thing. All color or naiveté had been snuffed out, filled with this new thing: a new way of being, of understanding; an awareness for what the world really was—large and strange and more terrible than they had ever dared believe.

"HELP!"

The cry came from the trembling lips of the eldest child, Quinn Tremrow's boy, Lionide. Clutching an old, corroded spear, he stood slightly ahead and to the left of the pack, a distance hardly discernable but enough to solidify his role as the leader. His youthful eyes implored William to do something, anything. To just *be* there. "Please…" the boy said. "Please help us."

The intruders were children? Just children? William eased the tension of the bowstring and, with it, felt his own body unclenching. *Just children.*

Younglings in need of assistance, those war cries in fact pleas for help. But then, from what? From whom? Was there still some kind of threat out there, or was this all just some ridiculous misunderstanding?

What the hell is going on?

PART SIX

DISCOVERY

The mind is a vault;
The truth is a key.

CHAPTER TWENTY-FIVE

Something wasn't right.

An obvious thought, what with the war of two primordial forces—Man and fire—occurring just a block down the street. Even from here, Natalie Willow could feel the blaze upon her skin, a heat beyond heat, as if she'd been enveloped by a bubble of flame. Its pressure and stinging surged against her forehead, her arms, her legs. Against the very film of her eyes, like she'd stuck them right up next to a furnace. It reminded her of the time when, as a small girl, she had fallen asleep out on Sunset Rock watching her father's tiny skiff bob up and down in the bay. She'd woken hours later, the sun low in the sky, to a terrible throbbing along every inch of exposed flesh. All of it was a blistery red, as though there were a fire within her trying to force its way out.

The heat scalding her now felt like that, but more immediate. Not a burning trying to escape, but a searing wanting to get in, to consume her. And all of that was to say nothing of the noise. Natalie kept her eyes fixed on the flames even as they begged to be averted; a few blinks were all she would allow. She wanted to see this—needed to, even. Because it didn't make sense, this fire. It shouldn't have been real. Things like this weren't supposed to happen, not here anyway, not in boring old Norick with its boring old adults and boring old traditions. A hundred years of monotony—and now this. It was totally surreal. Which also made it kind of thrilling.

But alas, it wasn't the fire that was the source of Natalie's disquiet. Nor was it the carcass lying in front of the stable. A mass of limb, belly, and hair, the horse was crumpled forward on its front legs, as if kneeling before a flaming altar. Its coned head rested upon buckled knees. Its throat had been slit. A wide swath of blood spilled forth and doused the sinewy muscles of its legs, the near-black fluid pooling between the cobblestones like sullied water into miniature canals.

Like an offering.

No, it wasn't this repulsive, incomprehensible sight but something else: a kernel of unrest nagging at the deepest edges of her mind; a prodding that simply refused to cease. Staring at the unfolding destruction of her town, Natalie tried unwrapping the truth of it. It took some time, but she eventually understood. She had forgotten something.

What, exactly, she didn't know. Still it refused to reveal itself. But now she knew—*I'm forgetting something.* Which of course didn't help the matter any.

Beside her, Thomas Calvin, Betsy Til, and the Reins twins gawked at the nightmarish scene. The five of them watched as the adults scrambled back and forth between the water tanks like panicked fleas. What seemed a whole parade of them came racing by, hollering for their children ("Timmy? Timmy!" "Please—have you seen Kel? Have *you*? Kel ... *Kel!*"). Others shouted the well-intentioned though vague commands of the untested ("We need more people over there. Quickly!" "Keep fighting!" "More water—more water, I said! Hurry—do what you must."). Some of the adults seemed to be speaking simply because they weren't sure what else to do.

Natalie and her friends really should've been helping out, but at the moment they were spellbound. Some wizened, flustered old man had squawked at them to, "Get back! Just stay back, *dammit*," so here they stood, unmoving, staying back, *dammit*, and finding themselves both horrified and elated at this turn of events. Thomas was actually *smiling*. Natalie could see it in his narrow, hard-set eyes: a smug satisfaction; *Serves them right.*

Disturbed, she turned back to the flames. For her, the night had soured. Earlier its sense of freedom and power and uncaged desire had felt liberating; now she mostly just felt stupid. The idea that they could do anything they wanted, without consequences... What were they thinking? And then there was this stubborn nagging in her head—poke, poke, poking. Natalie rumpled up her lips. *What am I missing? What can't I see?*

Of all things, it was the mutilated horse that finally provided the answer. Some of the soot-covered townspeople offered it grimaces as they scurried by; others, in their urgency, ignored it altogether. For Natalie, it was the way the beast was positioned: bent forward, belly down, its limbs twisted unnaturally. Bowing in a posture of defeat.

It was a posture of undeniable familiarity. A posture she had witnessed—had helped create—less than an hour earlier in a dank wall-side alleyway.

Her mind lit with recognition like straw to fire. Every nerve roared with heat. Gasping, Natalie fastened a sweaty palm against her lips. *No no no no no no...* Then she was saying it aloud, the string melding together into one long, horror-stricken syllable: "No!"

The others ripped their gazes toward her, but it was already too late: In a blur of movement, Natalie sprinted away. They called after her—"Natalie, what's wrong? What are you—? Where the hell are you going? Are you raving mad?"—but she ignored them. Arms flailing, hair tossing, she barreled down the street, straight toward the fire.

What have I done? What have I done what have I done what have I done...?

She elbowed past a man who tried to stop her. She shirked the line of adults passing pails, their faces rosy and sodden and hollowed out. She dodged more probing townspeople intent on thwarting her, kicking and slapping when forced. Keeping tight to the burning buildings and hurrying down the sidewalk, she avoided the horse carcass. The flames bellowed beside her. And, all the while, she wept.

What's wrong with me? How could I have been so—bloody—stupid?

They had departed the alley almost an hour earlier, moving toward the Market Square in search of more ale. They'd left him lying there in the mud, slumped forward on his belly and thighs. Bruised, bloodied. Unmoving. A sparring dummy for their sticks.

They'd all watched as Thomas had his final go at the boy, swinging until he'd exhausted himself, until his own breath was ragged; by the end, the vintner's son had broken his own rule ("Not his face. Nothing too noticeable...") and was aiming almost exclusively for Vernon's head. Satiated, Thomas had dropped the branch at the boy's side. Putting his hands on his hips, he stared down at the crumpled form in the mud before leaning forward and placing two fingers under Vernon's nostrils. There was a wheeze of breath, the slightest of rasps.

With a nod, Thomas turned and declared: "We're finished here."

Face cloaked in shadow, he'd started down the length of the passage without glancing back. His gait had been relaxed, resigned almost, as if he'd just completed some burdensome chore and wished to be near the thing no longer. Brushing past his friends, he exited the alleyway.

And without a word, they'd followed him.

Natalie had given Vernon many a thought since, though she hadn't considered the proximity the alley shared with the stable, the apparent epicenter of the fire. Nor had she considered the possibility that, because of their beating, the boy would be unable to pull himself from the passageway and would thus, in effect, be trapped.

She knew now though. She knew—and she hated herself for it. Because of her, Vernon would die in isolation—were the flames there already, the smoke? Was it fear he was feeling, or a resignation, a letting go? Was he begging even now for someone to take notice and save him? Or did he realize, as with all things, that he was alone?

Just a child—beaten, forgotten, and facing death alone.

No one should die like that, Natalie thought as she rushed toward the alley. Inside her somewhere were the vestiges of her personal childhood nightmare, long since put to rest but never quite vanquished. It was a byproduct of a story her father had once told her about his own father's demise—out fishing and caught in a tempest. The dream proceeded with a pious consistency: Like Grandfather, she would find herself alone on a skiff as it was tossed about by a violent sea. The storm was bad; the worst of it was the isolation, what could have been a character in its own right, tormenting her without cease. Each time, she would beg the sky for some sort of company, for even just a hand to hold, despite knowing none would come, despite knowing she'd been abandoned. *No one should ever die alone.*

The entrance appeared ahead. As she neared it—towers of flame on either side—Natalie pled with the universe and the fire and the alleyway itself. With every ancestor and god she could think of. Begging them to please—just please, please, *please*—let it not be too late. To let that endearing little boy, with his plump, dorky grin, still be alive. To take her life in his place if they must. She no longer cared, just as long as Vernon was safe. *Please...*

I'm coming, Vernon Rose, Natalie sobbed as she slid to a halt and pivoted to enter the alleyway. *Don't you worry, I'm coming.*

I won't let you die alone.

CHAPTER TWENTY-SIX

The children found him just after midnight.

They shouldn't have been out beyond the walls, especially so late. They knew that. Their parents and those old curmudgeons on the Council had practically battered this into their skulls since the first yowling cries of their birth. *At night, you stay inside the town. You listening now, child? There are things in those woods ... things that only come out after dark. It's not safe out there for a kid like you. You could wander too far, get turned around, and then...*

Now, the younglings understood the words, they did; they understood the rationale behind them even. But weren't adults always coming up with silly things like that, an endless list of rules and regulations meant only to hamper their fun? Sure there might be bears and lions way up in the mountains, but what were the odds of chancing upon something down here? The woods surrounding their valley were wild, yes, but not *that* wild. Certainly not *that* dangerous.

Couldn't the adults just learn to live a little?

It was with these notions in mind that a group of children came together on the evening of Milgrin's Day, early into the night. One of Night-Eyed's productions was being put on: a tedious affair, with stilted acting and jokes that weren't all that funny. Of course, their parents were collectively awed. They cooed and laughed, absorbed in the melodrama playing out on stage, while their younglings looked on in mute boredom.

No words needed to be spoken: One by one, the children, as if bound by some wordless agreement, monkeyed their way through the crowd, aiming for one of Norick's four main thoroughfares. Gathering beneath

a sign for The Wandering Cask, they counted their lot: fifteen in sum—
nine boys and six girls, all under the age of thirteen, some as young as six.
Most belonged to the same friend group, while others were tacked on for
the night, bonded in solidarity against the tedium of the adults.

"This is unbearable," one older boy groaned. "How do they enjoy
this?"

"Beats me."

"They wouldn't know a good time if it lashed them across the back."

"What else is there to do? All I can think of is eating, and I literally
can't eat anymore."

"Literally?"

"Yeah. I'm ready to burst."

"Sunken hells, mate, it smells like you already have. Was that you?
Who did that? It *reeks*. Milgrin might come back from the dead just to plug
his nose. And his tomb's not even close."

"Milgrin wasn't buried, that's what I heard. Some of the older kids
were talking about it. That tomb's empty."

"That's a bloody myth. They were trying to scare you. Where else
would he be?"

"I don't know. Burned on a pyre? They swore they'd seen—"

"We could try to steal some ale?" interrupted another boy.

"Nah, I can't stand the taste."

"Me neither."

"I saw Nannette Zander baking pies for the contest later," suggested a
mousy-looking girl. "Bet we could sneak some of those." Already her eyes
gleamed with the prospect of syrupy fillings.

"What don't you understand about, 'I'm not hungry'?" spat the husky
boy who, at the moment, was *ready to burst.*

"It's not all about you, pinch-face," the girl returned. "Maybe if you
didn't always insist on eating so much." Several others nodded their agreement. The boy opened his mouth for a retort but then thought better of it,
his eyes darting about the group.

"Let's go swimming!" said another girl with a map of freckles across
her nose. "I'd wager there's no one watching the docks right now. The sea is
perfect this time of night."

"How would you know? Two hundred joricks you've never done it."

"Have too!"

"You've swam at night—in the sea? When? Do you even know how to swim?"

"Yes! I once—"

"Hush it, you dolts. It's a good idea. If there's no one there, we could have the docks all to ourselves."

"Yeah. Yeah!" A refrain of agreement went up.

Lionide, son of the Town Guard's first lieutenant, Quinn Tremrow, stepped forward. "It's patrolled, you block-heads. My pa's in the Guard. They always station someone out there, no matter what festival's going on."

"We know your father's in the Guard. You insist on telling us all the bloody time."

"Either way, it's not an option."

"You don't know that."

"The Guard's a joke anyhow."

Lionide bristled. "Watch it, runt, or I'll—"

"Guys? Guys, how 'bout Star Glade?" Long-legged and dark-skinned Kel Pollor was grinning at the idea. "Yeah, it's nothing new, but it's not that far, and there won't be any parents around … and we can play barrows!"

The group was silent as the thought hopped about their circle. It made sense: Even on regular evenings they would sneak out to the meadow, a vast clearing nestled against the base of the mountains. On clear nights, while lying on its lush bed of brome grass, there was no better vantage for gazing at the whirling galaxies above. The stars capped the glade in a great celestial dome, near enough that it was as if you could reach a hand up and glide your fingers right through their midst. The meadow's existence—and the youngling's sneaking forays to it—was a shared secret, one kept between them and their friends. Little did they know that their parents, too, had once claimed the space. Little did their parents, who had no time now for such amusements, know that their former haven possessed new owners, a gift they'd bestowed by the mere fact of their absence.

First one girl nodded at the suggestion then another, and then two boys in near unison: "Aye. Let's do it." The others voiced their approval, and just like that, it was decided. Let the adults do what they wished; screw 'em.

They would go to Star Glade.

Stealing their way across town, the fifteen children pilfered a handful of supplies—torches, blankets, and, despite protests from the overly sated boy, a basket of bread loaves and two jars of honey. A few of the older children, wearing self-serious expressions, elected to stop at home for their fathers' old spears. By the time the group was ready, the sun had inched behind the mountains, sending impish shadows creeping through the streets.

They picked the eastern gate. It was easy, really: One of the guardsmen on duty had fallen asleep, and the other was hardly better, staring with drowsy eyes toward the fields beyond. The children, crouched behind a wagon across the street, simply waited for his attention to be diverted. It only took a minute or two; clearly in discomfort, the man did a little one-two shuffle on his feet, glanced up and down the block, then hiked the point of his spear into the earth and waddled out to take a piss.

Crouched in a line, trying not to giggle, the children tiptoed their way past the guard and made for open space. Soon the town was no more than a grid of buildings beneath them; here and there some had begun popping into illumination, candles and lanterns pressing back against the night. Moving through the first reaches of the forest—teeming with the sounds of a nocturnal populace coming awake—the children angled northeast, giving the Eastern Outpost a wide berth.

They found the path quickly, a snake-like trail of dirt and trampled vegetation meandering its way through the woods. In some places, it was difficult to say if there was a path at all. There were forks and turns, roots and brambles; there were cutbacks and a dead-end at a wall of sheer granite. But the children weren't concerned. They knew this route intimately, could have trekked it with their eyes closed. Ahead was Sparrow's Plunge; over there was Spider Tree, just off the trail to their left. And there was Yurwin's Peak, a mountainous crest just visible between those two hollowed-out oaks. A bit further in and they would come across Weeping Stream—gurgling and stunningly clear, almost like glass (no good for drinking though, unless you desired a bellyache). For them, the path to Star Glade was no more difficult than finding their way through the streets of Norick. There were markers everywhere along the trail. You just had to know where to look.

As they neared the meadow—inclined step after inclined step, grooves worn into the dirt like makeshift stairs—the children's anticipation swelled. In the deepening twilight, they strolled freely, unencumbered, gossiping and telling jokes. A teen in the back called up to a boy in the front, yelling over the line; a pair of girls near the center chatted about the day's events, about the vibrant dresses their mothers had worn. Two lads, just ahead of them, started a game of tag ("Grow up, would ya?" groaned Kel Pollor after one of them shoved past).

They pointed out oddities to one another: branches warped like skeletons and scarecrows and giant nebulous claws; the moss-ridden boulders that, in just the right light, appeared to hold faces. They gazed about in wonder, admiring the way the failing sunlight floated through the trees, a memory of light more than the thing itself, as if it were evaporating right before their eyes.

They hummed and whistled tunes. They kicked at the dirt and bent to examine chips of grated stone.

They could all feel it. They were close now…

They had arrived.

A hushed reverence overtook them as they broke through the tree line. Together, they paused to take it all in, the meadow unfolding before them like an island amid an ocean of trees. Cicadas chirped beneath a sky stained a deep shade of violet; the brome grass, chest-high in some places, was awash with the silvery light of the stars. The Observatory, a delta of compressed grass where the children watched the universe turn, loomed on the right. The barrows square lay near the center. Nestled against the furthermost edge, Lovers' Arch beckoned from the shadows. The older kids would sometimes sneak off to those two entwined trees, privately holding hands.

There was a moment of reverence from the children … then they were whooping and hollering and dashing in. Winking spheres of light rose with their charge: a curtain of fireflies ascending up and away and back down again. A hundredfold upon hundredfold, dancing as the children's eyes gleamed.

As was their custom, they started with barrows, a simple game involving hide-covered boulders and a half dozen hemp-woven baskets. Those who held torches gouged the handles into the earth and sectioned off the playing square. Others readied the boulders or repaired the bins, retying loose threads where needed. They divided up the teams: older kids versus the younger. After a dozen alternating rounds of possession and siege, the elders handily claimed the title of victors, as was their custom.

Another match ensued. With each spent breath, their elation grew.

They paused for a short break and passed around the loaves. Some of the younger, more ill-mannered of the group scooped their hands directly into the honey jars and shoveled out their portion ("You slobs!" said Kel, rolling her eyes). Together the children shared this simple meal, nodding to one another and to themselves. They were accomplishing something here. A sense of joy and camaraderie that their parents were incapable of. *This* was how life was meant to be lived, what true community looked like. *This* was real, and it was intoxicating.

It was *theirs*.

The following hours passed in a blur of laughter and motion and spirited adolescent activity.

Some of the children took up another match of barrows. Some spent their time wandering the boundaries of the meadow, giggling and chasing fireflies. A few, needing nothing more than the sky's company, plopped themselves down in the center of The Observatory, slung their arms behind their heads, and, grinning dreamily, gazed up toward the heavens.

Lost in their merriment, the children ignored the peals of the fireworks detonating in the valley below. They ignored how dark the forest had become, as well as the approach of thunder. Forgetting altogether about their childhood nightmares (*What kind of baby still had nightmares anyhow?*), they surrendered themselves to their play. They didn't think about the legends whispered around Norick's hearths late into the evening: tales of wandering spirits searching for lost loved ones or for a way to move on. Stories of untrustworthy water nymphs in the river and crafty dryads in the trees; of half-men and giants and the undead rising.

No, they forgot all about those stories. Forgot about everything save each other.

Which nearly blinded them to the figure observing from the trees.

Jacob Willow, a thin boy of a scant nine years and three months, spotted it first. Frail and aloof, but with a curious mind, the fisherman's son had wandered off from the rest of the group chasing a firefly. He'd seen his older sister, Natalie, collect them in aerated jars and wished to do the same. This particular insect, however, was proving elusive, repeatedly veering off at the last second. It bobbed its way to the northern edge of the meadow and drifted up into the lowest branches.

It winked out for good among the pines.

Pulling up, Jacob stared panting after the creature, wondering where it could have gone. He squinted into the woods. Away from the other kids' torches, the darkness between the trunks was smothering, absolute. Wind funneled through the gaps in a rhythmic inhale/exhale, as though the forest itself were breathing. The longer Jacob stared into it, the more it seemed the darkness was also moving, tunneling away somehow.

He felt an urge to stroll forward and see where it led.

Lips parted, Jacob took a step. The trees responded in kind: The branches chafed against one another, their fluttering leaves like flutes harnessing the wind. The thorns and thistles of the undergrowth swayed in silhouette. Another step forward, another moment more of losing himself in that swirling, stretching darkness. Two steps further; a wall of shadow rushing up, the other children vanishing behind. Somewhere in the distance, a herd of whitetails—two fawns, a doe, and a full-antlered buck— jolted at his approach. Whether Jacob actually saw them or just sensed their presence, he wasn't sure. He imagined them shooting him a melancholic look with their round, glassy eyes before darting away in agile vaults. Elsewhere, closer, a dray of squirrels scampered through the brush; suddenly startled, they scurried up a nearby oak.

He was at the cusp now, poised between the open air of the meadow and the forest's oppressive covering. Between darkness and a sprinkling of light.

Jaaaacooob… The voice seemed to come from nowhere, from everywhere. It tumbled around in his head; it pulled him like a string. It almost sounded like a gust of wind, stretched between the spinning particles of air. He didn't so much hear it as he felt it. Entranced, he moved for the pines.

Jacoooob…

He would have made it, too, and kept on walking—for how long or how far, he didn't know, only that he needed to go, to see, to be lost beneath that threaded canopy—but nature interfered. The sky overhead bellowed with concussive force, and a flare of lightning streaked across the mountainside, casting the forest floor in an otherworldly glow.

Snapped from his daze, Jacob now noticed the figure lurking at the edge of the clearing twenty paces to his right.

He jolted, his stomach cratering toward his limbs, leaving nothing but empty, aching space. Only a glimpse from the corner of his eye, but it was enough. He could feel that figure's presence as if the thing were on top of him already, pinning him down. He could feel its sharp fingers about his biceps, its chill along his spine. He could taste a foulness in the air, a disorientation, warm rancid breath blown across his eyes. He could sense every fear he'd ever known, every horror he hadn't yet dreamed. All of it swelling in that moment, taking on life.

He craned his head toward the figure not because he wanted to, but because to feel this degree of terror and not know its cause was a sure path to insanity.

Jacob reeled where he stood.

Down the line, the figure turned to face him. He could make out what appeared to be a head, an arm. A heavy mass of darkness around the shoulders. A cloak? A shadow? Something much, much worse? Backpedaling, he watched horrified as the figure, what now seemed vaguely familiar, started to wave.

The other children, deeper in the meadow and in the midst of their play, didn't notice Jacob's hyperventilating. They did, however, hear his screams.

They startled in unison, whipping their heads toward the fisherman's son. "Jacob— What's the matter?" asked a square-jawed boy named Timmy Kerian who stood closest to the scene. "What do you see—?" Following Jacob's line of sight, Timmy abruptly went quiet.

His mouth dropped.

The others were spread about the glade—some in loose clusters, several in pairs. A handful lounged in the grass. All felt the same terror worm its way through them at the sight of that figure; all knew a flood of inexplicable shame.

They stood. They gaped. And as Jacob retreated toward the meadow's center, they all rushed to huddle together.

They didn't speak. For a moment, nobody could. They simply gawked while the figure took a silent, gliding step toward them. Closer now, it caught the edge of their torchlight and drew into focus. The children stared at the place where its eyes should have been. They felt their knees go weak.

They stared, and they *saw*.

And, as one, they bolted for the nearest trees.

The figure watched them go. It didn't pursue.

Not yet.

Another sputter of lightning above, another moment of perfect stillness.

It vanished from sight.

As the woods would allow, the children sprinted. Mostly, they slid and staggered and lost their footing. It was too dark and they were too disorientated—and just too plain scared—to consider whether they were heading in the right direction. In some ways it didn't seem to matter, as long as they were moving away from the glade. Away from that *thing*.

Down the children went, always down, cutting back and forth as the trail dictated. On either side, vegetation and darkness rose up like the walls of a dungeon. Whereas before the forest had felt safe and familiar, it now seemed strange and threatening, a place incensed at having been awakened. With every step the children could feel the figure's eyes-not-eyes upon them. They could hear its rustle through the branches. Down, down, *down*: The word had acquired a primal, singular importance. All else faded.

It was this single-minded focus that would set into motion a string of events throughout the valley. None of which the children could've anticipated, as they weren't aware themselves of their meandering. A missed turn here, a gradual drifting there, and suddenly they found themselves much further north than expected. This detail was of little significance, however, for they cared only that they had finally emerged from the forest.

The white-planked fence of the Grove was there to meet them. Situated atop a shallow bluff overlooking the harbor, the orchard consisted of two dozen neatly aligned rows, a handful of sheds and outbuildings, and a spindly ten-foot watchtower placed near the center. The compound was maintained by Wilkes Loren and his small but industrious crew; the children begged the Founders for that gentle, big-bellied old man to be moseying about through the orchard right now. If anyone could displace this nightmarish terror, it was him.

But Mr. Loren wasn't there. They understood this almost at once, their eyes roaming over the fence and into the nearest fruit trees. The place felt vulnerable, exposed, filled with a palpable sense of absence. Like an invitation.

They kept moving. In the distance, the town was nestled in a bowl of light. The children clumped together as they raced toward it, many of them shivering—and not from the growing cold. A fresh chill slinked its way over Lionide's arms; more than once Kel Pollor darted her almond eyes back toward the forest, just to be sure. And still: darkness, only darkness.

And a legion of unseen eyes.

Curving around the fence line, the children arrived at the Grove's entrance, a gate of carved timber crowned by a rolling arch. The doors were open, drifting toward Norick as if issuing a summons. The movement was accompanied by a creaking from the hinges, an unnerving melody of ungreased iron.

The children stopped. They couldn't help it. Despite their fright, despite seeing what they had, the urge to look cut deeper. The impulse was almost beyond their capacity to resist. Something about that open doorway… It beckoned. It intrigued.

It sent their hearts careening.

Through the gateway, the darkened heart of the orchard stretched away in a labyrinth of silhouettes. The children's torches seemed to extract greater mystery from the compound rather than reduce it—shadows begetting shadows; flames unveiling that which was better left unseen.

Gone was the soft, jubilant spirit Mr. Loren's presence engendered; gone was the feeling of rebirth, of things growing, mending, starting anew. In its place a swelling fog of perversion pumped through the rows: not purity but rot. Whatever had occurred here—and the children understood then that something vile had indeed happened—had left its mark.

Their eyes found him then. First one—a youngling named Kylee, who gasped as if struck—and then the rest, who discharged a panicked symphony of their own. Overhead, the dead man swung on—a tight little loop, almost like a dance, unfazed by the interruption of their cries.

The details of the scene rushed over the children, superseding all other thought. The man hung naked from the watchtower; frayed and water stained, a rope was fastened around his neck in a carefully woven noose. It bit into his throat, purpling the flesh immediately in reach. The cord, disappearing into the joists of the tower, bobbed as it twirled in a leisurely circle first one way and then the other, nudged on by the thunder-churned buffets of the storm.

Then there were the other details, such as his wrists, which were bound together with strips of fabric at the crest of his buttocks. Each was leaking a dark viscous fluid, smears of which seeped down through the channels of his fingertips.

There was the bloated quality of the man's cheeks. There was his tongue, puffy and dangling. There were his eyes, two tortured orbs popping from their sockets and staring down toward the gateway—toward *them*.

There was his nakedness itself, a detail of profound strangeness. Nudity was at all times forbidden in Norick; to expose the flesh, even partially, was considered an impropriety of the gravest sort, an assault on the town's very virtue. But now here this man was, stripped bare, and it wasn't only that. In the simple removal of his clothing, it was almost as if other things had also been taken: his rank, his honor, his sense of personhood—all tossed away. He was now something more carnal, more animal, a hunk of meat strung up to cure.

Perhaps most alarming of all were the vibrant red symbols adorning sections of his flesh. Those, and the ominous message scrawled at his feet.

The markings were bizarre, blocky things; each was similar in design but a few degrees off from one another, as if the same rudimentary shape had been given to different children to reproduce. All told there were six of them: two on his shins and on the caps of his knees, one centered between both nipples, and a single mark stamping his forehead.

If the children had been able to avert their eyes—which they were not—they would have seen that the icons were also painted on the barks of the nearest trees. At any rate, the markings were nothing they could decipher, and so the children didn't try. Instead, they dropped their gazes to the words smeared in a rosy hue upon the grass. The message faced outward, positioned so as to allow passersby to read.

THIS IS MY VALLEY
YOU ARE TRESPASSERS HERE
HE WILL NOT BE THE LAST
I WILL COME FOR YOU ALL

Those of them that knew how, read it. And then reread it, letting its implications sink in. Their eyes lifted to the murdered townsperson. Back to the orchard floor. Up once more. Still they remained frozen, every fear and anxiety and nameless dread igniting like oil within them. Fifteen mouths gaping; fifteen young faces drained of color.

None of them moved. They didn't seem capable of so much as breathing.

It was the screech of Kel Pollor that finally shattered the spell. At the group's initial discovery, she'd staggered back and tumbled onto her rear, clasping a palm over her lips. She recognized whom this bloodied, defiled corpse belonged to—knew immediately that she was staring at the body of her best friend's father, Peter Ash.

Her hand could do little to hold back the ascent of her screams. They tore at the membrane in her throat; they spewed past her long fingers and erupted into the night. The noise was enough to release the children from their stupor. Some took up Kel's panicked cry. Two or three sprawled onto their backsides. Several merely twitched where they stood.

Then—in a press of bodies, a veritable mob of human flesh—they were lurching outward, hurtling themselves from the Grove in a flurry of screams.

They steered south. Away from the town—which, to their horror, they now realized was burning—and aimed for the Eastern Outpost. Shrieking, the children swept down the hillside, certain they were being pursued by any number of unspeakable things—or by the dead man himself, reanimated back to life. They rammed and elbowed past their peers, struggling for leverage. A few, beneath the shove of the group's momentum, plunged to the earth. None stayed down for long.

Their hearts thumped in their ears like exploding munitions; their breathing wheezed like wind through broken sills. None dared to look back, not even a glance. None dared to do anything but run. Run, run, *run*: to the shelter of the outpost and its tower; to the protection of a guardsman, an adult. To the simple reassurance of light.

None but Jacob Willow, who was once more transfixed. As the other children scurried away, unaware they were leaving one of their own behind, Jacob stood unmoving, staring at Peter Ash's bloodshot eyes. Almost purple now, they shimmered in the distant light, as if the man had only recently been crying.

Jacob forgot about the figure back in the meadow. He forgot about his fear. For a moment, he forgot everything save those eyes.

They were calling to him. Like an insistent whisper in his head, only he wasn't entirely sure it was just that, *in his head*. In some ways, the voice seemed more real than all the people in Norick, than the very ground beneath his shaking feet. In its presence, all else was smeared away. All else simply ceased.

As he stared up at those eyes, Jacob could almost feel the voice *watching* him. He could sense, despite the panicked flight of his friends, that he was far, far, from alone.

Taking a tentative step toward the watchtower, and then another, Jacob Willow, son of a fisherman, began to scream.

PART SEVEN

THE TOILS
OF THE VIRTUOUS

Against the night,
The righteous clash,

Not realizing
That the darkness
Against which they struggle

Dwells already
In each of them.

CHAPTER TWENTY-SEVEN

"Slow down, just slow down." He held up a hand, palm out, and titled his head, inching it forward like a coraller attempting to steady an agitated horse. His eyes were sympathetic, his voice calm. "Just take a breath, and then speak. Start from the beginning, I want to hear it all—hush. Just one of you at a time. All right ... there—good. Now tell me exactly what you saw out there."

And they did. With Quinn Tremrow's boy taking the lead, the pack of younglings recounted the disquieting turn of events that had led them to the outpost. Throughout the telling William listened with an uncertain frown, one hand resting upon the pommel of his sword while the other stroked the stubble on his chin. Off to the side, Brade slung his arms across his chest like the limbs of some great, spindly beast. He appeared bored, with one eyebrow cocked, though William knew this to be an act. Surely the lad's heart was reeling like his own. Surely he felt the same crawling dread.

"You're positive?" William asked, dipping his head toward Lionide. "What you saw out there? A person in the woods?"

"On Milgrin's ... and ... and ... my mother's names, sir," stammered the boy. Usually poised and articulate, Quinn's son had to search for the proper words. "Not a person ... a ... a ... *thing*. We all saw it. It had to have been what did that to him. What ... killed Mr. Ash."

"He's scared himself shitless," Brade muttered with a disgusted shake of his head. "Listen to him. Bloody younglings, I tell you what." William shushed the young guardsman with a wave of his hand and studied the panicked faces clustered around Lionide, looking for signs of mischief. Nothing: a cold sobriety all around; a graveness beyond their years. William knew it was likely many of them would never fully recover.

"And the body," he pressed as gently as he could, "it was Peter Ash, the master of trade? You're absolutely sure?"

"I ... I swear it. It was him, all right. We ... we all recognized him. Kel did straight away." The girl, standing somewhere near the center of the pack, had her arms clasped about her middle; she wouldn't so much as glance at William. The captain's frown deepened; her shell-shocked look was answer enough.

Nodding absently, William bit at the peeling membrane of his lip. He averted his gaze, trying to process what he'd been told, trying to make sense of the children's blanched faces, their sunken eyes. Peter Ash, a magistrate of the High Council: dead. Murdered in grisly fashion. He'd had a wife, William reflected, a young daughter. The thought of them receiving the news stunted his heart cold.

There was a killer stalking these woods, that much was clear. One of the townspeople, obviously (William didn't have time for superstition or the paranoia of younglings). Whoever the perpetrator was, he or she had a penchant for theatrics. Could the same person have also started the fire? It seemed likely. But why? As some kind of demonstration?

A distraction?

"Wait ... where's Jacob?"

A boy's voice, shrill and uncertain, broke the quiet. William spun toward the sound and fixed a flat-nosed child with a stare. "What did you say?"

The youngling gulped beneath the captain's gaze, peeked at the ground. "I ... my friend ... Jacob. Jacob Willow. He's not here. I coulda sworn he was just..."

William knew of the boy in question: a fisherman's son. He blinked, trying to call to mind the lad's appearance. *Chestnut hair? No ... wheat-blond.* He scanned the assembled faces. Nothing—as far as he could tell, Jacob wasn't among them.

So then, where in the sunken hells was he?

"You're certain he was with you?" The kid nodded, timid. The other children were glancing about as well, perusing their ranks. Their silence said plenty. "Could he have gone home sooner? From Star Glade? Left without your knowing?"

"I ... I don't think..."

"No," said Kel, as if deep in thought. It was the first word she'd uttered since their arrival. "He was there." She lifted her gaze, her eyes puffy, red, and so pained as to be almost hollow. "He was the first one to see it. Back in the glade. I remember running next to him. I remember—" Her head gave an involuntary twitch.

A couple feet ahead of her, Lionide nodded his agreement. "I'm pretty sure I saw him too, in the Grove. Which means he must still be..." His eyes widened at the realization: imagining what might be happening to Jacob; picturing himself in the boy's place. "By Milgrin... Sunken hells."

William stabbed a finger toward them all. Their faces were wrenched with guilt; most wouldn't meet his eye. "You left him behind? There's a killer loose out there! What've you done?"

Lionide was frantic, his eyes pleading. As their de facto leader, he was receiving the news hardest of all. "We didn't know, sir! Please ... I thought ... I thought we had everyone."

William cast his gaze toward the Grove. It lay in darkness, a realm of shadow and night, distinguished only by the blurred tops of the fruit trees. To its left, Norick shone with peaks of destructive color fanning out over the walls. William pressed this thumb and forefinger into the bridge of his nose, thinking.

"Okay. Brade." He turned toward the chancellor's son. The lad regarded him coolly—unsure, after their altercation, where the two of them stood. Something in William's look must have assuaged him, for a second later he uncrossed his arms.

"What's the plan?"

William dipped his head toward the children. "Get them back to town as quickly as you can, and make sure their parents know they're all right. Then alert the Guard and bring as many reinforcements as can be spared. We still don't know exactly what we'll find up there."

"And you?"

"I'll head to the Grove and see if I can locate the boy." He shot Brade a stare: *And I might need help, sooner rather than later. I'm counting on you.*

"Understood."

"Don't forget: There's a killer out there. Don't take your eyes off them for a second."

"I won't."

"Good. Quickly now."

With his long, agile gait, Brade maneuvered around the mass of younglings and made for the entrance. Reconsidering, he hesitated, turned back, and seized a torch from one of the nearest children, who looked ready to take up a wail. Brade didn't seem to notice, or to care. "Come on, you little shits. Stick close and don't wander. I'm not slowing down."

A couple lobbed William a skeptical glance. *Are you sure we can trust him? Will we be safe?* Rolling his eyes at Brade, William gestured toward the gate. "It'll be okay. Brade'll look after you. Now go. Get yourselves home. And Lionide—I'm gonna need your torch as well."

The boy handed it over. Then—as one, as if they were a single panicked organism—the children shuffled after the guardsman. William brought up the rear, feeling their nervous heat as he shepherded them along. Overhead, nature itself was spiraling out of control—and here they were, charging into the heart of it.

Brade started off at a jog down the lazy, rock-strewn slope. Eyeing the nearby trees, the children hesitated before finally following after him, hurrying to catch up. For a moment William simply stood and watched them go, overcome with an emotion he couldn't quite explain. Children: the innocents, the dreamers, the promise of a tomorrow. Any of them might have been Landon, had fate chosen differently. But it didn't matter; Marcus Calvin was wrong. Norick—despite its flaws, despite the suffering it caused him day after day—was still his home. These were *his* people in danger, *his* children. Their destiny belonged to him now—*they* belonged to him now, as they always had, if only he'd had the eyes to see it. They were his, and he was theirs.

He was theirs.

Blinking past loose beads of sweat, William shifted his eyes from the pack of younglings—no more than a dark stain against the backdrop, herding away—and gulped. He would need utmost vigilance during this journey, lest he be waylaid along the path. It was a tactical nightmare if there ever was one; an ambush might await around every turn. And that was the thing: He couldn't shake the feeling that all of this was some sort of trap. A snare that anticipated his arrival.

But what choice did he have? Jacob Willow—just a boy, one of the fifteen children he now felt a sudden and profound call to protect—was still out there somewhere, scared and alone. Vulnerable. William could only hope he wasn't already too late.

His sword rang out with a ghostly melody as it emerged from its scabbard. Descending the bluff in a sprint, William headed north, angling toward a swath of woods bisecting the foothills. Angling toward a darkness that, just then, felt eager to swallow him whole.

CHAPTER TWENTY-EIGHT

The fire was winning. Of this, Skylar Higgins was certain. Bent double with his spade-like hands pressed against his kneecaps, he tipped his head up and watched as the town—his town—burned down around him.

Standing before the charred remains of the stable, he offered the mutilated horse a frown. No one had bothered to move the mare; what purpose would it serve? It was too late for the creature; too late for them all. The flames had spread beyond any hope for containment. Even now the inferno was bifurcating, churning outward with uncanny precision: identifying the weak spots, cleaving whole sections of the town in two. Above, the storm was a petulant child: stubborn, implacable, intent upon withholding its life-giving sustenance. Instead it had chosen to align itself with the fire, to be a collaborator in their demise, using its howling breath to push the flames on.

Before sunup, the two of them would take everything.

Through the swirling curtain of smoke, Higgins squinted at a woman as she wobbled past, her eyes unfocused, her garments drenched. If pressed, Higgins might've said she was drunk. Muttering to herself, the woman vanished into the smoke. Elsewhere—perhaps close by, perhaps only in his mind—a child was weeping.

He craned his neck after the woman. Down the block, just faintly visible, a cluster of townspeople was still toiling. Their blurred silhouettes scuttled like ants between a water tank and the blazing struts of the granary. Even from here Higgins could sense the panic and disorder pulling them along, the misplaced hope. They were waging the great struggle of their days. They were fighting for their children, their lives, their home.

All in vain.

Others nearby had, like Higgins, dropped their pails and resigned themselves to gawking toward that which had sealed their fate. They, too, understood that there was no more to be done, no effort that wasn't now futile. The town's water tanks were too few, the reserves all but spent. Higgins could've attempted to organize a bucket line from the harbor, but the distance made the effort almost pointless. Even if they could manage to douse a section or two, the other areas of Norick would still be burning, out of their reach. It was, Higgins thought, like trying to scoop water from a boat riddled with holes.

Sooner or later, that ship was going down.

It isn't supposed to be like this. Their virtue was supposed to mean something; their legacy was supposed to matter. Since the beginning, the people of Norick had risen above those baser instincts that kept so many of their race benighted and low. Yet none of it had made a lick of a difference. Here, on the very anniversary of this sanctuary's founding, all of their achievements were proving themselves to be worthless, to be false. A mere fantasy.

They weren't a chosen people. They were the victims of a lie.

As if from a distance, Higgins felt his eyes watering—and not just from the smoke. A sob boiled within him like a geyser, beginning first as a low rumbling in his chest and then as a fiery swell up his throat.

He fastened his mouth shut, catching it at the last second. No. *No.* He wouldn't allow the sobs to come, wouldn't allow himself to falter so.

Still, he couldn't bring himself to wipe the tears from his cheeks.

CHAPTER TWENTY-NINE

On the wall, guardsman Riley Ford waited impatiently for his town to be sieged.

Below, the adjoining fields stretched away in darkness, by all appearances empty. Though this was merely a deception, Riley knew, a ploy their enemy was leveraging against them. But he wouldn't be misled, not private Riley Ford of the Norick Town Guard. He was no fool. When they finally came—and he knew they would—he'd be ready. Sure, he was only a private in the Guard and had only recently enlisted; and sure, he had a fondness for pies and watching sunsets and, on occasion, painting. But he was still a soldier. Still a military man from a proud family. He would do his part; he would do more than that. Soon all would know—townspeople and the enemy alike—that he wasn't someone to be trifled with. That he was, in fact, someone to be feared.

Tonight he would prove exactly that.

Squinting into the gloom, Riley released an exasperated sigh. He fidgeted with his armor, his bow, his sheath. Behind him, within the town, the fire continued to rage. It consumed a handful of buildings just off to Riley's left, tearing at them like ravenous claws through tender flesh. He could feel its heat upon his neck and back and the skin of his calves, but he refused to turn and offer it a glance. Not again; he was resolved now. Lieutenant Tremrow (a better leader, in his opinion, than old drunk Breeve) had stationed him and six others upon the walls, commanding them, in no uncertain terms, to stay and defend them until the last. And so he would.

He revolved in a half circle, scanning the landscape from north to south. Still nothing. He frowned, again wondering what might have happened to Peter Ash, if the man had returned in time before the gates were sealed. Riley hadn't seen him since the magistrate's stroll beyond the walls, and he had related as much to Tremrow. The lieutenant, flustered, had given it only passing consideration before waving the thought away ("If Ash isn't back yet, then that's on him. We don't know what's out there, and we can't risk sending a search party for one man."). The idea didn't sit well with Riley; twice he'd been tempted to abandon his post and go scour for Ash himself. He imagined the Council's faces when he found and safely returned one of their own… But orders were orders, and he was determined to hold true to that.

Sometimes heroism isn't always the right course of action. Sometimes discipline is its own kind of courage.

He also thought about the figure he had seen. How that hooded individual factored into any of this—a scout or lookout, perhaps?—he couldn't say. He did know the memory unnerved him. It was the stately way in which the figure had carried itself from the Grove; it was that horrible, *horrible*, little wave: five-fingered and taunting and all too intimate, as if it were meant only for him. Riley shuddered to think of it. He knew the recollection would haunt his dreams.

Enough of this. Mysterious figure or not, he would do his job. Which meant he needed to focus. Even now a great company might be out there, probing their defenses, deciding where first to strike. Riley, despite a nauseating sense of anxiety, hoped it would be right here.

And if that cloaked bastard happens to be with them, then he'll learn what happens to those who threaten my town. Riley nodded to himself. *Yes. Yes, he will.*

A minute stretched into two; two turned into ten. Still nothing. Just buffeting wind and swaying grass. "Come on," Riley found himself mumbling, "come on, you bastards…" Two minutes more and the fields remained empty. His pulse felt like avalanching stones. "Come on … attack." He ground his teeth. "What are you waiting for? Attack!"

Then suddenly they were.

A host of black figures poured over the eastern foothills. It was too dark to gauge how many there were—he would have guessed at least twenty—though several held torches aloft. One man, larger and more defined, ran slightly ahead of the pack, leading them on.

Riley huffed in a massive gulp of air. This was it, then. This was the chance he'd been waiting for. The opportunity to prove himself. To truly matter. After tonight, he would be worthy of everything the Founders had given them, of everything Norick stood for.

He would do whatever it took.

Riley pulled in another breath, squared his shoulders, and reached for an arrow. "Sighting!" he shouted, casting his voice to the other guardsmen along the walls. From the corner of his eye, he saw them hurrying toward his position. "Enemy spotted, eastern front. I need reinforcements over here."

The invaders dashed closer. A few paces more and they would be within the shimmering sphere of the town's glow, where he would finally get a good look at them.

He couldn't wait.

He hauled back on his bowstring; shut one eye. The group of attackers drew into the light. They slowed up, taking stock, their heads rearing up toward the burning buildings. At the sight, some seemed intent on breaking off, on fleeing, but a few sharp words from their leader effectively corralled them once more. They headed for the gate.

For a moment, Riley didn't understand what he was seeing. *Oh*, he thought once it finally registered. *Oh.* The bowstring relaxed. *They're children. Only children.* Shoulders slumping, he sighed. He couldn't help it: He was disappointed.

Lowering his weapon, he turned and informed the others it was a false alarm, that it was only younglings out there. He yelled for the guardsmen below to raise the gate. Down the line, his comrades echoed the call: All clear.

Not enemies, Riley thought as he watched the iron slab ascend. It rumbled on its gears and shuddered into a corresponding cavity, and then Brade Higgins and his strange company were trotting through, passing right beneath Riley's feet. *Not enemies, but children.*

Damn.

CHAPTER THIRTY

Her only option was retreat.

Hunched like a beggar within the alleyway, sixteen-year-old Natalie Willow understood, with clarity, that she needed to turn back. There was no hope in this enterprise, no victory to be had. Her mission here was futile: She would never make it to the end of the passage, and even if she did, logic told her it would already be too late.

Nobody could survive this hellhole.

Above her, the flames discharged wave after wave of heat, smothering every inch of her skin. Despite the deafening torrent, the only light came from a muted halo flaring periodically through the draping belly of the smoke. Not that it mattered: Natalie had long since clenched her lids and given herself over to navigating by touch. At first, she had used a hand to feel her way along; soon however, the bricks of the adjoining house, heated until they were scorching, proved too much to bear. With luck, she'd stumbled upon a tree branch lying half submerged in the mud. She'd known, without having to see it, that it was the same bough they'd used earlier. She'd retrieved the branch with a shudder before holding it aloft as though it were something accursed. A substance glossed the stem and lower spurs, making it difficult to grip. A combination of mud and moisture? The oil of smelting timber? *Or ... more likely ... blood?*

Oh Milgrin, what did we do?

Natalie gingerly pushed her way deeper, sliding the branch along the base of the wall, feeling her strength dwindling as she went, failing by the second. Already her limbs were unsteady, almost watery, as if they'd lost their form and weight. The ashy particulates congealed like a gooey paste in her mouth, and her eyes, even shut, felt desiccated and shriveling, crying out for moisture though there was none to be had.

She couldn't keep this up. Not like this. If she stayed much longer, she would faint—or worse. *And then...* And then her fate would be the same as Vernon's.

Retreat. The voice snuck up on her slowly, tender in its offering. *You need to get out of here, before it's too late. You can't save him. He's already gone.* Maybe so, but Natalie couldn't just walk away. Could she? If she did, she knew that, for the rest of her life, her mind would return here, to this moment. Even if she departed now, she would never truly leave this alleyway.

No, she thought, a sob building, *I have to try. This was us; we did this. I did this.*

Casting aside the branch—it'd only slowed her down anyway—Natalie sprinted toward the entrance with what little energy she had left. It didn't take long; within seconds she emerged onto the cobbled street and paused to guzzle air. It was threaded with fine particles of smoke, though it was no less glorious for it. She breathed deep, thinking to herself how extraordinary it was that something so simple, so forgotten, could be so wonderful. She heaved in another string of breaths; her lungs screamed in gratitude. And then she was off, launching herself down the sidewalk to a nearby water tank. The last dregs of its cache—cloudy and grimed, coating the bottom of the trough in the thinnest of layers—smoldered with firelight. Natalie studied the liquid for a moment before deciding. *It'll have to do.*

She shimmied out of her overshirt, took hold of one of the sleeves, and ripped the garment in two. Next, she severed one of the halves into a tattered yet lengthy strip. She held it up to her head, stretched it. It would work. Balling the strip in her hand, she plunged it into the trough and scrubbed along the bottom and the sides, soaking up all the moisture she could find. The cloth was soon adequately doused; with a grimace, she secured it around her lips.

Natalie inhaled; the air came shallow and moist. Already the potency of the smoke was diminished. *Okay.* She nodded to herself. *You can do this. It's gonna work out. It's gonna be fine.* Before she could reconsider—before the fear could again seize control and send her fleeing from the town altogether—she scampered back to the alley and rushed inside.

She was halfway up its length when disaster struck. Perhaps if she'd shown more caution she could have avoided what came next. Perhaps she would've had time to brace herself. But, in her desperation, she heard nothing: not the groaning of the timbers above, nor the whistle of the shingles. Not the sudden splintering of the siding as the foundation beneath it loosened and cracked … and the whole structure came toppling down.

The avalanche of debris walloped Natalie in the midst of a stride. Too shocked to scream, she yelped as wreckage crashed into her shoulders. Her hips crumpled; her back caved. A board snapped her head to the right. There was a moment of pure momentum, a terrible forfeit of all control, before the rubble completed its sweep and flung her against the far wall.

And then she was engulfed, buried beneath a mountain of mortar and wood. The debris, much of it still alight, flattened her.

Crushed her.

She grunted—the only thing she could manage—and a wave of darkness rushed over her, flooding all sight. *You never should have come back,* her mind rebuked in the seconds before the black stole her away. *What were you thinking? This was suicide.*

Vernon, Natalie thought as she faded, and she fixed her mind there, on him, on his dorky little grin.

It was for Vernon.

CHAPTER THIRTY-ONE

Crouched at the midway point between the outpost and the Grove, the man in the cloak waited for William Breeve, captain of the Town Guard, to scurry on by.

Overhead, the trees wailed. Their branches scraped. The sky split with fissures of light. The man in the cloak, burrowed in darkness, propped his shoulder against the trunk of an elm and, listening to the processions of thunder above, stared at the forest floor. A patch of knee-high grass strewn with weeds stretched out in front of him; a rotted, capsized log covered him from behind.

His wound had reopened. Lowering his hooded face, the man in the cloak inspected the hand in question, where a slight tingle had worked its way up into his fingers: not so much a pain as a curious sensation. After imparting the message on the magistrate's door, he'd wrapped the cut in a thick band of cloth, now soaked through. Twin streams of warm, sticky fluid trickled over his wrist and down his forearm, dribbling to the weeds below.

For a while, he let it. Measuring by feel rather than sight, he cranked his arm one way and then the other, relishing, with a simple sort of pleasure, the way in which the blood seemed eager to respond to his commands, oozing as directed. When he curled his bicep, the man in the cloak felt a third rill branch off and make for his elbow. It curled about the joint, seeped into his cloak. The blood covered just one arm, and not even in its entirety, but his whole body felt coated, submerged somehow.

With his right hand, the man in the cloak yanked a handful of vegetation, roots and all, up from the ground. Clods of dirt crumbled from their veiny moorings and pattered onto his knees. He flung the tuft aside. Pressing his palm into the leftover crater, he rubbed the cut against the soil, feeling his life force leak out, feeling himself join with the earth. He scooped dirt directly into his palm. Swirled it around. The soil, lumpy and cold, stung as it found the gash. Ignoring the pain, the man in the cloak squeezed a fist, holding it until the gush of blood had slowed.

Good enough. The dirt drizzled out through his fingers.

There was a rustle in the underbrush nearby: the snap of twigs and fallen branches; a series of grunts, a discarded curse. As predicted, Breeve had all but swallowed the bait, the idea of a child in danger a lure he couldn't ignore. He tramped his way through the interlocking cathedrals of sprig and bramble, his passage marked by a bobbing sphere of light floating just beyond the next gully—a graveyard of boulders, moss, and toppled trees. The man in the cloak didn't have to look to know Breeve's intentions; he could hear the captain pulling up (a spill of dirt and gravel, a whoosh of dust), panting, and preparing to descend. Unfamiliar with the terrain, he would take the slope at an angle, using his foot as a plow to furrow his way to the bottom. He would then catch his breath before starting up the other side. Shallow though it was, the man in the cloak knew the ravine would prove a difficult climb.

Hauling in a draught of air, Breeve sheathed his sword. He adjusted his hold on the torch.

He started down.

The man in the cloak tensed, pushing himself off from the elm. Any moment now, he thought as he rotated toward the gully. Not that time mattered. For the voice—and, by extension, for him—such a construct, so painfully human in its design, was of little real consequence. Time was an illusion; time was nothing at all.

Baiting the magistrate to the Grove might have happened years ago. Or perhaps merely seconds. It was hard to tell. All the man in the cloak knew for certain was that he had done his part: leaving the summons on Peter Ash's front door; filching the paint, rope, and knife from that cottage in Coastline; and, in the Grove, stringing up the noose, marking the ritual (the symbols floating behind his lids like foreign characters he didn't understand but had once memorized), then lying in wait for the master of trade to arrive.

He'd observed from the storage shed as the voice drove Peter Ash to madness. The man in the cloak couldn't make out the words, but whatever foul secrets the voice whispered proved sufficient: Discovering the flaying knife set out for him at the base of the watchtower, Ash slit both wrists, collapsed crisscross into the grass, and continued to scream. He bled out minutes later, arms spread wide, tears on his cheeks. Once or twice, the man in the cloak thought he heard the magistrate calling for someone—one name, over and over, sputtered out between those tortured cries. *Heather ... Heather ... Heather...*

The man in the cloak wouldn't allow himself to look away. Nor did he move to intervene. Even as Ash gurgled and flailed and sputtered that name, the man in the cloak stood still. Beneath the hood, one of his eyelids twitched. He scratched at his beard, clenched a fist. He reminded himself that Ash was an adulterer, a corrupter, someone who'd brought this upon himself. Still, the man in the cloak felt a flutter in his stomach as he watched the magistrate die.

Then he'd set to work.

At the bidding of the voice, he stripped Ash naked and stowed the soiled garments in a corner of the shed. Next, using a piece of twine, he fastened the magistrate's wrists behind his back. A bubbling layer had hardened upon the surface of the paint jug; the man in the cloak plunged the fisherman's brush straight through and swirled it like a wheel. When he pulled it loose, gobs of red dye plopped from the bristles and flung to the grass below. He paid them no mind. Closing his eyes, letting those floating characters guide him, he marked up the magistrate's body in similar fashion to the Grove: symbols upon the man's shins, chest, and knees.

And one for the forehead. A stamp, a crown.

The noose slipped over the master of trade's head easily enough. Its accompanying rope, levered over the tower's sturdiest beam, chaffed at the man in the cloak's fingers as he towed the corpse skyward, the magistrate's dirtied heels dragging through the grass before finally going airborne. Once Ash was sufficiently raised, the man in the cloak secured the end of the line, winding it around another joist and fixing the body into place. The rope offered a groan when he released his hands but otherwise held steady. Above him, Peter Ash swayed.

The bait was set.

The man in the cloak retrieved the brushes and the paint. With the voice whispering in his ear, he scrawled out the instructed message below the magistrate's dangling feet. Stepping back, he took a moment to study his handiwork and wondered, in an abstract sort of way, if the townspeople would be wise enough to heed the warning. Even if they did, the man in the cloak suspected it was already too late. The voice, like always, would have its way.

The voice. If it had a name, the man in the cloak didn't know it. Nor did he want to. Some regions might've referred to it as a demon. Other cultures had coined it a kalikan, a yurif, a tulmok. Each of these was merely an ineffectual attempt at grasping that which couldn't be grasped. A word was just an arbitrary label chosen to express a concept or a thing; language itself was little more than man's struggle to bring order to chaos, meaning to mystery. But this voice—ancient, elusive, all-reaching—existed beyond simple classification or finite order. It was so far beyond paltry human intellect that to try to understand its essence was an exercise in futility. Can a person describe the sound darkness makes? Can he or she explain the shape of the wind? Does music have a smell? Does infinity know an end?

Such musings were worthless, as was any attempt to comprehend the nature of the voice, and so the man in the cloak didn't try.

The sound of grunting rose up from the gully, followed by the swish of displaced leaves. Breeve was nearly at the top now; there was a crumbling of dirt as he hauled himself over the edge by a loose knot of roots. For a moment, he lay on his back and panted up toward the canopy.

Rolling over, Breeve reached for his torch—tossed over the embankment ahead of his approach—and pushed himself up. His sword screeched as it slid from its scabbard, its blade shining with a fiery gleam. Steeling himself, the captain took off, his eyes locked on the path ahead. So absorbed was he that he charged past the man in the cloak without noticing a thing. The lurker slunk out from behind his hiding place; Breeve raced on toward the Grove, oblivious.

Only a couple of paces back, the man in the cloak followed.

He wouldn't harm the captain. Not yet. His job was simply to observe: It was the voice who'd set all of this into motion; it was the voice who would bring it to its proper resolution. The man in the cloak was just one piece of its plans. An instrument. He had done everything it'd commanded because he had to. Because of everything that was at stake.

If they knew the truth, would the people of Norick still blame him? Doubtless. But what choice did he have? His fate, and theirs, had been decided long ago.

Hurdling over a rotting stump and through a patch of nettles, Breeve and his bobbing torch sped up. Behind him, the man in the cloak likewise quickened his pace. He sidestepped the stump and its treacherous mesh of roots. His hood flapped in the wind.

It was time, the man in the cloak thought. Time for Norick to face its past.

Time for all of this to end.

PART EIGHT

THE VOICE
IN THE NIGHT

Speak to it,
And the darkness will answer.

CHAPTER THIRTY-TWO

The knife was waiting. Protruding hilt-up beneath the body, it was lodged in a trampled tussock of grass. Both were glossed in a spray of blood.

The other children hadn't noticed it previously. Their eyes had immediately flown to the dead man and to the strange, ritualistic markings dressing his flesh. But Jacob, who'd been around every variety of sharp implement in the span of his brief nine years, felt the blade's presence from the outset, from the moment his eyes locked with the magistrate's.

Certain the corpse was speaking to him, Jacob screamed and screamed and clawed at his ears. He clenched his lids. Still that murmur buzzed, guzzling through his awareness like a deep-water riptide. It dragged him through the murk, ratcheting his terror with every plunge. And underneath it all, that knife. A simple fisherman's tool jammed into the earth like a stake marking territory. *That's it,* Jacob thought. *There's the knife that did it. That's what cut Mr. Ash's wrists.*

Of course it would still be there; why wouldn't it be? It was at home in that grass, where it could relish its handiwork. Jacob sensed it doing so, just as he sensed it reaching out to him in the dark. A wave of familiarity surrounded the blade, a sense like déjà vu, as if it had belonged to him in another life. And maybe it had.

It didn't matter. This was his part to play now. The discarded knife was the inevitable destination of a path he only just realized he was on, one he had no choice but to follow. Because Jacob *had* seen this knife before; it *was* familiar. It was one of his father's blades, but more so did he recognize it from a dream. *The* dream—his childhood nightmare.

In it, Jacob would wake in their family's cottage as if from a deep slumber, a sleep within a sleep. For a while, he would simply lie there, silent and uncomprehending, blinking past strands of blond hair. It was after midnight, the dream-Jacob knew, likely deep into the morning during that final crest of darkness before dawn's approach. The air was stagnant, the ocean muted. All seemed frozen, as if the heartbeat of the Earth had stalled. Lying in a stupor upon his straw mattress, Jacob was also held suspended, though his eyes were free to roam the water-stained ceiling above. Two things would happen then: He would become aware of a curious sensation upon his hip, and, from the corner of his eye, he would detect the dark form hovering over the bed.

Spell ruptured, the dream-Jacob would slowly crane his neck to peer at the black shape—featureless, without distinct limbs or edges, almost like a fog that had materialized from the air. While it didn't have eyes or even the semblance of a face, Jacob could feel it watching him. He didn't need to glance about the sleeping quarters to know his was the only cot occupied; he and this shadowy presence were alone.

As if arriving at some conclusion, the figure would lift what could have been an arm and motion for Jacob to follow. Turning, it would disappear through the hut's dividing curtain into the communal space beyond, the drape fluttering quietly in its wake. And each time, Jacob would rise, swivel his legs over the cot, and follow.

He brought the knife with him; it'd been clutched in his hand when he awoke, the flat side of the blade lying snug against his hip, the steel like ice. It'd been kept hidden for this moment, for the emergence of this nighttime visitor. As he crossed the room, Jacob's mind was numb, sanded clear. In four steps, he drew level with the curtain and breached the divide.

The profile of darkness floated in the room's only uninhabited corner. The visitor seemed, as best as the dream-Jacob could surmise, somewhat distracted. As if it were lost in other, more pressing thoughts. Turning his eyes from the granular figure, which had fallen into an indomitable bout of stillness, Jacob would examine the room. Besides the supper table—which was centered and wiped clear—the space matched his family's real cottage only in structure. This dream adaptation was stripped of its adornments. Other than the table, it was devoid of all indicators of human habitation. There were only the walls and a lurid darkness—separate from that of the lingering figure—that filled the space with a tangible sense of emptiness.

Though this wasn't the truth, at least not entirely. There were other things in this room, hovering at the edges. Merely waiting to be discovered.

There were other people in this place.

It was then that Jacob's eyes would find the first body. It belonged to his father, the fisherman Christopher, who was slumped in the corner, chin resting on his chest as if he'd only just nodded off. Across the way was Jacob's mother, Janae, equally comatose. Unlike her husband, she was standing with her back pressed to the wall. Knives were driven through both shoulders and through the pale flesh above her knees, pinning her to the wood. She looked like a scarecrow. From what Jacob could see, the knives were his father's own blades, normally used for carving fish and cutting lines. Each wound leaked a cascade of blood that pooled at Janae's feet. Her mouth and eyes were open, her look not so much pained as surprised. Jacob glanced back at his father. Blood seeped from the fisherman as well, trailing down from his throat and pasting his sleeveless tunic to his chest.

Not allowing himself to process the scene, Jacob completed the circle and lowered his eyes to the last corpse. His older sister, Natalie. She was curled into a ball, legs tucked to her chest, back exposed. All along her spine were the thin, slanting incisions of stab wounds—dozens of them, showing angrily through the tattered fabric of her nightgown. The configuration of the cuts held no clear sense of order; they could only have been produced in a mania, a rage. Natalie's strawberry-blonde hair was equally disheveled, crusted in blood and dirt and draped over her face like a veil. Jacob hardly recognized her. He hardly saw her at all.

Once he was aware of the bodies, the nightmare would mutate, evidence of the slaughter appearing everywhere: It soaked the walls in wide, splattering swaths; it saturated the floor until the dirt was spongy beneath his feet. It doused his own garments, splashes of blood fanning across his belly and up onto his cheek.

The horror of this scene was nightmare enough. Even worse, upon waking, were the questions that plagued Jacob for days, churning long after the dream should've ended: Had *he* done it? Why? Was he, in real life, capable of something like that?

The end of the nightmare almost unfolded as an afterthought. The dream-Jacob would raise his eyes from the carnage and gawk at the figure, hovering like a hole of darkness across the room. It seemed content now, satiated in some primal way. Jacob, numb, couldn't avert his gaze. *It's time,* the darkness would say without saying anything at all. *You know what you have to do.*

And he did. That table had been cleared for a reason.

Under the scrutiny of the figure, Jacob would step mechanically toward the table, spin himself to face the sleeping quarters, and, drawing the length of the blade across both wrists, stretch himself out along the wood. As he waited for his body's essence to drain, he would conclude the dream just as he'd started it: staring numbly at the ceiling.

At present, kneeling in the Grove before Peter Ash's corpse, Jacob thought of his nightmare and that knife and the tortuous period of waiting before he woke. He understood now that the dream and the scene before him were connected, that the two knives were in fact one and the same—as were the voice and that congregated darkness. As was the figure back in Star Glade. Ever since coming face-to-face with it in the meadow—ever since he'd dreamed that first nightmare all those years ago—the voice had been steering Jacob here, to this blade.

The question had its answer; he now knew what the nightmare meant. The knife wasn't intended for Peter Ash. The knife was for *him.*

Use it. Jacob could hear the words plainly enough—the voice smooth, gentle, sliding through him like honey. *Take up that knife, boy, and do what you've always been meant to. Cut yourself, like you deserve. Cleanse yourself of your transgressions.*

Jacob found himself overcome by a tide of guilt, a visceral remorse at what he'd done in that dream. *Mother and Father, Natalie … I slaughtered them.* The voice was right: He was wretched; he was unworthy. He deserved every fate the darkness could decree.

Opening his eyes, he rocked back onto his haunches. He took in the watchtower, the trampled grass, the swaying trees. And the knife—just where he knew it would be.

Good, purred the voice in his head. *Come now, Jacob. Do it quickly.*

He pulled himself to his feet and started forward, blundering after only a handful of steps. He landed hard, and the world about him jostled and bounced. Stalks of grass bristled against his cheek.

Get up. Move.

He groaned; blinked dizzily.

Come on, boy. Rise. Pull yourself up. It's waiting.

He lowered his eyelids. Opened them. He reached an arm out, thrusting his hand downward, and grasped for purchase.

One time, that's all it will take.

He dug his nails in; pulled. He slinked forward, winding like a worm, the blades of grass tickling at his stomach.

One time, Jacob, and I promise you'll be free.

His knees bent.

Two little cuts, that's all. Easy.

He drove a kneecap into the earth, regained his leverage. Pushed.

That's it. Good boy. Now come. Bleed for me.

Through a film of tears, Jacob Willow clawed himself up and, unleashing a sob—seeing again the mutilated corpses of his family, struck down by his own hand—he started once more toward the hanging body, and the awaiting knife.

CHAPTER THIRTY-TWO

How much time had passed, Skylar Higgins couldn't be certain. After what seemed hours, perhaps even days, he became aware of somebody calling out his name.

He cracked his eyelids; the voice, like meager birdsong in the midst of a maelstrom, hollered from across the fire-hemmed street. The man kept shouting, though less as a display of emotion than with a simple desire to be heard.

"Chancellor Higgins!" The man, a blocky apparition pushing his way through the funnels of smoke, approached along the cobblestone. Higgins didn't turn, reflecting instead on the thick layer of filth covering him. In spite of it, he felt almost weightless, as if at any moment he might merge with the smoke and up and float away.

His searcher arrived. Skidding to a halt, the man buried his nose into the crook of his elbow. "Milgrin's courage," he mumbled between the folds of skin. Higgins rolled his eyes. Like the chancellor, Lucas Illhap's face was black with grime. His cheeks—abnormally slanted, as if the man were perpetually sucking on the wedge of a lemon—were streaked with sweat. Charred edges framed a tattered tunic, while little singed holes perforated the legs of his trousers, revealing pockets of white flesh. The tavern owner looked as if he'd just ventured through some calamitous battle—*Through the very nadirs of hell*—and, Higgins supposed, in some ways he had. As they all had: a fight like none the town had ever known.

A fight they had lost.

Illhap lifted his elbow a fraction of an inch. "What now?" Higgins cast his gaze deep into the heart of the inferno, watching those flames tumble and swirl as if they were children at play. Uncaring, innocent. There was almost a beauty to it. "Higgins?" Illhap pressed.

"I don't know," he murmured. He had the strangest urge, just then, to amble forward and cast himself into the flames.

As steadfast as ever, the tavern owner wouldn't be deterred. He positioned himself between Higgins and the fiery rubble. "I spoke to Quinn. Other than for some children out there, his men on the walls are still reporting empty fields. It's all clear. The warning bell must have been a mistake—maybe the guardsman saw the fire and was trying to warn us. I think we should start moving people beyond—"

"No."

"What?"

"No."

Illhap's face wrinkled. "Every second that passes—"

Higgins was staring through him. "There is nothing," he said, "nothing at all we can do."

Illhap flinched as if he'd been slapped, realization dawning in his eyes followed by pure, unbridled rage. "Listen to yourself, you fool. Snap out of it! We have to get the people out. Right now. We *elected* you—so take charge." He waited, his begrimed face a surface of hard lines. Higgins didn't reply. "Give the command, dammit." He gestured wildly. "*Lead them.*"

"I failed them." Higgins's voice was hardly more than a whisper; he doubted Illhap, standing just a foot apart, could make out a syllable. He didn't care: The words were for himself, a confession. He wasn't a leader—never had been. He was a fraud.

He was nothing.

Hopelessness cinched his throat; he dropped his stare. Smoke and ash whirled about his shins and drifted off to some unknown destination. *Darkness, destruction: always in motion.* "It's over," he said. "It's all over."

"What are you talking about? It's not over—nothing's bloody over. Get ahold of yourself. We'll rebuild. We'll get past this. You hear me? We'll find a way—together. As we always have. You said so yourself: always."

Sickened to hear his words repeated back to him, Higgins just shook his head. "We'll starve together, that's what we'll do. We'll never survive the winter. We'll sit and we'll starve and we'll watch our children waste away." He scoffed, as if lecturing one of those children. "So, no, it doesn't matter what we do. Either way, we're all going to die."

Higgins finally gave the tavern owner his full attention. "Norick is finished."

Illhap glared back. The two men's silent exchange stretched, each of them measuring the other; each, in his own way, pleading. A tremulous bout of coughing wracked Illhap, and he stooped over, his chest shuddering with the force. When next he straightened, a new resolve had emerged in his eyes. "So be it," he spat. "*I'll* save the bloody town." He held the chancellor's gaze a moment longer. "I thought there was more to you than this, Higgins. I truly did." He offered a melancholic wag of his head. "I thought there was more."

With that, Illhap raced away. The murk quickly swallowed him, but his voice rang out clearer than ever: "Listen to me. People of Norick, retreat—retreat! Get outside, get to the hills. It's over—save yourselves."

Higgins remained stationary even as a wave of townspeople scrambled past. They came first in clumps of twos and threes, and then there was a whole school of them, clambering like salmon upstream. Watching them concede their homes to the flames, Higgins felt a fatalism like none he'd ever experienced: a stag caught in a hunter's snare; a condemned man waiting for the ax to fall.

His life: everything he'd believed himself to be; everything he had hoped for and planned and dreamed—all of it reduced, like this forsaken town, this cursed valley, to ash.

I thought there was more, Illhap had remarked.

So had he.

So had he.

CHAPTER THIRTY-FOUR

What happened next shouldn't have been possible. And maybe it wasn't. Maybe it was only a flittering apparition of a failing mind, a reverie manufactured in that tenuous realm between life and death.

Maybe this was all that death was: an infinite dream of the impossible.

Whatever it was, reality or figment, miracle or delusion, sixteen-year-old Natalie Willow knew one thing to be true: One moment she felt herself waning, dwindling into the darkness, and then, in the next...

She heard singing.

It came to her as a variegated thread of light, hued and woven like the strokes of a rainbow. It began first as a soft, pulsating glow hovering in the uppermost regions of her awareness. She didn't hear it so much as she felt it. The tune—no words, just a melody so somber it seemed almost to contain joy—contracted into a single strand weaving its way through the dark like an iridescent lasso. At moments it was so bright almost to be colorless. Then it would dip and soar, and the lustrous shades would return, more vibrant than ever before.

It pulled her back, that light-song fused into one. Cutting through the fog of her mind like a scythe, it led her up and away: away from the darkness, away from the void. She was rising; she was enshrouded in music so wholesome and cleansing it stung. A warm and buoyant ocean drifted around her, through her, moving only with the rhythmic swelling of the song.

She returned to herself, the physical parameters falling into place one by one: the cataclysmic weight bearing down upon her hips and chest, the swelling abrasions, the heat. For a moment, buried beneath the heap of rubble with her eyes shut, all Natalie could summon was surprise—surprise at being alive.

Why am I not dead? It doesn't make sense. I should really be dead.

She contemplated this with a vague sense of wonder, more a curiosity of the fact than an appreciation of it. How strange, she thought, to be alive when you had no right to be. How curious to have let go only to find that life had more it wanted from you. Gloriously numb, Natalie detached herself from these thoughts, wanting nothing more than to linger in the song's airy embrace.

The song...

Natalie snapped her eyes wide. Thick ashy smoke assailed them at once. Flinching, unprepared for such an assault, she lifted a hand—the left—to paw uselessly at her sockets. The movement quaked a thrust of agony up her side; she could feel something sharp and heavy lodged there. Despite the smoke's fibrous onslaught, she again cracked her eyelids and saw that she was pinched up against a wall like a toppled tree, buried to the chest in stone and wood paneling. Chunks of mortar and a ruptured board formed a jagged knoll on her hip, the timber's splintered edge burrowing deep, its nails mining for blood. Somewhere below, both ankles were ensnared, though her head, neck, and left arm remained free.

Natalie blinked, pulled in a frenzied breath through the dampened cloth. Screamed.

She was alive, and she was trapped. Yielding to a spout of chest-rattling coughs, each driving fiery aches through her ribs, she wriggled herself up and glanced at the bedlam of her surroundings. A smoldering embankment of rubble—more split timbers, the tattered remains of shingles, a mountain range of collapsed brick—stretched from wall to wall and heaped skyward: a graveyard of unknown length and design.

She really had no business being alive.

Natalie swiveled as best she could, grimacing from the effort, and peered toward the alley's opening. Empty, save for the mud and the smoke. Not that that was surprising—as far as she knew, no one realized they were in here. *The song.* She had heard a song. Had it only been a dream, or something more? Could it have been *him?*

Vernon—are you still alive in there?

The singing was gone now, but that was all right. *I'm alive when I should be dead. And so is he.* A desperate momentum coursed through her, every nerve flooding with energy. She needed to move; she needed to act. And she needed to do it now. The desire was a physical impulse as much as a mental one. It swirled inside her; it surged forth like water through a ruptured dike.

She needed to move, she needed to move, she needed to *move.*

With a roar—heedless of the pain, the pressure, or the stinging cuts crisscrossing her arm—Natalie squirmed for better leverage, pushing herself to tears as she maneuvered for space. She plowed into the surrounding rubble using her free hand. Grunting, she lobbed pieces both large and small toward the street, toward the ground, toward the sky overhead, uncaring of the bite of fractured timber and misshapen nail. She discovered a section of charred wardrobe; all along its surface the wood finish was bubbling. She hurled the chunk aside, surprised at her own strength. It was a thing like rage that consumed her, a force beyond understanding, and she bellowed with it as she continued the excavation.

She was erratic. She was implacable. She would not be denied.

Seared in her mind's eye: an image of Vernon—bruised, broken, and covered in rubble. Trapped, but alive. In her ears: the memory of that plaintive melody. Its inherent plea. *I'm coming, Vernon. Hang on just a little longer. I'm coming.*

She attacked the wreckage with renewed ferocity. Slabs of mortar ricocheted off stacks of brick before tumbling away. A toothed board had pierced the skin just below her armpit; it offered a wet sucking sound as she pulled it free. Beneath it all, her ankles were still caught, pressed to the mud by blocks of mortar. She could hardly feel their weight. The pain, along with every physical sensation, was now curiously abstract. She felt preternaturally focused, capable of any undertaking.

She panted and heaved. She clawed at the rubble like a canine foraging for a bone. The pile dwindled, and a path to her ankles opened up. Natalie gritted her teeth; placing both hands on the mounds beside her, she tugged. Her foot slid an inch, but the blocks shifted ... and wedged themselves tighter. She continued to yank, grunting all the while. Her feet remained lodged.

Abandoning the effort, Natalie set to combing the piles around her. *Come on...* She rubbed at her eyes, clearing away the tears. *There has to be something.* At last she spotted a piece of timber, remarkably unscathed, projecting from the wreckage. She didn't know how deep it was buried, but it'd have to do. She could only hope it was long and sturdy enough for the task she had in mind.

For the next minute, she worked on clearing the semblance of a lane. Once one had been established, she craned her body across it, belly pressing into the serrated debris, and strained her limbs as far as they would reach. There was a moment of tortuous proximity without contact, her fingers scrabbling through the dust for purchase. *Come on... Come on...* Sweat bristled upon the nape of her neck. She stretched further; the sharp edges of the mortar dug in. She shut one eye, tried to make herself as elastic as possible. Her tongue lolled from her lips. *Dammit ... come on. Just let me—*

First one finger grazed wood ... then the rest followed suit. A second later and Natalie had fastened a grip on the board. Relaxing, lying prone on the debris, she exhaled a pent-up sigh. Okay. She could do this. She was almost there.

The next part was the tricky bit. She squeezed the timber as tightly as she could, then, slowly transferring her weight, she sidled back toward the hole, dragging it along with her. The board wobbled, if only slightly, and Natalie allowed herself a smirk. *See. It's not stuck. It just needs a little more—*

In one final laborious tug, the piece came free.

The sudden release took her by surprise; she uttered a gasp as the momentum tossed her against the wall. She rattled to a halt, the board pinned beneath the crook of her elbow. Though, as she'd hoped, it was perfectly intact. And just the length she needed.

I'm almost free. You hear that, Vernon? I'm coming.

Blinking to clear away the sweat—and to steady herself—Natalie lifted the board. She thrust it downward and tilled it through the mud. The far edge caught a groove in the mortar, and she lugged on the upper half until she was sure the hold was secure.

She pressed down with a snarl. The edge levered itself further against the block, which offered a slight shake. She tried dislodging her foot; it remained fixed, refusing to slink free. Grinding her teeth, Natalie again heaved upon the board. Her muscles strained; her veins bulged. The mud slurped away.

Heave and wriggle. Yank and writhe. The progression took on a re-hearsed quality, as if she'd performed these movements hundreds of times. Heave, wriggle. Pull, squirm. She could feel the pressure on her foot diminishing with each new attempt. The top of the board wrenched the fragmented stone up while the bottom edge wore a deepening groove into the sludge.

All things considered, it took very little time. It happened almost without her being aware. One moment she was trapped ... and then she wasn't. She pried the mortar just enough, and—mechanically, without thought, almost anticlimactically after everything that'd happened—she slid her foot out in one smooth pull. With the new leverage, the second quickly followed.

Natalie blinked. For a while, she just gawked at those liberated feet. *I'm free?*

I'm free.

She didn't squander another breath. Tossing aside the board, she scrambled from the narrow pit, using her hands and knees to propel her up over the lip. She ignored the sudden spin in her skull, the pain accompanying her every breath. Her ribs may have been cracked, crushed even, but it didn't matter. She was free.

Wobbling some, she stood, hugged her arms to her chest, and clambered to the opposite side. The air hung thicker here, and the flames seemed louder. Natalie lowered herself to the mud. A few feet ahead, she remembered, was a section of the town walls. Where they'd left him.

Eyes closed, she crawled forward. Knowing it foolish, she nevertheless cast her thoughts outward, searching for some glimmer of his presence. *Vernon? I'm here. Please be okay, please be okay...* Sliding her hands through the debris, she worked her way toward the rear. The sludge squished between her fingers and smeared along her arms. But so far, nothing.

Natalie continued on; she stretched and she panted and she cursed as her shoulder joggled against a loose stone.

And then she was there.

The tips of her fingers nudged soft flesh. She started, a spark-like tingling racing up the length of her forearm. She flung her lids wide.

He was sprawled belly-down in the mud, his arms swollen, bruising, and scrunched like broken wings. Sweat and something dark coated his hairline, while his garments were likewise charred and filthy, clinging to him by the slimmest of tethers. The image of the mutilated horse returned to Natalie, and she shuddered. As far as she could tell, Vernon hadn't moved.

What have we done? Her lips split with a whimper. *Oh Milgrin, what have we done...* She closed the distance between them. Collapsing to her rear, she slung both arms about his middle and lugged him into her lap. "Vernon?" He felt so empty now, so small, almost weightless. She cupped his head between her hands. "I heard you singing. It brought me back. It saved me." She smiled between a cascade of tears and shook him gently. "*You* saved me. So you gotta wake up now, okay buddy? We have to leave."

The boy didn't stir. Natalie, uncomprehending, simply stared into his lifeless face.

"Okay. Come on now, enough of this. You need to—" A sob, the first in an onslaught, tore its way through her chest. Natalie placed a finger beneath Vernon's nose. His chest was still, his body limp. Even in the ambiguous lighting, his skin was pale.

"I said, *wake up* dammit!" She jerked a hand forward, striking him. His cheek quivered with the blow, but he seemed otherwise not to have noticed. Natalie slapped him again—still with no effect. "Wake up," she screamed before succumbing to another hitching sob. "Wake up..."

The realization dawned like a smack to her own face. She recoiled with the knowledge, moaning in tortured heaves, and crumpled to the floor beside him. "No no no no..." This wasn't right; this wasn't how it was supposed to be.

Overcome with a sorrow like an eradication of breath, Natalie nuzzled Vernon's head into her shoulder and rocked him back and forth, as a mother would her child. "I'm sorry," she whimpered, glancing again at his slack, youthful face. Looking almost peaceful, he could have been mistaken for napping, caught in the harmless embrace of sleep. Just that, Natalie thought miserably. Sleeping.

But she knew better. Her tears splashed on unresponsive cheeks.

She was alone in that alley.

CHAPTER THIRTY-FIVE

From inside the Grove: screaming.

William, fresh from the forest, tore up the side of the hill at a full clip, his lungs billowing like the whipping canvas of a sail. The orchard's entrance, two panels of corded timber, lay just ahead, illuminated by the bobbing sphere of his torch. The gate stood ajar.

Not knowing what he would discover inside (*What could make a child scream like that? What's that bastard doing to him?*), William launched himself up the incline and, using a shoulder as a makeshift ram, smashed the panels aside. The timber reeled away; the innards of the Grove unfurled before him.

What in the— William skidded to a halt. This wasn't at all what he'd been anticipating. Frankly, this didn't make a lick of sense. A few paces in, Jacob bowed low to the ground, kneeling before Peter Ash's corpse in a posture of defeat—though it just as easily might've been one of reverence. As William peered closer, he noticed the fisherman's son was trembling, his limbs jerking around as if they were under some great, invisible duress. Bloodcurdling screams punctuated the intervals between tremors. Somewhere between weeping and a panicked howl, the cries could have belonged to a prisoner at the rack. *What's happening to him?* William managed to think, seeing nothing that should cause the boy such distress. There was no madman or killer tormenting him. In fact, there didn't seem to be anyone else in the Grove at all.

Which wasn't to say the boy was free from danger.

Jacob pitched backward. Falling to his haunches, he swung an arm across his chest. It was then that William spotted the knife clasped in the boy's fingers: a glinting sheen of metal flashing through the darkness. His eyes widened with the observation, and his sense of dread deepened as understanding finally dawned.

The boy intended to harm himself.

No, thought William as he hurled forward. *Not after everything. I won't let you.* Ahead, Jacob had stilled, his screams tapering to a low, submissive moan. The knife, suspended just over the boy's wrist, was poised to make an incision up the length of his forearm: a critical blow. The tip of the blade was already tilting, ready to penetrate the milky sinews of his flesh.

No you don't. No you bloody don't—

Flinging aside both torch and sword, William launched himself into the air. In a bone-rattling collision, he crashed into Jacob, looping one arm through the boy's elbow while the other wrapped itself about his torso. He ripped back with all of his might, sending the two of them toppling in a sprawl of limbs and breath. The Grove careened around them; fruit trees spun, danced, and sprouted from the sky. Twice a gleam of metal whirled past.

It took William a moment to recognize it when Jacob's movements changed. What before had been a helpless tumble adhering only to gravity had now mutated into something else. The development caught William by surprise; it was nothing he could've foreseen, but, with the volatile state of the boy's mind, he still felt foolish for not having done so.

Jacob was fighting back.

Hollering himself raw, he squirmed and thrashed. "No! Let me go!" He swung his legs, his bony knees. He clamped down on William's bicep and bit deep.

William howled, less from pain than from shock. He loosened his grip, and Jacob used the opportunity to jerk his head forward then back, slamming his skull at a full tilt against the captain's nose. Motes of light coiled across his vision.

Jacob scrambled out from beneath him. Sometime during their floundering, the knife had been jarred loose from the boy's grip; at present, he clambered toward it, muttering and kicking out behind him as he went. A foot caught William squarely on the jaw and he staggered. Jacob continued on, murmuring all the while. Two words, repeated with a near-religious intonation: "Do it. Do it do it do it..."

Blinking against the throbbing in his skull, William watched as Jacob crawled the final feet and retrieved the knife. The boy spun around; breathless, he fixed his eyes on William. His eyes: red-rimmed and shimmering, hollowed out with an aloofness William found genuinely chilling. Eyes that contained madness.

He stared in horror as Jacob lifted the knife. "I'm sorry," the boy whimpered.

"Jacob, no..." That dizzy, chaotic feeling had returned to William's gut—the sense that things were happening too quickly, and were too widespread, and that at every step his efforts were doomed to fail. Again, he'd fallen for the lie, the belief that he could prevent the world from spiraling out of control. But for him—for everyone—there was no control. There was no meaning or order, no point in any of it.

In this world, there was only chaos. Chaos—and the futility of his actions.

"Please," William said as he deflated with this knowledge, "please don't do this." In his mind's eye, he saw the faces of his wife and son, the latter reaching out an infant's grasp, begging for a hand to hold, a finger to squeeze, a father's touch to keep him warm. He knew then that—however misguided, however absurd—he was speaking to them as well as to Jacob, sending his consciousness back through time. *Just once,* he called, throwing his voice over a rift that could never be crossed, *let me be able to save you.*

Please let me save you.

Jacob, fresh tears welling, wagged his head in return. He glanced down at the knife, considering, then back up at William, both their expressions fraught and miserable. "I have to," the boy said, his head bobbing with the words. "I'm sorry... I have to."

"Jacob, wait—"

The tip of the blade plunged.

CHAPTER THIRTY-SIX

He needed to go home.

A foolish notion—perhaps even an insane one, in no small measure reckless—but an impulse that riveted him all the same. It was a compulsion he could neither comprehend nor altogether quell: *Home. I need to go home.* He considered it without emotion or any acute sense of reason; the desire was something much more instinctual, almost physical, like hunger or the abrading chafe of thirst.

And so, Skylar Higgins—forgotten, invisible, a being out of place and out of time—loped forward across the street, into chaos.

Minutes earlier—or was it hours?—the evacuation order had been issued. First relayed by Lucas Illhap, the cry was soon taken up by members of the Guard and other passersby. Within moments it achieved its desired effect: The townspeople tossed their pails, abandoned their stations, and, scurrying like forest animals from a woodland blaze, hurried to one of Norick's four primary gates.

Guardsmen, looking rattled, screeched over the commotion, the streets suddenly seeming too narrow, the cobble corridors far too labyrinthine. As they fled, the citizens trampled and shoved, stumbled and dived. Some pulled themselves up; others—the elderly, the infirm—simply lay where they fell, pressed into the stone like mats.

At the gates, bottlenecks formed. The guardsmen—looking no older than teenagers in their oversized uniforms—scrambled to raise the barricades. The crowds swarmed them, hollering out instructions for more efficient ways of achieving the task. Young and old alike cursed, clawed, spat. "Get back!" the guardsmen yelped in return. "Let us work, dammit! We need room, you hear? Get back, all of you. Just stay back." Fed up with the guards' incompetence, the mob at one gate simply seized the two lads on duty and flung them aside. In an oppressive crush of bodies, they cranked the levers wide.

The townspeople, scarcely waiting for the iron to pass over their heads, stormed through. Once beyond the walls, they lifted their fists, spun, and inspected every possible avenue for assault. Finding no obvious threats, they turned to one another. They clung to their children. They attempted, rather hopelessly, to clear the soot from their eyes.

They locked hands. Collapsed to their knees. Peered at the burning town in defeat.

Together, the once-proud citizens of Norick wept, and they wondered what on earth they would do next.

Inside the town, Skylar Higgins felt no such uncertainty. Tearing through the smoke-infested streets, his purpose remained clear: *Home.*

Racing through Norick, he was guided less by conscious thought than by his limbs' innate memory. He spotted a handful of laggards as he went; disoriented, they drifted in and out of doorframes, ducked into storefronts. They called out for missing loved ones, children and the wayward husband, their voices like the refrain of some dreadful song. Others teetered beneath the weight of salvaged possessions: crates, chests, and oil paintings; threaded garments of silk. Arms laden, they ambled forward with grim-faced resolve. Some, Higgins knew, were looting their neighbors' belongings. He didn't care. The town was lost; let them do as they pleased.

"Higgins!"

The voice erupted from an intersection on his right. Higgins glanced at the man jogging toward him—Quinn Tremrow, the Guard's second-in-command—then continued down the street. "Sir," Tremrow panted once he'd overtaken him, "what're you still doing in here? Everyone else is outside. I'm just searching for stragglers." The first lieutenant's eyes, in a manner somehow both alert and unfocused, brimmed with worry. "Thank Milgrin I found you. We have to go."

Higgins brushed off the man's hand and kept moving.

"Don't be a damned fool." Tremrow was still pursuing him. "There's nothing in here that can't be replaced. We have to get clear before the fire rings us in. The people need you, Higgins. *Your son* needs you."

It was obvious the guardsman wouldn't be easily dissuaded. Slowing just enough to utter a few words, Higgins grunted over his shoulder: "There's a portrait … Teresa … at my house. I must retrieve it. Go… I'll be fine." Tremrow pulled up, frowning. As Higgins had hoped, there was pity in his eyes. Just enough to make him hesitate.

Perfect.

Higgins cranked hard to the left; Tremrow retreated up the block, back the way he'd come. The next intersection opened onto Higgins's lane. A street of carved granite separated two rows of houses, all three-stories or more. Short stone partitions divided the properties, and each possessed a small but tidy lawn. This far east, the fire had yet to arrive.

Higgins's house, situated at the end of the lane, sat untouched. Its elegant shutters were open, its windows darkened, and it seemed unaware of the chaos approaching. The structure—where Higgins had lived his entire life; where he, Teresa, and Brade had made a home—would be one of the last dwellings to go. It seemed cruel, that fact, almost like a tease. But what did it matter? Either way, now or later, the entire town would burn.

Higgins bounded forward; houses washed in firelight peered down on either side. He was halfway up his front stoop when he paused, blinked, then froze altogether. *The door…* He was certain: He hadn't left it open.

Fearing the worst, he crept up the last of the steps and palmed the door wide. It swung inward with a creak before colliding with the wall. Higgins caught the handle on its return and tiptoed into the foyer, dim light spilling in from the shutters and casting the foyer in a tepid glow. Stealing into the dining room, he squinted through the darkness in search of damage, of pillagers caught in the act or even now stowing themselves away. But the room was empty, all as it should be. The table's elegantly woven cloth, an heirloom of his mother's, was as smooth as he'd left it. The silver cutlery was impeccably arranged and, in cabinets along the far wall, an assortment of chalices sat undisturbed. Higgins pivoted and surveyed the area immediately adjacent: no sign of ransacking whatsoever.

He released a breath, one he wasn't he had been holding, and felt his muscles unclench.

Despite the fire's present distance, it would be best to finish this swiftly. Stumbling through the murk, Higgins moved down a short hall and into the hearth room. Furniture was positioned about the fireplace in a decorative grid; he dodged lavish armchairs and tea tables and one particularly elaborate settee on his way to the mantelpiece. It was adorned with treasures, though there was only one of them that mattered: Eustace's vase. *His* vase. Manufactured of gold and twin bars of unalloyed silver, it was engraved with a brocade of jewels about its base. It was a symbol of virtue for Higgins. A prize worthy of the family name. If all else in Norick burnt away, *it* would be the one thing he chose to keep.

There was just one problem: The vase wasn't where it was supposed to be.

Higgins stared open-mouthed at a faint imprint, cleared of dust, where the vessel had once rested. Baffled, he spun and glanced about the room, eyes peeled for a glint of gold. He bent, scanning the surrounding floor space and peering into the hearth itself.

Nothing.

Breath coming in dense, viscous pulls, he scrambled from the floorboards and heaved himself up by the edge of the mantelpiece, uncaring of the strain upon its fastens. He swept his gaze along the rich dark wood and examined the other treasures, which appeared untouched. He leaned in closer. Blinked.

In the center of that imprint, something had been left behind. So small, and so dark, as to have blended in during his first inspection. Now, he whisked a hand forward, pried the thing from the shelf, and held it up for examination. A coin: brown, flimsy, and oval in shape. Norick's crest was stamped dead center, though the seal was crudely fashioned, without distinct texture or form.

A fleetle.

Little more than a bronze shaving, it was the smallest currency the town possessed. Higgins turned it over between his fingers, searching for additional markings or other peculiarities. Anything to provide a clue as to its meaning. But there was nothing: It was just a coin. Once more, Higgins found himself perplexed, unable to register what his eyes were taking in.

A fleetle? Why...?

Then the memory arrived, recognition slamming into place. Sudden-ly Higgins *knew*, and his heart spiked for his throat while a rage like fire consumed him from the inside—more forcefully, he was sure, than any physical blaze.

A fleetle. *His* fucking fleetle.

I'll kill her, he thought.

CHAPTER THIRTY-SEVEN

Before she heard the flames, or the screams; before the swell of destructive color blossoming over the town proper, an unnatural kindling of day amidst the inky threading of night—before any of that, before the desecration of everything she'd known and loved, Heather first smelt the smoke.

Crouching in her parents' bedchamber, she was trying, without success, to placate the woman crumpled beside her. Face cupped in her hands, Mumma wept, her whimpers so hysteric and irregular they could have been laughter. They emerged from beneath an unruly curtain of hair split over her long fingers, while the rest of her body, heaped in a blanket, visibly trembled. Her previous declarations—horrible, feverish things that hadn't made any sense—still twisted through Heather. In the dark, all but alone, she fretted over their meaning and shuddered with the implications.

It's coming for us. All of us.

You need to run.

The sudden tolling of the warning bell only served to amplify her dread. Heather froze, her heartbeat faltering in its rhythm. She swiveled and shot a glance toward the closed bedroom door, though the pealing came as much from the shuttered windows as from the entry. Next to her, Mumma went eerily silent.

Heather stumbled to her feet and lunged for the lever that would turn the shutters; Sara, crawling like some subterranean creature, pitched herself onto a mattress and, with childlike sniveling, pulled the quilts over her head. "Noooo…" she muttered beneath the covering. "Noooo. It's happening, it's—"

Heather wound the lever, and the slats cranked open to reveal the townscape beyond. She could see the grid of neighboring houses and, down the way, the roof of the Council Hall. Further on, the town walls rose rigid and earthy. Because of the echo, the chiming seemed to be originating from their stones. "Mumma?" Sara, buried beneath the blankets, said nothing in return. Heather kept her gaze out over the town and up into the foothills, tracing the source of that sound. "Mumma?" she said again.

"It's happening it's happening it's happening…"

Heather backed from the window, the peals excruciating in her ears, and spun to face her mother. "What's the bell mean? What's going on?"

"Peter," Sara whimpered, "come down from there, love. Please come down."

Stepping closer, Heather gently drew back the covers. Sara didn't resist, though she kept her back turned and her face shielded. Heather swallowed and considered poking the woman with a finger. "Come down from where? What're you talking about?"

"Peter… Peter…"

"Papa?" Heather's eyes widened. "Do you know where Papa is?"

"It has him now. He's screaming in the dark … I can hear his voice in my head."

Heather gulped, considered retreating. "What—?"

"He's telling it where to find us. He's telling it our names… It's coming, Heather." With a gasp, Sara bolted upright and flung the quilts aside. *"It's here."*

It was at that moment that a draft of wind shoved its way through the window, ruffling past the drapes and tousling Heather's hair. It veered toward her candle, whose wick had been a nub from the start, and snuffed out the light. Heather yelped as darkness, materializing from nowhere, from everywhere, swept in upon her. She staggered backward, disturbed by her mother's reaction, by the sudden black, by those two ominous words. *It's here.*

Immersed in darkness, eyes yet to adjust, Heather finally smelt the smoke.

At first, her recognition was a purely physical one: Her nose crinkled. Then her mind caught up with her senses and she sniffed. Another inhale later and she was sure. *Smoke.* She could smell smoke.

Her initial thought was that the scent belonged to the extinguished candle. But this was different, reminding her more of a burning woodstove, of things stripped and purged and reduced to ash. Void of the perfume of smoldering wax, the smell was actually a stench: chafing, caustic, invasive to the nostrils. A smell belonging to only one thing…

A fire. Heather's heart miss-stepped once more. *There's a fire somewhere in town.* Which would explain the tolling of the warning bell. Eyes adjusting, she whipped her head toward Sara, who'd gone silent after the candle blew out. The woman was again lying prone on the bed; Heather reached a hand forward and rolled her onto her side. She didn't react, her body as limp as a doll's. A glaze covered her eyes.

"Mumma…?" Sara didn't twitch, didn't blink, didn't seem capable of hearing a thing. There were just those same flat, gray cheeks; those same unseeing eyes. Heather checked Sara's pulse: faint, but there was still a heartbeat. With both hands, she rattled her shoulder; the woman flopped around like a fish. "Please wake up." Her pupils rolled aimlessly. "Papa says if there's a fire we need to get outside right away."

She didn't budge. For half a minute, two, Heather simply stood gaping at the bundled form sprawled out on the sheets. When she removed her hands, Sara wilted facedown into the mattress, dead to the world. *It's coming,* Mumma had said. Heather wondered now what that *it* had done to her.

Crippled by dread and an inexplicable wash of shame, Heather slumped to the floor. She couldn't wake Mumma, that much was clear. Nor could she carry her. Drag her, maybe, though the notion was overwhelming. She could run for help, but something about the scene—Sara's mania, her vulnerability, a sense that the woman was somehow exposed—made Heather hesitate. And so, scooting beneath the window in just the spot where she'd found Mumma, she did nothing.

Minutes vanished; an hour came. Time lost its meaning for Heather altogether. Mind on the disappearance of her father and on Sara's catatonic state, she huddled against the baseboard and wept—and listened as the flames advanced. Shouts filled the streets. Smoke choked the alleyways. Seething shades of orange and red flared across the tempest-covered sky.

The air warmed. Whole buildings seemed to be rending in two.

Still she didn't move.

Even after the evacuation order went up and a searcher crashed into the foyer below, hollering for stragglers, Heather remained silent. She couldn't say why, but as the man scurried between rooms and clomped halfway up the staircase, she huddled even lower to the wall and willed him from their home. It was only later that the thought came: The two of them, mother and daughter, were meant to be alone.

Finally, the man left, tramping back down the stairs, through the hearth room, and out the front door. Heather waited nearly a minute after he'd gone before raising her head. When she did so, she knew at once that everything had changed.

Sara sat vertical on the bed, ghostly in the near-darkness, her legs swinging over the edge with a childlike rhythm. Her eyes had lost all vacancy, but there was no warmth or affection in them, no trace of confusion or sorrow. The look Heather discovered there frightened her more than anything she'd ever seen; was worse, even, than the nightmare that plagued her dreams.

This look… This look was the end of everything.

"Milgrin's courage," her mother chuckled in a voice several octaves too deep. Strands of loose hair hung over her nose, her lips. "You should go now, little girl. Before you can't."

"I won't leave you. We'll go outside toge—"

"She's mine now, girl. Gone to see Papa. Do you wanna see Papa, too?"

Heather stiffened. She pushed herself to her feet. A corner of the windowsill caught her between the shoulder blades, and she grunted as the ledge scraped along her back. Across the room, those legs kept swinging, swinging, swinging.

"Wha—what are you?" Heather breathed.

"I'm your friend from the nightmare." A flash of white teeth shone through the darkness. "Don't you remember? Circling, getting closer and closer… You can never spot me, though, can you? I sure love listening to you scream."

Heather's palms were pasted against her earlobes, her fingers curled about her neck. The windowsill at her back wasn't enough to quell a sudden fit of trembling. Pinching her eyelids tight, she yelled to block out all other sound, to distract from the whirl of images circling in her head: "It's not real it's not real it's not real…"

"Shut your filthy mouth." Eyes bulging, teeth jutting, Sara plunged her nails into the curved edge of the mattress and pulled herself forward, preparing to pounce. "I told you to leave, you little bitch." The floorboards offered a horrid creak as her feet dropped roughly to the wood. "Now go— or burn."

And Heather did. With a yelp, she dashed for the door.

While, behind her, Sara offered a single throaty cackle, went suddenly rigid, and then collapsed to the bed.

CHAPTER THIRTY-EIGHT

Ellen. Ellen was reaching out for him, and if he could just meet her touch in time, just brush the merest ends of her fingertips, then he'd be able to save her. He knew he would. That's all it would take. He would pull her back from the brink; would draw her into his arms, wrap her tight, and tell her everything was going to be all right. I'm here now, love, he would say. I'm here now. I won't let you go. Never again. And Ellen would respond in kind.

Ellen. The light of his days. A midnight flower on a moonlit field. The anchor of his soul. The best person he'd ever known.

William reached for her.

And at the same time, in some distant place—away from her searching hand and the gleam of her black shoulder-length hair; away from those eyes, dark and astute, that seemed to hold all the vastness and complexity of galaxies—William reached also for the fisherman's boy, for Jacob Willow, who logic said was real.

Jacob Willow, who knelt across from him clutching a flaying knife.

Jacob Willow, who thrust that same blade into the veins of his wrist and, in one quick jerk, pulled it back along his forearm in a rush of shriek and blood.

Mind half in one realm and half in another, William lunged for the boy—who was also Ellen—and together they spiraled over the grass, grappling for possession of the weapon. Ellen—or maybe it was Jacob—yowled as they spun. Pushing his advantage, William looped both arms around the boy and attempted to lock his fingers. Jacob sensed the snare and countered with even more thrashing. William held firm, gritting his teeth, and swung both legs over Jacob's own, pinning them to the ground.

"Stop, Ellen." She continued wriggling. "I'm trying to save you, don't you understand?" A carnal grunt issued beneath him, and the squirming intensified. "It's me, Elle. It's Will."

"Ellen, stop!"

Ellen—the boy—froze, her resistance vanishing. Other than the wheezing of their breaths, everything went silent. Then, softly, a whisper between pants: "What…? Who?"

"Ellen, it's…" But now William wasn't so sure either. His mind felt fragmented, the pieces all jumbled and rearranged—and not in any proper order. He could feel Jacob snug in his grip; at the same time, he was also with Ellen, back on that icy winter morning as she bled out on the midwife's cot. For a moment, he couldn't decide which of these scenarios was real. Each seemed tenuous, shadowy, like the fragments of a dream infiltrating the first light of dawn. "Ellen, I…" As his voice faltered, he reared his neck and stared at the patch of hair bristling against his chin. The hair was blond—wheat-blond.

Not black.

William's stomach lurched with vertigo. *How did that— Did I really just…?* He felt foolish, but more so was he alarmed at the ease with which his mind had misplaced itself, ignoring all parameters of time and logic to shunt itself back into the past. *I'm going fuckin' mad.*

Head reeling, he surveyed the ground on either side. The knife lay a few yards off to their right, flung there sometime during the course of the melee. If he were quick, he thought he could reach it before Jacob did. "Don't move," he commanded in a low tone. "Do not move."

He released his hold gradually, ready to reapply pressure if the boy attempted a dash. Jacob, however, remained still, his body limp. Whatever force had propelled him was gone.

William slid out from beneath him and stood, blinking to clear his head. *Don't think about her. Just don't think…* No longer supported, Jacob sagged to the prickly cushion of grass and, with a whimper, clutched at his wrist. A new sense of dismay passed through William at the sight: He'd foiled Jacob's attempts but, if he didn't act swiftly, it wouldn't matter. The boy would bleed out.

Jogging to the knife, William slid it into his belt. Next, he retrieved his torch and sword and returned to Jacob's side. The boy's eyes were closed, his lips quivering. He was curled nearly into a ball. His face had lost all color.

William swallowed, rethinking his approach. "Jacob? Can you hear me?" The boy mumbled something incoherent. His right hand covered the wound loosely, far from the center of the incision, as if it were an afterthought. Crimson threads leaked out from beneath his fingers, spilling to the grass below.

His movements rapid and precise, William set to work covering the wound and fashioning a tourniquet. His belt, stripped of its adornments, was the perfect size. He lobbed both his sword and the knife to a safe distance, then cinched the band tight. Jacob grimaced as the leather constricted about his elbow but made no further indication he understood what was happening. Nodding at his handiwork, William shifted back and prepared to hoist the boy up. It was rough terrain getting back to town, and the shock of the journey could very well kill Jacob, but William had no choice. *I'm going to save you*, he thought.

Accepting that he would have to leave the torch and the weapons behind, he scooped his hands beneath Jacob and secured a hold. As he did so, the fisherman's son opened his eyes, blinked groggily, and spoke. "I didn't mean to," he breathed, his voice pinched and wavering. "I swear I didn't mean to."

"I know," said William, bracing to lift him. He didn't meet Jacob's eye.

"It ... it made me."

William grew very still. Jacob was staring off over his shoulder, toward Ash. "Who made you? The person who killed Mr. Ash? Is he still here somewhere?"

The boy wouldn't look at him. "It made me..."

"*Who*, Jacob? Where is he?"

It was as if the fisherman's son couldn't hear him. The look in his eyes had gone from guilt and panic to outright terror. Finally, his gaze settled on William. "It killed 'em. It killed all of them."

"What are you talking about? Is someone else hurt?"

"It'll make me do it." Jacob was sobbing now in earnest. "One day, it'll make me... It's my fault, it's all my fault."

"Quit speaking nonsen—"

"I deserve this! I deserve to *die*." William drew back at the boy's outburst, startled by the words themselves but more so by the urgency that bore them. "Just leave me here," Jacob continued. "Let me die."

"Don't be a bloody fool. You're going to live, boy. I'm taking you back to town. Right now." And William meant to. He slid his arms beneath Jacob, pulled him tight to his chest, and, driving the ground away with a kneecap, began lifting them both from the grass.

"It won't let you." Jacob's voice—quiet, timid—emerged halfway up their ascent. "It's not going to let us go anywhere." William peered down at Jacob, but the boy's eyes looked past him, gawking in horror at the swirling storm clouds above. All night, a nameless sense of dread had pestered William's every step, all the way back to the call of that wine. All night, he'd tried to ignore the disquiet, but the feeling had never truly faded, and he could feel it now deep in his bones as he stared into Jacob's eyes. The boy had seen something. Something horrible, something beyond words.

Something that's still out there.

A tremor of fear jolted through William, and his skin crawled with the touch of invisible eyes. Not daring to turn around, he continued studying Jacob's petrified face.

"It's coming," the boy whispered.

William's own voice was little more than a breath. Dreading the answer, but incapable of suppressing the question, he asked, "Who?" But Jacob shook his head vigorously, refusing to answer. "Who's coming?" William pressed, still in an undertone. "Jacob, tell me who."

There was a moment of nature's ordered chaos—thunder rumbling, wind howling, the Grove's laden branches grating out a mournful song—then the response finally arrived.

But it was not the boy who answered.

CHAPTER THIRTY-NINE

"Willllliaaam…"

From out of the blackness the voice came: came from nowhere, from everywhere. From inside him and from afar; from all things at once. It danced about him in a befuddling arrangement of sound, skittering through the rows of fruit trees, mingling with the clouds. It tickled his neck hairs; it crooned into his eardrums. It emerged, last of all, from the site of Peter Ash's demise: that ugly encumbered tower, as if the dead man himself were speaking.

One word, that's all it was. Whispered and drawn out like an opera singer's vibrato. It was dressed up in a certain playfulness, a certain wicked glee, but beneath its slick veneer lay a rotten core.

One word, but it was enough.

William reeled, spinning his head like someone deranged. He could feel his mind unraveling within him, a disintegration of every belief he'd held to be true. *I'm losing my mind,* he thought, *I'm—*

"Willllliaaam…"

Once more the voice funneled through him, and he winced as if struck, mouth flapping open. In his arms, Jacob released a whimper and burrowed himself against William's chest. The captain's eyes raced across the orchard, though he knew intuitively that the sound hadn't come from the trees. Fear quaked its way up his thighs as he regarded that cool, empty darkness. There appeared to be nothing present—nothing physical at least.

Which didn't mean they were alone.

It can't be, he thought. *It can't—*

"Can't it, William? Are you so quick to doubt?" The words sliced through his nerves like a grated spike. This time his legs gave out completely, and, in a plunge—the world upending around them—he and Jacob toppled to the earth.

They crashed hard. Jacob yelped; William grunted. Carried by their momentum, the boy tumbled from William's arms and rolled away. He buried his face into the grass. The development was nothing William could process; winded, lying on his side like a broken vessel, he shielded his eyes. *It's not true, it's not true, it's not true.* He hadn't so much heard the words as felt them; they flared like the worst throbs of a migraine. A personality existed behind them, the feel of inner workings, but most of all there seemed to be anger: a sense of loathing, thinly veiled, underpinning every syllable. William knew this voice; he'd heard it before, during the nightmare. Its resurgence rang like a death knell in his ears, in his skull, in every frayed nerve of his being.

It suddenly became clear: The wine, the fire, the children, the corpse— all of it had been a misdirect. From the beginning, the voice had been leading him here, to this very moment. Manipulating him—though for what purpose, William didn't dare speculate.

"William, William, William," chanted the voice as he desperately willed himself back into sanity. "Foolish, doubting William. Do you not remember? I showed you so much. And we're not finished yet. No, Captain, there is still so much left for us to accomplish..."

William dug his nails into his scalp. "Stop! Please stop..." The torch rested on the ground nearby, though it may as well have been a thousand leagues away. Just then, its light seemed the dimmest in all the earth. Losing sight of it, William writhed upon the ground.

"Oh, William," the voice warbled, softer now. An unnatural chill blotted the air, accompanied by a foulness, a reek: the stench of burning hair, festering fruit, decomposing meat. Nausea tossed about in William's gut; he retched, but nothing came up. Elsewhere, the voice continued its ebb and flow, converging upon the watchtower. William could feel its chuckle as it peered down from the perch. Its sneer as he dry-heaved.

"William, William, Willlllliaaam..."

He attempted to claw himself up. "What. Do..." He had to grind the words out over the turmoil in his stomach, the compression of his bowels. "You. Want from me?"

"Come and see."

The corpse and its rope loomed in shadow, Peter Ash's bloated face all but concealed. Across his limbs and torso, those crude markings caught the torchlight and danced before William's eyes. As they seared through his consciousness, he at last understood their meaning: They were a ritual. A summoning.

"Come, William. See what I have to show you." Propped on an elbow, clutching at his sides, he peered up at the cone of darkness centered around Ash's head. The dark leered back, and William's awareness slid.

"This can't be. This can't—"

"Come, come, come…"

The call was nothing he could now resist. He heaved himself up and, huffing air in gasps, he started toward the watchtower.

He glanced at Jacob as he passed. The boy, a mere pawn in the voice's schemes, lay inert, having succumbed to shock. *Or he's dead*, William amended. *Just like the rest*. He didn't have time to consider it further; the watchtower and the voice were waiting. Staggering forward through a rush of vertigo, he crossed the final span of the orchard and, in a half-trip, half-dive, flung himself before the dead man's feet.

He looked up; the soles were caked with mud and loose gravel. Dried blood spattered one of the ankles. Like a dancer's, Ash's feet twirled first this way and then that, this way and then that: a creaking coil of rope and flesh.

William realized he'd landed in something moist. A sticky fluid coated his arms, belly, and chest. Some had smeared on his throat. His first thought was that it was blood, but as he raised himself onto his forearms, he saw the substance was an artificial red, all too vibrant. He scrambled to his rear and shoved himself away.

With the extra distance, the shape of it became clear: four sentences, scrawled onto the grass in thick, glossy smudges. There was an appearance of haste in their composition, some of the letters quite large, others bafflingly small. Three of the lines veered off at a peculiar angle, almost as if a young child had drawn them. William read the message once, twice, a third time. His heart stuttered. *You are trespassers here … I will come for you all.*

"Yes, William," hissed the voice while he read. "Yessss."

These words were not just arcane statements or idle threats. Neither were they the ramblings of some desperate, delusional man. These, William understood, were promises.

Air coming in fits, he scooted back even further, the surrounding fruit trees lifting their branches in grim salutation. "That's right, William," the voice whispered from Ash's eclipsed face. "*I* brought you here. You belong to *me*."

William gaped, unable to muster a scream. The priests and holy men of the South had been right, he thought. All along, after all this time, and they had been right. Skeletal, elusive, more outline than actual consideration, these notions drifted by as his insides quivered like the plucked fiber of a bowstring. *We made a mistake*, he thought, this time more solidly. *We never should have come here.*

"No," returned the voice, "no, you shouldn't have."

CHAPTER FORTY

Out beyond the walls, the people of Norick waited, and they grieved.

They were the daughters and sons of explorers. They were the progeny of the righteous and the seekers and those bold enough to venture into the unknown. They were sired of hope, raised in virtue.

They were the last in a line.

Like mice fleeing a flood, they scattered from the tavern, the Market Square, the dingy side streets. Mindless, becoming something less than human, they surrendered themselves to their instincts: escape, survival, at whatever the cost. They soon remembered themselves, however, as they congregated at the base of the foothills—gathering together for one last communal purpose, one they all felt obligated to fulfill: watching their home perish.

Norick blazed like a funeral pyre before them. A cloud of ash—all that was left of their belongings, all that was left of their hopes, their memories, their dreams—swirled off toward a horizon of sharp mountain peaks. Women wailed as they watched it go; their children shrieked. Fathers, lips trembling, pulled their families close, shielding small eyes with big bodies. As if they could somehow—if only for moment—block out fate.

Thomas Calvin, the winemaker's son, observed the proceedings with, curiously enough, a growing sense of boredom. He didn't know where Natalie was, though at the moment he didn't care. (*What does it matter to me? The idiot ran off.*) She'd always been temperamental, that one. Shrewd and levelheaded one minute, then emotional to a fault in the next. (*Like all bloody women. She's probably staying away on purpose so that we worry about her. Bloody selfish, I tell you what.*)

Christopher Willow, Natalie's father, stood a dozen paces to Thomas's left and shivered as his mind was pulled back into the past. His thoughts were set on his own father, Old Joe, who'd perished in that squall all those years prior. The feeling in his gut now—roiling with a palpable sense of unease, like a bundle of tightening knots—was the same as when he'd watched that lethal tempest approach and begged for Old Joe to come home.

Behind Willow, town guardsman Riley Ford gripped his wide-set hips and wheezed. He stared at Norick in vague disappointment, knowing none of his efforts could alleviate the assault of those flames. In this fateful battle, he was just like the others: helpless—*Useless*—and unable to prove his worth.

Lucas Illhap, the tavern owner, attempted to wipe a trail of soot from his puckered lips. Already he could feel a smear coating his tongue.

Close by, little Codiah Longford thought not of fire but of horses, and the one he'd guided from the stable. He wondered now if it had been painful, when he slit Bravia's throat. He wondered if he should have instead left her inside to die alongside her friends. At the time, the killing had felt like a mercy.

The winemaker, Marcus Calvin, thought about all the bottles and casks he'd left inside. He clenched his meaty hands in fury. His entire livelihood … gone, boiling up into the night. He couldn't have said why, but he suspected all of this was somehow that damn captain's fault.

Lerrick 'Night-Eyed' Rose stood on shifting feet. Alternating his weight from one foot to the other, he peered over the mass of townspeople and tried to ignore the fuzziness muddling his view. Ashamed of his failing eyesight, the eccentric theater head had decided against searching for Vernon amongst the crowd, instead choosing to assume his son was safely huddled somewhere in the back.

Off to his right, near the throng's eastern flank, the barmaid Julie Temult was freshly returned from the wharf. Slinking into their midst, she paced and fiddled with her hands. Her palms, just then, felt unaccountably sticky.

The misplaced younglings, latecomers as well, clustered near their guide. The chancellor's son, equal parts entranced and disturbed by the flames, had forgotten about the murdered council member, about Jacob Willow, about Breeve's harried flight to intervene. In his stupor, Brade wouldn't remember to send help until it was already much too late.

The people of Norick: the daughters and sons of explorers. The progeny of the righteous. They were sired of hope, raised in virtue.

They were the last in a line.

CHAPTER FORTY-ONE

She would have to leave her. A horrible, unforgivable thought, but there it was: if Heather wished to survive the night, she would have to abandon her mother.

Abandon her to the fire. Abandon her to that *thing*.

Racing down the staircase, Heather could still hear its voice in her head. Could still see those glossy, unfeeling eyes piercing through the dark. *I told you to leave, you little bitch. Now go—or burn.*

She hadn't looked back. She couldn't have even if she'd wanted to. Terror pumped through her veins like a swollen river; panic threatened to rip her lungs in two. She stampeded into the hearth room, its assorted furniture lying like snares waiting to trip her up. She shoved a decorative table, a whole sofa, aside. Between the bookshelves, the portrait of Rufus Milgrin shuddered on its rivet, awakened by the thudding of her footsteps.

She was out the front door without hardly having taken a breath. Free of the house and its unholy occupants, Heather guzzled air with her arms draped over her head. She looked around. Every house on the block—every structure in sight—shrieked beneath the onslaught of flame. Plumes of smoke funneled over her like fat, voracious fingers prying for space. Eyes smarting, lips trembling, Heather squinted through the sooty miasma and tried to hold back a cough.

Inside the house, she'd come face to face with unspeakable terror. Out there: She was ensnared in a valley of flame.

A landslide of foreboding crashed down upon her, and claustrophobia tightened like a noose. She was trapped: No matter where she turned, no matter what she did, disaster would always follow her. She was cursed.

She was helpless. She was—

You can still make it out. The thought drew her eyes toward the road. There were flaming mountains on either side, but the lane itself remained unclogged, merely sprinkled with debris. If she moved quickly, she could still escape without much trouble. Who knew what the rest of the town looked like, but if she could just rid herself of this street—and its proximity to the monster—then that would be enough. She'd figure out the rest from there.

And Mumma? Heather's stomach cartwheeled, and she whipped around, peering up over her shoulder toward their second-story windows. Tears flowed freely as she bit at the side of her cheek, knowing it too late, knowing there was nothing at all she could do.

That wasn't her mother up there. Not anymore. Whatever that thing was, it had taken ahold of Sara's body and ferried away her soul. The woman she'd known was long gone, and if that were the case, she wouldn't really be leaving Mumma if she left now, she would simply be doing the sensible thing.

Right?

Mumma would want her to save herself; she would understand. There wasn't any hope in fighting a creature like that. Its power was too great, its hatred too deep. And—most of all—Heather was scared, so desperately scared.

Fight that thing? She wouldn't even begin to know how. Her only choice was to flee. "I'm sorry, Mumma," she whispered up toward the windows. "Forgive me. I'm so sorry..."

Eyes closed, she wobbled from the stoop.

CHAPTER FORTY-TWO

The voice was a thunderous echo in William's skull. It shredded through his awareness. It burrowed like a claw.

Were he able, he would have fled. If his legs had still been functioning properly—if they were solid and accessible rather than watery and abstract—he would've scampered up and away and never once looked back. He would've abandoned Jacob to his fate and not felt a moment's qualm about it. He would have run until he collapsed.

Instead, he was left to tremble and stammer for breath.

"But why go?" asked the voice, mindful of his intentions. "You and I are friends. Can't you see that? We can help each other."

William shivered, not daring to look up. A friend of the voice—a friend to this *thing*? The thought was enough to sour the scant supply of air he had left. "This is how it's meant to be," the voice went on. "You and I together. That's why I brought you here—so we can be friends. All you have to do is invite me in. That's it. And then I can fix you."

"I don't need fixing. I'm … I'm … I don't need fixing." But as soon as he'd spluttered out the words, a familiar wretchedness cut through him, summoned as if on cue.

"There's no need for falsehoods here. I know you, William. I know all about Ellen and Landon and what happened to you in the South. And I can make all of it go away. I can make you feel alive again. You just have to let me in."

William's mind burned with memories of them: all the bad—but the good ones too, which were worst of all.

Gagging from the stench permeating the air, he tumbled forward and buried his face into his hands. The wind, in its madcap dash through the trees, seemed amused. "As I'd thought," said the voice, mirroring the sentiment. "There's no sense deceiving yourself, William. It's obvious: Their memories haunt you. But they don't have to.

"As I said, I can fix this. I can fix *you*. I know what you desire. You want to save the town. You want to belong. I can give you all that. I can grant you the strength to rescue them, to stop the fire." The voice was as smooth as silk now, a masterful stage performer guiding along a rapt audience. "You will be a hero. The champion of Norick, beloved by all."

William said nothing, though the offer was more appealing than he would ever admit.

The voice pressed on. "Better yet, I can help you overthrow the Council. I know how they've treated you. All the lies and little games they play. Those swine; those greedy, self-righteous bastards. I can destroy them for you. I can make them into fools before the people, can drive them into madness until they're the brunt of every joke in Norick. The High Council will be yours for the taking." William had gone rigid. The longing was now almost a physical need. "You'll rule this town; it'll be your kingdom. Whatever you wish to do—own any object, bed any woman, kill any man—no one will stop you.

"I can gut that prick, Brade Higgins, for you. Remember how he mocked you, how he spat on Ellen's memory... Don't let him get away with it. Show him who you are. Show him what happens to disrespectful little fools. I will make him squeal until he begs for mercy."

The impulse to rise, take up his sword, and hunt down the chancellor's son nearly overwhelmed him. Instead, he jammed his fingers into his ears and shook.

"You're so lonely, William. After all these years, and still alone. I can get you any woman you like. I can make them quiver with longing at your feet. Just name one and I'll—"

"No." It was his first word in what felt like hours. His grief, cold and sharp, had pried him loose. *It's pushing me toward madness,* he thought, finally able to summon an idea independent of the voice. *It's trying to weaken me, to tempt me away. I have to stay strong.*

His resolve vanished the moment the voice next spoke. "I can take you to *her*. All you have to do is let me in. Just say yes, and I'll show you

Ellen—and Landon. You can be with them again. You can be a family."

The voice might be nudging him toward madness, but so be it. *Let it,* he thought. Damn it all, let the thing do with him as it pleased. He no longer had the strength, nor the desire, to resist.

"Let me show you, William. Don't you want to see Ellen again?"

The words emerged in an outpour, nothing that could be stopped. "I want to see them! *Please.* Show me … just show me—"

The air in William's lungs outright fled as movement caught his eye. He jerked his head up: To the left of the watchtower, a shadowy figure had appeared. His mouth flopped open, his eyes blinking of their own accord. *Ellen.*

It was Ellen, come back to him at last.

Which couldn't be.

Dressed in a flowing black gown, she seemed to float above the carpeting of grass, her features blurry, indistinct, though growing clearer with each passing second. Milky white skin shone in sharp contrast to the orchard's gloom, while sleek black hair hung in straight lines down her cheeks. Regret—and a strange emptiness—clouded her eyes. "Elle?" he whispered, inching closer, trying to focus the image in his mind. Not yet daring to believe. "Elle, is that you?" Her form wavered like a mirage in the summer heat, though William had never felt colder. He may as well have been buried in ice.

She offered him a slow, sad smile as the details of her body solidified. Hazy curves hardened into concrete edges; patches of skin darkened into a more natural hue. As her bare feet kissed the grass for the first time, she nodded and held back a sob. It was a gesture of such humanness that William nearly wept. Instead, pushing right through the painted message, he clambered forward like a beggar and cast himself at her feet. "Ellen… I've missed you so much. I couldn't save you. I lost you. I—" A sob halted the flow of his words, and he nestled his face into the ground, forgetting altogether about the glide of the voice and the weight of its sting.

He sensed her leaning down: not so much a noise or a shuffle as a peculiar charge to the air, as though the molecules themselves were being rattled loose. "Do it, Will," she whispered, and the hair on his forearms prickled. "Invite it in."

Overcome by the smell of her—the rich floral fragrance of her perfume—William struggled to raise his eyes. Ellen now knelt in front of him, her legs tucked away neatly, and cradled something in her arms. William whimpered as the bundle took shape.

It was an infant. Swaddled in a tattered green cloth, its face was just visible: two pressed wedges for eyes; a flattened nose; thin, pink curves for lips. A wisp of downy black hair. Skin that was a soft, translucent blue.

It was a boy—*his* boy.

Landon.

Across from him, Ellen was absorbed in that little green bundle, her arms taking on a gentle sway. "Say yes, Will." Her voice was light and airy, as if he too were just a child. "That's all you have to do. Don't you want to be with me again? Don't you miss us? I need you." She tipped her head affectionately toward Landon, who didn't seem to be moving at all. "*We* need you.

"Just say yes."

William blinked. Such a simple command, with such a simple answer. Over the past four years, he would've given anything to have them back, would've traded any amount of gold or friends or pleasure—even his own life—just for few more moments. Now he had the chance, and all he had to do was say this one word? It was almost too easy.

Too easy...

Something's not right, a morsel of logic whispered, sneaking its way to the forefront. *She—it—is pushing too hard. It's desperate. Don't say a word.*

Feeling like a traitor, William kept his mouth shut and begged her with a stare. *Please be real. Please let this be true.* But it was too late: The spell was broken. He could hear the groan of the rope overhead; he could see the dead man's dirty feet. And that baby—that strange, beautiful, blue-skinned baby—still hadn't moved, its little arms tucked uselessly out of sight. *Why's he so still? Why's his skin so blue?*

Because he isn't living, William's logic responded as the pieces reassembled. *Because he's already dead.*

That wasn't Landon over there. Landon was gone—had always been gone, had never even taken a breath. William remembered holding on to his lifeless body, no bigger than a grapefruit, before laying him in the soil next to his mother. He remembered the pile of dirt. The shovel. How the sun had seemed to shimmer that day: pale winter light peeking through a migration of cloud.

No, that wasn't his son. It couldn't be.

So then, what *was* that thing?

William ripped panicked eyes from Ellen's arms to her face. "No. That's not him. That's not Landon. It's impossible."

Despite the outburst, Ellen was still smiling—smiling and rocking the baby, though there was a strained quality to her expression now, and it wasn't from sorrow. "What are you talking about? Use your eyes. It's our boy. Our baby boy. Remember all the dreams we had for him? All our plans?"

"No. That isn't him. It can't be. I *buried* him."

"You buried me, too, Will." Her tone was casual, off-hand. She could have been remarking upon the weather.

William was backing away now, retreating. "I know I did. I can still feel that shovel. The blisters. You're not her. This isn't real."

"It's me, Will," she said, reaching an anxious hand after him—though still not making contact. Her figure flickered like a candle flame covered and uncovered in rapid succession. "Don't you remember me? Don't you love me?" Tears pooled in her eyes as she went on. "You just have to say the word, Will. You just have to say yes. Let *it* in and then all of this will be over, and we can be together again."

"No… I can't."

"You must, my dear. I love you. You know that. More than anything. So come back to me."

William shielded his face with his hands. "No… None of this is real. It's just a dream…"

"Say it, Will. Please. I love you. Say yes to inviting it in."

"You're not her, you're not her, you're not—" He rolled onto his side, knees curled to his chest, his entire body quaking.

"Say the words!" The sudden change in pitch cut through his nerves like a blade. It was still Ellen's voice but deeper, misshapen into something darker, more animalistic. It was enough to summon his gaze.

The change in her voice was chilling; the sight that awaited him was much, much worse.

Ellen's cheeks had tightened. Her eyes were slits. Imperfections, previously concealed, were now rampant: the sagging skin beneath her

jawline; a host of scars, moles, and wrinkles; a cemetery of stained and broken teeth. The shape of her arms—once natural, healthy—was now a rigid
contour of bone, grotesque in its sharpness. Gone was her floriated scent,
replaced by the musk of ripening hide and moldering wheat. Her entire
appearance, her very essence, was one of decay.

The transformation was ghastly enough to send William skittering
away. "What the fuck what the fu—"

"Say it!" In a rage, the wraith leapt up and hurled the child from its
arms. The bundle bounced once, soundlessly, before tumbling out of view,
all of it happening too quickly for William to scream. He tried not to look.
Tried not to imagine the ground's impact with those little bones. Instead,
he thrust himself to his knees.

"You're not real!" he shouted, his voice notching up to match the
wraith's. "You're not bloody real!"

The spirit froze, and once more it seemed to flicker, just briefly. Rolling its tongue over those horrid teeth, it glared at him. "I'll show you real."

The change was instantaneous. The wind, impossibly, up and stopped.
In its wake, an uncanny silence descended, one deeper and more piercing
than any sound. The sudden stillness had the effect of altering the torch's
burn, sending its flame in a new direction and thus illuminating a different
section of the Grove. Ash's swollen face was now fully illuminated.

The magistrate was bleeding from his mouth, nose, and those two
gaping eye sockets: huge waterfalls of black-crimson fluid that spilled
down his cheeks and plummeted to the grass below. A gash formed at his
stomach; it ruptured, and a chute of blood poured out from there as well.
One of his legs moved. It kicked up, then halted midway through its ascent.
Seconds later, it jerked to the right, snapping at the knee with a bone-shattering *crunch*.

Terror impaled William like a spear. He averted his eyes. What he saw
next was better only by the slightest of degrees. Jacob, too, had begun to
move. Though unconscious, the boy convulsed as if he were being probed
by a legion of unseen hands. His body rolled first one way then the other.

It rose.

It hovered there, levitating two or three feet above the grass as a series
of long, tracing cuts webbed up the boy's forearms, stomach, and legs. The
wounds flared a bright angry red, each incision grisly in the capsized torch's

wavering glow.

Unable to endure the scene a moment longer, William dropped his gaze. "How is that for *real*?" the wraith snarled. At its words, the wind roared back into existence. "Shall I snap his neck just so you're sure?" William didn't dare return his eyes to Jacob. He refused even the thought of glancing up toward Ash. Just then, he may as well have been chiseled in stone.

"Let me in. Surrender your flesh." Mustering every ounce of willpower he had left, William shook his head. "What, you think you can save him? You think you can still rescue this pathetic town?" He stayed quiet, cowering beneath the spirit's gaze. Ashamed at the truth of those words. "This is *my* home. *I* decide who lives or dies."

The wraith, never once touching the ground, drifted to him. "I never loved you," it said, the voice fully Ellen's now. William understood, in some far-off way, that it wasn't actually her speaking, but it didn't matter: The words cut. "You understand that? I hated you. You were never good enough. You were never more than a lost cause. I didn't love you, William. I *pitied* you."

William seized as if struck, and he crumpled to his forearms. The spirit towered over him. "Poor, poor William. Forced from his home, forced to fight in the wars. How often did I have to listen to that sob story? How often did I have to hold you while you sniveled and begged for forgiveness? What kind of man is that? What kind of husband? I wasted my life on you. You and your self-pity—and all because you couldn't let the past die."

William moaned, nodding into his palms. Because that was the thing: The spirit was right. It was right about everything. He was pathetic. He was unlovable. He was the most wretched human to ever live.

"You didn't deserve me," the phantom growled. "You always knew that. Yet still you brought me down with you. You're selfish. You're filth. *Invite me in.*"

Tapping a reserve of strength he didn't know he possessed, William said nothing. Though he wanted to. He wanted nothing more than for all this to be done with. He knew what awaited once he spoke those words, but he didn't care. He deserved this.

"It's because of you I died. You know that, right? Deep down, you always suspected your sins would catch up to you. Always thought you might be cursed. Well they did, and you are. All sins require an atonement. A head for a head. My life for theirs. *You* killed me, William. Only you."

William shook, and he wept. *Stay strong*, some inner part of him counseled. *Endure.* Another part, a roar over the tenuous breath of that whisper, urged him to concede. He desired then, above all else, to die.

"I promise you," the spirit continued, "if you don't do as I say, you'll suffer like no man ever has. Every step will be agony. Every breath like fire in your lungs. I'll never let you sleep another night in your life. You'll hear your boy crying out for you. You'll hear Ellen fucking another man. I'll hollow you out until there's nothing left. You will never know peace."

He tried to lower himself further into the grass: tried to disappear, to fade into nothing. *Help me*, he begged the universe at large. If this creature was real, then maybe there were other forces out there as well. Ones that just might intervene. *Somebody—anybody. Please.*

"You will be cursed, an outcast. The people will spit on you. They'll attack you openly in the streets. And still I won't let you die. Not until I take everything." The wraith drew closer, its presence—and its reek—smothering him. "Do you know what will happen then? You will go mad and kill yourself. And then I'll be waiting for you on the other side.

"So invite me in."

He looked up without meaning to. Teeth bared, the apparition dissected him with its eyes. William stared into their depths and again yearned for the release of oblivion. *Endure*, that inner whisper insisted. *Don't let it win.* He didn't know where these thoughts came from; he was hardly aware of them. They were a flickering ember in an ocean of darkness. They were one last blossoming of hope, waiting, like always, to be quashed for good.

They were nothing.

The wraith shattered the silence with another barrage, its voice a force of unfathomable rage: "Say yes, you fucking maggot!"

The strength to resist vanishing at last—thoughts of Ellen and Landon drifting through him though providing no measure of comfort, instead serving as reminders of his guilt and shame—William Breeve, man of sorrow, man of death, opened his mouth to speak.

PART NINE

THE LIGHT
BENEATH THE DARK

Even in the darkness,
Stars shine.

CHAPTER FORTY-THREE

Out on the jetty, Mary Fern stood alone. She wasn't moving, old Ms. Fern. She didn't need to. The battle was here already. The great struggle for them all was already being waged.

And *it* was winning.

Mary Fern, who had lived over a hundred years and ventured to the uncharted waters, a horizon without name. Who had visited, and dwelt, in the Silent Lands. Who'd walked through the fires of Fwenlock, unmaimed.

Mary Fern, who had lived so long now her inner self was like an ocean of stars, the pinpricks of light all the days and days of her life. Between them flowed the great current of the universe, a fathomless tide on which she was eternally adrift. From it came the *knowing*—a separate stream, somehow deeper, more elusive, a presence like pure light, older than time itself. She was connected to that presence; how or why, she didn't dare speculate, but she was, and it flowed through her in a flood of purpose and peace. It was apart from her, that presence, apart from all the world, and yet it was still in accordance, still sown into the very fabric of their being: a mystery beyond all comprehension.

Mary Fern—a founder, a wanderer. Someone who had glimpsed the very truth of the universe but, at times, still felt like that fraught little girl from all those years before: so lost, so broken; a memory of a dream, a dream of a memory. An unrelenting curse.

Mary Fern: dreamer, keeper, warrior.

With her back turned to the town and the inferno within, she stood looking out over the bay. Searching. The current stirred within her, but it was silent and distant. The sea was as black as tar, churning as the world itself threatened to boil over. The voice, a darkness of another sort, cackled in the roaring buffets of wind. Some primordial balance had been severed, and the pendulum was now suspended upward, frozen in place.

Darkness; there was only darkness.

Mary's heart threatened to rupture with the terror of it. As she struggled back, pushing against its weight, her reedy limbs nearly collapsed.

But then, as if from nowhere, as if the very air had breathed it into being: a flash of lightning. Just that. A sheet of white-green luminescence flaring between the folds of the clouds. In its wake, Mary could feel a curious prickling on her forearms as its static spread.

That light: so transient, so brief. Receding before it'd even completed its entire tract. But so too was it brilliant, dazzling even. A show of irrevocable beauty, like a simple child's song.

Evil assaults with a roar, but the light wins with a whisper.

As Mary recited the old adage, a stirring began in her gut—and with it, power. *Yes... Yes!* How could she lose sight of this? How could she doubt? She smiled at herself then while another streak of lightning burned across the reef of clouds overhead, spreading through every crack and covering every ridge.

The light. It was so simple really, so assured. A truth she had always known. The light: Even in the darkness, the light would find a way to crackle and shine. Even now, in this blackest of hours, it had refused to flee.

Even now, they were not alone.

CHAPTER FORTY-FOUR

The sobs overtook Heather halfway up the block. Her chest shook with the force of them. Her knees threatened to cave. Robed in a garment of smoke, she jarred to a halt.

A memory had returned to her: watching her father depart, alone, into the night. She thought of her indecision and failure to follow him. She thought of the racking guilt that'd seized her ever since. *Not again,* she decided, her hands squeezing into fists. *Never again.*

It didn't matter whether or not Mumma was already gone. It didn't matter how powerful that monster back there really was. She couldn't just leave. Not now, not without trying. If there was even a chance of saving Mumma, she had to take it. The woman would do the same for her. *She needs me. I can't abandon her.*

I won't.

Heather pivoted. Down the street, their roof cavorted with heavy spurts of flame. The walls below it were haloed in a hellish orange glow, their windows flaring like giant spiteful eyes. The front entry, meanwhile, loomed in darkness, tendrils of smoke snaking inside.

Heather tensed, her balled-up hands trembling at the sight. Blinking past fat droplets of sweat, she gulped. She prayed.

She sprinted toward home.

CHAPTER FORTY-FIVE

It was rage as much as a yearning for survival that finally pushed Skylar Higgins from his home.

I'll kill her, he thought. *I swear to Milgrin I'll strike her dead.*

His limbs were not his own; without guidance, they led him from the hearth room, down the corridor, and out the front door. He stumbled over the steps and into the street, where his senses were immediately flooded. Nevertheless, he found himself incapable of dwelling on anything save that singular, insatiable impulse: *I'll kill her.*

If he found her, he would. By Milgrin and all the Fifty, he swore she would regret the day she'd chosen to cross him. The barmaid—that filthy barmaid. He wasn't even sure of her name, but it didn't matter. He could recall her face perfectly, could picture the peculiar shape of that nose. He would find her all right, and when she begged for mercy, for even an inkling of kindness, he would offer nothing more than saliva in return.

She'd stolen it—stolen *everything.* This was her fault. Because of her depravity, weakness had been allowed to infiltrate and fester among them. *She* was the reason Norick's integrity had failed; *she* was the source of the breach. Higgins would see to it that she was rooted out like a weed. He would make her pay. He would enact a punishment that fit the crime.

He would—

Boot catching a loose chunk of pavement, Higgins careened toward the street. He flailed like a clipped pigeon before hurtling against the cobblestone, striking face-first. There was a terrible jolt through his teeth, and the tang of blood coated his gums. He'd bitten his tongue.

A groan was all he could muster. A chip in his front tooth revealed

itself as his tongue slid by. Bracing an arm beneath him, Higgins tried getting up. He slipped and fell once more. "Fuck." He rarely swore and then,
only in private. Now, the release of that one word felt necessary, therapeu-
tic. "Fuck. Fuck." Shards of debris hopped into the air as his fist collided
with the cobblestone. A second blow produced a tiny *crunch* in his hand.
"Fuck!"

The fall had shaken something loose, something that went much
deeper than his teeth. With each gasp of air, his rage dissipated. *It's over,*
he thought as his former resignation caught up at last. *And no bloody vase
can change that.* More than ever before, he was aware of the buildings' fiery
crowns, their confining hulk. He felt ringed in, entrapped. *Any moment
now, those houses are going to topple. And I'll be smothered.*

But what did it matter?

It doesn't, Higgins thought, and then it wasn't so much a question as a
statement of purpose, a hardening of his resolve: What did it matter.

Higgins pressed a cheek against the surface of the street. The stone
felt surprisingly cold. Shivering, eyes closed, he pulled in a breath, longing
for the smoke to fill his lungs; longing for the warm drift into that eternal
sleep.

The end was upon him with wonderful swiftness. Coming from every
direction at once, there was a cataclysmic detonation of sound, the noise
not so much a *boom* as a horrific rending of the air. It shuddered the cobble beneath his cheek, tunneling into the depths of his skull, while searing
pieces of wreckage drifted down from above.

Relief soared through Higgins. So this was it, then. This was how
he would pass from life: trod into nothingness by the collapse of his own
home.

It seemed right that it should be so.

A second crack pealed over the block. Higgins, needing to see,
snapped his eyelids wide and peered up at his house. The dwelling, while
under siege, wasn't toppling. In fact, with its inordinate crown of flame, it
loomed higher than ever before.

His house wasn't crumbling to a heap? *No.* Then what?

He twisted his gaze toward the sky. Another concussion tore through
the clouds, and a bolt of lightning zagged. Not a structure collapsing, Higgins realized. Thunder.

CHAPTER FORTY-SIX

Vernon Rose: cradled in the arms of an angel.

He became aware of her gradually, gently, like a slow ascension from a deep sleep, feeling her presence as one feels the first golden notes of an early spring morn. Before she arrived, he'd been incapable of feeling anything. He simply *was*. Was, and was not: a boy between worlds; a melody without sound. Mind broken, thoughts scattered, he clung to the edge of oblivion with only a trace of resistance, unaware of holding on even while doing so.

But then the angel's breath unfolded upon him, her arms circled about his middle, and she pulled him in close. He drifted toward her through the darkness as best he could, only mindful of the movement after the fact. Some part of him suspected she was merely an invention of his mind, some sort of hallucination that would vanish the moment he reached for it.

But she didn't.

Like few others ever had, she stayed.

Following the departure of his five assailants, Vernon had wilted in and out of consciousness, quivering and gasping into the mud. His body—covered in a swarm of welts, bruises, and cuts—felt ruined, incapable of even the most basic of tasks. Just then, he could scarcely summon the strength to open his eyes.

Alone in the alley, he slipped away...

...before being jarred back into reality, the pain a tormentor who refused to let go. As it renewed its assault, Vernon clawed at the earth, pleaded with the sky. He collapsed back into darkness. Later he stirred again, and the cycle continued. And the flames approached.

At their arrival, Vernon finally managed to muster himself into action. Between spells of fainting, he crawled his way to the corroded bars of a storm drain set into the base of the town wall. He slumped forward and thrust his lips between the slots, lapping in all the fresh air he could find. Above, the flames were a horde of cackling demons sneering down at his efforts. Smoke descended from them like a separate sentient creature searching out his lungs. Vernon huffed, spat, and pressed his cheeks tighter against the bars. Beyond, so torturously close: crisp coastal air, the perfume of seagrass, a whiff of salt.

As his mind wandered and languished, he tried to do the one thing that still made any sense, an act as natural to him as breathing: sing. It took a while, with several false starts and missteps, but eventually he brushed up against a song. Snagging onto it, Vernon cleared his throat, traced the tendrils of its melody, and sang.

He kept it up as long as he could: a bright, wistful gush of music that filled his mind with color. Then his strength failed him completely and he retreated into the void, its sheer vastness devouring the song.

After that, Vernon drifted, his awareness no more than a lonely speckle on a deep and soundless night. He clung to the edge of oblivion, he faded, he let go...

But then something unexpected happened. Someone came for him.

The angel.

His father's productions—the more allegorical of the bunch—sometimes featured beings such as angels. Ambassadors of peace and light, the creatures always had rich, singsong voices, giant floppy wings, and beaded halos like miniature suns. Occasionally, the performances also included the angels' nefarious counterparts: ancient beings of malice who, with their glowing red eyes, would cackle and hiss at the audience from beneath the stage. For many years, these portrayals had frightened Vernon, and he had tearfully begged his father to cease production of them. Lerrick, ever patient, had gently refused, instead introducing his son to the men who played the villainous parts and reassuring him that none of it was real. *It's only a show, my boy. Look—they're actors. Demons don't exist.*

Nevertheless, an entire legion of them now surrounded Vernon and roared down from a fiery perch. But the angel was there, too: a guardian of the downtrodden, a protector of the weak. Rocking him like a child, she cradled his head and sang soft assurances into his ear.

The angel's voice, as sweet and as pure as mountain air, pulled Vernon back from the darkness, freeing him from the tangle of his own mind. He drew in a breath. Felt himself rise.

"Vernon...?" she whispered, and it revived him further. Overhead, there was a booming in the clouds, a sound not unlike the clashing of bombi drums.

"Vernon," the angel said again.

CHAPTER FORTY-SEVEN

A wallop of scalding air met her at the door.

As she shoved her way through the bubble of heat—which seemed eager to push back, to deny her entry—fresh tears found Heather's eyes. Her skin flared deeper than ever before, and sparks fizzled down from the eaves, singeing her hair, her tunic, the bright rosebushes bordering their lawn. Several windowpanes above were webbed with heat-induced cracks.

She didn't have long.

Heather lowered her head and bull-rushed into the foyer. Ignoring the sudden rush of darkness, as well as a portentous creak of the hardwood, she sprung into the hearth room, dodged an armchair, and snagged another candle from her father's candelabrum. She held it aloft, realizing that, sometime during the intervening hours, the embers in the fireplace had gone out. The candle was worthless.

Aside from locating a striker and some flint (and spending precious seconds trying to ignite the wick), the only option was to proceed upstairs as is: in the dark.

Where anything might be hiding.

Heather breathed in thickly through her nose. Unable to suppress it a moment more, she released an agonizing bundle of coughs, the act like a violent scrubbing of her lungs. All the while, she kept her gaze fixed on the staircase, a black cutout framed in softening darkness, and expected at any second for something horrendous—a sneering, razor-toothed jester perhaps, or maybe the giant furling wings of some demonic hound—to come lurching out from the gloom.

The darkness around that rectangular opening continued to brighten;

her eyes were adjusting. This realization more than any helped steel her nerve. Though conditions were far from ideal, she would soon be able to see. At least well enough to continue on.

She could do this.

The candle bounced when it struck the floor, vaulting up once before wheeling away on its side. In the shadows, the portrait of Rufus Milgrin appeared to be smiling—whether for encouragement or out of malice, Heather couldn't decide. She tried to ignore those crafty, hawk-like pupils as she bolted past, instead concentrating on putting one foot in front of the next. She took the staircase at a sprint, not waiting to see what was inside. Its steps grumbled as she climbed.

It's not real, it's not real… Heather repeated the mantra, but this time she wasn't referring to the monster so much as to her own fear. Maybe that was what Papa had been trying to say all those months back, when he'd held her close and whispered it like a secret. Maybe the true enemy here was fear itself.

Maybe confronting that fear *was* the battle.

I'm not scared. I'm stronger than this fear. The darkness is only scary if I let it be.

With her father's words echoing, Heather reached the top and charged down the hallway. Her parents' bedroom door wheeled on its hinges when her elbow connected and slammed against the wall. As she rushed toward the bed, Heather's fists lifted of their own accord. "Give her back," she shouted, dredging up every ounce of bluster she had. "You can't have her! I—"

Her voice faltered, and she slid to a halt.

Heather didn't know what she'd expected to find upon arriving, but it wasn't this. Before, she had come face-to-face with fear incarnate, a creature of pure evil; this present scene, lit by yellow firelight slashing in through the shutters, was so completely antithetical to the one she'd encountered earlier that, strange though it was, it nearly frightened her more.

Sprawled out on the bed as if she'd been tossed there, Sara lay stock-still upon the rumpled quilts. Cataleptic eyes gawped at the ceiling, and tendrils of hair floated about her head like a smooshed, sand-colored crown. The bedchamber itself was eerily quiet; the growl of the flames outside didn't so much break the silence as compress it, sealing in the room's stasis.

Heather scanned the rest of the space. The wardrobe hulked like a monolith beside the windows, its ornate doors fastened shut. Beneath it, the bearskin rug stretched across the floor. Its soft matting was smooth, unrumpled. Mumma's dressing table sat undisturbed in another corner; a variety of hair brushes, a washing basin, and a half dozen jars of facial pigment lay scattered beneath a gilded mirror. Several evening gowns were piled beside a sowing kit, and a riding cap teetered on a peg. Her mother had never been a tidy person; for Heather, the vanity's clutter was in fact a marker of order, of normalcy.

Everything was as it should be. No monster, no ghost, no scary demon lurking.

The place was empty.

On the mattress, Sara was still frozen; she would have looked almost peaceful if not for those glassy, unseeing eyes. Heather glanced over her shoulder, out the bedroom door. She didn't dare go check the other rooms—nor look under either of the beds—but her gut told her things were different now. She could no longer feel the monster's presence, not like before. Its aura of rot was distant, imprecise. Diminished somehow. Which meant… The two of them were alone? Her mother was free? Or was all of this some sort of trap?

Heather crept toward the bed and its lifeless occupant, ready at any moment to spring back, out of reach. Once she'd drawn level, she stretched an arm forward—balancing on one leg to retain some degree of distance—and prodded Sara's shoulder. "Mumma? Mumma, it's me, Heather. I came back. I'm here." Sara's skin felt leathery and cold as Heather brushed her cheek with a thumb. Her eyes remained unfocused, unblinking.

Heather swallowed, tears again threatening to emerge. Was she already too late? Had the monster left behind only an empty vessel? Was Mumma's spirit gone for good? Or could Heather somehow draw her back?

She knelt beside the bed, driven by instinct more than any rational thought. She clasped Sara's hands and gave them a desperate squeeze. "Mumma, it's gone now. You don't have to be scared anymore. You can come back. Please come back…" She stared at Sara's pale, expressionless face and waited for a reaction, for even a hint of recognition: a twitch of a cheek, a crease of a brow—anything, she would have taken anything at all.

But the woman's face was empty, her sagging lips offering nothing. There was only—

Breath. Wafting in shorts spurts from both nostrils. Tickling the hairs of Heather's forearm. It was so subtle she'd almost missed it. It was so wonderful she nearly screamed.

Her mouth fell open as her gaze flitted over Sara's body—nose to eyes to lips to chest, then back around. A smile bloomed on Heather's face, elation erupting like the colors of a sunrise. She blinked away tears, not because she wished to dismiss them, but so that she could see.

Mumma was breathing.

Mumma was *here*.

Discarding caution altogether, Heather sprung to her feet. She seized Sara by both shoulders and, in a near panic, shook her. "Wake up, Mumma. I know you're in there. It's me, Heather. You're safe now. I love you. You're safe."

Heather froze when her mother suddenly blinked. Her lids held shut—behind them, a roll of movement—while Sara offered a low, muffled groan. "Heather," she whispered sometime later, eyes still closed, "is that you, dear?"

Heather snatched up her hands. "Yes! It's me. It's your Heather. I'm here. I came back."

Sara cracked her eyelids before tipping her chin in Heather's direction. Her fingers were cold and trembling; Heather got the sense that, with even the slightest squeeze, her mother's bones might snap. "My sweet, sweet little girl. I'm so glad to see you again." She attempted a smile, the expression immediately lost between her two sunken cheeks. "I missed you so much."

"I missed you, too. I'm sorry I left. I—"

Sara gave a sudden start, and panic rippled through her eyes. "Wait— Are you down here with me? *Now*?" Her head whipped to the left, to the right, as if searching for threats. "No no no... You can't be here. You have to get out, baby, before it comes back. You have to ru—"

"No, it's okay. Shhh. We're in Norick. We're home."

"We're home?" Sara blinked, her hysteria subsiding, and took another peek at the room.

"Yes. In your and Papa's bedchamber. You never actually left." Sara's forehead wrinkled as she struggled to process the information. She looked more disoriented than ever.

"It didn't get you, too? You're safe?"

"Yes." At that, Sara breathed a sigh of relief and collapsed into the bed. "But we have to go," continued Heather. "Okay? There's a fire and—"

"You have such pretty hair. Sara's fingers slid from Heather's hand to reach for a dangling blonde strand. A glaze had returned to her eyes.

Heather took a gentle hold of Sara's arm and steered it away. Like her fingers, the woman's wrist felt brittle, infirm. Heather peered toward the shuttered window. Smoke rushed through it like a swollen river. "You have to listen to me. We need to leave—right now—before it's too late."

"I still need to teach you to ride sometime. I loved riding ponies when I was your age."

"I know. But that doesn't matter right now. We have to go."

"You came back for me?" Sara was staring idly at Heather's soiled shirt. Confusion tightened her brow.

Heather bent to meet her gaze and offered an empathic nod. "Yes. And I won't leave you again. I promise. It's gone now—it can't have you. I won't let it."

"You promise," parroted Sara. "You promise..."

"Yes, I promise. Now let's go."

"It's gone now..."

"Yes—"

"You won't let it..."

"No, I already told you—"

"You're Heather..."

"YES! Now come on"—she seized Sara's wrist, not bothering to be gentle, and heaved—"I'll help you down the stairs, but you have to get yourself up."

"Go without me." The response, an elegiac rasp beneath the thickening layer of smoke, stopped Heather cold. Sara's eyes were bleary, as if she'd just woken from a deep sleep. "Save yourself," she said. "Leave me."

Heather ground her teeth. "No," she said, eyes narrowing. "I won't." A throb of heat that had nothing to do with the fire reddened her face. She shook Sara roughly. "I said, no!"

"Your father..." Sara wagged her head in the gloom. "It made me watch what it did to him. It made me stand right there while it…" Her voice trailed off and she shuddered, something between a sob and a dry-heave. "I can't bear it. I'd rather feel nothing at all."

The sound of rending timber and toppling stone surged in from the window: A section of their neighbor's house was crumbling, disintegrating beneath the fiery inundation. Both of them gave a start as their own walls quaked in response. They whirled around, Sara emitting a frightened yelp. Through the shutters: nothing but the vibrant flush of inferno.

Sara jerked back to her daughter. Grogginess had been replaced by fear. Her mouth hung open in alarm, the particulars of their situation finally becoming real. "Heather—"

She shushed her. Leaning over the bed, she fumbled for Sara's hand amongst the quilts and entwined their fingers. "I don't know what it did to Papa,"—she fought back a sob of her own—"or what you saw, but right now we have to keep going. It *wants* you to stay here so the fire will get ya. We can't let it win."

Sara wiggled her head miserably.

"Look at me." Heather fixed Sara with a stare. She squeezed hard. "I know he's gone, but I'm still here. *I* still need you. You're my mother, so *be my mother*." She yanked on Sara's arm, digging her feet into the rug for leverage. "Now … come … on."

Another heave and suddenly—wondrously, the most incredible sensation she'd ever felt—Heather stumbled back, losing her footing. She watched in amazement as, with only partial reluctance, Sara allowed the momentum to pull her up into a sitting position. Recovering her balance, Heather rocked forward and met Sara's gaze head-on. Understanding passed between them, and Sara nodded, just once. At the gesture, Heather brimmed with a current of color and light she possessed only one word for: hope.

Allowing herself the thinnest trace of a grin, Heather gave her mother's arm a gentle tug. Sara rose from the bed completely and, wobbling some, followed after Heather as she moved like a tour guide for the door.

The next moments passed with the surrealism of a dream.

Before she could process, before conscious thought could again take hold, they were in the hallway and racing down its length. Heather's feet didn't so much strike the floorboards as float above them. Her breath, blooming in her ears, was a familiar escort leading them along: not just filling up the darkness, but pushing it back.

Outside, entire buildings broiled and warped. The inferno, ever gluttonous, descended upon the town, but the two of them—mother and daughter, flesh of flesh, heart of heart—didn't hear it. They were aware of nothing but themselves, of the feel of each other's palms. Hand in hand they went, embarking not merely on an exodus of escape, but a flight of possibility. Time was a fluid substance about them, predisposed to their will. In this journey, this casting aside of the old things, it seemed not to exist at all.

They were exiting the bedchamber; at the same instant, the flight of stairs loomed in a sharp descent. Heather pulled her mother down the steps and, in some parallel dimension, they dashed through the hearth room, this time dodging the furniture and ornaments and stacked copies of books.

The seconds elongated and shrunk around them. The world tipped and spun. An infinity, and no time at all, passed them by. Then—as if they had always been there; as if, all along, all they'd had to do was take the step—they were out the front door, together.

CHAPTER FORTY-EIGHT

A peal of thunder cleaved its way through the sky. A twitch of movement stirred in her arms.

Natalie Willow—tear-stained and broken, strands of her disheveled hair glowing golden in the shimmering firelight—fell silent and, more perplexed than shocked, looked down at the boy she cradled like a doll.

Heart igniting, she blinked at the subtle rise and fall of his torso, at the slight vibration now apparent in both nostrils. She gasped as his eyelids started to flutter, and her mouth dropped all the way to her chest.

The alley and the fire fell away. All noise ceased to exist. Right then, the two of them were the only creatures left on Earth.

"Vernon…?" A fresh flow of tears waterfalled down her cheeks. "Vernon."

She couldn't believe it. She couldn't make it make sense. Against all odds, the son of the theater head had survived. She whimpered with this knowledge, this miracle; she shook her head with a dorky grin, one that would've rivaled any of his own.

Vernon Rose was alive.

CHAPTER FORTY-NINE

A clangor of thunder overhead. A portent of his fate.

Kneeling before the spirit, William understood it was over. Once he spoke, all of this would end—his memories, his fear, his pain. His very existence. He welcomed it. Whatever waited on the other side couldn't compare to this present agony. Every cell within him protested; every breath was afflicted.

Above, a smirk had formed on the creature's face. It looked pleased—and more horrific than ever before. Its lips—*Ellen's* lips—were warped into a terrible grimace. Then there was the lack of humanity in her eyes, a vastness so empty and unfeeling as to invoke terror. William cowered beneath the gaze, certain those pupils were boring into his skull.

Don't speak. That still-small voice was back; this time, it came in the shape of his former commander, a man of such grit and resolve, ordering him to persevere. *Don't you speak, soldier. Don't even think about uttering a sound.*

It was too late. He wanted this, truly he did. He yearned to let the darkness rush in, consequences be damned, and smother him. He willed the words that would make it so up through his windpipe, onto his tongue, and out through his lips: *Yes. Yes, I invite you in. Take me—take it all. Just make it end.*

But as William's lips parted, he felt a curious sensation on his head: a patter—slow and rhythmic, like fingers tapping upon a schoolroom desk. *Fingers?* The wraith's? In this final moment, was the spirit at last willing to touch him?

No. Along with the tapping came an airy, agreeable sound. William's ears perked up as he recognized the whistle of falling liquid, and the soft drumming as the Earth received its stream. One of the droplets splattered on his forehead. It trickled pleasantly.

William's mouth clamped shut. He sensed it immediately: Things had changed. A balance had shifted. In a rush of wonderment, he jerked his head toward the wraith. But the beast had forgotten him; its attention was glued to the sky.

It was trying to hide it, but William caught the look all the same. A trace of shock—as well as alarm—dashed across its face. Emboldened, William shifted focus, turning from the spirit to the glorious host of droplets plunging overhead. His eyes found an individual bead high up, and, as if it were in slow motion, he traced its fall.

Raindrops, he thought, temporarily baffled. The word felt new to him, strange, as if he were experiencing its related phenomenon for the first time. As if such an occurrence belonged only in the realm of dreams. *Bloody hell. Raindrops...*

A goofy smile widened across his cheeks.

Disoriented, benumbed, intent upon watching the fire until it exhausted itself to embers, the nine hundred or so residents of Norick gave a start, almost as one, at the titanic eruption of thunder that detonated over the valley.

Some tore their eyes from the burning town and planted them onto the clouds eddying overhead. Others, more stoic or uncaring or simply unaware, didn't bother to look, instead keeping their gazes fixed on the fire's ingestion of their homes. What did a little thunder matter now? Nature had denied them its bounty; in fact, with its wind, it had sealed their fate. They were fools to have ever believed it would be otherwise.

Another growl fissured through the sky: the storm's response to their cynicism. A fizzle of lightning followed, and the countryside was suffused with a white-hot radiance that sent the darkness scampering back. Attentions now fully drawn—their heartbeats sputtering back into rhythm—the townspeople diverted their eyes upward. A third rolling utterance came from the tempest; the foothills rumbled in its wake. In spite of themselves, the people of Norick dared then to do the one thing their logic told them not to: hope.

Hope: that cursed word. That beguiler and cheat.

And yet ... this thunder, this lightning: After all this time, could it be? Would the storm finally unleash? Had the moment truly come?

It had.

First one drop fell, streaking silently from the sky and plopping on— of all people—little Codiah Longford, who'd first set Norick ablaze. The droplet, an asymmetrical tuber that sparkled in its plunge, drizzled upon the boy's cheek with the lightness of a snowflake. It wasn't until the liquid began trickling downward that Codiah became aware of its existence at all.

He pawed at it like a bear cub to a pesky bee; vaguely, he wondered if he might be crying.

First one drop—and then another. The second splashed on the hair of a gangly townswoman with hollowed out cheeks. A third, in a different part of the crowd altogether, landed on a redheaded child of five. Each droplet was separate, arbitrary, and uniquely received—but each was also a herald for the same master, announcing an amending of fate.

One drop; two; three.

A tease. As if the sky itself were hesitant, shy. *Is this okay?* it seemed to ask. *May I?* The moment of suspension lingered like the space between two new lovers dancing around a first kiss. But the tension was drawn, the emotions were welling, the breaths mingling already. There was no option now but an outpouring.

A marshalling of raindrops gathered at the storm's belly. Numerous beyond count, they finally charged—slowly at first, then all at once, in a great sweeping curtain.

A thousand buoyant faces tilted skyward; a hundred flailing hands stretched to receive the offering. The rain, ever gracious, showered down upon them, infusing the air with the music of its descent. Drenched from heel to crown, the townspeople rippled with gooseflesh—though they weren't cold. The grime covering their faces oozed away, dribbling into the soil.

They were rinsed; they were cleansed; they were born anew.

They were the first in a line.

Hundreds of cheers erupted into the night sky. The townspeople leapt up, shared embraces, wept. Many, in gratitude, sank to their knees. Dozens of others dashed through the downpour, splashing their way through the widening puddles. No matter the reaction, each of them felt like a child, reduced to the most basic of human impulses: the expression of joy.

To an audience of rainfall, and to a cadence of thunder—a consecration, as if the storm itself were voicing approval—the people of Norick began, for a second time that night, to dance.

Thunder: a shattering of the sky's foundations; a jeering reminder of their fate.

Lightning bolted across the rectangle of purple-gray sky just visible through the flames. Watching it, Higgins—weaker than ever, a mere shadow of his former self—was nevertheless overcome by a compulsion to rise, to be nearer that which would bring about their ruin.

Sliding a forearm beneath his chest, Higgins attempted to prop himself up. A sob blindsided him. "You bastards!" he hollered at the churning clouds above. "You *bastards!*"

With that, the once-great chancellor of Norick, who'd ushered his town into an unrivaled age of prosperity and virtue, buried his face into his palms and wept. But that's when something amazing happened; that's when—miraculously, after all hope had fled—it started to rain.

CHAPTER FIFTY

Raindrops. *Bloody hell. Raindrops…* A goofy smile widened across his cheeks.

The wraith ripped its sneer back toward William as if sensing his newfound joy. But its eyes didn't just hold contempt or malice. There was also panic: a horse losing its footing upon a rocky outcrop; a gambler, over-zealous, called on his bluff. The spirit watched, open-mouthed, as the rain poured onto its palm. As if it, too, were perplexed by this intrusive liquid.

Recovering a semblance of its poise, the wraith turned and glowered at William, its blackened teeth flashing. "Say yes!" it hollered. But its bluster was merely an act, a last-ditch effort to regain control. The creature had been bested and knew it.

And it was afraid.

William could sense its fear almost as plainly he could smell its stench. Perhaps that was what the odor had been all along: the reek of ancient dread, long festering. For, wasn't it possible that in order for something to be capable of instilling such fear that it, too, had to first feel and reside within that terror? That the beast couldn't impart the emotion if it hadn't itself already experienced it? The idea, though paradoxical, bolstered William with a newfound conviction. It seemed an advantage he now held over the wraith, a secret to its true nature. Filled with a strength not his own, William stared directly into its narrowed eyes—no longer seeing Ellen, no longer feeling his shame—and shook his head no.

A vein on the creature's forehead threatened to pop. "So be it." It turned to glance over its shoulder toward the rear of the Grove; toward what, to William, looked like nothing at all. "The hour has come," it called to that patch of darkness, as if there were someone hidden back there, watching from the ordered rows. "Come forth. Reveal yourself."

William observed the summoning with a cold sense of bewilderment. "Who are you—?" He stopped, a chill riddling its way through his spine.

There was somebody approaching from the trees.

A man in a cloak glided toward them, his black hood adhering itself to a gaunt jawline. He ambled closer, pushing through the sheets of rain, before pausing at William's discarded torch, whose oily flame was still holding out valiantly against the storm. In a strange blur of shapes and shadow, he stooped to retrieve it and William got a glimpse of a red, splotchy nose, one as bumpy and swollen as any lifelong drinker's.

The man in the cloak straightened. With the increased proximity, the torch had little problem now in illuminating the man's face: His beard, while slicked with rain, nevertheless looked thin, desiccated, a white moss spread every which way. It crawled up his cheeks like an overgrown fungus, reaching nearly to his eyes. Beneath those strands, thinning as they were, lay an entire landscape of craters and scars. One looked as if a whole spoon had been dug into his skin and then scooped away. Another could have been the result of a child's fingers, trying unsuccessfully to peel an orange. The right side held a wide, jagged blemish: an old burn. There was a history written on that face, William reflected, and it wasn't a pleasant one.

Despite the beard, the scars, and two bushy gray eyebrows, the man in the cloak didn't appear old. If pressed, William would've estimated that, beneath it all, he lay somewhere in middle age.

The man in the cloak's thin, emaciated legs hauled him near. He stopped beside the wraith, neither of the two acknowledging the other, and then—expression blank, eyes unreadable—he turned his gaze onto the kneeling captain.

"Show him," the spirit growled.

Using a hand swaddled in a blood-stained cloth, the man in the cloak took hold of his hood, and, in a fountain of displaced drops, flung it back. A jungle of hair—expansive, hoary, and matted with knots, what could have belonged to any stray hound—settled upon two bony shoulders. The man's mute, tight-lipped expression didn't change as the entirety of his face came into view, though his hawkish eyes searched for recognition. William, peering past the busyness of that face to its essential components, blinked as a vague familiarity washed over him, a feeling not unlike coming face-to-face, at long last, with someone you've heard about but never met.

Someone I've heard about but never met...

William's jaw plummeted. His eye sockets were mere suggestions, incapable now of their most basic charge. Mind whirling with all of the oaths and discarded mentions—with a hundred memories of seeing that face peering out from oiled canvas—William floundered back, striking his tailbone, and scooted away. The man looked different now, there was no denying that. He was shrunken and feral and all but beat to hell, but it was still him all right. Definitely him. "That's ... that's not possible," William said.

"Oh yes," responded the wraith in Ellen's corrupted voice, "I assure you that it is."

Beside the beast, Rufus Milgrin, founder of Norick, dipped his head to agree.

CHAPTER FIFTY-ONE

William couldn't move for the incomprehension mashing the conduits of his mind.

Shock threatened to cover him in darkness, to eradicate all thought, and a ringing took up residence in both ears. Streams of rain gushed over his chin while his mouth bobbed—moving but unable to speak. Seething, the wraith turned to its famed companion. "Deal with him," it said, "then meet me in the woods. I'll find you in the dark.

"And don't let any of the other wretches see you." The spirit cranked its neck around, piercing William with a malevolent stare. "Not yet. I want the fools to drown in their ignorance."

"Understood," Milgrin said.

The wraith offered William one last scowl before turning its back. It drifted toward Peter Ash and paused to run its fingers possessively along one of his heels. Then—in a puff of wind, a warping smear of black—the creature vanished. William blinked, dumbfounded, and checked to see if Milgrin, too, had disappeared. The founder—with his pinched skin, beaklike nose, and skeletal limbs—gazed silently back.

A weighted hush filled the wraith's absence. William's breath thickened. Rufus Milgrin: an explorer, a trailblazer, the epitome of honor, reason, and virtue. A man whose endeavors were so often lauded—his name so casually praised—that, over the years, he had taken on the quality of a myth, a legend, more god than man. He had discovered a new world; he'd given his people hope.

He was supposed to be dead.

"You're not real," William managed, pushing himself to his elbows.

"You're just another hallucination."

"No, Breeve." The founder's voice was just as William had always imagined it: deep yet regal, coarse but fatherly. As he spoke, the ropey muscles of his neck strained, his vocal cords raw from disuse. "Not this time."

"It's impossible. It can't be—"

Milgrin crouched between William's legs, and the air flooded with his stench: an odor like old, wet pelts. With droopy, dead eyes, he reached forward and—gently, like a father blessing an infant child—cupped William's cheek in a palm. William flinched at the contact, at the immediateness of that smell, remembering how the wraith hadn't once touched him. How it'd seemed reluctant to, perhaps even unable. This present hand, however, possessed no such limitations. While withered, it was constructed of flesh and bone, neither hallucination nor ghost.

Rufus Milgrin was here, now—very much alive.

William's eyes darted between the hand and its disheveled owner. Noticing the reaction, the founder traced William's jawline all the way down to the cleft in his chin. William observed the movement in a riveted silence; so intimate was the gesture, so strangely tender, he couldn't find the nerve to resist.

Milgrin drew closer, and William received another pungent whiff. Still he couldn't bring himself to turn away. "Soon my fate will be yours," whispered the founder, holding his stare. Ensuring he understood. Despite the insinuation, Milgrin's tone contained neither threat nor scorn, just a simple statement of fact.

William couldn't decide if that was worse. Nor did he seem capable of finding anything worthwhile to say. "The tomb," he stammered. "There's a—"

"It's empty," said Milgrin, matter-of-fact.

"The Council… The Founders—"

"They were wrong."

"They said you died."

"They were deceived."

Quickly tallying the years—noting again that the man hadn't so much aged as *decayed*—William sputtered out his next inquiry. "*How* are you here?"

Milgrin paused before responding. "*It* can do a great many things.

Keeping me alive is nothing." Then, softly, almost to himself: "Its power surpasses all understanding."

William processed that, anxiety coiling like a snake in his gut. If that were true ... if the entity could do *this* ... then that meant—

Sudden movement tore William from his thoughts. Milgrin's free hand had disappeared into the depths of his cloak. With a quick jerk of his wrist, he pulled out a knife.

Adrenaline catapulted through William. Stasis shattered, he lunged for the founder's wrist before the man could take a swing. Snatching a hold, he spun both of their arms toward the ground, using their combined weight to propel the blade from his chest. Milgrin didn't resist, instead limply allowing William's momentum to pull them down. The torch twirled out of reach. William growled, fighting for purchase; Milgrin, meanwhile, slithered to the right, to the left, and then, in one nimble tug, wriggled free. Planting a foot in the grass, he shoved himself away.

Still carrying the knife.

William fell back onto his haunches, searching for a weapon with which to defend himself. Both his sword and the fisherman's knife were out of reach. But Milgrin wasn't launching another assault; instead, the founder lifted a gesture of peace. "I will do you no harm," he said, inching closer, as calm and detached as ever. "It ordered me not to kill you. It has other plans, you see."

"Bullshit, you bastar—"

The knife glinted as Milgrin flipped his wrist and caught the blade in his palm. Stepping forward gingerly, he proffered its hilt. "Take it. It's yours." William inspected the outstretched weapon but made no move to accept it. Milgrin anticipated his next question: "Why give it to you? So that you remember what happened here. When the time comes, you'll know what to do with it. Take it," he said again, this time with a nod.

Dumbstruck, William did so. The man didn't intend to harm him? This was some sort of truce? He studied the knife. It was light, flimsy even. Jagged notches scarred the length of the blade, and a sheen of rust darkened its tip. As William examined the weapon's bone handle, a dreamlike heaviness hanging over him, Milgrin slowly withdrew.

"Wait..." Something the founder had said earlier prickled at William's subconscious, and his head shot up. "What did you mean? What plans?"

From beneath the watchtower, Milgrin offered nothing more than a blank stare. Already he was backing away, merging with the night.

The man's retreat unnerved William in ways he couldn't understand. "You can't just leave. Tell me what that thing wants. Why did it choose me?" Milgrin slung the cowl over his head. He turned to go. "Why now?" William called after him. "Why do any of this?"

Milgrin hesitated and rotated his face partway around. "I had no choice."

Memories of the entity's furious insistence returned to William. All the pleasures it had offered. All the curses it'd vowed. "You said yes? You let it in?"

"No. Not in the manner you speak." Milgrin shook his head, and for the first time William thought he saw real emotion etched across those unkempt features. A silent melancholy curtained over the visible half of the founder's face. He glanced toward the orchard floor. "It took something from me, long go," he said, still facing away. He fiddled with the coiled cloth cinching his palm. "It swore an oath, promising that if I helped it, it would…" His voice trailed off, pained, and his eyes returned to William's. "This is the only way."

A pang of sympathy, unexpected though not unwelcome, spread through William's chest. He frowned, thinking of Ellen, of Landon, of all the things he would do. "If you're speaking the truth," he said, voice rising hopefully, "then we can be allies. Together, we can find a way to beat that thing. Come back to town, and we'll—"

"Goodbye, Breeve."

Milgrin adjusted the cloak's placement upon his shoulders. He strode away.

Startled by the abruptness of his departure, William fumbled for words. "Wait! This is your bloody town, Milgrin. *You* brought the people here. So save them. You owe us." But his words fell on deaf ears: Like the wraith before him, the founder simply vanished in a swirl of rain and night.

William stared after him. He looked down at the knife. Back up. The blade fell from his grip. Milgrin's words ricocheted through his skull; with their tumble came a titanic wave of that same ominous dread, that same worming shame. *Soon my fate will be yours.*

A tremble seized William's limbs. The voice was there now, in his head, saying nothing, saying everything, drawing him back. He clawed at his temples in an attempt to shunt it away. He howled at the sky.

No, no—not again...

Now he knew: Though he'd survived, though Norick itself had persevered, none of it mattered. They hadn't truly won. This was but one night, a single contest in a much larger war. The entity was ageless: What of all the nights still to come? What of the vengeance it would seek?

None of them could escape.

William, it called, sounding like Ellen, like Milgrin, like every person he'd ever known: his dead comrades in the South; that former commander who'd gifted him his sword; maybe even himself. *William*, it purred in its unholy song, filling him up like wine into a flagon, like blood into a cup. *William, William, William.*

All but choking on his breath now, too scared to close his eyes—fearful of what, behind those lids, he would find—William screamed toward the heavens, buried his face into an elbow, and, for the first time in his adult life, submitted to a weeping born of absolute terror.

CHAPTER FIFTY-ONE

Perfectly at peace, cocooned in a warm pocket of air, Vernon Rose discovered he once more had the strength to open his eyes.

And so, without thought, he did.

He fluttered his lids, testing them out, and then he found her, this angel of light hovering like a shield against the darkness. Her complexion sparkled like a thousand polished stones. The very air, in its proximity to her, seemed to be aglow. She smiled down at him, her holy tears dribbling upon his face; where they landed, his flesh tingled and pleasantly burned. Overwhelmed with her warmth, her light, with a flood of giddiness spreading through him like a chorale of rising suns, Vernon returned the angel's look, nodded, and lifted his eyes toward the heavens.

He was alive—he was more than alive. A current of *knowing* swelled within him, accompanied by a vast, unfathomable presence, one older than all the earth and the sky and the molded molecules of the sea. Infinitely benevolent, it churned through him. It urged him to see.

To see and to hear.

And he did, he did, *he did*.

Vernon giggled with the tide of music gushing through him, a song like no other. It lifted him up upon an endless strand of melody. It infused his mind with color. All the universe was held in those notes; Vernon heard each of the threads in turn, isolated and magnified, as well as all of them together, a divine chorus, coalesced into one:

There was the gurgling of mountain brooks, the rustling of a hummingbird.

There was the call of every avian species—the trilling and the squawking, the playful chirps. The hooting of owls. The cawing of crows. Early morning birdsong filtering through a webbing of leaves.

There was the swishing of grass upon softly rolling meadows. There was the voice of the wind caressing wheat fields and fallow pastureland. There was the slow, primordial creep of the Earth's woods, nature's eternal outward expansion. There was the seeding of moss, the stringing of vines, the pollination of flowers.

There was the seasonal shedding of the cottonwoods: a flurry of snowfall amidst the humid summertime heat.

There were grains of sand leapfrogging across the desert's endless warping dunes. There was the fissuring of glaciers and their crawling plow across the high country. There was the pandemonium of an avalanche, a sudden detonation of ice and snowpack.

There was the lazy trickle of frost as it thaws beneath an infant spring-time sun. There was the flowers' unhurried bloom ... before an escalation, all at once, in their pace, pattern, and hue. And all the other sounds of spring: a glorious song of cleansing and rebirth.

The hum of a sunrise—an abeyance just before dawn, then the noise of a world coming awake: a mounting flush on the air, an eruption of up-roarious color.

There was the great sigh of the Earth as it turns finally toward night. There was the breath of the whirling stars above and a universe in motion: gases expanding; comets colliding; whole planets seeding with life.

There was the erosion of rock and soil, the tumble of boulders, and the workmanlike drone of water as it eats away at a piebald canyon side. There were the wrinkles and grooves, like patterned memorials, it leaves behind.

There were ribbons of cloud surfing across a robin-blue sky; there was the smoky baritone of thunder as those vapors turn toward darker designs.

There was the ocean's eternal dance with the shoreline: a choreogra-phy of surge and retreat, surge and retreat. A courtship as old as time.

There were deer vaulting, and lions roaring, and fireflies sparking; there were squirrels rummaging, geese honking, and the thunderous stamping of oxen. There was the baying of wolves, the frenetic buzzing of bees. There were great alien creatures of the ocean, diving; there was an or-chestration of fish, rising. There were the guileless snouts of dogs, panting and drooling and plunging into mud-rimmed puddles.

So, too, were there the songs of Man: fiddles and harps and every assortment of stringed instrument, each plucked to the whims of countless imaginations. There was the soft trilling of flutes, the stomping of percussions. There was the giggling of children and the cooing of infants. The bustle of celebrations, tavern games, athletics. The whisper of lovers, and the tender, infinite press of a kiss. There were the prayers and congregations of the pious; there were the schemes and murmurs of the downtrodden. There were final breaths, and the first yowling cries of birth.

There was death, and there was life, and there was everything in between.

All of it, a diverse and ancient symphony, passed through Vernon in that moment. But he wasn't just a receptacle for it; he was a conduit, an orchestrator, channeling the light through song. With his guidance the music went streaming out, dispersing into the world.

Vernon Rose: marred, broken, lost. But he was not alone. He was a carrier of the song now, a witness to the very secret of the world.

He was transcendent. He was *free.*

As the angel looked on, Vernon's song turned once more to giggles and then to outright laughter as he stared up at the flames and the teeming night sky. For lastly, in the symphony of the universe, there was now this, showering upon them from above:

The joyful flight of rain.

PART TEN

REBIRTH

The world spins—
Onward, onward, it goes.

But for all its motion and vigor,
Newness and hope,
One truth remains:

The world is stuck,
Ensnared in a loop.

For all things upon the Earth
Will one day
Know a return.

CHAPTER FIFTY-THREE

"What in Milgrin's name..."

Skylar Higgins, who—beneath a silent, pointed stare from Lucas Ill-hap—had recently retaken command of the town, stepped into the Grove with a sword drawn. Behind him, equipped with oil torches, a detachment of the Guard followed. The soldiers, the most capable of the town's outfit, formed a protective half-ring about the chancellor. Like their leader, they eyed the surrounding fruit trees warily, their capped heads skittish and swiveling.

Higgins stalked deeper into the orchard, struggling to make sense of what he was seeing. The steady rainfall was blurring everything; the scene took on the dizzy quality of a smeared painting, the entire Grove seeming to smudge right before his eyes. The unmoving form of Jacob Willow rose up abruptly enough that Higgins nearly tripped over him. Recovering at the last second, he paused, wiped at his eyes, and bent to take a closer look.

The boy's arms and legs were covered in thin, winding cuts. His tousled blond hair, thoroughly drenched, hung down in a mourner's veil. Higgins studied the outlandish symbols, now seeping away, that adorned the tree barks surrounding Jacob. Next, he considered—blinking to be sure—the ball of human flesh that was William Breeve, curled in a fetal position. The captain didn't appear wounded—at least not physically. As Higgins strode closer, he could just make out a soft babbling coming from the man's lips. The sound presented Higgins with not only a chill of unease, but a secondhand humiliation.

He averted his eyes from the display, partly out of deference for Breeve's former dignity and partly because to look on such weakness reminded him of his own. He sensed a similar reaction from the captain's subordinates: embarrassment and pity all around, then a merciful diverting of their attentions. Whatever respect they'd had left for him was now gone completely.

"Get him out of here," Higgins said. "The youngling, too. Make haste. Get them both to the infirmary. We don't yet know the extent of their injuries."

Four guardsmen hustled forward. "He's alive!" one of them called after laying two pressed fingers against Jacob's throat. Another, crouched beside Breeve, was gently encouraging him to his feet. "Come on, Will," murmured the soldier, whom Higgins recognized as the Guard's first lieutenant, Quinn Tremrow. "You're all right. It's over now. Let's get you up."

Higgins changed focus, moving in grim-faced silence toward the watchtower. Brade had informed him of its occupant; the description had done little to prepare him for the real thing. He peered up at Peter Ash—a colleague, a friend—without breaking eye contact. "Silas. Carrington." He gestured toward the rows ahead. "Search the trees. I want no section left uncombed. The perimeter as well. Every inch—however long it takes. I want every clue we can glean."

"Yes, sir," the two men replied. They set off for the leafy corridors.

Higgins took another entranced step. "Sir?" He stopped; the soldier who'd spoken—a rotund, beetle-looking fellow—stood slightly apart from his comrades near the end of the line. Even in the pouring rain, his face looked flushed.

"What, soldier?"

"May I suggest I accompany the other two? In case they need reinforcement?"

Higgins rolled his eyes. *Of course, an overachiever.* "No," he replied with a glower toward the interloper, possessing no patience for this sort of game. Come to think of it, he couldn't recall having invited him along to begin with. "Leave us. Go monitor the front gate."

The guardsman stiffened. "Oh," he muttered. "Oh. Okay. Right away, sir." Head bowed, the lad turned and fell out of line, shambling off toward the entryway.

Higgins continued advancing toward the tower. He didn't glance at Breeve and his helpers as he passed, instead directing his stare at the killer's message. Light-headed with the words, Higgins hardly noticed when another guardsman trod forward.

"What the hell, Breeve?" the soldier hissed as he, too, passed him by. "Have some self-respect and *get up*." Higgins realized the voice belonged to his son, who drew alongside him. "What next, Father?" asked Brade once it became clear the chancellor had no intention of acknowledging his son's presence. "What're you thinking?"

Higgins ignored him, blocking out this and all other sound. For the better part of a minute, he simply stared up at the body and its strange markings. He examined the grotesque, bone-shattering bend to its knee; he forced back a gag at the sight of the blood pouring from its eyes and mouth and from the explosive rupture in its side. Meanwhile, the wind and rain flounced down upon him, baiting for a reaction that never arrived.

He forced himself to look at the corpse until the sight no longer made him queasy, until its mutilated features began to waver and run. Finally, spotting a glint of light below, he bent and retrieved a knife lying discarded at the dead man's feet. He held it up to his eyes, turned it over in his palm. Its handle was pitted and worn; its blade, meant for flaying fish, was bloody and streaked. "Huh," Higgins remarked, perversely intrigued. He glanced toward the corpse's severed wrists and then at the fisherman's boy, who was at present being whisked away by the soldiers.

Frowning thoughtfully, Higgins slid the knife into his belt.

He returned his attention to the watchtower. Searching for meaning, for something beyond words, he set his gaze onto Peter Ash. The moment he hadn't realized he was dreading had come. Swallowing against the lump rising in his throat, Higgins offered his former colleague a stiff nod, motioned a signal toward the awaiting soldiers, and then turned away.

"Cut him down," he said.

CHAPTER FIFTY-FOUR

For town guardsman Riley Ford, the request was a simple one: He just wanted to know what in the sunken hells was going on.

As his comrades ferried Captain Breeve, the boy, and Peter Ash's corpse back to town, Riley had been forced to observe from the fringes, relegated by Lieutenant Tremrow to the rear flank. During the journey—and in the hours since—no one would tell him a damn thing. Which was imprudent on their part, reckless even. He was a sworn member of the Guard, for Milgrin's sake. In order to do his duties, he had to know what was happening. He needed to be kept informed, dammit!

But every time Riley attempted to glean information from one of his fellows, they pretended not to hear him, or they feigned ignorance, or they just scowled and turned away. Even after Riley himself was questioned by the Council about what he'd seen from the walls—during which he was every bit the embodiment of militaristic decorum: straight-lined spine, rigid as an iron rod; politely folded hands nestled in the crook of his lap; an expression of eager obedience, all of his senses focused and attuned—the magistrates denied him any insight into their conclusions. They simply told him to go home.

It was clear he needed to make amends for that moronic stunt he'd tried pulling in the Grove. And, as Riley saw it, the best way to do that was by being the most capable soldier possible—which, circularly enough, meant he needed to know what orders were coming in, the status of the investigation, the condition of the people. Unlike Norick's leadership, *he* understood a military organization was at its best when each of its members was kept privy to the lines of communication. So, if they wouldn't share their knowledge—and, by consequence, allow him to do his job—then he would gather the intelligence for himself. He'd make his own way. This night had taken so much already; he wasn't about to allow his reputation to be another of its casualties.

After the debriefing, Riley approached two guardsmen posted at the edge of the Market Square. "Milgrin's courage," he said, raising a hand in salute. "What news? Have you heard any word on a suspect? On Captain Breeve?"

"Piss off, rookie."

"Get lost before we flog you."

Another tactic, then.

Frustrated, though not deterred, Riley shambled off toward other occupied areas of Norick, pausing every so often to look around. The downpour had all but quenched the inferno. While the northern half of town was a total loss—and would continue quietly smoldering for days—the southern half had gone mostly untouched. The contrast between the two halves was striking. On one side, chaos and ruin; on the other, possibility and order.

There would be a coming dawn for Norick after all. *Together, we'll rebuild our future.*

Riley spent the next hour scouring for information. This time, he consigned himself to listening in from the shadows, or dropping into conversations unannounced. He casually inquired with several citizens at their homes. He eavesdropped at the infirmary. He pressed a loitering gaggle of younglings to spill what they knew. With each interaction, a clearer picture emerged:

After taking stock of the damages, the Council had ordered a census to evaluate the toll of human life. In the end, despite the fire's fury, there were only two parties unaccounted for: Gregory Millons, the stable head; and Mayrin Malecko, a laborer. The general consensus was that they must've been caught unaware in their respective homes—and hopefully weren't made to suffer long. A renewed hunt for their bodies would be conducted at first light.

News of a separate incident, however, had also spread amongst the townspeople, and the story served to alleviate their numbness and grief. Two teenagers had been discovered in an alleyway near the fire's epicenter.

The discovery, a small miracle, really, was made even more baffling by the fact that the two of them were giddy and smiling—even singing—when the searchers had pulled them free.

But word of Peter Ash's demise had also circulated, swiftly diluting any optimism. The Council stressed the need for calm; as of yet, they explained, there was no proof the two events—murder and fire—were related. Until they knew more, it was best not to rush to conclusions.

Of course, such calls for reason hadn't worked: The people were horrified. Tales from the fifteen recovered younglings recounted a malevolent presence stalking them in the woods, the same creature that'd slaughtered the master of trade. Rumor or not, the story had, over its many tellings, accrued the veracity of truth. Even the more practical of the citizens shivered at the thought of that horrendous scene up in the Grove. Most wouldn't dare speak Ash's name. Many wouldn't venture into a room not well lit.

Riley didn't blame them; he'd seen the orchard for himself.

Partly because of the risk of a panic, and partly because of the threat of an unchecked killer, the Council ordered a mandatory curfew in effect for the remainder of the night, and all subsequent nights thereafter, until the ordeal had been seen to its proper resolution. Other than the Guard and the magistrates themselves, no one was allowed on the streets or beyond the walls. The gates were sealed, with guardsmen posted throughout Norick on high alert. Those citizens with homes in the town's northern half were boarded with those owning houses in the south. Any overflow—and there was plenty—was assigned lodging in Coastline, despite halfhearted bickering from both sides. Downplaying the people's fear, the Council announced that the reconstruction of Norick would begin first thing in the morning: Their starting over, their rebirth, would commence with the dawning of a new day.

Later, at the barracks, Riley overheard several of his comrades discussing the recent detainment of a fisherman. The bloke's knife (engraved with his initials and later verified by his own son) had been found in the Grove, as had his mooring ropes, brushes, and a jug of paint. The herbalist, Trinity Weston, confirmed she'd sold the dye to Willow; apparently the fisherman had claimed to be painting his skiff for his wife. Perhaps most damning of all was the man's lack of an alibi: Several townspeople loosely recalled Willow's departure from the Market Square, but none could attest to his whereabouts afterward nor to the exact time of his return. This placed him beyond the walls, unsupervised, from before the start of the fire all the way up to its eventual termination at the storm's outpouring, during which he'd been officially sighted amongst the crowd. Even if he'd returned sooner in order to help combat the inferno (as one citizen alleged), this still allowed a wide range in which to commit the murder, as the period between his initial departure and purported return still encompassed nearly two hours.

The collected evidence seemed rather circumstantial to Riley, and he suspected the arrest had more to do with assuaging the town's fears than any genuine certainty, but that wasn't his call to make. The Council had spoken; until they said otherwise, Willow would remain in irons.

That's power, Riley thought as he slipped from the barracks and out into the night. *To be able to control the narrative.* The fisherman didn't have to *be* guilty; it was enough that the right people said that he was. The facts would eventually fit the charge, because they were assumed to. Because so often perception *was* the truth.

The notion gave Riley an idea. Eyes widening, he waddled to a halt beside the charred statue of a founder. Could it work? He nodded to himself; it could. But *should* it? That question was trickier to answer. As a member of the Guard, his duties went beyond material defense and simple policing; he was charged, too, with safeguarding the town's virtue. Could he, then, in good conscience, undertake this course of action? Was he willing to dirty his own hands—to sully his very honor—just for this chance?

Riley considered the question while he shuffled for the Council Hall, feeling the founder's burned-out eyes upon his back as he went. This could be his fresh start, he thought, the first step in achieving his dreams. It didn't matter if they believed him or not; all he had to do was sow doubts, to distract from his own inadequacies. There was opportunity in chaos. He just had to tell one little lie.

A pair of guardsmen, Silas Lairen and Carrington Welsh, flanked the entrance into the towering granite palace. The two soldiers, thick and ugly, swung their spears to bar his entrance. "What'd you want, rookie? The Council isn't receiving visitors."

Riley puffed out his chest as much as his snug leather breastplate would allow. "I must speak to the honorable magistrates at once. To

Chancellor Higgins, especially. It's urgent."

"What, did you forget how to lace up your armor again?"

"No, I—"

"You want permission to go search the Grove all by yourself?"

"It's none of that. I have pressing information that the Council needs to hear."

"They're occupied—and even if they weren't, they don't have time for the likes of you."

"I said it's urgent."

Carrington waved him off. "The Council's holding court tomorrow. Come back then." The two brutes shared a sneer.

Riley exhaled sharply, thinking about the eye-rolls those brawlers had given him earlier; about Higgins's mortifying dismissal at the Grove. He clenched a fist: He'd had enough. "I will see them *now*. The Council was eager to hear my testimony earlier. I have more to add. Now move aside."

He didn't wait for a response. Tapping a source of daring he didn't know he possessed, Riley shoved past their crossed spears—registering a flash of surprise on both their faces—and then marched straight into the building. He hustled down the dim corridor, fearing they would soon follow, until he had arrived at the amphitheater. Its heavy metal door was slightly ajar.

He peeked inside. Below, down a slope of tiered seating, the nine remaining members of Norick's High Council were seated at a table in a row of plush, highbacked chairs. Flaming sconces burned along either side of the chamber, the firelight casting the magistrates' faces in heavy shadow. A patrol of guardsmen kept watch from the first few stairs.

Riley carefully nudged the door wider and wriggled his way into the room. For a moment nobody noticed him, and he took the opportunity to gulp down a calming swig of air. "Chancellor Higgins," he called, knocking sheepishly on the doorframe as though he'd just entered. "Excuse me, sir." Startled, the guardsmen raced to intercept him. Riley grimaced as Brade Higgins's long fingers tightened around his biceps. "Hey—easy! It's me. It's Riley Ford." He raised his hands in a gesture of goodwill, but Brade made no move to release him.

The elder Higgins, looking exhausted, peered up from the table. After a pause, he flicked his wrist dismissively, and the guardsmen released their hold. "What is it?"

"Sir, can I have a word?" Riley shimmied out from between Brade and a soldier named Cas Melick, and, glancing from side to side, he stepped up to the landing. "I … I have something to tell you."

The chancellor's expression remained impassive, unreadable. "Regarding what?"

"Well, you see…"

"Get to it, boy."

Riley gulped. This was it, he thought. If he did this now, everything would change. But that was a good thing, right? Because in order to fulfill its calling, the Guard *needed* to change. To start over, as the town would. Furthermore, if Riley wished to restore his reputation—if he desired a place in that future—*this* was what it would take. He could see that now; there was no other way.

Glory required a sacrifice. A little bad in order to bring about the good.

The High Council regarded him now with open displeasure. He saw several of the magistrates roll their eyes. He saw Higgins preparing to signal him away.

Opportunity in chaos, Riley thought. Here goes.

"It's about Captain Breeve."

CHAPTER FIFTY-FOUR

Seagren Lake: Before the sun rose, he would go to Seagren Lake, to die.

Fuck them, William thought as he staggered down the sparsely lit corridor, his vision shimmering with hot, salty tears. *Fuck them all.*

He'd just been debriefed by the High Council. Earlier, their lackeys had pulled him from a cot in the infirmary and lugged him to the amphitheater. Along the way, he'd tried to concentrate on what he would tell them, but his mind seemed incapable of formulating even a hint of coherence. Memories from the Grove kept spinning and spinning in an endless loop. Peter Ash, butchered. Rufus Milgrin, alive. All of the old legends, true.

So horrifically true.

He tried to tell them. He spoke as clearly and succinctly as possible, willing the magistrates to understand. But those stubborn wretches upon their dais—upon their *thrones*—wouldn't listen. Deferring to skepticism on principle alone, they wouldn't even entertain the possibility that the tale might be true. Instead, William was mocked and scorned. Laughed at even. A demon stalking these woods, wreaking havoc? Rufus Milgrin, still drawing breath? The story, they told him in no uncertain terms, was patently absurd.

William had anticipated this response, though expectation was nothing compared to the real thing. Their ridicule left him fuming. Their stubbornness made him want to scream. Worse yet was the betrayal that occurred only minutes later.

From the moment Brade discovered the flagon up in the outpost, William had assumed the younger Higgins would report him to his father.

But he was wrong. The demise of his captainship didn't come at the hands of the lanky guardsman—who observed the proceedings with a look of genuine surprise—but from one of his peers, the beetle-looking novice, Riley Ford. Emerging from the shadows, the rat bastard swore he often saw William drinking while on duty, and that he could personally attest to the captain partaking that night too. By *his* calculations, that made Captain Breeve partly culpable for everything that had happened. In *his* humble opinion, the Guard needed new leadership.

William's response wasn't a choice on his part. "Liar," he hollered. "You scheming, fucking liar! How dare you spout this bullshit—and right to my face. You pathetic roach. You don't know one bloody thing."

Ford ignored the outburst. "I'm afraid it's true, sir," he said, directing his words at Higgins while doing everything he could to avoid meeting William's eye. He adopted his best impression of a concerned citizen: overly solemn, maddeningly self-righteous. "I would not have presumed to address Norick's esteemed magistrates if it weren't so. But alas, Captain Breeve's behavior of late has left me no other choice. The integrity of the Guard is at risk."

From the chamber's central dais, Higgins was studying the two of them in silence. A soft, humorless smile turned the corners of his mouth, and he nodded. "So be it."

William whipped toward the chancellor. "*What*? Tell me you don't believe this load of filth, Higgins. It's utter nonsense. The bastard's clearly lying. Look at him—he can't even stand there without fidgeting."

Higgins's chair creaked as he stood. "It's settled, Mr. Breeve. The hearing is over. Based on conclusive evidence brought before the Council's attention, you are formally discharged from the Town Guard, effective immediately."

"You're playing right into his hands. He's setting me up. This is the first time I've seen him tonight."

"During your tenure, our town has grown vulnerable and weak. The Guard has deteriorated into mediocrity. But no longer. You are dismissed."

William took an involuntary step toward the dais. "What don't you get? What happened tonight isn't over. The beast is still out there. You're gonna need me."

"I know this little charade is attractive for you," said Higgins, glancing at the table as though he were embarrassed, "but we have precious little time for your delusions of grandeur."

"What in the sunken hells are you talking about?"

"It's obvious. You're a broken man craving a sense of purpose. And I empathize—I've been where you are, after Teresa died. You want to feel some kind of significance again, so you're crafting conflict where there is none."

"Why the fuck would I—"

"Because," lectured Higgins, "for years you've been nothing but a shadow of your former self. You yearn for redemption, and what better way to achieve it than to orchestrate a scenario in which you alone can save the town."

"I never said—"

"Wake up, Breeve." Higgins's voice had iced over. "Quit cowering in denial and accept what you are. Your grief has made you erratic. It has for years now. The shock from what happened tonight simply pushed you over the edge."

"You lost Ellen," another magistrate added, not unkindly. "We understand, and we grieve with you. But we can't let your anguish compromise the safety of the town."

"Fuck your pity. I know what happened up there. I know what I saw."

"What happened," Higgins broke in, "was those poor younglings discovered a murdered council member. As awful and horrendous as that is, that's the sum of it. The fire, in all likelihood, was just a coincidence. There're no spirits haunting these woods. No resurrected Founders. We're alone, just as we always have been. One dead body doesn't change that."

William's fingers curled before his face. "Things *have* changed, you halfwits. I already told you: That creature is still out there. And it's not done with us. Can't you see? We were wrong—*the Founders* were wrong."

"Stop." Higgins thrust a palm forward. The other magistrates appeared just as insulted. For them, William knew, questioning the Founders was the same as questioning the very truth of Norick. "I know you're from the South," said Higgins. "Maybe that's it. Maybe you're just upset. But make no mistake: Those two things do not grant you unchecked allowances here. The Founders—rest their souls—erred only in not coming to Norick sooner. Don't let your fear steer you into blasphemy."

William gaped. "Listen to yourselves. You claim to have no religion, but it's clear who you worship. And it's blinded you."

A cacophony of chair legs raked against the floor as the Council bolted to its feet, each of its members ready for violence. Standing off to the side, Riley Ford wore a smug grin.

The expression only amplified William's fury. "Forget your bloody egos for once and open your eyes. I know you don't wanna hear it, but there's something out there. Something the Founders overlooked. If we wanna survive, we must act immediately—and leave. Until we do, none of us will be safe. I swear it. Don't let your pride get these people killed."

One of Higgins's eyelids twitched. "Get him out of here."

And then the soldiers—minus Brade, who stood by looking uncharacteristically conflicted—seized William from behind and dragged him from the room.

At present, he staggered down the Council Hall's main corridor and tried in vain to hold it together. He was done now, done with everything. If they refused to see reason, so be it. That was their choice, not his. Let the stubborn fools march proudly to their own destruction; let the beast have its way with them. He'd done his part; what did he care.

He didn't mean it, of course. Resentment was simply an easier herb to swallow than the truth: No matter what he did, no matter how hard he tried, he couldn't save them. He'd never been able to—not his comrades in the South, not Ellen or Landon, not this bloody ungrateful town. Over and over his efforts had proven themselves insufficient; *he* had proven himself insufficient. Who did he think he was? He couldn't make a difference. He couldn't change a damn thing. When it came down to it, he was just another fool who'd thought he could outrun fate.

Even if he tried to warn the townspeople, they would never heed his word over the Council's. He would be deemed a lunatic, a rabble-rouser, someone desperate for attention. Someone who didn't belong. And that was the thing: He was truly alone now. There was nobody left to believe him, no job to give him purpose, no ally to help shoulder the weight of this terror.

William now grasped the true cunning inherent in the entity's schemes: Not only had it inferred a culminating act of retribution in the future, it was also ensuring an ongoing torment in the present. It'd cursed William with a perpetual state of loneliness and unease, of never knowing exactly when it might reappear. The constant dread would chip away at him; the uncertainty, the waiting, would eventually drive him mad.

And then, when he was at his most vulnerable, when all hope had fled, the beast would once again steal close and exact its revenge.

Soon my fate will be yours.

Milgrin's words scraped at his mind like talons. William believed the prophecy without question. Back in the Grove, the sudden downpour had shifted the balance of the night—an alteration that had, at the time, felt momentous, ordained—but then the entity had shrewdly reasserted itself by revealing Milgrin and all that his return implied. The founder's existence demonstrated the spirit wasn't just powerful or ageless—it was damn near *godlike*. Temporal parameters were of no concern to it, nor were the natural laws governing death and life. After such a revelation, after merely glimpsing the entity's plans, how could William ever feel safe again? How could he go on knowing a creature like that was out there, biding its time, orchestrating its revenge? How could he go on after seeing everything he had?

William shuddered. As he walked, he hugged his arms tightly about his gut and stared at the tile floor with bleary eyes. He reached the end of the corridor and shouldered past the stationed guardsmen, not caring if they glimpsed his tears. Across the Market Square, piles of rubble and half-eaten structures continued to smolder. The rain had slackened, reduced now to a light patter, but spirals of steam still scurried from its touch. Stumbling, ignoring the accumulating moisture, William turned for a wide alleyway spanning the Council Hall's eastern flank.

The southern gate would be quickest. From there, he would hop on the path, bypass the farmland, and turn south toward the mossy banks of Seagren Lake.

Ellen, William thought as he heaved his sagging body through the alley. He didn't care but for this one thing: to be with her and Landon again. All his life he'd struggled to find purpose in a cold, unfeeling world. He knew now that whatever meaning life offered had died with them four years ago. He hadn't been able to save them then; he couldn't overcome the darkness now. So his words were a prayer, a desperate entreaty: *Ellen, I'm coming. I'm sorry. I'm finally coming.*

He closed his eyes as he rounded the bend in the amphitheater. He could almost feel her presence beside him, a somber and tenuous warmth, beckoning him along. *Come to me, Will. It's okay. It's over now. You can rest.* He could already picture their graves, those two soft mounds covered in knee-high grass. He could imagine her standing over him, keeping watch as he lay down between the unmarked crests. He could see her sad smile, her approving nod. He could hear the rain's elegiac procession upon the waves.

He would do it swiftly, with his eyes closed. He would do it as he listened to those twirling droplets fall.

Milgrin's knife, snatched up before the guardsmen could whisk William from the Grove, rattled at his belt. Though short and rusted, its blade would be more than adequate. Perhaps this purpose was exactly what Milgrin had intended for it. Perhaps the knife was a gift.

Tears found William's chin. He quickened his pace, determined to not be waylaid by sobs, but it didn't matter: There was sobbing in the alley already, and it stopped him cold. He pulled up, sliding a little on the wet stone, and blinked dumbly into the gloom. The lament, its source just out of sight, echoed against the granite walls.

William crept closer; a small figure drew into focus. A youngling—no older than nine or ten, wearing garments soiled with rain and smoke. Soot streaked through her white-blonde hair, and her hands formed a white-knuckled grip upon a windowsill. The girl, not yet noticing his approach, sobbed into the wall beneath the opening, the stone muffling the sound. A sob tilted her torso toward him, and William got a better look. His shoulders slumped as he recognized her, and his heart—what he'd believed permanently numbed by a permafrost of despair—broke open inside of him.

Heather Ash. The master of trade's only child. A youngling overcome with grief.

William dropped his eyes. Why had she come here? And where was Sara? Did she realize her daughter was out here alone? Studying Heather's posture against the wall—as well as listening to the self-important voices of the Council streaming out from the window—William suddenly understood her purpose there: She was eavesdropping.

She'd snuck away to discover what she could about her father's death, despite knowing the things she might learn, despite knowing the pain it would cause. Because hers was a spirit of a warrior, of someone who wouldn't—couldn't—just sit and do nothing. Even now, in the midst of her sorrow, William could see it plainly: an inner fortitude, a relentless strength.

"Heather?" He whispered so as not to startle her. His own misery forgotten, he inched down the alleyway, approaching her as one would a cornered animal. "It's William Breeve. The captain of the Guard. You shouldn't be out here by yourself."

She acknowledged him with a whimper, her chin bobbing up and down, her lips folded in tight. Seeing him, her fingers loosened from the windowsill, and she turned away.

William, blinking past his own tears, knelt beside her. "Shhh, shhh." He placed a soothing hand on her back. "You poor girl. I'm so sorry."

Her resolve crumbled at the words; with a sob, she spun toward him, threw her arms around his neck, and buried herself into his shoulder. "Papa… My papa…"

"I know, I know." William smoothed her hair softly, tenderly. Like a father. "Your papa loved you," he whispered, nodding earnestly, willing her to understand. "You and your mother both. He was proud of you— so proud. He's still with you, even now. And you never have to let him go." He said these things because he'd often dreamed of telling Landon as much. *I love you, and I'm proud.* Such simple words for expressing the inexpressible, for attempting to go where language failed. The words weren't enough—would never *be* enough—and yet no others would do.

I love you, and I'm proud. I love you, and I'm proud.

For a time, they simply stayed like that: two survivors in a vast and broken world; two wanderers, sharing an embrace. A halo of calm suspension shrouded them, and all else faded away. Right then, they were the shared recipients of all the anguish the world could afford. But so too, in their togetherness, did they discover the strength to endure.

Sorrow passed over and around and through them. Like smoke

upon a breeze, it drifted away.

The shores of Seagren Lake relegated far from his thoughts, William pushed himself to his feet and gently guided Heather along with him: away from the window and the conferring voices inside, away from the deliberations and the ugly realities of the night. Reluctantly at first, and then conceding with a wearied slump, the girl followed.

"Come on," said William. "Let's get you home."

CHAPTER FIFTY-SIX

For the first time in recent memory, the High Council of Norick was entangled in total gridlock.

After Breeve and Ford were dismissed from the room, the magistrates had again turned to the subject of the fisherman Christopher Willow: namely, his recent incarceration and the legality of such a detainment. On this point, the nine men were divided.

"We've gone too far," said one magistrate, jabbing the table to accentuate his point. "This is a gross overreach."

"Every piece of evidence alludes to him," countered another. "It's irrefutable."

"But there's still no clear motive," said the master of justice, an elder in the group. "All signs indicate they lived entirely separate lives. It's unlikely they ever crossed paths."

"Ash was master of trade, and Willow's a fisherman. It's not unfounded to think the two of them might've had dealings in the past."

"Even if they had, that's circumstantial at best. It proves nothing."

"You can't deny he's suspicious. I'd wager he's guilty of *something*."

"That's pure speculation. What of the presumption of innocence? What of reasonable doubt? We've confined the man to the dungeons based on conjecture alone. We're better than this. Wiser. Shouldn't we at least conclude the investigation before throwing a citizen beneath the scrutiny of the town?"

"An investigation rife with evidence—all of which leads back to him. His ropes, his dye, his knife—"

"It's possible someone's setting him up."

"That doesn't negate the fact that, for much of the night, his whereabouts can't be verified."

"The same could be said of half the townspeople."

"The man has no alibi to speak of."

"He was inspecting his skiff—"

"Nonsense."

Seated at the center of the room, Skylar Higgins listened to the debate without intervening. He slouched a little in his chair, his chin resting on a fist. His eyes, grainy from overuse, struggled to focus on the table's ancient grain, a river's worth of thin dark lines flowing across the surface of the wood. His thoughts, meanwhile, though set on Willow, weren't fixated on the man's culpability or innocence; instead, the chancellor's mind lingered elsewhere, on the ramifications of this meeting.

The decision to detain Willow had been his own. Though cursory, the Guard's investigation had brought to life a number of discrepancies surrounding the fisherman, and Higgins had quickly recognized an opportunity. One that was apparently beyond the grasp of his colleagues.

"We cannot rush to conclusions based off evidence not properly surveyed," the master of justice was saying. "We need to allow ourselves more time. Otherwise, fear will blind our deductions."

"Whether we grant the investigation an extension or not," said the master of town development, "it's obvious. The recovered clues—the pattern is too convenient, the thread too seamlessly weaved. That evidence was left *for* us."

The master of labor's cheek lifted in a tic. "I don't believe it."

"We're making a mistake," said the master of virtue. "One that could tarnish the color of several lives."

"Consider for a moment if Willow *is* guilty. Can we afford to take such a gamble? What if, the moment we release him, he kills again?"

"Or kindles another blaze!" interjected another.

"This is not who we are."

"I concur. The sanctity of the law *must* be preserved."

"Wake up, you old fool. The town was nearly eradicated tonight. This was no accident. We were *targeted*. Would you have us do nothing?"

"All I am advocating for is patience. I—"

"Don't be naïve. Or perhaps you've already gone senile."

"How dare you—"

The room descended into chaos as several council members shouted in unison across the table, many of them now leveling personal insults. Looking uncomfortable, the guardsmen above rocked on their feet. Higgins could stomach it no longer. A member of the High Council murdered, half their town destroyed, and here they were bickering like younglings. It was infuriating. And, on top of all that, he was tired. So bloody tired.

Higgins threw up his arms, righteous anger supplanting all other emotion. "That's enough! Quiet yourselves at once!"

The magistrates' voices tapered off in short, peppering bursts while Higgins chastised each of them with a stare. "I know we're in discord, but we're better than this childish squabbling. We are allies here, gentlemen, lest you forget. Even if you can't presently agree with that, surely you recognize we're the only thing still holding this town together."

He waited. The men beside him continued huffing for air, several of them red in the face, but none dared voice any objection. Higgins, eyes softening, inspected them anew. "My brothers… I understand emotions are high; I know this night has strained us more than ever before. Losing one of our own … and especially in this manner. It's incomprehensible. It's catastrophic. But need I remind you, we are the *High Council*—we are Norick. Even if we can't agree on this matter—even if we ourselves are terrified or exhausted or unable to discern the path ahead—we must endure. The town's very future depends on it.

"I understand this is a moral quandary. One all of us would much rather avoid. But circumstance has found us here, and, as Norick's guiding light, we cannot turn away. We must press on, my brothers. We must make the difficult choices. We must *lead*."

This oration earned him a few nods, the familiar notions a balm for their anxieties. Along the table, the magistrates' breathing steadied, slowing in anticipation of his next remarks. Higgins waited until the room was graveyard-silent before carrying on.

"And that's why I recommend we keep Willow right where he's at: in a cell."

Another eruption overtook the room. Higgins motioned them quiet. Two places down, the master of justice cocked a wispy brow. "You intend to exploit him," he stated, matter-of-fact.

Higgins offered a quick bob of his chin. "Aye, I do. And while I know that decision is a controversial one, I believe it is our best available option. Let me explain," he added when several of the council members moved to interrupt. "Right now, it matters not whether Willow is guilty or innocent; what matters is the preservation of our town.

"Can't you see it? We're teetering in the balance. One little nudge, and all of this ends. The greatest threat to Norick right now isn't some shadowy killer—it's panic. If we let the people succumb to delusion and terror—if we allow hysteria even the narrowest of footholds—order will decline, morals will wane, and the people will tear this town in two. It'll be the end of Norick, the end of the Council, the end of every dream we've ever had. If we release Willow tonight, we may as well spit on the Founders' graves and head south right now."

"You have an astounding penchant for hyperbole, Higgins."

"You think this is a jest? An exaggeration? I *know* these people. They're animals. Domesticated, yes, but just so. The moment they suspect we can no longer protect them, they will turn on us. We must project strength, now more than ever."

"Ignoring the law isn't strength," spat the master of education. "It's tyranny."

Higgins threw up a hand. "And what decrees would we be breaking? Do tell. As we've already established, the collected evidence is already enough for us to detain him."

"He's supposed to receive a trial."

"And he shall. In due course. Once we know more. But right now, the people need someone to blame. Better to have an innocent man in custody than to let them think a madman is still loose among them. Imagine the panic. Imagine what they might do. Conveying anything but absolute certainty right now will be tantamount to giving the town over to chaos. Is that what you want? Do you want to see the people tear each other apart?"

"What of our morals? Our pledge to integrity, to unwavering virtue?"

"I know, believe me. *We'll protect the town, but at what cost?* That's what you're all wrestling with, is it not? Should we risk sullying our honor in order to keep the town safe? I've considered it thoroughly, and I would argue yes. We would be acting in defense of our morals, not against them. If we wish for Norick to endure—if we wish for our children to carry on the

Founders' legacy—then this is our best hope. The state of the town necessitates it. The future requires it."

"And what about Willow? The accusations alone will likely destroy him and his business. Not to mention his family."

"These are desperate times," said Higgins. "Some degree of sacrifice is inevitable."

"Easy for you to say," interjected the master of education. "You, and you alone, made this decision. It was on your orders that Willow was imprisoned to begin with—without the direction, or approval, of this assembly. Perhaps *you're* the tyrant, here to dictate the course of our lives."

"Watch yourself. Everything I do is for this town and for its citizens." Higgins's eyes were a pair of twin suns blazing upon the man's face. "Even the ungrateful ones."

The master of education squirmed beneath the glare. "All I'm saying is that the precedent we would be establishing … it's unheard of. It's staggering, even."

"Perhaps. But that doesn't make it the wrong course of action."

"Say we keep him locked up. Say someone else turns up murdered."

Higgins acquiesced with a nod. "Aye, it's possible. I submit there may still be a killer out there. But this remains the wisest step we can take. The people need somewhere to direct their fear. Willow provides us that. His captivity—his *temporary* captivity—will help keep the panic in check and will allow us the time we need to make sense of all this. It will help the town heal."

"And we'll continue to investigate?"

"Aye, until we're absolutely certain. And in the meantime, we'll keep the townspeople on guard without them knowing the full reason as to why. They'll be none the wiser." An uneasy silence settled as the Council considered it. There was misgiving etched upon their faces; more prevailing was a growing sense of resignation. They couldn't argue with his logic. Morally dubious though it was, detaining Christopher Willow was, for Norick's sake, the proper thing to do.

"Okay," conceded the master of education. "Okay." The other magistrates followed suit.

Higgins knew the next moments critical. While compliant, the Council was nevertheless divided. It was up to him to make them whole.

Buzzing with a sudden rush of adrenaline, he clenched a fist and waved it at his colleagues. "Stand with me, brothers. You hear? Even now. Even in our disagreements. Stand strong, stand united, stand proud. Stand against superstitions. Stand against fear and turmoil and doubt. Stand in the light of our future. Stand with the Founders."

The master of labor slammed a palm against the table, and a soft chorus of approval crackled about the room. The magistrates couldn't help it: They were a proud, zealous lot—and Higgins knew it.

He pushed his advantage. "We are a chosen people. Though flawed, we are the hope for a dark and uncultivated world. We are evolved; we are anointed. We shall hold fast to our legacy, to our ancestors, to our virtue. Despite everything, we *will* prevail.

"Tonight was a setback; we shall overcome countless besides. We are resilient; we are born of champions. Together, we will remain vigilant. Together, we will transcend every obstacle cast our way. Together ... we will soar!"

This time, to a man, the Council responded with boisterous ovations. Higgins could see it in their eyes: They remembered; they trusted; they believed. Shouting their endorsement, the magistrates drummed the table in a thunderous display, and, for a moment, the amphitheater was beautifully assailed with noise.

To Higgins, it was purified. He was just as moved as the rest. All of his efforts; all of his doubts; all of the humiliation following his breakdown: All of it had brought him here, to this very moment. His body was now a thing beyond his control. Upending his chair in the process, he launched himself to his feet. "To Milgrin!"

"*To Milgrin!*" the magistrates echoed, intoxicated on the promise of his words, on the surge of their recovered belief. Even the guardsmen above contributed to the creed.

"To the Founders!"

"*To the Founders!*"

"To the Council!"

"*To the Council!*"

"To Norick!"

"*Aye, to glorious Norick! May ever she prosper, may ever she reign!*"

This last declaration bellowed loudest of all. Just then, Higgins knew all had righted itself in the valley. Despite what'd happened—despite the damage and the fear, and even his own failings—the town would endure. What awaited Norick now was merely a new age in its glorious history: an unfolding future that would soon prove itself triumphant and hopeful.

Drunk on the feel of their voices, the nine remaining members of Norick's High Council continued their salute for several rounds more. Around them, the amphitheater's draping shadows looked on, in silence.

CHAPTER FIFTY-SEVEN

A short distance from town, seated on a lonely bluff overlooking the River Torinth, the man in the cloak settled in to watch the sun rise.

His flesh insisted on shivering; the cloak hung drenched and heavy, drawing forth goosebumps along both arms. He ignored them. Compared to the breadth of eternity, corporeal sensations were nothing. Neither pain nor pleasure resonated; for the man in the cloak, neither warranted consideration at all. Even his own name was a mooring he'd long since abandoned. Like everything, its significance had faded through the years, swallowed up by the sheer vastness of time. It was easier, when faced with that immensity, to be nobody at all.

But why, then, had his pulse quickened when that Southerner had called him by his name? And why did it feel now like some small part of him was awake after hearing it?

Milgrin. I am ... Rufus Milgrin.

He shook his head; it was just a name. A bygone identity belonging to an altogether different man. The emotions it aroused were inconsequential; more pressing was what he'd just learned.

As instructed, the man in the cloak had rendezvoused with the voice in the forest, and the creature—if it could be called that—had shared its plans. "Remember your oath," the voice admonished, after a flicker of doubt had sparked through him, "and I will remember mine. Soon, if you do as you're commanded, I will give you what was promised."

What was promised. It had been so long now that the man in the cloak sometimes forgot why he was impelled to do any of this. Sometimes, he wondered if the object of that promise even still existed. In light of the voice's proposed scheme, he was even beginning to question whether the tradeoff was worth it.

Of course it was. One hundred years couldn't change that, neither could the numbness, or the doubt, or the price the voice demanded. The man in the cloak couldn't allow himself to waver, not now, not when he was so close. Not when there was still hope.

But was there? Could the voice be trusted to deliver on its end? Or, as he'd long suspected, would a snare lie at the end of this path?

There was also what Breeve had said. Watching the river gradually soften from charcoal to silver, the man in the cloak heard the captain's words anew, their stinging accusation cutting deep. *This is your bloody town, Milgrin. You brought the people here. So save them.*

You owe us.

Could he—help them? But how? The voice wasn't omniscient, though it was close. It fed on human fears and could sniff out emotion like a blood-crazed hound. Not only was it astute, it was transcendent: Its perception would always be leagues and leagues ahead. Nay, the voice would sense a betrayal before the man in the cloak could even formulate a plan. And its punishment for such treachery would not be slight.

Helping the citizens of Norick was hopeless. Perhaps even impossible. Even if he could manage to come to their aid, the people would reject him. Once they discovered what this valley really was ... once they learned what he'd done ... they would tear him apart, limb by limb, before casting him into the sea.

Perhaps that was exactly what the voice had in mind.

The man in the cloak picked up a chip of stone. Tossed it. He couldn't help the townspeople, not without risking everything he'd worked for. Not without risking certain ruin for them both. But still... The voice was deceitful, conniving, treacherous. And then there were those three accursed little words: *You owe us.*

The man in the cloak—who, in some small way, was also Rufus Milgrin—decided he had much to think on.

And, courtesy of the voice, he had plenty of time to do so.

CHAPTER FIFTY-EIGHT

The flow of rainfall had at last terminated, though its slurping mud remained.

Julie Temult, grimacing in the faint light just before dawn, dug her heels into the sludge and thrashed against the rough hands pulling her along. "Let me go," she hollered. "Let me go! You have no right to detain me. I've done nothing wron—" The two soldiers, looking almost bored, dumped her into the slick, cutting her off.

She landed face-down. Mud invaded her nostrils, flooded her gums. Darkness covered everything.

Overhead, someone was speaking, his voice distorted by the gooey froth. "Right?" the man thundered. "I have no *right?*" Julie pushed herself up shakily, first to her elbows and then to her palms. She spat; still a residue of grime coated her tongue. Through the muddy film, she struggled to take in her surroundings. A sagging plow-shed, its planks bleached and rotted, dominated the view. The soldiers had brought Julie around to its rear, near a wooden chopping block standing waist-high. Meant for shearing crops and cleaning fish, the slab was empty save for a single implement, one fashioned of smooth Dobë wood and a rusty iron head.

Julie gasped when it registered.

An ax.

She whipped her gaze toward the speaker, a towering behemoth of a man hovering beside the chopping block. His tree-trunk-sized arms were crossed against a mountain of chest, though not tightly: They seemed ready, eager even, to snap forward and take up the ax. His eyes, meanwhile, were two blazing beacons of scarcely suppressed rage, both doing everything in their power not to pop out from their sockets. The man was dressed down, and he was haggard, but Julie recognized him immediately.

Skylar Higgins, chancellor of the High Council and mayor of Norick. Victim of her thievery.

Julie's eyes, rimmed in muck, widened at the memory. Her stomach free-fell. She shot a glance past the plow-shed, toward the rolling landscape beyond. But there was nobody there to help her. Judging by the pitch darkness and the rows after rows of crops, the shed was located somewhere along the outermost reaches of the agricultural fields. Somewhere isolated. Somewhere private. Somewhere where no one would hear her screams.

The terror returned then in droves. Above her, Higgins was still bellowing. "*I* have no *right?*" he repeated, lips toothed in a snarl. He lunged toward her, then stopped, as if reconsidering. He settled instead for a knifing thrust of his finger. "*You* had no right to violate the sanctity of my home. *You* had no right to sabotage the virtue of this town. *You* have no right to remain here at all.

"Get her up," he said.

The two guardsmen—Silas Lairen and Carrington Welsh, the latter a man she'd once been involved with—stepped forward and hauled Julie to her feet. With vise-like holds about the cuffs of her shoulders, they shoved her toward the chopping block.

"Wait—wait! Carrington, listen to me. Please. I swear it: I'm innocent."

The brute ignored her, but not before making a show of averting his eyes. Together, the pair lugged Julie to the chancellor, who studied her while making a soft *clucking* sound with his tongue. "So not only are you a thief, you're also a filthy liar. Alas, most of your kind typically are." He scoffed. "To think you would take advantage as you did, in the midst of a crisis. It's pathetic, loathsome. A despicable deed from a despicable wench."

Julie squirmed. "I didn't do it. I'm telling you, Mr. Higgins, you have the wrong person. I don't know where your vase is."

With a sharp intake of breath, she realized the severity of her mistake.

Higgins cocked an eyebrow. "My vase, huh?" He smiled at her, though the expression contained only a compulsory sort of pleasure. "As I'd thought." He stepped away from the chopping block, dragging the ax along with him. He gestured toward the slab. "Hold her down."

Everything was suddenly happening too fast. Silas and Carrington, now with adequate room to maneuver, slammed Julie into place, the impact rattling her bones. The chopping block's coarse surface grabbed hold. Julie renewed her struggle, writhing and kicking out behind her. The soldiers' iron-clad grip held fast.

"It wasn't me," she spluttered through the mud and the splinters. "I was fighting the fire, just like everyone else. Ask around—people saw me." Higgins leaned on the ax's upturned handle and considered her mutely. Disturbed by the chancellor's silence, Julie continued floundering. "Somebody told me about it—that's all. You'll see. It was a rumor going around. People were discussing it … a boy, I think it was—yes, a youngling! I'm sure of it. He told me all about the vase. Maybe *he* took it during the chaos."

At last, Higgins shook his head. He appeared disappointed, even mournful. "The denials of the accused truly are their own form of poetry. What a shame."

"I'm supposed to get a trial." Trying to deceive him now was pointless; if Julie desired a chance, she had to appeal to his reason. "There are laws. You're the chancellor—you know this isn't right. You know this isn't true justice."

Higgins cackled at the assertion, and that's when she saw it: in the chancellor's eyes, that same reckless sense of detachment, that same wild uncaring. Earlier, it had been a brazen, insatiable yearning within her—and the reason she'd stolen from Higgins at the start. Now, in the hands of another, it would ensure she paid the price.

Julie's breath fled her. Against that black tide, she knew, there could be no victory. Until the urge was satisfied, nothing would stand in its way. "I'm supposed to get a trial," she entreated nonetheless. "I have a right to a hearing and to the—"

"What're you gonna do about it, you little thieving bitch?" Julie stared in disbelief; the expletive disturbed her not because of its intended insult, but because of its disparity to the chancellor's customary degree of eloquence. Never once had Julie heard him utter a swear word. Until now. His voice, laced with venom, was not his own; his face and eyes belonged to another.

He almost seemed not to be a man at all.

"I'll tell everyone! I'll have you arrested. I'll—"

"Who will possibly believe you? Who will heed your word over mine? I make the laws here, wench. *I* decide who lives and who dies. You are nothing. You are a blight on this town's history. You're a traitor to your people."

"Please—" Gasping, Julie wriggled along the slab, though she found herself gaining no marked advantage. Her captors' hands held steady at her shoulder blades and at the small of her back. "I'm sorry, okay? I'm sorry! I've learned my lesson, I swear it. I've changed."

Hefting the ax with one hand, Higgins cushioned its handle against his shoulder: He could have been lumberjack resting before the day's work. "You know the punishment for thievery. That which takes, shall be taken. That which sullies blood, shall be bloodied."

"Mercy—show mercy! What of our morals? What of forgiveness? The Founders always said..." Higgins took a step toward her, his expression set. "I'll return the vase to you, I promise. I tossed it in the sea—I can still swim down and get it. I know just where it lies."

Higgins slung the ax across his chest, into the clasp of two meaty palms.

"Please," Julie begged. "*Please.*"

Carrington swung her arm around, yanking it forward on the slab. Without expression—as if he, too, were merely completing a chore—he pressed the brunt of his weight against her elbow.

Higgins emerged beside her. His mountainous chest invaded the liquefying sphere of her vision. Hooded in shadow, his face held not only a recklessness but a dark pleasure. He smiled, and Julie trembled at the sight.

Then: movement. The ax was reeling up and away—a shadow like a soaring bird, a streaking bat. It was simultaneously too sluggish and too swift, a disruption of time's usual course. She waited an eternity; she flinched and it was over.

The ax arced downward. Cold iron found warm flesh.

And then the screams of Julie Temult split the dawn.

EPILOGUE

THE PATIENCE
OF NIGHT

The dark is patient.
The dark is clever.

Even in retreat,
It plans. It schemes.

Its power does not dwindle
With the mere turning of the earth;
Its resolve does not wane.

The dark can be expelled, aye;
It can be beaten and banished and shoved aside.
It can be trampled.

But, unlike the light—
Unlike that fleeting span of day—
The darkness can never, ever,
Be put out.

The dark one had come.

It hovered behind her, motionless, having materialized moments earlier between the thrashing of two breakers against the shoreline.

Out on the jetty, Mary Fern had been observing the approach of sunup with squinted eyes. The tempest had passed on; at present, it doused the sharp slopes of the Remos Mountains to the north. The sea, however, remained incensed, stirred like a swarm of wasps within a jar. On the horizon, the first murmurs of dawn had arrived, peeking through the toothed crags and highland vales. Little more than a hint of paleness beneath the thunderheads, the pseudo half-light seemed to exist only in memory.

Leaning on her pinewood cane, whose history was bound inextricably with her own, Mary waited for the dark one to come, knowing its nature would allow for nothing less than a face-to-face meeting. One moment the space about her was empty, then, in the next, there was an elemental *crash*, and *it* was there. As if coalescing from the wind, from the very fabric of air. A concentration of living darkness about a single, punctured point.

Mary didn't deign to turn around—partly out of defiance, partly out of fear. Still, she could make out the looming silhouette floating behind her, off to one side. It was tall, though in a way that was still somehow compact. Its core wavered in the remnants of the wind and in the pale glow rising from the east. Its outline, however, remained steadfast, unyielding.

For a long while, they stood in silence, just paces apart. Mary could hear the reeds chirruping against each other along the shoreline. She could hear the groan of the rocks and the soft twinkling of the sand. Elsewhere, there was a lull in the turn of the Earth as if the world itself were waiting, poised on this encounter.

Finally, the moment arrived—and with it, a voice.

"You," came a rasping snarl, somewhere between a hiss and roar. "Maaaarrrry. Fern." Each syllable was elongated, drawn out like the notes of some obscene melody. Despite her preparation, despite everything she had seen, Mary felt her hair stand on end. "Little, little girl. And now an old, forgetful hag. We're quite familiar, aren't we?"

Shutting her lids, Mary steeled herself against the voice. To hear her name upon the tongue of such a creature, a beast of such foulness and hate... It was torture. The thing behind her was the very spirit of darkness, the unholy song of night. It was the destroyer, the corruptor, who held all the world in contempt. It was the hunter, the defiler, the cheat: the one who smothered and drowned and thieved. Ageless, it roved over the land in a vast cloud of perversion, spinning an infinite reverie of darkness, a nightmare the world didn't realize it was dreaming. It was one as old as time: From it, like a great wellspring, all fear and sorrow came.

The thing hovering behind Mary was Death itself, and it knew her well.

"You think you've bested me," it spat. "You think this light can hold? You're wrong."

Mary refused to turn, to even open her eyes; she cast her mind out, searching for an anchor on which to cling. *The light will come*, she thought, and then amended: *The light is already here, within me.* The dark one's eyes—if it had any—inspected her in the haunted silence that followed, its glare a length of flaming steel upon her spine.

"This isn't over. Do you understand? They're mine. You can't protect them."

Mary said nothing. The fear was a hammer to her breastbone; the shame, the ache of a million tortured deaths. Just standing upon that jetty required every ounce of her will.

"You think this display proved anything? This land is forsaken. *I* was granted dominion here, to do with it as I please." The mass of darkness crept closer; she could smell its fetid breath. "No matter what course you take, no matter how you prepare, my hour will come again. I will rise up, and this time in full. In material form. And I will claim what's mine."

The hair on Mary's head rippled. Her lips trembled. Whether

imagined or not, she could taste the dark one's stench on her tongue.

"My claws are already in each of them. I *own* them. Not you, not the light. No matter what you do, they won't listen. You know it as well as I. They're too stubborn—and self-righteous—to see otherwise. It's worthless: Your efforts are nothing."

The dark one paused, as if thinking. "You believe the town proved its spirit. You think I was defeated. No, no, silly girl. That spirit will crumble beneath my roar.

"You have won nothing. I will destroy them from the inside, stirring up division until they tear themselves apart." The beast was working itself into a rage, her silence infuriating it. Its subsequent growl was a wallop against her cheek. "I swear it, you hag. I will make this night seem to them the most pleasant of memories. I will soak this land in their screams. The light will be but a candle as I drag you all into the abyss."

Recognizing the effect she was having, Mary stood silent—and held on.

"I will come for you, too, Mary Fern." The dark one bit her name off like a bitter curse. "When you're among others or alone. When you're sleeping or praying or strolling through fields of flowers on the brightest of morns, *I will be there.* Whatever beauty you hope to find, know that darkness follows your every step. I'm going to drain you into the earth, woman, you hear? This is only the beginning."

In the east, a band of fledgling sunlight soared past two bowed summits and fell upon the jetty, shattering the suspension that held them. At the intrusion, the dark one—a shadow within a shadow, an amassing of all the foul things upon the Earth—dissolved at once from the seawall, departing just as it'd come: between the crash of waves.

Mary opened her mouth to respond, the world's primordial current of color and light finally blossoming within her, but the beast was already gone.

For a long time, perhaps even days or weeks, old Mary Fern stood upon the seawall and regarded the unfolding sky. The dance of the waves gradually softened; the howl of the wind altogether ceased. Far away, the embankment of clouds parted, and the storm veered off toward distant shores.

Mary considered the dark one's final utterance, words of malice slosh-ing like poison through her gut. She thought of its resentment, its rage. She pondered all that lay ahead of them: a long and arduous journey that, for many years hence, would see no end. Then at last she responded, be-cause she knew the creature hadn't spoken frivolously, that even now it was bound to be near.

This is only the beginning.

"I know," she said.

THE END

The Norick Saga will continue in Book Two,
A Song of Night.

ACKNOWLEDGMENTS

Writing can be a solitary, and often lonely, endeavor. But it is never a wholly independent pursuit: Just as every novel is made up of many words, so, too, is a writer made up of a many lives and experiences and people.

All those who have helped and believed along the way are, in some respects, woven into the very fabric of a story. Looking back on this journey—back to when I was just a small, wide-eyed kid in our family kitchen, furiously scribbling away in a beat-up spiraled notebook—I recognize I never could have achieved this dream alone. There have been so many gracious people who've inspired, championed, and supported me throughout the years. There isn't enough time to convey my gratitude to all of you, but just know I *am* grateful. Just know your belief *mattered*.

As a former educator, I understand the immense impact teachers can have on their students' lives, both for the positive *and* for the negative. Fortunately, I have had so many remarkable and affirming instructors of my own along the way, people who have helped me become not only a better writer, but a better man. I can't think of a more fitting place to start than with them.

Mary Fisher assigned me one of my first fiction writing assignments—"Dr. Templeton's Time Machine"—but more importantly, she taught me my first real lesson in grace and kindness. Christina Odom, freshman Religion, believed in this dream from the moment she read one of my stories and has spent every year since lending her wisdom and encouragement. I'm honored to now consider her a friend. My time in Kate (Cavin) Michaelson's classes—freshman English and, later, Creative Writing—was some of the most formative for me. Her Greek mythology project (which I somehow turned into a murder mystery) is one I'll always remember, as I don't think I ever had so much fun in school. Charlotte Clovis was an ally when I didn't know I needed one, going above and beyond to champion my writing (and she's also an incredible writer herself). Taylor Warntjes, senior Government, opened my eyes to a wider world, and always did so with such humor, positivity, and wit.

Fate was exceedingly kind when it placed me in the homeroom of Pat Sitzman, who deserves her own paragraph here. In truth, I could draft a separate book on all she's done for me: on the measure of her selflessness, on the excellence of her teaching, on the depth of her love. Throughout her nearly half a century in education, she has changed so many lives—and all for the better. I'm blessed to have gotten to be one of her "homeroom children." Room 401 will always stay with me.

Additional gratitude to some of the other educators I was fortunate enough to learn from: Wendi Alessio, Dawn Boeshart, Jill Bork (favorite—and only—second grade teacher), Tom Brunkan, Brendan Burchard, Keri Clifford, Justin Coury, Charlie Curran, Kristen Dale, Beth Dalton, Laurie Dougherty, Bryan Farris, Nanette Fladung, Bob Geary, David Gisch, Laura Grebasch, Dennis Hirschman, Mary (Halligan) John, Nan Kiel, Ann Martin, Dan O'Brien, Marla Pluim, Greta Prichard, Sr. Colane Recker, Megan Schettler, Michele Schorg (homeroom teaching partner/unfortunate Hawkeye), Ron Schultz, Kenneth Strouse, Jeri Lynn Sturges, Rebecca Wolf, and Jay Wright. Also, to the infamous and the incomparable Andy 'Mr. Hollywood' Umthum ("Uuuuuuuuuu!"). Thanks to my student teaching instructors, Matt Davis and Bill Dimon, for taking me under their wings … then subsequently pushing me out so I could fly.

College is an uncertain time for any student; the phenomenal professors I had at UNL instantly made me feel welcomed and at home. In particular, I'd like to thank Drs. Stephen Bueller, Lauren Gatti, Joe Gecke, and Sarah Thomas. Their guidance and support—their way of helping students look at the world through a lens of nuance, creativity, and hope—were instrumental. Their classes were legendary; their compassion, uncommon.

I am grateful as well to *my* former students (this includes you, Alicia; please don't burn my books). I know all of you asking about my novel was just a stall tactic in order to waste time in class, but it meant a lot to me all the same. I'm still rooting for each of you, and I can't wait to see where you end up.

The story itself is just one aspect of the audience's overall reading experience; just as important are the countless small (and often invisible) details that go into a book's production: those design, editorial, and promotional elements that, in effect, make a book, *a book*. Throughout the entire publishing process, I was blessed to work with an incredible production team, without whom I never could have made this book a reality. Obigas, Carlos G. Rios (RemyArt), and Cristina Tanase brought Norick to life with their haunting illustrations. Anamaria Stefan, meanwhile, delivered an impeccable interior design that perfectly aligned with my vision. Upon seeing Damon Freeman's gorgeous cover for the first time, I was met with that old childhood feeling of being at a bookstore browsing covers, wondering giddily what worlds and adventures waited inside... Taylor Maurer turned a frigid February day into a series of wonderful author photographs (my face notwithstanding) that I'm extremely proud of. Nathan Schulz went above and beyond in designing my website; the man's a genius—and big-hearted, to boot.

Additionally, Robert Liparulo blew me away with his feedback, encouragement, and life-giving words. Jane Friedman offered editorial assistance and query letter insight, and the industry research I received from the Grad Student Freelancers remains invaluable. Lastly, this story wouldn't be what it is without the patience, enthusiasm, and eagle-eyed professionalism of my two editors, the aforementioned Pat Sitzman as well as my proofreader Rachel Mann, both of whom are true masters of their craft.

I suppose I'm a stereotypical millennial in that I've had several jobs over the course of my brief adult life. What hasn't been conventional, though, is the quality of the people I've met and gotten to work with. Heartfelt appreciation to my colleagues at the Willard Community Center, Sacred Heart, Sterling Computers, P's Pizza (particularly Kaylee Hughes, Jaymi Leif, and Joe Sitzmann, whose generosity helped make my first book signing a dream come true), and all those at Bishop Heelan Catholic Schools. Thanks as well to all of my former coaches (especially Jerry Steffen), and to Dan and Kari Nelson. I'll always savor our discussions on sports, books, and life. Finally, eternal gratitude to Father Jerome Cosgrove, the most selfless man I know. One day, we're going to have to have that talk.

A massive shout-out to Nick Wankum, whose passion for this story not only blew me away but kept me going on those nights when I was sure I would never finish. I will forever relish those hours-long phone calls discussing the plot, analyzing characters and themes, and—my favorite part— listening to him rant after a cliffhanger. Even in its formative stages, Nick treated this novel as a real story worthy of discussion—and he even wrote my first (!!!) piece of fanfiction. I love ya, brother. I hope the wait was worth it; I hope I made you proud.

Another behind-the-scenes champion to whom I owe a great deal is my cousin Kristian Freed. From reading each new draft and providing feedback, to helping me navigate the seasons of doubt, he was always just a phone call or a text away. I'll never forget our epic adventures back on the farm (imaginary or otherwise), nor can I relay the depth of his wisdom, humor, and strength.

Cheers to my friends both near and far. Our shenanigans always bring me joy and life—and way too many headaches. I don't have the space here to list out everyone, but believe me when I say I'm thankful for each and every one of you. Next time we're together, beer's on me.

I'd be remiss, however, if I didn't mention a few special people here. Ever since he rode with me to that football meeting back in seventh grade, Brady Van Dusen has been my wingman, my ride-or-die, my "quartaback," my co-head coach, my 'gator. Mostly, he's a brother I couldn't imagine living without. Shane Kleier helped reignite my love of seeing the world and was the best travel buddy a guy could ask for (even when he was encouraging me to jump off cliffs and out of airplanes). Landon Mattison (BASK) attended my second birthday and has been a lifelong best friend ever since.

I'm likewise indebted to those who've read earlier stories and offered feedback/hounded me for more: Carli (Tritz) Berger, Kaitlyn Brown, Jon Buck, Angel Cancino, Gina 'Mama G' Cougill, Judy Doyle, the Fitzsimmons brothers, Andres Flores, Kylee Hickman, Casey Johnson, Emily Keane, Kyle Kinney, Matt Koley, Joe and Marlene Kruse, Alex Mallory, Mike and Raejean Mattison, my extended family (the Bauerlys, Bodes, Freeds, Kruses, and Starostkas), Morgan (Welte) Palmer (I still have my shirt!), Sam Raybine, Sean Roberts, Betsy Ronspies (DB), Nick Sawin, Adam Smith, Corinne Spears and the entire Spears family, Megan Vander Mullen, Katelyn Walsh, the Wankums (my second family), and Jared Weaver—cow tipper, speech giver, friend.

Most importantly, thank you to my family. Words fail, but I'm gonna try: Mom, despite being a gomer pile and quite possibly the worst dancer alive, you have the biggest heart and the deepest love. Thank you for sharing books and movies with me (even when you can't remember their names) and for always helping the less fortunate (yes, even the frogs!). You sent me my first acceptance letter all those years ago—it meant more than you'll ever know.

Dad, you're my hero. You've shown me the true meaning of hard work and success (as well as how to make a proper Captain-diet). I'll never forget how you dropped everything to fly me to Nashville for a writing conference, just because you believed in this crazy dream. You would do anything for our family, and have. One day, I hope to be even half the man you are.

Tyler, whoever claimed you should never live with your siblings got it all wrong. You own *way* too many water bottles, and you hoard more licorice than a Doomsday prepper does canned goods, but I'm so lucky to have you as a roommate as well as a brother. Thanks for always being there for me—*especially* on couch Sundays—and for everything you do for our community. You make me so proud.

Nicole, over and over you've pushed through life's setbacks and kept on going. Your sense of humor is wacky yet infectious, and it always brings a smile. I look up to you, big sis, even now.

Emery, you're the cutest little sister alive, the butt-wagging center of attention, and the purveyor of so much joy and laughter. Never lose your curiosity, or your spark. I love you all the way to the moon and the sun and the stars and back; I love you all day long.

And to the three best doggos ever (don't @ me): Cassie, Abigail, and little Peyton.

Last but not least, thank you to the Author of all things. You're my words and my wisdom, my hope in the night; you're my joy with the morning, and the coming of the light. Thank you for these stories and for a heart to tell them.

Thank you for your love.

ABOUT THE AUTHOR

CORY KRUSE has worked as an English teacher, marketing communication specialist, and, most recently, as a fundraiser for a local nonprofit. A graduate of the University of Nebraska, he now resides in South Dakota, where he spends his free time with friends and family, watching college sports, and nerding out over all things *Star Wars*. This is his first novel.

CPSIA information can be obtained
at www.ICGtesting.com
Printed in the USA
LVHW090607210920
666618LV00009B/60/J